DOWNTOWN NOIR

-a Bozeman apocalypse novel-

PATRIK HILL

FIRST EDITION: August 2015
SECOND EDITION: October 2016

Dedication:

This work is dedicated to Adam, Lacey, and my bro Schaap, who without the experiences and frigid temperatures of the day, these voices would have no meaning or substance.

In the days when the hours were too long, the tea in short supply, and the meager sunlight unable to thaw the maddening cold making it almost too much to bear, it was the laughter that has kept us going.

For the times when we had to make those zip trips because "we were new here" and had to bite our tongues….

Andora, my friend and probably my first legitimate editor, should also get a mention because she was one of the very first people to tell me to stop telling her *about* the story and to just "shut up and tell the Gods-be-damned story."

…and to Jo, my first true believer – I love you forever…

Furthermore:

There are a few more people that I am pretty sure I need to be thanking...

"B", Bodhi, Charley, Clint, Derek, Dia, Lindsey, "Ranger", Ricky, Rio, Zach... Thank you for letting me beautifully, and I think flawlessly, capture, model, impersonate and then publically assassinate your characters for reference to this particular publication. Thank you for being such damned good sports about the whole thing, regardless of whether or not I really gave you a choice in the matter.

Your beautiful essences gave breath to the characters in ways I could never have imagined; suddenly two dimensional characters on paper gave birth and the offspring were given life in a truly graphic and alternate world.

I appreciate you all *Love You All* more than you will ever know, or could possibly imagine.

Table of Contents:

noir:

noun 'nwär -- crime
fiction featuring
hard-boiled cynical
characters and bleak
sleazy settings

A DOWNTOWN MEETING

Friday. 17 July 15. 2230 hours.

Sitting in this gaudy downtown, tawdry excuse for a restaurant named Roger's Pit Stop, I'm watching the party goers and drunken young adults going back and forth through the establishment, moving with all the skill of frenetic undead zombies. Picking at a half-eaten falafel concoction, a semi dejected *SIGH* escapes my lips; this is nothing like the stuff we've got back on the east coast.

Foreigners are running rampant all over the east coast, flowing into the major cities as if a dyke had burst but I'll be damned if they don't bring some decent cooking with 'em. This isn't the worst shit I've ever had; no the worst shit I ever had had come from some rolling food cart dive in Phoenix a while back, and I'm pretty sure that whatever *it* was had given me an intestinal parasite. I remember being glued to the seat of toilet with all the enthusiasm of a colonoscopy patient enduring their hospital issued prep kit for the following morning's procedure while my bowels seemed to explode out my ass end.

This stuff, though, it wasn't half bad. Even had just a hint of spice to it, or at least just enough to set it apart from any other fast food chain garbage. Mixed with a premade yogurt spread passing for tzatziki sauce it was easy to swallow and didn't cause a rash when it went down the pipe; or was coming out the other pipe.

Teenage kids behind the counter threw the ingredients into the sandwich, wrapping it up with vegetables that were actually fresh. I didn't even know that places like this still used fresh vegetables anymore; not when everything came prepackaged and precut, essentially tasting like the sterile cardboard shipping packages and hermetically sealed plastic bags from which it was produced.

Why did Vincent insist on meeting in this place? This particular joint was loud; the volume of the music, the styles and colors, even right down to the obnoxious clothing that people wore. The slick, clean, freshly scrubbed and brightly colored Kelly green walls and red accent border trim clashed with the rough hewn authentic oranges, browns, and tan brick of the walls, as well as the steel I-beams that supported the second story apartments above the restaurant.

Industrial heating and cooling piping was exposed near the ceiling, and heavy gage speaker cable crisscrossed the walls and ceiling tiles, blaring out music that sounded something akin to a cat being neutered underwater. *Who the fuck makes the decision to paint the walls these colors, anyway?* I was trying to stomach the food and then this garish coloring just runs right into your eyeballs and gouges at them, really skull fucking you and turning your stomach in knots. This particular choice of music wasn't helping with the digestion process, either.

It had to be some awkward corporate decision that was designed to entice the college age frequenters and people who had a tendency to drink too much at the surrounding bars. It seemed as if the bright colors called to the drunks in the dark hours of the night, beckoning them in, to be sustained long after normal human sleep cycles began with food and sugared beverages. Looking up, again, I felt a much more calming vibe from the natural brick and metal accents of this joint. I found they were much more pleasing to the eye than the obscenely bright colors of these walls and chair rails. There was a certain authenticity to the brick, if not a tomb-*ish* feeling to it. If this joint had been downstairs it could have come across as creepy, but now it could, with some serious reworking and a small prayer, easily resemble the gastro-pubs and ale houses that had become all the rage on the West Coast, and sadly, my beloved East Coast.

Those damned hipster people with their bad moustaches and sickening fetishes trying to bring back drinks that tasted like badly fermented apple juice. Shit, they just needed a frigging sippy cup and a spill proof bowl. They even had a name for it, they were starting to call themselves "lumber-sexuals" because of their feelings on how it made them look more like lumberjacks. In reality they looked like damned cartoon fairies reborn in flannel shirts and those shitty skinny jeans. *Jesus Christ, what a nightmare for the future generations...*

Across the small dining area a petite gal with red painted lips, spiky black hair in the shape of the ever popular pixie cut, and Echo 8 band T-shirt kept making eyes at me and glancing at her cell phone. I gave her a look like "Late for something?" and she returned to her textbook parked on the windowsill beside her.

Who gets any actual study work done in a place like this, at this hour? Someone was going to miss a very important date if they weren't careful because this gal was all business, by the looks of it. I pity anyone foolish enough to stand her up.

The exterior of these downtown buildings was far more pleasant to look at, however. Enticing, authentic brick accented with wrought iron window frames and coverings gave the impression of back alley jive and a flare for something new, hell something akin to the true meaning of *hip*. There was a sense of reborn 1930s Prohibition Jazz begging to get out. Even the open grate, metal staircases in the alley, just outside the back door that led to the second floor apartments above, had that beautiful industrial look that I just about get a hard-on for.

I'm no architect but I know what I love, and when it comes to style and the raw beauty of brick and metal, that will get my dick hard any day of the week. A beautiful marriage of old and new, that's what I live for. It's as if there is a story inside the architecture, aching to be massaged out, and the melding with the newer, metal version, tells me someone sought out that story and begged to coax it out, even if it wasn't the exact story, but a hint, or a reinterpretation of that story. That's where the true beauty was.

I had a sudden urge to don a classic zoot suit and step out on the town with a fedora to match. A classic black with white pin striping silver watch fob chain and pipe to match. Hot damn, if that wasn't style, I don't know what was.

Whomever this particular artist was that had recreated this particular neighborhood had certainly understood the story of this area and had done a helluva job with this particular building, even. Fittingly enough the alley out back had a cobblestone retouch that turned a blacktop paved road into a quaint passage that young thunder cats would come blaring through with their turbo bikes and race cars, listening as the roar of the engines echoed and reverberated off the urban canyons created from all the brick and metal.

Surrounding this restaurant was more than one hundred years of sordid history, emanating from a town that was born from cowboys, rough riders, and mountain men looking to stake a claim in a newer territory of the so called "new world." Bars with dirty, plank floored basements and restaurants with canopied entrances of metal and glass that descended from hidden and forgotten alley ways were the norm in this part of town. Street facing shops had the look of good and modern while the rear kept the shady appearance of a dark, seedy underbelly in polite society. Hell, there were rumors that the official "red light district" was still alive, and in full operation not two blocks from here. It could easily be the perfect subject for a

18

new book, assuming that one wasn't lost in the overall research of the subject matter, that is.

Dammit, Vincent. There was a perfectly good coffee joint next door, open until late in the evening, that served reasonably priced lattes out of real porcelain cups and saucers, and had very comfortable leather couches to relax in; the kind that still had the antiqued brass furniture nails in the arms and had once been overstuffed but now sunk down to allow you to comfortably relax and put your feet up on the checkerboard coffee table that occasionally held stacks of old clay checkers, the chipped red and black paint still clinging to the molded edges and clinging on for dear life.

Unlike this joint, said coffee shop kept subdued feelings and dark undertones of jazz music; sensual saxophone and bassoon mixing with the ancient leather and brick of the store. Well mannered patrons kept their voices and conversations low so as not to disturb the person sitting across the way, reading from a shared and battered copy of Keats, or Ginsburg; they themselves daring to believe that once upon a time *they* were the angel headed hipsters. I could almost smell the hint of cigar smoke mixed with old hair cream, creeping in from years gone by when it was fashionable to smoke indoors, wafting up from the wooden floors worn smooth and polished from thousands of shoes over the years. There was an even an honest to God brass ashtray stand in the corner, next to the front door. I bet that if I picked through the ash pot there would even be a few antique, half chewed cigar butts from said days past. Rumor has is that on certain nights, a local legend, calling himself *Rio,* held court after hours with selected guests while he read works of his own divination while puffing a curious blend of vanilla and Cavendish pipe tobacco from an authentic hobbit clay pipe.

I shook my head in dismay. These flimsy wooden chairs that my ass was currently precariously perched on wouldn't stand a chance if some fat drunk bastard decided to cut loose on one; worse, if one of these horny half dressed college coeds with their thongs sticking out decided to pull an impromptu pole dancing strip tease. I guess shit like that happens in college towns like this. These tables would be kindling in seconds, and based upon the way they already wobbled, it had all the appearance of someone who had given it a fair go. God knows there are certainly enough rowdy bitches, hopped up on booze and meds, unaware of their sexuality that caused their hormones to go running wild moving about through places like these. Randy young men looking to score would have no trouble hooking up in this dive.

What scared me was that there was no one around to keep a sexual pervert from having his way with a few of these young ladies. There wasn't even a hint of human security, just some cheap plastic cameras. I would love to see what some of the security footage would look like from these cameras, mounted to the walls and ceiling. The fact that there are even cameras in a place like this makes me wonder more than just a little bit as to what kind of shit goes on after the *OPEN* sign gets turned to *CLOSED*. I'm guessing the party doesn't stop. *Was that steam, mist, or bong smoke coming from the cooler?* I suspect that at this point it was anyone's guess, and with the amount of unsupervised teens and young adults running through here, it was anybody's game.

Squeals of mock protest erupted from the dish pit, at the back of the kitchen, and two young girls in their uniform short shorts came running up from the back, attempting a sad protest at the equally young male who was making a pathetic attempt to wash the kitchen ware had given them a friendly spray from

20

the hose. Lord knows, he'd love to spray them with something else if he got the chance. *Dear Christ, was he the one washing the dishes my food was prepared in? I'm going to most likely need to get a course of antibiotics and some antacid in me if I'm going to survive tonight's little escapade.*

This falafel isn't bad, though, and it certainly could be worse. Even with the ratty table and the spindly chair, the scene in here was overwhelming and every time someone brushed passed me, I half expected to be wearing the contents caught in the waxed paper wrapper that was now spread on the table, covering my lap, my own vain attempt to prevent the food from making a hellish mess of my freshly pressed and hemmed slacks, tailored just to my liking.

I had stopped wearing shitty leftover, hand-me-down clothes about the time they handed me my diploma that had the words "Master's Degree" stenciled on it. These slack jawed shits looked as if they don't even give a good God damn, and maybe they don't, but for the love of Christ, I pay good money to look even better and I don't need some spoiled ass, money spending, wet nosed, dripping dick mama's boy who spends their stepdad's money spilling their food and drink all over my *freshly laundered,* and *perfectly tailored* clothing.

It's not that I feel as if I am a fashion model, far from it, with my extra baggage around the midsection, but I keep a clean look that the ladies respect and it is extremely important to me. Yes, my hair is starting to go the way of receding and starting to show a few hints of salt 'n pepper silver in it, but the closely cropped black hair had just the slightest hint of a faux-hawk in the middle, with cleanly shaped and shaved sides. My beard was kept jaw line perfect and the wire rim designer sunglasses perched on my forehead gave a look, as I saw it that was both beautiful and ominous. Or, so I had been told. I like the name brand labels and they look good on me, so why shouldn't I be able to splurge once in a while. Shit, who am I kidding, lots-in-a-while. A freshly pressed, slim fit, grape wine purple button down shirt with sleeves rolled up to the elbows, along with these black slacks and matching black skate shoes had already turned a few heads tonight, from girls and guys alike. It certainly wasn't hurting my feelings, not one bit. With a matching black dress vest and black silk tie with silver tie pin and fob chain there was a hint of royalty to the look, without the snobbery, of course.

People tended to notice guys dressed in a manner like that. Correction, *women* tended to notice men like that and as a single guy, it was nice to have a few warm bodies to keep a fella company every once in a while, yaknow? It also made for a slick-as-hell back cover photo for the book jackets.

Or maybe these young punks thought I'd be more at home in the coffee shop next door, and while I tended to agree with them, this is where I agreed to meet.

Where the hell is Vincent? As I look around and prepare to gnaw on the hardening pita bread I spot Vincent walking down the hallway from the back door of the restaurant. He's carrying a leather satchel, like the ones that old school lawyers would carry, maybe even Gregory Peck in *To Kill a Mockingbird*, and damned if he wasn't grinning from ear to ear, like that sadistic cat from *Alice in Wonderland*. *What the hell was his name...? The Cheshire Cat...?* Vincent's whole posture told the world he had just ducked the bouncer at a club and was now in the VIP room, heading for free champagne and cocaine, not just walking into a downtown dive, clutching that battered satchel as if his very life depended on it.

I can't stand those animation flicks with elves and fairies dancing and singing; that shit scares the hell outta me. I'd prefer a good true crime drama, any day, or a damn good war movie. I can usually figure the bad guy out with a little luck, and the gratuitous release of violence in war movies was always good for some plot filler, but with those fairy dancing flicks and all the animation you never know what the hell was going on, even when the credits were rolling. *Did the good guys win?* Who knows because everyone in those movies all lived happily ever after and everyone knows that is bullshit and that it never happens that way, not in real life.

"Where the hell have you been? I've been sitting here for the better part of forty five minutes," glancing at my expensive watch, with custom cut and tanned leather watch band, "Do you know how bad it smells in here? It's like beer, sweat, hormones and bad breath. And what the fuck is this music, I mean can you even call it music?

"It stinks like bad sex, I mean really bad sex from a cheap hooker in here. I'm pretty sure that there are two people who have no business being out at this late hour right now fucking in the bathroom, creaming all over the toilet seat. It's fucking noisy as shit and I've got a headache." Vincent's gaze followed my finger down the length of the hallway.

"Let's go next door. It's quieter there. My wallet is starting to jam me right into my left ass cheek and I'm not in the mood to be fucked like that tonight. Well, not in a place like this, anyway." It was the best I could manage at humor and maybe I had come across as too harsh, but still, this was just too much too late at night and the stern tone in my voice made sure my displeasure was known.

Vincent's head turned back to me and without asking permission, he leaned in close to me, occupying a lot more real estate on this flimsy table than I was comfortable with. Cheap aftershave and booze *(Was that really booze?)* mingled on his collar. *Oh God, was Vincent shitfaced, too?* I don't think I could deal with another stinking drunk, not in this close proximity. His crooked teeth were in desperate need of a dentist's chair and maybe probably some serious orthodontic surgery. "It's... *He's* called Skrillex, and he's a new artist on the scene. It's some trip house stuff the kids are just shitting their beds for these days. I've been told that the music is supposed to be an audible representation of a drugged induced orgasm."

Without managing to lose my food in my stomach I asked, "Who the fuck thinks this shit up? And what kind of, *who's kind of* fucking orgasm is this, anyway? Who would think to record something like...*that*?"

Vincent just smiled back, "Why are you so interested in the sounds and smells in here? Yeah, it stinks, welcome to a college town late at night. If people are out at this hour they aren't going to be smelling all that pretty now are they? They're looking to score some drugs, score some sex, and generally get into all manner of shenanigans. It's hot as hell outside, and it ain't much better in here. Probably gonna storm too, by the feel of it. Kids this age are filthy and stinky and they are oozing Gods-be-damned hormones through their skin. Seriously, I thought you were like some sort of a smart guy, or something."

I shot Vincent an extremely disapproving look that related I was not amused with his side show commentary.

"Anyway, shut up about the music and the smells, I've got some news for you. You wanna hear about it?" He had a tone in his voice, and his head cocked like a late night info-mercial salesman. His eyes sparkled like he knew I was hooked on the newest product fad and was going to buy two of them.

Apparently my face continued to convey that I was less than enthused about this current situation as that look on Vincent's sour face quickly dissipated. It was the hardest thing I could do

24

to not be reaching over the table and throttling this little shithead. Vincent continued on, acting as if he hadn't heard me, though I am pretty sure he had.

"I'm sure this music will allow a fair cover of anonymity so people don't hear what I have to tell you. This is the kind of information that can get people killed, and unless I've missed my mark, I think that it already has. The kind of people that are involved in this narrative, these narratives that I would like to impart to you, are the kind of people that have eyes and ears everywhere. They have the ability to get to people and ensure that those people who are 'gotten to' don't do a whole lot of speaking after that. Or walking, or breathing, yaknow?"

Vincent mimicked a finger gun to his left temple and the impression wasn't lost on me. I stare at him, "Already has...*what*...? Gotten someone killed?"

Vincent nodded, "Yes, I think so."

Dejectedly, I drop my cheap paper napkin on to the waxed paper. Wringing it through my fingers has done little more than to smear the food over my hands. With another dejected *SIGH*, I hold my arms up, hands open, as if to say *Please, continue on; give me all of your secrets.*

"Vincent why would I give a shit about what you are going to tell me? There's no one here who is sober enough to remember tomorrow morning that they were even *here* tonight," gesturing towards the plethora of odd people scattered across this shabby dive, "Look at these drunk motherfuckers; they're fucking animals. Look at that whore over there. She's fucking got her pants riding so damn low that Victoria doesn't have a whole lot of secrets left."

Gesturing to the blonde haired Nordic beauty who could have easily been a fashion model, a volleyball player, or a rodeo queen; shit she could have been all three at once. Standing

25

against the soda fountain her tight fitting tank top showed enough side boob that I was pretty sure she was hoping to score, or really going out of her way to prove what a feminist she was. Her cut-off jeans turned hot pants had her well toned, and well tanned ass cheeks hanging out the bottom and even the rear pockets were showing fabric.

Vincent didn't give her more than a passing glance. Was he queer? All of a sudden a thought like that made me even more uncomfortable. I didn't give two shits about a person's sexuality, but suddenly a person like him intently wanting to be alone in a room with me was so much more disconcerting. Maybe it was a good thing we had met in this place.

"Vincent this place is a raging basket of teenage and 20 something hormones. No one gives a shit."

As I continued to try and read Vincent's face, a man wearing mirrored aviator sunglasses and khaki pants, button up shirt and flip flops walked past me, with a messenger bag across his back. He stopped long enough at the soda fountain to admire the Nordic girl's tits, then pulled a neon paper copy band poster from the bag and tacked it to the corkboard near the front door. As he exited he turned to give the Nordic girl's rack another long and healthy glance. She noticed and gave him a very flirtatious smile. He smiled back, touched his fingers to his lips as if to mimic a parent *SHUSHING* their child, and slipped out the front door. I didn't see this so much as catch the highlights out of the corner of my eye. I was still fixed on Vincent's face, trying to get a read on him, and where he was going with this story of his.

I had first met Vincent a few years ago when I was on one of the required tours my publisher set up for my newly published crime novel *Detective Stories after Dark*. He was in the receiving line and he insisted that he had a story that was going to "blow me away," it was going to "knock my socks off," and generally get me all wet and excited because of, as he put it, "the darkness involved." I thought that perhaps he was taking this whole *darkness* thing a little too far, but I was happy to hear him out. I figured if he had a good idea or two, hell, I might borrow them for a new novel. It's amazing how quickly art can start to imitate real life, and vice versa, and if you are ready with a mental note pad, you can glean some of the best ideas from just watching people. Hell, these ideas were often the rough draft lyrics to a brand new opera; I just needed to add a backbeat and some rhythm. Then I could really have a brand new tune to put down on paper.

Listening to him talk though, you'd think he had uncovered the secret resting place of the Holy Grail, and I really didn't think it polite to point out that a certain critically acclaimed author had already done that story line, quite well I might add, and it was of no use to make an attempt at rehashing it. Honestly, I didn't think that I had a snowball's chance in hell of retelling it any better.

No, Vincent claimed to be on the track of a serial killer who had never been caught, much less one who had even been labeled a serial killer. He claimed that he had found, stumbled upon rather, some clues that were so obvious that they had never been connected. *Hiding in plain sight*, he'd said. I'd heard stuff like this before from everyone and their dog that had had a great idea for a true crime or detective novel. Thing was, every once in a great while, these people were half right.

I listened to him as briefly as etiquette would allow and when it was time for him to move on, I tried to gently, but firmly, shove him off down the line. As I switched focus to the next person in line, Vincent took the hint and promised to contact me soon with the *pertinents*, as he called them. At that point I had actually been a bit excited but that enthusiasm, as well as my patience, had started to fade soon after. I have enough on my plate and enough things going on that I can't keep a mental note pad of people I meet and the ideas they have, especially when said person doesn't bother to get back to you within a reasonable amount of time.

That was two years ago, well beyond what I believed to be a reasonable amount of time, and it was just last week that I had received a voicemail from Vincent saying he'd like to meet me, here in Bozeman, Montana. My most immediate concern was how he had tracked down my personal cell phone number. Hell, my own agent didn't even have this number and I preferred it that way. Sometimes anonymity was the best policy, and as a writer it helped to keep a healthy and safe barrier between myself and some of the "adoring throngs".

I don't know, or see, what's special about this town. I'd much rather be somewhere warmer, but the mountains aren't too bad, I guess. I've seen worse scenery. Seattle was pretty shitty, rainy and generally grumpy people with their grunge music. If there wasn't so damn much snow, this town might have a chance to be somewhat beautiful. There were too damned many yuppies and rich college kids running through this town to make it the quiet hamlet everyone thought it was, or pretended it to be. I can't ski so the whole mountain thing really doesn't do much for me, aside from an occasional back country trek with one of my West Coast buddies, Reef. High school injuries prevented me from ever again strapping on a pair of skis, or worse a snowboard, without landing myself in the office of a good orthopedic surgeon, or worse, under said surgeon's skilled (hopefully) knife.

My place in Boston was a far nicer place than this town, and the anonymity it allowed me was far superior. Put on a Redsox cap and you could disappear on damn near any street in just about any neighborhood. Well, except Southie. Piss the wrong person off there, and you just might disappear, permanently. Or if you were lucky enough to be found, it would be later in Dorchester Bay. Either way, not a good vibe. Like any major city you had to know where it was safe to be and when it was safe to be there. This town, for all its fluff, hell I could walk the streets at any hour and not have to worry about a single thing. Maybe an occasional transient bum looking to hit you up for a buck or two to buy some cheap wine from one of the many casino liquor stores that dotted the city map would cause a bit of harassment, but nothing more.

Currently I called a nice corner brownstone on Dartmouth Street in Back Bay my home. It blended in nicely, fit my lifestyle and lived up to my style demands. I looked like the folk, I talked like the folk, and dammit, I was pretty good at living there. I did some of my best writing from the third floor loft that overlooked the bay. Even the granite tiles and black marble pillars in the entry lent themselves to my creative talents. With a build year of around 1870 I was pretty sure it was indeed haunted and that gave me some great writing inspiration. I don't think that I was ever going to find something like that here in this town. Besides, the convenience that Boston allowed me to escape to Puerto Rico, or other Caribbean islands, could not be matched by this particular town.

As if to punctuate my thought process a reflection of jagged, angry purple lighting streaked across the hot summer night's sky. Looks like Vincent was right, after all. Maybe that was the reason for my current mood. Whenever the weather changed like it was right now, I got testier than a basket of bees being rained on. Tingling spikes of radiating pain shot down my left arm leaving my fingertips numb and about useless. The weather in Boston was for more predictable and workable and I was able to keep my temperament on more even keel. Also, I was currently up well past my normal bedtime and if I was going to make my lecture, tomorrow, I was going to need to get some rest, some real sleep at some point tonight.

I was scheduled to give an early morning guest lecture to some writing students on how real world and writing can overlap, at the campus of Montana State, and Vincent had said he could drive up and meet me at my hotel room. I wasn't near as comfortable with that idea as Vincent would have liked and I counter suggested we meet in more of a public place. Maybe it was the writer in me, or maybe I had started to take my own work too seriously, which was easy to do when you put as much research into the novels as I did, but I wanted a public venue where we sure to be seen if something happened. Either way I certainly didn't want to be in a secluded space with him, I barely knew the man and I damn sure didn't trust him. Him and those damned crooked teeth of his. I really should have carried a firearm for things like this. A nice little snub nosed .38 would have worked, but the permitting for those things, especially on the East Coast was a bitch I didn't want to deal with. A nice spring assisted folding gentleman's knife, clipped to the inside of my pants pocket kept me feeling safe and it kept a cleaner look, anyway. There was no clamshell holster to be digging into my kidneys while I waited on Vincent's story.

"Vincent, what's so important? I've been researching tomorrow's lecture for the better part of this day, this day that is pretty much over and I'm friggin' beat. You said you had an idea, let's hear about it, 'K? I need to get back to my hotel room, get some freaking sleep, and be on a plane, at six o'clock tomorrow afternoon, which means I have to be at the airport by four thirty. I'm scheduled to be lecturing and doing meet and

30

greets with various students and people from about nine o'clock in the morning until about three o'clock in the afternoon. That doesn't leave me a lot of precious time in between and as soon as I get back to Boston there is going to be even more research. There are more lectures and book signings to be done. Also, I have a meeting with a guy down in Tallahassee who is going to hook me up with some research and notes that are going to go into the next book. I'd like to make all my connecting flights, yaknow, if you are OK with that; if that's possible."

My particular hotel room was in a newer joint, Hilton style hotel out on 19th Avenue North, just down the road from the off ramp of Interstate 90, next to a semi decent burger joint. Hell, we could have met there. It was a classy enough joint but it was more of a sports bar cum throwback establishment that Mom and Pop never would have approved of. With all the tawdry neon and TV noise it wasn't conducive to normal conversation, but I would bet a fair sum of money that people didn't meet there for the conversation. With a TV turned on, turned up and tuned to just about any sporting event you could want, or bet on, it was an orgasmic digital joyland for those short on attention span and long on the current sports' odds. The university here in Bozeman had a going rivalry with the university in Missoula and apparently football team from Town A was playing football team from Town B, and there was quite the wager going on, or so I'd heard. My driver who brought me in from the airport was telling me all about it and you'd've thought he hit the million dollar lotto with his plans for the money if his team won. Whichever one wore the maroon jerseys, I guess. They weren't my New England Patriots and therefore didn't warrant much of my attention. I'd been told, in the past, that a local guy from Bozeman was now playing for the Patriots and that made my heart do a small flutter when I thought about it because even though I was considered, by many, to be famous, I still got pretty fan girl crazy when I happened to run into an equally famous person. Call it my modesty, but I still blushed when shaking hands with other literary minds and accomplished authors.

However, I'd been to that particular establishment in the past, on previous trips through this particular neighborhood, and I've had their burgers before and they were good, not *stellar,* but good. The beer was cold, though, and that certainly didn't hurt the argument. Even the gal that ran the game room, trying to pass itself off as a legitimate casino, at said sports bar cum burger establishment was cute; quite the looker, in fact. Her dirty blonde corkscrew hair always bounced when she saw me, and that smile of hers could light up the room. Her skin tight black shorts, and skin tight black T-shirt, fairly well accentuated by her ample breasts and hips. Shit, I could have easily walked her across the parking lot, taken her back to my hotel room, given her a bounce and a twirl after her shift was over and not felt the least bit bad about it. She couldn't have been a day over 21 but I'm sure she knew a few tricks to impress a fella in the bed room. I'm further sure she had some dimples on those round ass cheeks of hers that she wouldn't mind having squeezed while I watched that springy hair of hers, pulled back into a sporty little pony, tail bounce up and down...

Coming back to reality, as the image of the game room girl bouncing up and down on my crotch faded and slowly Vincent rematerialized while he spoke... *Was that a soft woody pressing against my slacks?*

"You remember when I told you I had a great story idea?" Vincent was still leaning over the cheap fiberboard table and grinning ear to God damned ear. His long, greasy hair was originally slicked back in what could have passed as a mobster haircut, but when it fell out of place, he looked more like the kind of gamer kid who sat in his mom's basement jerking off to cheap porn and wishing he could get laid. God he was just too creepy. His clothes were a stark contrast to my own. While I was proud of the fact I paid good money for my clothes, Vincent seemed very agreeable to purchasing his clothes, or dumpster diving for them, at a discount rate and the pattern of his ill fitting suit jacket didn't match the pattern and fabric of his equally ill fitting pants and his stained button down shirt that had once been white but was now stained to a dirty ivory coloring with an honest to God sweat ring around the collar.

"Yeah, I remember. I also remember you said you'd be in contact; *soon*, I believe is what you said. That was two fucking years ago. I'd hate to see if you were taking your fucking time. So, what's the big deal?"

Vincent's eyes gleamed like it was Christmas morning, "I've been following a serial killer around. I don't think they know it, yet, but I've been following their career, going back some twenty years. Maybe... Probably further than that, actually."

"They?" I was instantly skeptical. Serial killers rarely worked in pairs. My Master's Degree in Criminal Sociology told me that if killers did work in pairs, or tandem partnerships, it was often to satisfy a mutual need that the partnership served, or it was one killer asserting dominance over the other. Such was the case of a certain serial killer, dubbed the *Candy Man*, in 1970's Dallas, Texas.

Rarely, though, were there pairs of Bonnie and Clyde style killers running around, offing people and knocking over gas stations in an epic Hollywood fashion. Too often it became a liability and it often became hard for the alpha in the group to maintain a level of dominance required for volatile partnerships such as these to function for any length of time. Invariably, secrets begin to leak, trust was often breached, and after an extended period of time it becomes hard to keep the secret if you aren't able to trust your partner in crime, as it were. If the alpha were perceived as weak, or if the inferior partner began to become too inferior, it usually ended violently. Take the case of the *Candy Man*, for example, when his own protégée had straight up offed him, more for a self defense tactic than anything else, but also to assert a level of dominance. Maybe, just maybe, it was just to make the violence stop.

Vincent looked annoyed, as if I wasn't paying enough attention to him. "I'm saying *they* because I don't know if it's one or more people, if *they* are male or female; you get the idea." He waived his hand in front of his face, in a dismissive fashion, as if to clear phantom cobwebs from his eyes.

"No, *they* are a very peculiar killer. *They* seem to be more opportunistic rather than purpose driven. It's almost as if *they* are killing out of sheer impulse and not really to satisfy a need or to 'calm the demons.' There appears to be no rhyme or reason to this particular methodology. There is nothing logical, sequential, or even plausible about their patterns; if you could even call it a pattern."

Holding up my hand to pause him, I said, "Vincent, I have a college degree; a few of them, actually. I understand the criminal mind and criminal behavior pretty well, that's why I write stories about them."

I was a little annoyed, myself, right now. Vincent wasn't sharing anything specific regarding story information that was going to get my dick hard. Rather, it felt like I was back in a 101 class being taught by a pimply faced, first year teacher's assistant.

Vincent nodded in deference, "OK, I admit you're the better mind, here, when it comes to crime. But think about it, what are the two main factors that drive homicidal rage? I'm talking pure, homicidal rage." He motioned for me to pick up the conversation.

Nodding I said, "When you boil it all down, it basically becomes motive and opportunity. One doesn't necessarily have to be a predictor of the other, however, they generally, in some distant ways, come in contact with each other.

"However, if only one behavior is present, it can lead to a murder, often times, it would be a killer's first murder."

Vincent was nodding in agreement, "Exactly! But, does it *always* have to be the two? What if a sociopath simply one day saw an opportunity? Or simply had the means to execute a murder? That wouldn't leave a lot of clues or patterns for the cops to follow, would it? It would almost be downright impossible to trace, wouldn't it?

"Think about these kinds of murders spanning several states; over the course of several years. What if the victims had absolutely no connection, whatsoever, like hair color, height, skin tone, all the things that a serial killer might identity with. Let's say that the *only* connecting factor is that there are no connecting factors.

"You take all these unsolved murders and start to compare them, compare the elements of each murder. Even unintentional things, say for example whether a killer is right handed or left handed will start to leave comparing features. If a killer is right handed, X amount of feet tall, X amount of inches from shoulder to wrist, etc. they are going to leave a specific cut pattern on the victim, if the victim is stabbed. Gunshot wounds will have a specific projectile trajectory, even if the killer is methodical about using various weapons, altering their methodologies, that sort of thing."

Picking at my falafel, which was now stone cold and covered in the congealed tzatziki sauce, I said, "Vincent, something like seventy percent of the population in the United States is right handed..."

"Closer to ninety percent, actually," he interrupted.

Waiving my own hand at the phantom cobwebs I said, "Whatever. The point is that you're basing a lot of common factors together and trying to manipulate conclusions out of data that seems already biased towards one direction. It's a pretty flimsy argument."

Vincent was looking a little deflated, which I thought was good. Maybe he'd see a bit of reason. I'm guessing the reality that he's no Peter Faulk is slowly slipping into his mind at this very moment.

"See, you're the one who's already got tunnel vision. You're assuming because one situation is true, it's the only way it can be. What I'm saying is that we know these things are true, so let's use them to solidify the argument."

I sighed, "Vincent, what the fuck are we getting at, here? I'm tired. Get on with this thought process of yours, I'm getting way too tired, actually, to continue with this discussion."

"OK. Just listen. I stumbled across a case, a while back. It seemed pretty benign, but the more I poked around, it seemed a little *hinky*. Now it could be nothing, but I think after I tell you about a few of these cases, you'll piece it together." He opened the leather satchel of his and pulled a sheaf of papers that was clipped together with various colored paperclips, and rubber banded around the midsection.

"Hinky, huh?"

Vincent was nodding enthusiastically, nearly waiving the papers in my face. "Yeah, a lot of stuff that just doesn't seem to want to add up and the more I look at it, it could all be a fantastic coincidence, or it could be that it's something like what we've just been talking about."

I sighed, and once again put down my cheap paper napkin, this was going to be a long night, after all. "Fine, tell me a story."

Vincent unbanded the papers and spread a few of them on the table, opening his mouth as he did so, he began his tale.

TAKE THE 12:15 TO
BROOKLYN

"Bobby! Didjya tip the boy?!" DeeDee's shrill scream rang across the deserted gas station. Her thick Brooklyn accent, punctuated by a thick and persistent smoker's cough was a stark contrast to her lined Spanish features. The "boy" was actually a 34 year old delivery driver named Nick who, every week without fail, arrived to stock the shelves with the candies and small grocery items of this dilapidated and decaying business that sat in the intersecting shadows of Interstate 684 and Highway 35, just a few hundred feet down Old Deer Park Road. Even the updated Harlem Line tracks that ran past the station seemed to overshadow the building, and shake the building with their high speed locomotives that brought all manner of people into the heart of New York City, a glaring contrast of new and old. Bobby, was DeeDee's nineteen year old son and was the on-site mechanic and shop manager. DeeDee may have kept the books and court in the rear of the building, but it was Bobby who kept the doors open, the business moving, and the lights on.

The gas station was a simple affair consisting of a 1,200 square foot building that contained one small but efficient service bay that currently housed a sun faded robin's egg blue VW Vanagon in need of a new muffler that Bobby was currently working on at the idiot rate of $175 per hour. The owners were some free spirit hippies who were, in their words, "trying to retrace their roots" and in no need of a vehicle, or their money, as they floated around town. They paid the fee for the muffler and the work up front, as well as enough to store the Vanagon while they moved about the streets of the town. Bobby wasn't real sure what they were searching for since Woodstock was still another 90 miles north along the I-87 corridor. As long as the signature on the credit card receipt was good, and the card

41

didn't come back *DECLINED*, there was no problem in Bobby's books, or even DeeDee's books.

Whitewashed siding that was weathered and in desperate need of repair and repainting still managed to keep the harsh winter winds out, and the green shingle roof, while it too was in need of a makeover, still kept the snow and rain outside. Matching green storm shutters had been permanently nailed open, against the siding since Bobby had convinced DeeDee to spring for new windows that could sustain the harsh New York winters. A small apartment above the store served the needs of both Bobby and DeeDee nicely, allowing for sufficient living quarters without causing DeeDee's checkbook to have a small coronary. Bobby had, in the past, looked into separate living quarters but when DeeDee found out, that idea was quickly struck down.

"There's no reason to spend money when we don't have to," she'd chide him. Bobby, who was not really looking to get into another argument with his mother, just let the whole argument slide, and eventually he stopped looking for a new place, all together. More and more it seemed as if it was going to be just a pipe dream, anyway.

Four interior aisles of the store did indeed hold all manner of snacks and convenience items. A sad looking, sagging lunch counter sat in the back, often doubling as DeeDee's desk. A partitioned area behind it had once held a small kitchen where blue plate lunch specials had been dutifully prepared. These days the "kitchen" was more of a break room for DeeDee and Bobby and more and more was piling up a sad collection of office machines and furniture that was in disrepair that DeeDee was too cheap to shell out for.

Papers, invoices, and all manner of legal correspondence piled up on one side while a constantly overfull ashtray spilled half smoked Marlboro cigarettes on to the floor. Smoking was technically illegal in public buildings but the service station was far enough removed from the hustle and bustle that no one really thought to protest. The small amount of customers that did frequent the business either pretended not to notice the yellow pall of lighting and cigarette smoke that swirled about from the ceiling fans overhead, but never quite dissipated, or the customers were themselves smoking. Either way DeeDee wasn't near a stickler about the health codes as she was for the checkbook and the bottom line.

Once upon a time this had been a conservative, family friendly stop, but progress and technology had quickly overshadowed old ways and good old days. Industry and progress had moved the world on, around the store that DeeDee had inherited from her late husband, but her duty to his dream bordered on obsession. The land was a gold mine that she refused to give up, even when "some goons" had showed up bearing a marked bank case full of brand new, neat and crisp, one hundred dollar bills. No questions asked. But, DeeDee wasn't about to give up on Edward's dream, even if her late husband had been dead for seven years running. Like Marley he was dead as a doornail.

Businesses and individuals had, for years, been attempting to buy out DeeDee and Bobby, who was named as a co-owner in the business, because of desires to level the station, and rebuild it with a newer, fancier place that would be sure to attract new droves of clients, eager to appease their children on long road trips, or traveler's eager to relieve their bladder from the last station stop's sixty four ounce bladder buster soda fountain pop.

"Ma, for the last time, we don't tip the delivery boys. It's their job." Bobby had actually slipped Nick a greasy $20 bill from the pocket of his oily garage coveralls, but his mother would have shit a solid gold kitten if she knew he was giving away money so freely. While his father's life insurance policy had left them well enough off, there was no woman who was as tight fisted about money as his mother was. DeeDee even scoffed at spending money on the occasional girl that showed interest in Bobby and so often, the only woman in his life was his mother.

Bobby wasn't by any means ugly but his face still bore the scars of teenage acne that never fully went away, and the long, straggly strands of red hair didn't cover the scars, so much as draw attention to his neglected face. This self-consciousness often led him to shy away from people; Nick might have been the closest thing that Bobby had to a real friend. Bobby's slight build could have once been athletic, but neglect and a poor diet now made him look malnourished and sallow as opposed to fit and trim.

Katonah, New York, where DeeDee and Bobby currently called home, had once been a sleepy village, and in many ways still was. With a population that barely topped ten thousand on a good day, the only people left in these parts were the old and the filthy rich, sometimes these were one and the same. All of the younger folk had hopped aboard the 12:15 train to Brooklyn and joined a faster, modern world, seeking adventure, fame and the bright lights of the big city. This was a town meant to be quiet and to retain a small bit of colonial heritage. An odd mix of old and new was the staple definition of what this burg was all about. Christian Science churches moved into old three story houses. Cobblestone sidewalks abutted up to new asphalt streets. Old colonial architecture clashed with modern metal architecture for houses and businesses. Even the proud white heritage of the city left DeeDee more often than not getting the stinky eye from a few stubborn store owners. Her Spanish heritage was just off white enough to ensure that others would suspect for the least little thing.

Nineteen years earlier DeeDee, Edward, and newborn Bobby had themselves hopped the same rail line that took so many young people out of this town, and actually moved in. Edward's dream had always been to own his own business and after working for so many task masters over the years he had finally saved enough money to buy this small service station. In his dreams it was going to be a classic general store, where travelers could get all manner of goods and information as they carried on about their way; a very modern representation of 1950s Americana and American Dream.

Growing up in a small Midwestern town, Edward had brought his strong work ethic to a new change of scenery by moving to the East Coast when he himself was only 17. Edward was 20 when his brother, Dominic, joined him Brooklyn. The two shared a small flat above the bakery on Martense Street, across from the butcher shop that sold all varieties of exotic meats, with Edward's new bride, DeeDee.

Six months after his twenty second birthday Edward, along with DeeDee, welcomed their new son, Robert, named for DeeDee's father, into the world. Dominic couldn't see his nephew being called Robert and immediately took to calling him Bobby, and the name stuck. Bobby's shocking red hair could only have come from Edward's side of the family, and coupled with DeeDee's striking Spanish features, he was sure to be a handsome boy. He even took to toddling about earlier than normal leading his parents to believe he had unlocked a very special and wonderful sports gift.

When Bobby was four months old, too young to remember, his family buried his uncle Dominic in a small plot of a largely forgotten cemetery in an equally forgotten neighborhood. The victim of a mugging gone awry a would-be thief had plunged a knife into Dominic's chest, all for the thirty seven dollars that he had in his wallet. Dominic died, cold and alone, on a damp February night on the sidewalk in front of the walk up entrance to the shared flat. Police canvassed the neighborhood for the assassin, but no leads were ever brought to fruition and the killer was never caught, nor the murder weapon ever recovered. Eventually the neighborhood let the story die and it became the basis of myth and legend. Parents would often ensure their children were prompt with their curfew, however, as in some circles the story had grown to legendary proportions in which the killer was not merely a killer, but a dark demon sent to claim the souls of children who misbehaved and disobeyed their parents.

This was all the motivation that Edward needed to pack his family up and move them north, to the quiet streets of Katonah, New York. Dominic was buried in a pauper's grave beneath a cheap headstone in a cheaper casket, and that was all that was left to mark their time in Brooklyn. Katonah, was in of itself a small hamlet town to the larger town of Bedford. It was just the kind of environment that Edward and DeeDee needed to raise their son in, quiet and safe. Good school, great museums, a solid history. Hints of Neil Diamond still wafted from open windows during the warm spring months, marking the return of times when children would pull the covers to the town's fire plugs and entertain themselves in the small flood that would collect in the corner intersections.

That dream quickly started to deflate, and even more quickly unraveled, when the town council approved the construction of a new, high tech truck stop cross corner from the small town friendly service station that Edward had in mind. Gossip around

46

the Sunday tables stated that Albert Hause, himself an out of towner, and lead councilman, was in bed with some of these companies, and was lining his own pockets with small contributions from companies wishing to set up shop in the fair town.

All manner of lights and neon and chrome blinked on and off twenty four hours a day while DeeDee promptly closed up shop at nine o'clock. She needed to be in bed early, if she was going to get up early and have the station open by six o'clock. She was as prompt as the watch on her wrist that her late husband had bought her on their first anniversary.

"Dammit!" DeeDee slammed her morning copy of the *Bedford-Katonah Beacon* on to the makeshift desk of hers. Pages of the daily rag could be heard rustling all over the empty station. To call it a rag was more credit than it was due, as the paper was about two professional steps above that of a high school newspaper, but it was all they had. More gossip columns and movie reviews than actual news, it served the town's interests and kept the small subscription group happy enough to renew on a month to month basis. It arrived promptly on the station doorstep every day by seven o'clock, delivered by the McLaren boy whose father owned the hardware store. This kid was going places, DeeDee could feel it. He had a real sense of business about him, just like his old man.

"Ma, waddaya bitchin' about?" Bobby came in from the service bay where he had the old silver GE radio tuned to WRKI out of Brookfield, Connecticut. The classic rock that the DJ's favored on this station was a welcome change to the talk news radio blather that his mother insisted on listening to inside the main building. Bobby was sure the old kooks out of Mount Kisco only hired the absolutely delusional or the overly paranoid because every manner of conspiracy theory was thrown around like it was fact, debated until the callers were blue in the face, and argued about with the wisdom of drunks at the local pubs and watering holes.

If Bobby wanted politics he would turn on the C-Span channel that came free with the cable, in the apartment above, which was a rare occasion. Instead, he preferred to listen to the music his father listened to, while he was growing up. It seemed far more pure and wholesome than the news radio pundits, and Bobby didn't hesitate to agree that his father's spirit was just a bit closer when the music played, long and loud.

DeeDee turned down her radio and with the ever present cigarette stuck in her lip, folded over the thin sheet of printed news paper, quoting the *Beacon* stating "...Governor Andrew Cuomo has legalized gambling in the state of New York...guaranteed income for the state..." Her voice trailed off in disgust as she continued to scan the rest of the article, her quivering lips spitting cigarette ash over the counter top.

"Ma, I don't see what the big deal is. It's not like this is going to hurt us. It's just some innocent gambling."

DeeDee looked up, "Waddaya new here?" Jerking a thumb over her shoulder, she continued, "You know this means they are just going to install more of those electronic gambling machines at that big rig stop and go over yonder. What little business we got ourselves here in this little slice of heaven is gonna go south real darn quick if people find out they can gamble on those devil machines while they get gas jockeyed. People don't want authentic customer service, not like we offer here, no they want something to make their mind go mush when they get that few minutes out of the vehicle. They want a false promise of a quick payday."

Bobby did his best to hold his scoff back when his mother mentioned 'customer service.' That was about the last thing his mother offered. It was a wonder people didn't run in horror from the monster with the AquaNet sprayed hair and matching blue cloud of cigarette smoke that bellowed orders from the back of the store.

Continuing on, as if she hadn't noticed his smirk, DeeDee said, "Waddaya we got here? Blueberry muffins from the bakery? Nick only comes once a week and by then we are throwing out more of 'em than we are selling."

In truth, they were throwing out most of the baked goods, because no one came here for them. No one came for the muffins, or the lip balm that the Chamber of Commerce has printed with their slogan, "Authentic New York" on the white tube. No one came for the gas, unless the waiting line at the other stops was longer than usual, and they certainly didn't come for DeeDee's wise council, either.

Bobby twisted a greasy rag in his hands, "Well then maybe we outta get ourselves one or two of those machines..."

Before he could finish DeeDee's voice rose two full octaves as she shrieked, "You think your father would approve of that in his business?! This was meant to be a family establishment, not a den of evil!" Never mind that DeeDee could curse a blue streak that would have the sailors in port running for cover with red faces of embarrassment.

"Ma, Pop's dead. He has been for damn near a decade now. You really think he gives a damn what goes on down here? This was his dream, not mine, and I'm starting to wonder if it ever was yours."

"Robert Alvin Martinson you wash your mouth out with soap right now! Your father's ticker would kill him a second time over if he heard you say that!

"And don't you think for a second that I'm not his dutiful wife. It was, and still is my job to carry on the wishes of my husband, regardless of if he is dead or not!"

Bobby studied his shoes, "Ma, I love you, and I love Pop, but this is not my dream. One day I'm gonna wake up and be forty years old, still here, and not a thing to show for it.

"Ma, I'm thinking about taking the 12:15 down to Brooklyn. They have opportunities there. They have schools there. There's nothing here. It's becoming a black pit in my heart. It's literally sucking at my soul, Ma."

DeeDee used a nicotine yellow stained finger to lift her son's chin, and looked her son in the eye, "First of all, young man, you have plenty to show for it. You have your father's legacy, this station is his legacy." DeeDee waved the one hand that wasn't clamped to a stubby cigarette butt around as if to expound on the holdings of his kingdom.

"Bobby, they have schools here, too. Good schools. That's why your father came here. He didn't need you mixed up in a gang or shot dead like his brother, Dominic." Her voice had calmed down a bit and the volume was back down to reasonable levels.

"Ma, he was stabbed. Uncle Dominic was stabbed. I know Pop wanted a good life for us, but right now, the life is in Brooklyn, not here."

DeeDee studied her son's face, "You think you can just go down to Brooklyn and make a life for yourself down there? Who's gonna take care of ya? Who's gonna make sure there is food on the table? Huh? You gonna get shacked up with some street whore and maybe *not* get a case of the clap?"

"Ma, you and Pop raised me better'n that and you know that, and for the love of God, welcome to the real world, Ma. It's

50

called Chlamydia. It's an STD. And they can treat it with a shot, yaknow."

DeeDee studied her son, further. "Oh really, smart guy, since you know so much. You know they use penicillin to treat that? You forget you're allergic to that stuff? Bobby you get sick out there and it'll kill ya, son."

Bobby had had enough of this conversation and was looking for an exit to end it, "Ma, how come you seem to know so much about STD's?"

Faster than he could react, Bobby's mother reached across the counter and slapped him hard enough to leave bright red fingerprints across his face. Stunned by her sudden outburst Bobby recoiled. Never had his mother raised her hand to him, not in such a violent manner. Not even when he had argued his case for moving out and the ensuing threat of her being all by herself had she raised her voice, or her hand to him.

"Boy, you better watch how you speak to your mother. I won't have that tone in this house. You will keep a civil tongue when you speak to me, do you understand me?" Her sudden switch to a proper tone, all hint of accent and slang gone from her voice; that was enough to let Bobby know he had really crossed the line.

"Christ in a cartoon, Ma, this isn't even a real house. This is a fucking gas station on the edge of the sticks. We sold the house, remember? I sure do. I remember Pop kicking the bucket, and the insurance company dicking us around until we had to sell the goddamn house so we could eat! I remember the house, Ma. I remember because I had a whole damn floor to myself. Now I share a toilet with my own mother!"

Now DeeDee Martinson looked as if she was the one who had been slapped. The horror on her face would not have been more prominent if a master painter had put it on display in one of Katonah's chic art museums.

Bobby really did want to feel bad for his mother at that moment, but he also wanted her to know just how angry he was, and that for just one minute this wasn't all about DeeDee Martinson, that there were others in her globe of influence that had lives and thoughts of their own.

"Bobby, the insurance company paid the claim. You know they have to do the investigation. When a man that young dies of a heart attack in his own garage, of course they are going to investigate. They paid the claim, Bobby."

"Yeah, pretty convenient, Ma. They took just long enough that we had to sell off the house." Bobby was looking at the rag in his hands, again. "You think this is what Pop would want for us? Ma, if I go down to Brooklyn, I can get a job there. I can get a job earning some real money. Maybe even finish college. Then I could get you back into a real house. Ma, those stairs gotta be killing your back going up and down 'em every day."

DeeDee looked wistful, "A real house would be nice."

Bobby turned to walk back into the service bay, "Ma, just think about it. 'K?"

Before DeeDee could respond, a rare occurrence happened, a real life customer walked into the store. She turned to help the young couple that had walked in.

"Excuse me, ma'am? Could you help us with directions?" Dressed in outdoor clothes straight from R.E.I. they looked a little bewildered with their forest service map. "We're trying to get to Ninham Mountain State Forest. The map says we're close, but we've been driving around in circles for hours."

DeeDee smiled her toothiest, cigarette yellow grin. "Don't worry, you're only about 20 miles south of it. Ya must be new here, right?"

"Gee, ma'am, how'd you know?"

"Oh, I had a feeling."

* * *

Bobby was busying himself in the service bay with the menial tasks and chores that he needed to make the service bay right for the following day, before he closed up shop this evening. The bright red finger marks on his cheek had already started to fade. He knew he shouldn't have provoked his mother, it was his fault.

But, why couldn't she see that this life was going to kill them both, eventually, if they didn't move on in the world? It had always bothered Bobby, growing up without a father. Being a twelve year old without a father was bad enough, but when your father died of a heart attack when he himself was only thirty four was something else entirely. Investigations from insurance companies and law enforcement aside, it was a mark that never really went away.

Rumor mills are never more prevalent than in a small town rumor mill and while other young boys were spending time with their fathers learning how to throw a mean curve ball for Little League, Bobby was reading over autopsy reports. While other fathers and sons worked on derby cars and scouting projects Bobby was at the library trying to decipher autopsy findings in a vain effort to figure out how an otherwise healthy young father and husband had dropped dead in his own service station. He always went in early, to ensure the shop was prepared for the day and DeeDee would show up, after she had dropped Bobby off at school.

But on the morning of August 19, 2007, things were different. DeeDee showed up to find her husband lying face down in a pan of oil just recently drained out of the Chevy

Suburban perched on the hoist above him. Both the Sheriff and the town medical personal showed up in the town's lone ambulance, within minutes, but it was to no avail. Edward Martinson was dead. Autopsy reports showed he was alive when his face went into the oil pan, as signs of oil in his lungs and stomach indicated he had ingested some of the 5W-30.

Initially the sheriff investigated the crime as robbery gone bad; tragically poetic considering it was how his brother had died, but since no money was gone, and nothing had been disturbed in the shop, the rumor mill started up that it was drugs. Without any fact or evidence, Edward Martinson was labeled the victim of a drug overdose, even though the death certificate officially labeled the death a heart attack. In the eyes of the surrounding community a drug overdose made sense, since he was married to that gal with the dark features. She wasn't like the town residents and surely she must come from a shady background, and most certainly had to know some questionable people, themselves with nefarious backgrounds.

Throughout high school Bobby lived in a mild state of fear that the label would be placed on him, as well, though he never so much as took a puff off of one of his mother's half smoked cigarettes. He had tried out for sports but no team or sporting group would accept him. Officially he was allowed to be "on the team" but never receive any court time, or field time, or practice time. It wasn't long before he got the hint and stopped going out for sports, all together. No self respecting small town could afford to have the son of a drug addict on their team, much less be seen as to support such a hideous person. After graduation, right in the middle of the class of about three hundred students, Bobby drifted into anonymity and spent more time here at the service station than anywhere else.

Now, as Bobby was arranging his tools and making sure his seldom used machines were in pristine working order, he heard his mother bawl out his name from the other side of the building.

"Bobby! Get in here!"

Bobby set down his greasy rag and walked into the building, proper. "Waddaya need, Ma?"

"Bobby, get that Jeep out there gassed up for these young folks. They're going camping. Make sure they got a spare Jerry can, 'K?"

"Yeah, sure, Ma." As he turned to head out the door, Bobby noticed a faint smell in the air, above that of his mother's cigarettes. "Hey, Ma, what's that smell? Is something burning in here?"

The young couple began to giggle. The female reached her hand out to show a small, but expertly rolled joint. "You wanna take a hit?"

Bobby looked at his mother with incredulity on his face, "Ma, what the hell is going on here?"

"Oh, Bobby, don't worry, this is one of those natural herbal cigarettes. They say they're actually healthy for you, as they don't have the chemicals in 'em. I guess they even cure the glaucoma."

"Sure they do, Ma. Ring 'em up for fifteen gallons of the premium."

Bobby was a little over his estimation, as the Jeep only took twelve gallons to top it off, but judging by the look on the trio's faces in the back of the station, he didn't think they would notice. He was right. The young man handed over the money without so much as a second look. There was no need for a spare Jerry can, as there was a full one attached to the Jeep's rear bumper.

"Hey, bro. We've got some friends that are coming to meet us. Any chance they've showed up, yet?"

Bobby looked at the young man, quizzically. "They wouldn't be driving a VW Vanagon, would they?"

The young man's face lit up. "Yeah man! That's PJ's bus! Are they here?"

Bobby smiled, "Try the coffee shop on the corner of Grandview and Glenridge. I think they have been hanging out there."

"Cool, bro. That's pretty righteous of you."

Bobby went back to the service bay and continued to straighten up the shop. His father had instilled upon him a sense of tidiness and orderliness. All things that made for running a shop right. Why all the thoughts of Bobby's father, just now? Was it because of the discussion from earlier? Was it really that the conversation this morning had brought out the emotions that had been simmering under the surface? Was he ready to finally hop that 12:15 train and get back to Brooklyn? He hadn't been there since he was an infant, so there really was no way he could have any sort of real attachment to the place, could he?

Knowing that the answers wouldn't be found in a red drawer of metric sockets, Bobby closed up the bay for a lunch break. There were leftover sausages in the kitchen, upstairs, and he was pretty sure Ma could look after the place for an hour or so.

"Ma! I'm going upstairs for some lunch. Ya want anything?" He really hadn't expected much of an answer, but was surprised when he heard DeeDee holler back.

"Bobby, don't worry about me. I'm fine, down here. My friends and I can watch the place."

Shaking his head, Bobby walked up the stairs to the apartment above, already planning his lunch in his head.

Leftover venison sausage, some pickled sauerkraut, and a couple slices of the marble rye bread his mother favored. Then, possibly, if lunch was a success, there would be a nap. It wasn't as if business was gonna come knocking on his door in the next couple of hours.

* * *

Bobby woke to the sun shining through the living room windows. Evening already? The windows faced west, could he have slept that long? Yawning and stretching the sleep from his eyes, Bobby walked downstairs to find his mother not at her usual spot. Rather she was coming in the back door, having taken a load of trash to the dumpster.

Odd, thought Bobby, *she never takes the trash out.* However, he wasn't going to argue on his good fortune. One less cleanup chore for him, tonight, after the station closed up.

"Ma, where'd your friends go?" Bobby looked around but didn't see a soul in the store.

"They went down to that fancy joint you told 'em about. Bobby, I don't understand why people don't just go to the diner, just off of River Road. They have great coffee and it's still seventy five cents a cup. What is so special about that joint over on Grandview?"

"Ma, diner coffee doesn't have a label on it. That's why the kids go to that drive-thru joint. It has a label, it's known. It's known and trusted. The stuff from the diner tastes like watered down gasoline and who knows how many times it's been reheated. It's nasty, Ma."

Looking outside, Bobby saw the Jeep parked in the same spot it had been earlier. "Ma, I thought you said they left."

DeeDee looked outside, as if she had forgotten the Jeep was there. "Yeah, they said they was gonna walk over."

"Ma, it's like two miles away."

Jabbing a nicotine yellow finger into Bobby's stomach she fired back, "Yeah, Mr. Universe, like you couldn't stand to lose a little weight and get some exercise, yourself." An empty threat as Bobby was all but swimming in his father's old coveralls.

Bobby responded, "Well, did they leave the keys, Ma? They're blocking one side of the pump."

"You really think we are gonna be that busy that we need both sides of the pump, tonight? We close in three hours, Bobby. If we need to, we can push it out of the way."

Bobby knew that he was at the losing end of the argument. It was better to just walk away. "Ma, I'm gonna finish straightening up the shop, then how's about we go grab us a bite to eat, for dinner?" The reference to spending money would surely rile his mother up, he knew, but he was even more surprised when she agreed. "Just lemme run up stairs and freshen up." Bobby shook his head in amazement. Maybe his mother was starting to come around, after. Maybe he would be hopping that train sooner, rather than later.

While his mother was upstairs freshening up her hair and makeup, Bobby went over to the pump to check on the Jeep. Most curiously, the keys were still in the ignition. *Why would they take off and leave the keys in the ignition?* thought Bobby.

Checking the door handle, Bobby saw the Jeep was unlocked so he reached in, took the keys and locked the doors. Taking the keys into the service station, his intent was to put them on a hook where he kept other keys from repairs that he was working on.

Bobby didn't think there was going to be a whole lot more business today, so he made the command decision to lock up early. Again, a decision that his mother would most certainly scoff at. "Never pass up on a chance to make money!" she

58

would say. Standing in the front of the service station, Bobby surveyed the surrounding areas and even the interstate traffic was looking bleak; probably not a lot of chances for that almighty dollar tonight.

Flipping the sign from *OPEN* to *CLOSED* and turning off the neon signs in the window, Bobby made a last round for the trash and was taking it out the back door when he noticed a smudge, like dried chocolate, on the back door leading to the dumpster in the corner of the lot. He'd better get at that pretty quick, Bobby thought. If the stain set, his mother would come unglued. Setting the trash down, he grabbed an old, but serviceable blue shop towel and quickly ran it under the faucet in the service station. The stain came off quickly, but Bobby noticed a faint coppery smell. Lifting the rag to his nose he wasn't sure if it was from the shop or... No, that was definitely something else. Blood, it smelled like blood.

How in the hell did blood get on the back door? Did Ma cut herself?

Now, more worried than annoyed at the stain, Bobby ran up the backs stairs leading to the apartment above, to check on his mother. "Ma, you up here? Is everything OK? There was some blood on the back door. Did you cut your hand?"

Sounds of metal scraping and glass rattling came from the bathroom. Not bothering to check if his mother was decent or not, Bobby barged into the bathroom.

A sight he could never have predicted confronted him. His mother stood in front of the sink, the medicine cabinet falling out of the wall, a plastic freezer bag in her hands containing what looked like various wallets and money clips.

"Ma?! What the hell is going on?" Bobby had no idea if the cabinet had fallen on her, or if she had pulled it out of the wall. "Are you all right? I saw blood on the back door downstairs."

59

Letting the cabinet fall into the old freestanding porcelain sink, DeeDee turned to face her son. In her hands was the snub nosed .38 pistol that she kept under the counter, by the cash register, downstairs. It wasn't registered, a crime in the state of New York state, but not an uncommon one. In small burgs like Katonah it wasn't uncommon for shop keepers to keep a little extra security in their places of business. Sheriff Bartlett was well aware of it, and as long as there wasn't any trouble, he didn't choose to make an issue of it. Hell, Old Joe McLaren kept a sawed off shotgun and a spiked baseball bat under the counter at the hardware store. Everyone knew about 'em and though he'd never had to use 'em, they were a great deterrent. Rumor has it that this particular snub nosed piece was purchased off of the back of truck in Brooklyn, many years ago, by Bobby's own father, for a mere fifty bucks.

"Ma, waddaya doing with Pop's gun? Is everything OK?" DeeDee didn't answer, just stared at Bobby with a faraway look in her eyes. Reaching out and taking her hands, Bobby checked them over to see if she was cut, but there were no obvious signs of trauma. "What's in the bag, Ma? Where did all these wallets come from?"

DeeDee's shoulders slumped visibly, "Bobby, I don't know what to say. I was hoping you'd never have to see this. I don't know if you'll ever understand. Bobby, honey, was the sausage all right? It wasn't too over spiced was it? I needed to make sure the spice would cover up the taste of the sedatives I ground into the mix."

Bobby was sure his jaw was going to hit the floor, "What the hell are you talking about? Did you dose the food in the fridge? Is that why I was out for such a long time?"

DeeDee nodded her head drunkenly, "Honey, things aren't ever what they seem. Your uncle Dominic got in with some bad people, back before you were born, when we were still in that old apartment on Martense Street. He owed a lot of money to a lot of people, and they were coming around, threatening him, your father, us…"

Bobby recoiled a bit. What was all this stuff about his uncle?

"Ma, are you saying Uncle Dominic was killed for gambling debts? How do you know this? They never caught the guy that did it. How could you know? What does that have anything to do with the stuff in the bag?"

DeeDee dropped the bag of wallets into the sink, and with her other hand reached into the space behind the medicine cabinet. "Because the police were looking for the man that committed the crime, not the woman that committed the crime."

In her hands she held a small black switchblade that could have come from any backroom of any shady or less than reputable shop in Brooklyn, or SoHo, or any place with a sizable population. With a metallic *SNICK* the blade popped open showing faint rusty stains, blood stains, still clinging to the tip of the blade.

"Ma, what the hell is that?! Is that Uncle Dominic's blood? Did you kill Uncle Dominic?!" Bobby couldn't believe what he was seeing; his eyes wouldn't let him believe it.

"Bobby, I didn't have a choice. There were dangerous men coming around. They were threatening us. I couldn't take that chance. If your uncle was gone, there'd be no reason for them to come around anymore. So, I took care of it. I made sure that those dirty, vile men would have no reason to come back around anymore, or give us any trouble whatsoever."

In his head, Bobby could see back to the past, back to a dark and cold February night; the night his uncle was murdered. He saw him walking up the street, dressed in the khaki pants and his favorite blue button down shirt with pearl white buttons and wide Cuban collar that he wore when he went out for a night of gambling. Horses were his favorite, but Uncle Dominic would gamble on anything. Horses, cars, baseball games, basketball games, even the occasional hockey game. With the look on his face you'd never know that he owed just over sixty grand to a bookie out of Queens. This night was going to be a good night. He has just placed a small wager on a game that had turned out big. With the odds he had been given, no one believed it was going to be a sure thing, but it was. That one small bet had hit the right numbers and the gods smiled upon Dominic Martinson, who now walked down the street with four rubber banded bundles of one hundred dollar bills in his jacket pocket; ten thousand dollars that he planned on turning over to his bookie tomorrow morning before he headed off to work.

Maybe that's why he didn't see a figure wrapped in clothes to big for him (her) step from the shadows of the recessed bakery doorway. This mysterious figure's oversized sweater hid the breasts that would have easily given away the fact that the evil doer was in fact his sister-in-law. He never had a chance, only to turn around when he felt the tap on his shoulder. The dark figure plunged the surgically sharp blade of the switch into Dominic's chest with all the rage and fury he (she) could muster. The last thing Dominic saw, in this world, was the rage and fury and hatred in those dark eyes as his own eyes went dark and then saw no more.

DeeDee was right. The vile men didn't come around anymore. By the time the bookie from Queens, who ran his shop out of an old self serve laundry facility, figured out it wasn't one of his associates that had offed his biggest client, Edward had moved the family north. Insurance money from

Dominic's death had provided a safe passage and enough to purchase this station.

However, when the money started to run thin, DeeDee began to worry. Would they be able to survive here, so far away from the world she knew? From her family? It didn't matter that she had not spoken to her family in some years, but there was always a chance to amend her ways and come home.

When Edward began to start asking questions and reinvestigating his brother's death, DeeDee knew she had to act quickly. Edward's insurance policy ensured that they would be comfortable for quite some time. Insurance policies were an important part in both the lives of Edward and Dominic. They had been brought up knowing that they needed to be fiscally prepared, and all it took was one financial catastrophe and they'd be ruined for a lifetime. It was the right thing to do, and they both had been counseled about ensuring for their family's futures.

DeeDee knew there were poisons that could kill quickly, easily, without a lot of notice. She made quiet inquiries and eventually she found the potion to do the job. Arsenic, ironically, was the antidote to DeeDee's problem. A few healthy doses had been added to Edward's morning coffee and oatmeal, just to be safe, and DeeDee's poor husband had never stood a chance.

But, heart attacks in young, otherwise healthy men with no previous history tend to arouse the suspicion of the insurance company when they are being asked to pay out three quarters of a million dollars, even if they don't arouse the suspicion of the local coroner.

"Ma..." Bobby's voice trailed off, "Ma, you murdered Pop and Uncle Dominic? Where's the money, then? If there's all this insurance money, where is it?"

DeeDee looked around. "Bobby, it's right here. It's always been here." She tapped the floor panels of the bathroom and the loose planks rattled against the joists. Motioning with the pistol she pointed to a specific spot. Bobby knelt and picked up the loose plank. Underneath the board, between the joists, were piles of cash, wrapped in plastic grocery bags, stacked end to end.

"You mean we've been living in this shitty little apartment the whole time? You've had the money the whole time? Ma, what the hell is wrong with you?!

"You murder two people for money and all of a sudden you can't spend it? Why the hell did we lose the house, then, huh Ma? Why the *FUCK* are we stuck in this filthy dump when you could have at least kept the house?"

"Bobby, the insurance company didn't believe your father really had a heart attack so they took their time on paying out the claim. We were going to lose the house, anyway. We were too far behind on the payments. This dream of your father's sucked us dry and if all of a sudden we had the money to take care of it, it'd look suspicious. So we had to maintain the appearance..."

Bobby cut her off, "No, Ma. We lost the house after Pop died. So how did we get the money for the station to stay current? Is that where the wallets came from?"

DeeDee looked worn, older somehow. "We would have travelers come through, hitchhikers mostly. Even if they didn't have a car, I'd write 'em a receipt for a car repair. It's not out of the ordinary to have a significant charge appear on your credit card from a repair shop, and as long as we had one or two charges on a regular basis, spaced far enough apart, nothing seemed out of the ordinary."

"So what happened to the people, Ma? How come they never questioned the charges? Surely someone would have said something by now, even if they were complicit. Unless... Ma, you didn't, did you?!"

"Bobby, it was the only way. Besides the garbage is supposed to be messy at a service station. Oil covers up blood really nicely and the question never came up, so..." DeeDee's voice trailed off, again. "Son, we have so many of these hippy bastards that come through here, it was about time those freeloaders did something for us, yaknow?"

Bobby's face had gone completely pale. "Ma, we gotta do something. We can't let this go on, if you get caught, we'll both go down. Do you want me to get into trouble?"

DeeDee moved closer to Bobby, "No, honey I don't want you to get into trouble. This was my doing, and no one else's.

"But, we can't say a word of this. No one can ever know anything about this. If we wanna move on, we can."

Bobby had put his hands up and was walking backwards out of the bathroom, ready to make a break for the stairs. If he could get out of the station, he would certainly stand a better chance.

"Bobby, where are you going, honey?" DeeDee had the gun up, pointed at Bobby's chest.

"Ma, lemme go downstairs and move the Jeep. If we put it in the back, no one will notice for a while. That will give us some time." It was a lie and they both knew it. Enough people had driven by and seen the Jeep, enough that it could be something to be remembered, later on. Is this what had happened to the hippies who owned the VW bus?

"Bobby, don't go anywhere. Just stay right there. I'll take care of it."

"Ma, I got this, don't worry..."

"Bobby, don't you move!" DeeDee lunged at him, intending to pin him against the railing by the stairs. Instinctively Bobby dove to the side, and without realizing it, unable to grab hold of his mother, she flew over the railing, into the darkness of the empty gas station.

There was a sharp snapping sound, like the sound of twigs breaking, as her neck snapped. Bobby looked over the edge and saw his mother's head lying at an obscene angle to the rest of her body. Her body a gruesome display on the warped and chipped linoleum tile of the station floor.

"Ma, what did you do? Oh what did you do?" Of course, she wasn't going to answer.

Bobby didn't know what he was going to do, but he had to do something. Going back down the stairs, carefully stepping over his mother's body, Bobby grabbed the keys to the Jeep, and stepped out the side door. He made his way around to the front gas pumps and started the Jeep, pulling it around to the back of the station, next to the garbage dumpsters. Pillaging through the back he found a daypack with a sleeping bag and other camping essentials. These he took inside and locked the Jeep back up, replacing the keys on the same peg.

Walking back upstairs, Bobby went to his room, changing out of his dirty coveralls along the way. His mother still lay at the bottom of the stairs. Her hand wrapped around the worn wooden grip of the old pistol, her right index finger gently caressing the trigger. Realizing that it wouldn't be good if she was found with a throwaway piece in her hand, he walked back down the stairs, again, wearing only his boxers. Trying to mimic heroes in the movies he stuck the pistol into the waistband of his shorts where the cold steel barrel rested uncomfortably close to his penis. Walking back up the stairs, yet again, the pistol slipped in his boxers and what should have been a comical sight as a grown man fumbled around his crotch, producing the pistol now looked more like the antics of a tragic amateur magician, attempting to cover his latest blunder.

Putting on a semi clean pair of jeans, work boots and a worn, but serviceable paintball T-shirt that bore an old Nuclear Winter Industries *starflake* logo, he dumped the contents of the backpack onto his bed. A sleeping bag, inflatable sleeping pad, assorted amenities, even a few freeze dried camping meals. Repacking the bag, there was still room enough to pack the money from the floorboards. There was an odd sensation of bundles of money digging into his back, but they quickly dispersed as the money was distributed through the bag. The .38, unloaded, was tossed into the middle of the bag. Ammo in a plastic bag, tied off, at the bottom of the backpack. Grabbing his jacket from the closet, and his Bruins ball cap from the coat tree he very quickly transformed himself from Bobby the grease monkey to anonymous college student on a walkabout, or college hooky.

One last task... The oil pan from the VW bus was still in the service bay. With a little luck he'd be across the freeway and into the train station by the time the oil caught the old wiring on fire. Flicking a few lit kitchen matches into the oil pan, the greasy 5W-30 instantly caught, filling the service bay with think, noxious smoke.

Heading out the back door, he made sure it was latched and locked before he headed out into the cool New York night. Not paying too close of attention, he didn't realize that the precariously set oil pan was knocked onto the floor with the force of the building being shaken by a slammed door. He didn't see the flaming oil oozing out, to the drip trough, in the floor.

Looking at his watch he saw it was only 10:15 p.m. *Only?* It felt as if days had passed since his mother had lunged at him. In her desperation she had misjudged her position and that one fatal mistake had ended her life. Bobby wished he could feel bad, could feel anything about tonight, at all. Too long living in this mundane hell had numbed him to the possibilities life held outside the town boundaries. A chance to regain his missed youth from the treachery of a woman who no longer held sway over him.

Approaching the guardrail of the interstate, Bobby checked to make sure there was no traffic coming. No lights on either side. Quickly crossing to the median, he again checked for headlights. Not a single one. Looking back over his shoulder he wasn't sure if he really saw the first hint of flames licking out the door of the service bay. The orange glow was perceptible, but not absolutely noticeable unless you knew to look in the direction of the sad, dilapidated service station, specifically in the windows of the service bay doors. Time had forgotten the building and Bobby didn't think it would take much notice of it right now.

Crossing the grassy strip between the interstate and the tracks Bobby wasn't sure just where he was going or what he was going to do until he walked into the all night ticket booth of the train station.

"Where ya headin', hon?" The 1980s throwback girl behind the old-fashion wrought iron ticket booth snapped her gum in a manner that belied her bored nature. "You need a ticket to ride the train, babe, where ya goin'?" Without waiting for a response she flipped the pages of the beauty magazine she was reading to the next article.

Producing the same greasy, crumpled bills from his pocket that he has used to tip Nick this very morning, Bobby said, "I'll take a one way ticket. The 12:15 to Brooklyn, please."

Without a second glance, the fashionista behind the counter printed off the ticket, stamped it *PAID* and slid it through the cage with the appropriate change. Bobby took the ticket and walked to the old wooden benches, waiting for the train to arrive. Leaning back on the bench, he balled up his coat and closed his eyes.

Bobby never saw the man in soft shell windbreaker and jeans standing nearby. Tired as he was, and still suffering the effects of the narcotics his mother had slipped into his dinner, Bobby never heard the man take the pack, open it up and remove the monetary contents.

If the board blonde girl at the counter noticed a thing, she never uttered a word. More than likely she was engrossed with the new line of metallic nail polish that she could imagine herself wearing down the latest runways of Milan, if only she could lose another ten pounds, according to her mother.

The screeching sound of metal grinding on metal brought Bobby back to reality as the locomotive pulled into the station. He checked his watch and saw that it was ten minutes of midnight. Surely the store had to be in flames by now. Would anyone notice, or even care? He couldn't hear the sounds of any fire engines, or police cruisers. Bobby didn't want to go to the windows to check on the station, just in case someone remembered and thought back to talk to the police about it. No, he would wait until he was on the train, pulling out of the station and make some innocent glances over the interstate.

The platform man called for 'all aboard' at midnight. Bobby gathered up his new found belongings and mounted the car. Picking a window seat that showed the view towards the station, Bobby tried to imagine what the interior of the station looked like right now. He imagined the industrial metal shelving units melting down with this week's freshly stocked goods bursting into flame, smoke pouring into the back of the store, mixing oily smoke, competing for oxygen with the last vapors of his mother's cigarette smoke. There still wasn't a glow, at least a noticeable glow, anyway...

Closing his eyes, Bobby drifted off and imagined his new life in Brooklyn, maybe even the world beyond. It was the last thing he ever thought...

* * *

Later the fire marshal would call it a million to one odds on a freak accident. When the service station caught fire, instead of engulfing the entire building in flames, years of neglect and improper storage and disposal of motor oil into the drip trough of the service bay caused the fire to follow the path of least resistance. In this case it was a crack in the trough that led to the storm drain. A storm drain that led dangerously close to the buried fuel tank that supplied the gasoline to the pump that Bobby had forgotten to turn off. The buried tank had been buried long enough that it was often forgotten about and well past the inspection date. The leak in the tank wasn't big enough to cause a noticeable drop in the tank levels, but big enough to catch the flames roaring through the storm drain. This caused an explosion that launched the pump straight up into the air. When the pump came crashing back down it hit the external propane tank, also just recently topped up.

A combination of force, pressure, and fuel launched the one thousand gallon industrial propane tank across all four lanes of the interstate and directly into the path of the oncoming train. Flaming propane ignited the diesel in the locomotive,

70

immediately incinerating the first half of the train, including the car in which Bobby sat. Heat was so intense that many of the passengers were never identified. Police and inspectors were combing college campuses across the entire eastern seaboard, checking on missing students to see if any of them matched the vague descriptions they were given from the remains.

No one in town was surprised that the old service station sitting in the shadows of progress at the intersection of Interstate 684 and Highway 35 had simply gone up in flames. Most people were surprised that it hadn't happened sooner. There were a few that mourned the death of DeeDee Martinson, while just as many others simply shrugged their shoulders with the look of, "What do you expect from the wife of a drug addict?"

Traffic was diverted from other exits to circuitous routes around the crash scene. Months went by, photos were snapped, measurements recorded and statements taken. In the end, the fire marshal signed off on the final report that this was indeed a freak accident.

A year after the explosion the plank walls erected to keep gawkers out had been spray painted with graffiti and artwork, but no further progress had been made to repair the scar that was once a charming service station, reminiscent of days gone by. Perhaps one day, but until then it remained a subliminal warning to others. Buyers who were so eager to approach DeeDee about her valuable land now stayed away, as if a curse hung upon the scene, a palpable taste of death in the air.

The only mystery that remained was whatever had had happened to Bobby Martinson. Many believed he had finally hopped the 12:15 to Brooklyn and disappeared...

Friday. 17 July 15. 2315 hours.

"You know, that's a great fucking story, but you haven't told me shit. Some dude gets cooked on a train in the biggest case of cosmic karma that I've ever seen." I had waited all this time for that ending. I felt let down, no more than let down, I felt near abused of my time.

"Dude, think about it. What happened to the money?"

"You just said it was incinerated. Hell, according to your own words, the police weren't able to properly identify all of the remains."

"Exactly, yes, that's precisely my point! It doesn't matter how hot that fire was, there still *were* remains. There was something that was left behind. In this case there was no evidence that any money had ever been left behind. No paper residue, or linen residue, in this case. There was nothing to suggest that there ever had been money there, to begin with."

"Vincent, what you just told me, though, was that you heard all of this second hand. You got information from police reports. How did these people know there was money there?"

Vincent was grinning again. If he didn't have such a horribly crooked smile, he might actually look like the Cheshire cat. "I followed the money. See, according to all of this there was an insurance payout; two of them, actually. There was the one for our dear old Uncle Dominic, as well as one for the more recently departed husband and father, Mister Edward.

"Using the Freedom of Information Act, I was able to find out that there was indeed an actual insurance policy paid out to one Mrs. DeeDee Martinson, approximately seven or so months after the death of her husband. The timing matches up, near perfectly, for this particular scenario.

"Where things start to get hinky again, is that there was never a deposit to an actual account held by anyone named DeeDee Martinson."

I look Vincent in the eye, "Start to...?"

Vincent gave me a sour look of disapproval, "If there really was a three quarter million dollar payout, someone, somewhere would have taken notice. Especially if a deposit that size landed in a small town bank. But, there wasn't a deposit; there was nothing to raise any modicum of suspicion inside the little circle of influence in Ms. Martinson's life. Even her bank verified that at no time did DeeDee ever have more than five thousand dollars in her checking account. No savings. No safety deposit box."

I threw up my hands, "Wait, back up. How do you know what the bank said? They can't tell you this stuff, even if she is dead. They would be in direct violation of federal privacy laws."

That Cheshire cat grin, again, "I know, but when a federal officer walks into a small town bank with a badge, some very official looking paperwork, using phrases like 'Patriot Act' and 'domestic terrorism' people tend to get compliant pretty quick."

"*You?* You posed as a federal officer? Do you have any idea how many laws you broke?

"I think that it's a crime to even insinuate something like that, or to threaten that kind of action. There's a good chance that at the end of this you are going to jail, you know that, right Vincent?"

Sliding a shiny gold shield in a black leather folio wallet across the table, Vincent said, "I never said I was a federal officer, nor did I ever show them the actual paperwork, which by the way was an old college transcript with a blue paper cover around it.

As for the badge, well, it's amazing what you can buy on the internet.

"No, I showed up and the bank manager saw what he wanted to see. He heard what he wanted to hear. I didn't so much as demand the records as thank him when he provided them by means of cooperation. Besides the woman is dead, who's she gonna care who sees the paperwork, her bank statements and how much she spent online."

"OK, fine, so you didn't *technically* pose as a federal officer, though I think you should still go to jail for that. I'm pretty sure it's a crime to even have a badge, in this state, even if you are just using it for dress up. It's a pretty shady thing to be playing with titles and things like that." I nodded towards the badge on the table.

Taking hold of the badge, and replacing it in his inner jacket pocket, Vincent just shrugged his shoulders, as if to imply he didn't care one way or the other. "Maybe I should, but there are worse things out there than trying to pose as a federal officer."

Eyeing him, I asked, "Like what?"

Vincent smiled that grin again, "Like murder."

I was looking at him squarely now. "You never said anything about murder, at least not an intentional murder. You said this was all accidental. Where does the murder come in?"

Vincent theatrically sighed, "Did you already forget about the money? You can't just take a check for that large of an amount to a check cashing joint. You can't cash it at your local big box store or Qwik-E-Mart. So where did the cash come from?"

"I dunno, man, you tell me?"

Vincent put up his index finger, as if to accentuate the point, "Well, I have a theory on that, but you'd need a bigger bank, probably international, and someone at that bank who isn't going to question, or even bat an eye at a large cash transfer or deposit like that."

"You have a theory? Jesus man, I thought you had been tracking this serial killer? What the hell have you been doing for the last two years if you haven't been putting all this together?"

Vincent put up his hands in defense. "Hold on partner, let me tell you another story. It might put things into a bit of perspective."

My shoulders slumped. "Another story? Fuck, man. I'm getting tired of these stories.

"And, I'm not your damn partner."

Vincent produced a handkerchief from his inner jacket pocket and dabbed at the corners of his mouth. Sonuvabitch he was really salivating to tell this story. "Yeah, another story, and it's a good one.

"Just wait until the end and you see if we aren't partners by the end of this. I'm pretty sure you and I are going to make headlines with this."

This time, I was the one who sighed. "Fine, tell me another story."

BLUE SKY AT NIGHT

"Peek-a-boo, I see you." *CLICK.* Rick talked to himself while he shot still frames of the three men in the motel room. "C'mon, show me your pretty faces." *CLICK.*

His camera's shutter snapped open and closed, recording digital images on the CF memory card stored in the camera balanced on the steering wheel of the car he currently occupied, his images were sharp relief glimpses of the seedy underbelly this town often refused to show the trendy tourists and yuppy out-of-staters who showed up for the adventure and skiing that the nearby mountains had to offer, all year 'round.

Parked on the corner of Cyprus Street and Main Avenue, Rick could see his subjects, two dealers and another undercover officer through the motel room's window. Donald Schaap, code named "The Reverend" was often paired with Rick because the two were both effective at being cut off from the world, working in solitary conditions and having little to no contact with other officers, or higher ups. Rick and Schaap had been working together for so long that Rick wasn't even sure he could honestly say where the nickname came from, but he was pretty sure that it was one of those jokes from back in their younger days, that had stuck and no one was even sure of the original story behind it.

Rumor has it that Donald Schaap's middle name was actually Patrick and that he had once upon a time had a roommate who was fond of the drink and often the name Patrick, after a night of heavy drinking, would come out as "Pastor Rick" and eventually that was morphed into The Reverend. Either way, Rick couldn't think of calling Schaap by his God-given name anymore and for so long he'd been The Reverend, even the Chief of Police had started to call him The Rev.

Rick couldn't hear what The Rev was saying, but his body language suggested that they had gotten to the dealing portion of the buy, negotiating over money and weight.

"C'mon, beautiful, show me the money." Rick continued to shoot still frame after frame of the men, documenting everything in great detail. A set of binoculars would have been nice, but nothing would scream *STAKEOUT!* quite like a guy watching a hotel room with a pair of high powered binos.

Rick Walker sat in his used 2000 Chevy Cavalier, smoking Marlboro Menthol Ultralight cigarettes and drinking four hour old Starbucks coffee. What had once been a large, *venti*, toffee nut latte, was now a cold, congealed mess in a paper cup. But, it was caffeinated and it was keeping him awake. Donuts would have been a nice compliment on this particular stakeout, but instead peanut butter and honey sandwiches stuffed into a soft sided lunch cooler gave him a longer energy boost. Besides every time Rick ate a glazed donut his ass seemed to grow and he invariably dripped frosting on to his pants, making it look like he had jizzed himself for no apparent reason.

A gift from his late brother, the car had been purchased brand new, off the lot from a smaller scale dealership in Helena, Montana, and it was most likely the closest Rick was ever going to get to a sports car, at least on a detective's salary. A two door, five speed transmission, with wide chrome alloy wheels and a spoiler gave it the look of a sporty little car, but the fuel efficient V6 engine allowed him to drive for weeks at a time without ever using more than forty dollars to top up the tank. Officially the title stated the color was "black cherry" but Rick was pretty sure it was just maroon. It wasn't the classic, "write me a ticket red" nor was it the boring white of so many cars, it had just enough style to make it unique, just like Rick. With some aftermarket tinting and the replacement of the original factory sound system to a new Alpine stereo system, it was indeed a sporty little car. Even now, sitting at ninety thousand miles, the well cared for engine ran as smooth as it did with only four miles on it, as he and his brother Chris, drove it down the interstate, back to Bozeman. A 100 mile road trip was a perfect way to break in the new wheels as it hugged the mountain curves of Interstate 90, quickly exceeding the posted speed limit of 75 miles per hour.

Sitting in the passenger bucket seat were some of Rick's best friends. His used Canon Digital Rebel DSLR camera with a Tamron 200mm telephoto lens connected to his Panasonic Toughbook laptop allowed him to reach out and see people from a distance that diffused scrutiny. Lying on the seat next to the laptop, in a special ordered Headlock Holsters Custom Kydex creation was his Glock 19 pistol. Small enough to easily conceal inside his waistband, with the custom holster, but large enough to carry fifteen rounds of hollow points if he got into trouble, the pistol as well as two extra fifteen round magazines were his first line of defense, and had proven to be a great little insurance policy.

In the trunk, bolted to a custom mounting bracket and accessible through the fold down backseat was a Remington 870 shotgun with a folding stock and pistol grip, a cut down 18 inch barrel, fully loaded with six rounds of 2¾ inch triple aught buckshot. However, Rick knew that if he needed his shotty, or the "noob tube," as he was prone to call it, he was already in a world of shit. He would have preferred to have his custom built M4 rifle but it would be a lot easier for a civilian to pass off a shotgun, here in Bozeman, than a rifle that was as customized as a special ops weapon rolling around in the mountains of Afghanistan or the streets of Iraq. That fella down in Oklahoma had done a smashing job on the design, build and precision of

81

his weapon and it had served Rick faithfully for the last three years. Rick had received word through the grapevine this particular outfit was building weapons for various federal agencies and he wanted in on it.

Even with his time on the Special Response Squad, Rick had preferred the M4 over the MP5s that a lot of his crew had chosen to carry. While there was no hard and fast rule as to what each member could carry, generally it was the discretion of each member of the squad to carry what they preferred.

However, after seeing Rick's rifle in action, there were quite a few converts to the platform, and quite a few more orders to his builder in Oklahoma.

When it came down to brass tacks, Rick was doing exactly what he was supposed to be doing, and that was to pass as a civilian, pass as a transient, hell pass himself off as anyone *but* an undercover cop, and a paid civil servant employee of the City of Bozeman.

Rick didn't carry a police radio; again it would have been too conspicuous. Instead he had a customized smart phone that could easily blend in with any other personal mobile device in Bozeman. It was preloaded with a few discreet numbers that he could call, just in case, that were monitored by support agents round the clock, 24/7. All of this, coupled with dressing in a variety of casual and rough clothing, Rick was the perfect image for undercover work.

Tonight's attire consisted of loose fitting, scuffed khaki cargo hemp pants, black SmartParts paintball T-shirt with the always recognizable grey crosshair logo, grey three quarter top hiking boots and a well loved, and worn, navy blue Boston RedSox ball cap. With his scruffy beard and longer, curly unkempt hair that was marred with flecks of silver that he kept pulled back in a loose ponytail, no one would ever suspect that Rick would be an undercover narcotics detective.   That was just the way Rick preferred it.

At five foot, nine inches tall, and weighing in at a solid 210 pounds Rick Walker, who was affectionately called Rick Bull by his friends, mainly due to his physical size, told people that he was a freelance photographer and aspiring writer who had gone through college on a football scholarship, but lost the love of the NFL combine scouts when he blew out his knee during the homecoming game of his Junior year.   Pro football dreams and gigantic paychecks soon became pipedreams, causing Rick to switch his focus back to photography and media arts, honing his already considerable skills.   He coupled that with a Bachelor's Degree in Criminology and immediately set his sights on a career in law enforcement.   His story carried the credibility of truth because, like any good undercover legend, it was mostly true.   Rick only omitted the details that he also worked for the Gallatin Drug Task Force, here in Bozeman, and that he a very storied and impressive career in law enforcement.   Most of his friends knew that he was indeed a freelance photog, and only a few close and trusted associates knew where the true source of his cash, his real paycheck came from.

As a photographer, his images had been seen in publications like *Montana Life Outdoors* and *Country Wide Living*.   One freelance assignment for Yellowstone Park had even landed his crisp and cleanly cropped shots in an article for *National Geographic*.   All of this and some online magazine articles served as the perfect backstop for his undercover work.   It all made for great theatre cover while he was working undercover drug busts and stings at dingy, shithole motels like the one he was currently parked across the street from the entrance of.

People question people who go door to door, around apartments asking questions, snapping official pictures.   What people didn't question is a freelance photojournalist, a freelance photog, snapping pictures and asking people to do a bio on local people, getting their story, promising to have their stories told in magazines all around the globe, in publications that spanned from New York to Madrid. Sometimes that even happened.

More often than not, however, the story that Rick produced was usually just one of the many sordid details that were recounted in a courtroom in front of twelve useful members of an unbiased society and a very stern judge.

* * *

Once upon a time, the Blue Sky Motel was a very attractive and humble joint, on the east edge of Main Street, where it had once been the scenic edge of town, not a mile from one of the many off-ramps of Interstate 90. Offering clean rooms and a beautiful mountain view, it was situated directly across from a small gas station and casino combination and near the downtown night life, what there once was. The Swingin' Tree Bar, a true to style, sawdust on the floor, swanky dive country saloon and dance floor was close enough near to the Blue Sky such that patrons who had celebrated a little too much often found their way to the motel, either by foot or motor vehicle; sometimes friends, sometimes law enforcement, most usually just to sleep it off until the following morning.

However, continued progress and fancy lit billboards had moved the world on and most of the hotel chains with it. Like any other business entity, they sought to move their establishments with the changing times and progress to a newer, closer access off of 7th Avenue, on Wheat Drive. This left the Blue Sky Motel to start offering the discount rates and extended stay rates that often attract the less than desirable type of clientele that are quick to be associated with drug dealers, prostitutes, and the occasional transients who had a bit of extra coin after the day's earned hours of street corner begging and discreet liquor runs. It was even spoken of, though not widely nor with any degree of authoritative volume, that the bed sheets were more often burned than washed at said Blue Sky Motel.

What had been a curious blend of stucco walls and stamped concrete and rock façade walls that had been a rage of style in the early 80s, were now a horrific mess of disrepair that left the trim peeling, the windows cracked and taped, and curious stains of all shapes and sizes on the floors and walls, bleeding over on to the equally sad wallpaper of these shabby and forlorn little rooms of despair.

Shower shoes and sandals weren't a requirement of the hotel staff, but they were certainly recommended. A few years ago a small outbreak of bedbugs had quickly destroyed the little credibility the small motel had managed to hang on to; that and the small, portable meth lab explosion that had burned an entire corner of the motel to a charred chemical crisp; a scar that was never bothered with repairs.

Construction barrier tape billowed in the winds, a sad and neglectful reminder that the hotel would never again be the eastern jewel of the city. Such a sad reminder that big city life, and the detritus of such a life, could creep into any small town burg if left unchecked.

A sudden movement near the window brought Rick back to his duties. Schaap was standing in front of the window, stroking his chin, as if deep in thought. He had Rick's attention. With the subtle deftness of a practiced professional, he ran his index finger across his throat, knowing full well that Rick was watching, and just as quickly back to casually stroking his chin.

There would be no deal tonight; time to pack it in. Rick would remain at his position until Schaap emerged; later they would meet up for a debriefing. Rick wished he had some long distance listening and sound equipment, but it wasn't standard issue for the Gallatin Drug Task Force. He could get the equipment off the internet but again, if the wrong person saw it, it would more than likely raise more questions than anything else. Sometimes you had to run old school tech.

The front door to room 301 opened and out walked Schaap. In his hand he held the green nylon duffle bag that held the money that was intended for tonight's drug buy. Judging by the bulk none of the money had even made it out of the bag. Rick wished he could have heard the conversation go down, but no matter, he would get the details later on and send them up the chain to the right people. Why hadn't the dealers gone through with the sale? Were they spooked?

"Rev, waddaya doing? Get outta there. Don't be frickin' dragging ass if ya don't have to." There really was no point in talking out loud to himself as Rick knew that Schaap couldn't hear him. "Let's go, mate, my ass is starting to tingle sitting here, all damn night."

The sound of the gunshot was unmistakable and from this distance, and even in the dark, Rick could still see the blood spray. Through the lens of his camera, the look of shock on Donald Schaap's face was as sudden and unmistakable as the gunshot. Rev was on his knees, holding his stomach, one bloody hand pawing at the air. The part of his intestines that hadn't been instantly incinerated by the close range blast were slipping through his splayed fingers and dangling mere inches above the filthy ground. Steam from his exposed warm entrails perked in the cool night. Blood drooled from his mouth, the warm spittle mixing with the intense red, already on the pavement.

Rick has his phone in hand, as if by instinct, and hit the speed dial that connected him to the dispatcher. "This is Detective Rick Walker, badge number three-one-seven. I'm at the Blue Sky Motel on East Main Street. I have an undercover officer down. I need EMS and backup on scene, *immediately!*" Rick's calm and professional voice belied his demeanor which was rapidly switching into overdrive, straight into battle mode.

Without waiting for a reply he hit the END button, and tossed the phone on the seat. Grabbing the Headlock holstered Glock and shoving the holster's paddle into his belt, right above his kidney, he popped the trunk release. Jumping from the car, Rick grabbed the shotgun and his personal first aid kit, immediately making a mad dash run for the room. The kit was specially designed for gunshot and trauma wounds, so Rick wouldn't have to do any unnecessary searching for items he didn't need.

"Rev...Schaap! *Schaap!* Buddy, hold on, man!" Rick was screaming, now. He'd been on raids before where men were injured, but never when it was his best mate. Even back in 2005 when they'd raided that meth lab in the trailer court just off of 23rd Avenue, and the entry man had taken a 7.62 round straight to the vest, breaking ribs but by God's own grace nothing else.

Some poor slob had thought it was a rival producer come to raid his stash and without checking to see who was at the door, he had immediately grabbed his Romanian knock off AK-47 and fired off three rounds through the flimsy mobile home door. Even after the entry man was hit, he was still able to clear the door and the two men stacked behind him had immediately cut the meth head down with well placed shots from their MP5 submachine guns, their 9mm hollowpoints shredding the brain tissue and chest cavity.

No this was different, this was Schaap. He was the God Damned Rev, and Rick damn sure wasn't going to lose his best mate, not on an undercover deal, not in such a sadistic manner like this. Not bleeding out on the dirty concrete stoop of a shitty flophouse motel on the east end of town.

Running into the room with his pistol drawn Rick did a quick search of it and the tiny bathroom. In the few moments that Schaap had been shot, the dealers were gone. They had up and disappeared like a virgin on prom night. The bathroom window was open and Rick assumed that they must have gone through, using it as a prepared escape route. Even if he dusted for prints, Rick knew there would be none. This was too clean and these boys had to have known this was going to go down like this, or there wouldn't have been this much preparation. How the hell had they been tipped off? How did they know they were going to be dealing with undercover officers, tonight?

A sound like sludge water being sucked through a wet / dry vacuum came from the doorway. Schaap was still alive, though just barely. Rick ran back to where Donald Schaap was lying in an ever growing pool of his own blood. The wound was a particularly nasty one, straight through the stomach, from a rear entering jacketed .45 hollow point by the look of it. Disregarding the product's instructions Rick grabbed the QuikClot from his trauma kit and stuffed the trauma sponge into the entrance wound. Taking the battle gauze he stuffed it into the exit wound hoping to staunch the copious blood loss. Without even thinking about it, he grabbed the remaining entrails and shoved them back into the torn and ragged exit hole, causing Schaap to scream out in pain, spraying Rick, and the surrounding wall behind Rick, with thick, bloody phlegm.

Schaap's blood flecked lips were trembling and he whispered to Rick. "They knew. They knew I was a cop. I don't know how, but they knew. We're burned, Rick. You gotta find out who did this to us. You better fuckin' find 'em."

Rick was clenching Schaap's hand when Schaap's heart stopped beating. What Rick didn't know was that a fragment from the jacketed .45 caliber hollow point that had pierced Schaap's stomach had ricocheted off of his spine, traveled upward, and nicked his aorta, causing massive internal hemorrhaging. Schaap never had a chance. If he had been sitting inside a trauma room of a five star emergency theatre he might have had a chance. *Might have.*

Whoever had fired this shot knew exactly what they were doing. Schaap had been mortally wounded, but was alive long enough to deter anyone from pursuing the thieves turned assassins. This was as cold blooded a crime scene as Rick had ever been involved with.

EMS and backup officers arrived amid a myriad of screaming sirens and flashing lights and when Captain Silvan himself, head of the Gallatin Drug Task Force, walked in he found Rick still kneeling next to Donald Schaap's body. Captain was no slouch, he himself a veteran of the Air Force Para Rescue and at least three overseas engagements that Rick knew about, Captain Silvan was a man who led from the front and it was no surprise to see him clad head to toe in tactical gear, M4 at the ready, clearing the nearby area, along with the rest of the backup unit. If his face hadn't been on the front page of the newspapers and been on the local news channels, he too would have been pulling undercover assignments. He was truly the case of you could take the officer out of the field, but you couldn't take the field out of an officer.

Already officers were sequestering would be witnesses and taking their statements. People who might have seen anything or heard anything were being pulled away from the macabre spectacle, their contact information being recorded and asked to remain indoors until further notice.

A very tight and controlled perimeter had been cordoned around the crime scene and the body, Schaap's body. Without waiting for the crime scene techs to show up, the officers on hand immediately began marking the necessary characteristics of the scene, taking measurements and snapping photos on their hand held digital cameras. This was going to be done by the book, it would just be their book.

"Rick, come with me. We need to talk. I need to show you something." Captain Silvan slung his rifle on his back, and gently eased Walker up, herding him out the door, around to the back of the building. "Is this one of the men that was in the room, tonight?"

Captain Silvan pointed his SureFire G3 flashlight on a body that had been stuffed into the bushes behind the building. The head was hanging askew of the body, due to it being almost decapitated from the throat slash. So violent and jagged was the cut the head had near come clean off. This was not the cut of an expert killer. No this was the cut of someone who was in a rage or in a hurry, possibly both. This was not clean, not at all, it was truly a hack job.

Rick nodded, "Yeah that was the guy who was dealing with Rev, fuck, I mean Schaap.

"He was the one who set up the buy. We assumed he was the main man, the go-to guy, whatever..."

Captain Silvan nodded. "We've already talked to a few people, done some preliminary witness interviews, and some of them said they saw an old Volkswagen bus, possibly with out of state license plates, come tear-assing outta here about ten minutes ago. Did you see a van, or anything else?"

Rick shook his head, "No, I was on the opposite side, over by the cemetery." Rick jerked him thumb over his own shoulder. "We figured the best vantage point was to shoot through the parking lot and hope they wouldn't be able to see me that far away. There was good shade cover from the elm trees and the street lights were too far up the street to cast a glare on the car, so..." His voice trailed off as he realized the futility to explaining the tactics of a crime scene as fucked up as this.

Captain Silvan was nodding again, "OK. Let's get you back to the station. We'll have someone bring your car down.

"Leave your gear with one of these guys, and give 'em your weapons too, so we can clear everything. Make it all by the book. We're damn sure going to get the fuckers that did this to Schaap."

Too numb to really make conversation, Rick Walker nodded and walked over to Captain Silvan's personal car. Handing his pistol and shotgun to a uniformed officer, who cleared them and made them safe, Rick slid into the passenger seat of Captain Silvan's car and collapsed.

Monday. 25 June 12. 0830 hrs.

Rick Walker entered the Gallatin Drug Task Force headquarters through the north entrance. The last two days had been a blur, a veritable nightmare that had no apparent ending in sight. His partner was dead, lying on a cold autopsy table, in the private morgue in the basement of the Gallatin Drug Task Force's headquarters building, awaiting the confirmation by the medical examiner. Though there was no evidence to suggest Schaap's death had happened any other way in which the details were relayed, everything was going to

91

be by the books. Not that it ever hadn't been by the books; but there was going to be no room for error on this one.

One by one Schaap's organs were being removed, cut out of his central trunk cavity, weighed, cataloged and dissected, all to ensure that there was no other possible way to prove his death. Just below the floor on which Rick now stood, his partner was now becoming a lab experiment. Rick couldn't get the image out of his head, and no matter how hard he tried, every time he closed his eyes, he saw his partner's stomach explode outward, the terrified look in his eyes. Surprise. Shock. Disbelief. Defeat. All wrapped into one terrified final emotional toll. A death toll.

Headquarters building itself, was a veritable enigma. Like everything else about this particular department and the crew that ran it, it looked nothing like the purpose it served. Situated on the corner of Rouse and Tamarack streets was the city's road maintenance department and scattered throughout the lot were piles of sand, gravel and salt mixtures. Industrial trucks and constant traffic provided the perfect cover for cars coming and going at all hours of the day or night, even on holidays. On the west side of the lot was an aging khaki colored corrugated metal building that housed the Gallatin Drug Task Force equipment bays and main office.   Twenty five hundred unassuming square feet housed one of the most clandestine and necessary arms of law enforcement in Bozeman.

Abutted up to the east side of the Gallatin County Fairgrounds, headquarters building was a scant fifty foot walk to the indoor pistol range that encompassed their private shooting house and practice facilities where the Task Force worked their close quarters tactics and takedown procedures.

All of this served as literal camouflage, all the better to hide in plain sight, something that the Task Force desperately wanted to ensure when they were working. Often fellow officers didn't know members of the Drug Task Force from regular force officers because they were so much in the shadows and out of the mainstream policing of the city.

Despite the shabby exterior, the interior was retrofitted with high tech electronics packages and instead of individual offices, the entire office bay was made up of desks in a bull pen style to ensure that ideas and information flowed freely and that no one was left out of the loop. Large screen plasma monitors covered the west wall and scrolled through an ever changing ticker list of activities and missions that the Task Force had in motion. The north wall had a corkboard with wanted posters and BOLO alerts. A black outline of a male head with details penned in the margins above a grainy photograph that Rick had shot on Saturday morning was tacked up on the top. This particular cat had immediately gone to priority number one. He was Donald Schaap's killer and nothing else mattered, right now. As he walked by, Rick gave the photo an involuntary middle finger, something that was deeply juvenile and immature, but it was the only way to express the hatred and rage he was feeling.

Only one person, Captain Silvan, had his own office. It was this office that Rick Walker entered. A few heads had nodded at Rick when he came in, but no one said anything. A few of the other Task Force agents had lost partners and friends on operations, and all knew that nothing could be said that was going to lessen the hurt or guilt. A lost comrade was a failure, even if it wasn't anyone's fault, directly. Time would heal the wound, probably, but until then, it was a delicate healing process and no amount of words, phone calls or cards could make up for that loss.

Finishing up on the telephone, Captain Silvan motioned for Rick to take a seat. "No, I don't care what your budget is. You spend every last fucking federal dollar finding this guy, or you and I are going to have to step outside and have us a chat about this. Are we clear? If you spend all the federal dollars, you start delving into that county treasury that you know isn't going anywhere and you start to use those dollars. Use the damn city sanitation dollars because as far as I am concerned that finding this asshole is picking up the biggest piece of shit out there. You just find a way to make it happen.

"When we hang up, I want you to get back on your phone, and start making things happen."

When Captain Silvan was talking like that, someone's ass was about to get twisted up real good, real quick. The way he slammed the phone back into its cradle told Rick that Captain Silvan was not in the best of moods. No one was. When Captain Silvan sunk his teeth into something, there was no way that anything less than 100% satisfaction would suffice. That satisfaction had better come quick, too, because without it the captain was going to be out for blood and he wouldn't rest until he got his pound of flesh as payment for losing one of his agents.

"Rick, how are you holding up?" Rick knew that this was a dumb question, but Captain Silvan wasn't asking if he wasn't truly concerned. He'd been there and done that, and he wasn't going to mince words; not for something this important.

"Not too bad, Captain." He was lying and they both knew it. Rick was a mess. How could he be anything else during a time like this? Christ he was still wearing clothes from last night that he was pretty sure he'd fallen asleep in.

"Rick, right now the only thing that matters is finding the guy that did Schaap," Silvan nodded his head towards the phone, "and I was just having a chat with one of our sister agencies in

Park County to ensure they understand the severity of this search."

"Captain how sure are we that this perp bailed? Hell, I didn't even see 'em leave out the back. I'm not saying call it off, but maybe we should be focused on a more local search?" Rick wanted a search, and then when the motherfucker who did this was found, he'd take 'em a short walk down a dark alley. Just the two of them.

Captain Silvan nodded, "I know, and we are. Our brothers and sisters in the PD, as well as the Sheriff's Department, hell even the Highway Patrol, they are looking for this guy. But if he did bail, and he's traveling, we're gonna make sure that everyone knows what to be looking for. All the standard alerts went out, but I wanted to reach out and make sure that all our people know how personal this is for us. How personal it is, for you."

"Thank you, Captain."

"Rick, when's the funeral? Next week?"

Rick nodded. The state's Attorney General, himself, had called Schaap's parents to inform them of the death of their son. Donald Schaap had never married and had no children. There was an ex girlfriend from a few years ago but last time anyone heard from Becky, she was in Island Park, Idaho, tending bar at the Sawtelle Mountain Resort, just off Route 20.

No, Aldrich and Kelsy Schaap, Rick's father and mother, would be receiving the flag from the draped coffin at the funeral. What scared Rick, though, was that Schaap was going to be buried in the same cemetery that Rick had been parked next to on the night Schaap died, overlooking the Blue Sky Motel. Really, an almost cruel ending to the whole narrative.

"Rick, I gotta ask, how much have you had to drink today?" Captain Silvan could smell the cheap whiskey on Rick's breath.

95

The wintergreen mints weren't fooling anybody as a cover, no matter how many he had chewed up on the way over.

"Captain, I'm good. I had a shot this morning to clear my head, while I was getting cleaned up. I'm stone cold sober, though, you know that. Twelve years on this job, Captain. I'm not gonna fuck that up."

Captain Silvan nodded his consent. If it was only one shot, it was a doozy of a shot, but Silvan wasn't going to make an argument of it, not right now. "I'm just making sure. I don't need you collapsing now. We're going to take this fucker down, you can be sure. But I need you cool, calm, and collected.

"You need to do the standard psyche eval. If the shrink clears you, you're back in the field, as soon as you wanna be. However, if you go into the eval smelling like a whorehouse at low tide there is no way in hell he's gonna clear you."

Rick started to protest but the Captain cut him off, "Rick, this isn't me talking to you as your friend, but your fucking boss. You need to make sure you are one hundred percent, or you aren't going back out. Are we savvy?"

"Yeah, Captain, we're cool. I'll head over today and talk to the doc." Rick started to get up but the Captain motioned him back down. "Something else, Captain?"

"Rick, one last thing we need to talk about. What happened to the money?"

Thursday. 28 June 12. 1629 hrs.

Rick had done what the Captain told him to do. He went over to the law and justice center, and talked to the in-house shrink. He talked about his feelings. He ensured the doc that he, Rick himself, wasn't in any danger of putting a gun barrel in his own mouth and painting the wall with his brains. Rick assured the doc that he wasn't going to go rip shit riot with a bottle of Black Velvet. The fact that he had already gone rip shit riot two nights previous was of no further consequence and not worth mentioning to the doc, so it wasn't brought up. The fact that the bartender at Mixers Lounge, who was an old college buddy, had cut him off after the second bottle, did not need to be brought up because he had gone home, slept it off, and cured that bitch of a hangover with some leftover Mongolian food in the fridge that he ate cold. It masked the taste of stomach acid and bile as he vomited out the contents of his stomach on Wednesday, as the stench of sour sweat and booze permeated Rick's empty house.

Not on suspension, but certainly on leave, Rick had spent his time in his home, on Bozeman's modest west side, contemplating what had transpired. Was it his fault? Could he have been faster? Should he have parked closer? Why wasn't Schaap wearing his Kevlar fucking vest? Most importantly, what the hell had happened to the money?

All of these questions circulated in his mind while he tried to simultaneously push them out of his head and answer the questions. Rick, conveniently, lived alone. His marriage had ended shortly after it began when his wife realized that he was married to his job, and was cheating on that job with her.

Catherine was a strong woman, but even she couldn't bear the long weeks of not hearing a word and then all of a sudden Rick would show up, out of the blue, as if no time had passed. At first it was spontaneous, but after Rick and Donald started to work longer hours and go deeper undercover, it became a nightmare. Every time the phone rang, or someone knocked on the door, Catherine's heart would stop, and as a policeman's wife she would instinctively fear the worst.

It really wasn't all that much of a surprise to Rick, after he came home from an op, and found divorce papers on the kitchen table. There wasn't much of an argument to be had. Their life together wasn't a life, and it certainly wasn't together. Rick signed the papers the next day, before he went to work. While he was at work, Catherine packed up her belongings and moved back in with her parents. Rick knew they didn't approve of him much, anyway. They had wanted more for Catherine and last time they had bumped into each other, Rick saw a handsome young man on Catherine's arm, with a matching diamond ring on the third left. Good for her.

Their modest house they purchased together, meant to be a starter house for a new family, had now become a two bedroom reminder of his empty life. All Rick had left was his job and his mates, and a garage full of tactical gear. But, now Schaap was gone.

When Captain Silvan had asked Rick about the money, Rick was in total shock. The last time he had seen the money was when he and Schaap had counted it, marked it with an ultraviolet ink, and then packed the bundles into the green nylon duffle bag. All in all, there was better than one hundred and twenty five thousand dollars in that bag. Meant to be a good sized purchase, it was supposed to be the invite into the big card game that the dealers were working with. Their bosses were supposed to be the guys who were supplying all the drugs and party favors in the southwest corner of the state. To crack these cats would have been the career bust and given Schaap and Rick the ticket they wanted for any career posting. Hell, they could have written their own ticket.

Now, the money was gone. When the investigators at the scene opened up the bag, all they found was a stash of porno magazines that someone had put in there. The bulges looked right, and the weight felt right, so no one was the wiser until the bag was actually opened.

What didn't add up was how did these two dealers pull a switch without Schaap noticing? How could all that money go missing without anyone noticing? Preliminary toxicology reports showed trace levels of THC in Schaap's blood, but that was to be expected. Hell, he could have smoked a joint with those two goons, it was part of his cover. He didn't pop positive for anything else, so Rick knew he wasn't drugged. Schaap was a professional, he would never let that money out of his sight. How the hell did they make the switch, then?

A very unpleasant thought began to surface in Rick's mind. He had heard of agents, in the past, going native. With all that money being handled, sometimes some of the money would go missing. Not large amounts but maybe two or three grand, here or there. If an agent had to buy his way out of a situation, or had to make deals with gun dealers, whatever. Once again, this sort of thing was to be expected.

But, that was absurd. Schaap was a pro. He wouldn't go rogue, would he? No, he was a legit agent and there was no way that he was going to blow it. Even if he had the cash he couldn't deposit it, not without notice. As a Drug Task Force agent, guys like Rick and Schaap were under constant scrutiny, just to ensure that they were constantly on the up and up. If he tried to make a deposit, in that large of a size, someone would take notice, and Rick would have heard about it. Internal affairs would have brought Rick in to have a friendly chat. Not threatening, but just a quick back and forth, let him know that they knew that Schaap might need to have an extra set of eyes on him. No, nothing like that had happened. Unless... Unless they suspected him too. Captain Silvan had been a bit off putting these last few days. But, no, that couldn't be...

Captain Silvan had more or less insisted that a period of time off would be for the best. Did that mean that Rick was under suspicion? It was plausible. With any amount of money, especially an amount that large going missing, someone was bound to be asking some questions and wondering.

Rick decided that he would just let it go, and talk to his superior officer on Monday, following. There'd be no point in worrying himself over it. Just then, the oven timer DINGED to let him know that his beef pot pies were done. With a couple of cold Guinness beers to pair with, he'd be set for a vintage Star Wars marathon on DVD; a rare find since that bastardized company Disney had bought out his beloved franchise and locked the movies into the vault. He'd never get a chance to get 'em on BluRay before he turned 60, at this rate. Fuckin' Disney.

Friday. 29 June 12. 0700 hrs.

Rick recognized that kind of knock on his front door. It was the knock that he often used. It was the knock of law enforcement officials when they had something important they wanted to chat with you about.

"Hold on, I'm coming." Plodding to the front door in his pajama pants, minus a shirt, he opened the front door to find five armed men, all with blue wind breaker jackets and a myriad of yellow alphabet letters stenciled on the back. "You guys sure you got the right house?"

Rick stood there, rubbing the sleep from his eyes, wondering what in the holy blue fuck was going on right now. Who were these clowns and why were they on his doorstep so damn early? It was Friday morning, for God's sake, weren't these governmental clowns supposed to take the weekend off, starting right about now?

"Richard Walker? Are you Richard Walker?" One of the men in the windbreakers looked like he spent more time on his moustache than he spent money on his cheap suit. Had to be a fed. He was holding a very official looking metal clipboard with some very official looking paperwork on it. His mirrored aviator sunglasses reflected the early morning sun.

"Yeah, I'm Rick. Waddaya want?" Rick was thoroughly confused.

Now Rick saw him, standing in the back of the small group. Captain Silvan. "Mr. Walker, we have a warrant to search the premises." Moustache barged in without even giving Rick a chance to review the document that he slapped into Rick's hand.

Rick stood in the doorway while federal agents donned black nitrile exam gloves and began to paw through his personal belongings. In a very rough manner all of Rick's drawers and cupboards were turned out and dumped on the floor. Laundry and clothing were pulled from hampers and closets and drawers. Rick's office was turned upside down as case files and other important papers were strewn across the floor.

Captain Silvan spoke then, "Rick I don't know what to say. These guys showed up this morning and said they had a federal warrant. I'm not even supposed to be here. They allowed me to come along as a professional courtesy.

"They said that an internal investigation turned up some off shore accounts in the Cayman Islands. Your passport shows stamps to the Caymans. They seem to think that it's all somehow connected; the accounts, the missing money, the passport stamps."

Rick stammered, "Captain, you know I was down there in 2000 with Catherine. It was our fucking honeymoon. Yeah, it's gonna have a stamp on it."

Captain Silvan threw up his hands in defense. "I told them. I said you had a legitimate reason but they have a federal fucking warrant. There's nothing I can do, brother."

"Captain, you're telling me that these federal clowns, who couldn't get FEMA supplies to Katrina survivors for almost a month, found dirt on me in six damn days?" Rick was truly perplexed. He stood, mouth opening and closing like a dying fish on the line, trying to make sense of this early morning intrusion and utter violation.

Captain Silvan motioned Rick inside the house. "Rick, let's go inside and sit down. Let these jackasses do their thing, and when they don't find shit, we'll let them look like the fools."

Captain Silvan ushered Rick to the small dining table. Rick was finally able to sit down and unfold the warrant. Spelled out in no uncertain terms was a federal magistrate demanding that agents should indeed search the home of one Richard Walker, a resident at 1737 Tradewind Avenue. Specifically they were to search for documentation pertaining to offshore accounts held in the name of one Richard Walker, or any of his undercover aliases, located in the main branch of Cayman National Bank, Grand Cayman Island. Those aliases were supposed to be classified, part of his cover and legend. How had these feds found out? They weren't supposed to be privy to this sort of information, regardless of what agency they worked for.

Just then an agent walked up with some papers in his hand. "Captain, we'd like to talk to Mr. Walker. We found some receipts we'd like him to explain."

Rick looked up in total disbelief. "What are you talking about?"

The agent handed Rick several receipts sealed in clear plastic evidence bags. Some of the receipts had dates and amounts going as far back as 2000. "Can you explain these?"

"What…? No, well, some of them, but…" What the hell was going on, here?

"A simple YES or NO will suffice, here, Mr. Walker."

"My new wife and I went to Grand Cayman Island, for our honeymoon, back in 2000. We were down there for a month. We were advised, by our travel agent, to open a local account with one of the banks, before our arrival, to make our money handling a bit easier. We did currency transfers as well as pay our hotel bills and travel expenses from that account. When we left, we closed the account."

Agent Moustache came in, just then, still wearing his aviators. "Apparently you didn't. This particular account goes back to March 17, 2000.

"And, here's something interesting. This is a copy of your latest bank statement that we were able to get from Cayman National. One deposit, for instance kind of stands out; this one for one hundred and twenty five thousand dollars." Pointing to a line on the receipt. "Can you explain that? Maybe you were planning a little retirement down there?"

Rick came off of his seat. "You motherfucker! You planted that! When the hell did you think I was going to be able to get down to the Caymans to deposit that money? I've been in town all week, people can verify that!"

Moustache continued, "Well, there is always a wire transfer. You can do that locally."

Rick nodded, "Yes, I could have. But there are cameras in banks. If I made a wire transfer to another bank then the local branch would have me on video surveillance. Not to mention that something like that, a deposit that size, would most certainly be flagged. Any activity that size in an account like mine would be flagged as it is standard goddam policy. We all know that. There has to be an explanation."

"Oh, I'm sure that there is a perfectly logical one," Moustache continued, "and when that video surveillance surfaces I'm sure you'll have a few explanations for them, as well. I'm sure you'll have a whole host of excuses, but right now I think we need to go downtown and talk some things over."

While Moustache was talking, the agent that had brought the receipts in had produced a pair of handcuffs. As soon as Rick realized what was going on, he jumped from his chair and snatched the pistol from the open top leather clamshell holster that the agent wore on his belt. Favored by plainclothes detectives it allowed for easy access to the pistol but wasn't terribly secure, at least to someone who knew how to gain access to a pistol in a hurry.

Screaming in surprise, the agent freaked, "Gun! He's got my gun!"

Rick wrapped his left arm around the neck of the surprised agent, using him as a human shield. The lifted pistol was pointed directly at Moustache's head. "Captain, you know I had nothing to do with this. There has to be a legitimate explanation. Call these fuckers off so we can talk like men."

The rest of the agents, as well as Captain Silvan, had drawn their weapons and had them trained on Rick. Captain Silvan spoke softly, "Rick, I'm sure there is an explanation, but right now you are not helping that cause. You need to let that agent go, drop that piece, and get on the ground. If you are innocent, and I'm sure you are we'll get you figured out, right quick.

"But if you are going to go Rambo on everyone, I can't fucking help you. You have got to put that weapon down, brother. I'm talking to you as your friend, now. Put the weapon on the table."

Still using the agent as a human shield, Rick began to walk backwards down the hall, towards the bedroom. He had no fucking clue what was going to happen when he got there, but at least there would be a small barrier between these agents and himself. "Captain, I can't do that, and you know it. Something is going on, here, and I have to get it figured out. I'm being framed."

Reaching the bedroom, he opened the door, never taking his eyes off of the guns trained on him. Captain Silvan spoke, "Rick if you barricade yourself in there, we're going to have to come in after you. You know there are men outside. You're not going to escape. You need to end this, NOW!"

"Captain, I have no idea what the fuck is going on, but you have got to give me a minute. Let me figure this out."

Captain Silvan spoke with the firm tone that he reserved for suspects and offenders, "If you close that door on me, brother, I will give you sixty seconds to open it back up before I come in there, myself, and take you down. *How the hell are you going to put me in this position?!*"

"Captain, give me a few, will ya? You said it, there are men outside. I'm not going anywhere. Let me calm down and we'll go downtown. All right?"

Never lowering his weapon, but relaxing his posture, just a bit, Captain Silvan said, "Only because it's you, I am going to give you three minutes. And then I swear brother, I will come in after you. Three minutes, got it?"

Rick released the agent, and slammed the door in front of him. Locking the knob he had three minutes. Vest? No, if he put on his Kevlar the agents would surely suspect something. Better to leave it under the bed. Pulling off the fleece pajama pants and he grabbed a pair of drawstring hemp pants, flip flops and a Proto paintball T-shirt. He would never be able to outrun anyone like this, but at least he might be able to put out the air of his innocence, and not one that said he was ready for a battle.

This had to be a mistake. He would go downtown with them and answer their questions. Captain Silvan was right. He'd stew for a while, sitting in the same interrogation room where he had questioned so many suspects, but the Captain would get him out, for sure. He hadn't broken any laws. Well, unless you counted putting a loaded weapon to an agent's head and using said agent as a human shield.

Stuffing the pistol into the waistband of his pants, he called out, "I'm coming out. We're going to take it nice and slow, all right? I want Captain Silvan at the door, everyone else back the fuck up, for Christ's sake! You hear me? Back the fuck up!"

On the other side of the door he heard Captain Silvan, "All right. Everyone back up. Remember, as far as we know, he's still one of us. Let's not make this harder on him than we have to, OK?"

There were grunts of approval from the other agents. Captain Silvan said, "They're all down the hall, Rick. I'm here. Just open up, all right? Nice and slow, I'm going to escort you downtown, myself. Don't worry."

Very slowly Rick eased the door open. When it was all the way open he stood with his hands raised. Captain Silvan had his weapon holstered but had his cuffs out. The agents were indeed down the hallway, weapons trained on Rick.

Nodding towards his waistband, with hands still raised, Rick indicated to Captain Silvan that he had the gun tucked there. Captain Silvan nodded in agreement and in a very slow, deliberate motion Rick began to reach for his shirt to raise it, allowing Captain Silvan to remove it.

The chaos that followed was understandable. This whole situation was a breach of protocol. Captain Silvan should never

106

have been there in the first place. Rick should never have been able to get the agent's gun in the first place. The disgraced agent had grabbed his holdout piece from his ankle and it, too, was trained on Rick.

So, when Rick began to reach for his shirt, Moustache yelled out, "He's going for the gun!"

Captain Silvan immediately turned around to scream, "NO!"

Instinct kicked in, though, and the agents' trained muscle memory had them each firing two rounds before Captain Silvan could react. The rounds were perfectly placed and Captain Silvan had no chance at all to get out of the way. No less than four 9mm Black Talon hollow points slammed into Captain Silvan, one right into the center of his forehead. He was dead before he hit the floor.

The rest of the slugs all slammed home into the stunned body of Rick Walker. He was not as fortunate as his captain, though, and he didn't die instantly. Slumped against the hallway his arterial blood pumped freely through his fingers. He knew one of his major arteries was severed, though he had no idea which one. It was a big one though because the amount of blood flowing through his fingers indicated he didn't have a whole lot of time left.

By the time the EMS personnel got through the cordon and into the home, though, Rick Walker was dead. He bled out and died, still with no answers. His body was placed into a body bag of the same make and manufacture that his partner's body had been placed into. Rick was too dead to know, but it was the same EMS personnel that loaded the body of his partner into the back of their waiting ambulance that were now loading his still warm body into the back of the very same ambulance.

For hours investigators combed through the house. Agents spoke in hushed tones on their cell phones, talking with their superiors. All agreed that this was a terrible tragedy that could have gone differently. Should have gone differently; this was no way for an undercover agent as respected as Rick Walker to die. Speculations about Captain Silvan arose; why was he there? He should never have been allowed near this investigation but he was respected and sometimes professional courtesy overrode protocol. It was an unfortunate lesson that all the agents that day learned and vowed never to repeat.

Agent Samuelson, the unfortunate chap who had lost his pistol to Rick, was found the following day hanging from his shower rod, a makeshift noose around his neck and a heartfelt suicide note on his computer. His remorse over his part in the tragedy only added to the confusion as all on scene agreed that it was not his fault. It wasn't spoke of, but thought by many, that Agent Samuelson's death would also alleviate some of the paperwork necessary to this particular investigation, especially the form that was required to document just how in the hell an unarmed man was able to lift the weapon of a trained federal agent.

To further muddle the confusion, the agent with the cheap suit, bad moustache, and aviator sunglasses was nowhere to be found for his statement, regarding the role he played in the drama. Mysteriously, the receipts from Cayman National seemed to also be missing from evidence. The account in question was closed by an unknown person but the last transaction showed a transfer to a numbered Swiss bank account. All further trails for the money had gone cold.

In the end it was determined that both Rick and his partner, Schaap had been planning this for some time. The transfer from Cayman National to a numbered Swiss account was the product of a preset notation on the account to divert all funds and close the account. Normally this is done in the event of an accountholder's death, but can be set up for any number of reasons. Investigators spent months plying the Swiss government for access to the account, but were stonewalled.

No evidence of Rick Walker, either through video surveillance, or other electronic means, ever surfaced to show him making the deposits in question...

...downtown bozeman...

Saturday. 18 July 15. 0005 hours.

My falafel was well past the point of eating, and I was almost considering getting up to refill my soda but at this point I was becoming intrigued in Vincent's story. I might actually be able to run with a story like this. I would have taken notes but I didn't want Vincent to know that I was actually beginning to care about his story, his little narratives.

I did start to get up. I had a feeling that I was going to need some more caffeine to get through his bantering, and frankly, I was going to need it to even get back to the hotel room, at this point.

Just as I was about to dislodge my tired ass from the cheap seat, though, a man and a woman, both wearing horrendously loud clothing, so bright it would have had Stevie Wonder screaming, "Turn it off," walked past me, bumping my elbow and splashing the last of my soda into my lap.

"God. Damn. It!" Now I had no soda, my crotch was wet, and Vincent still wasn't going to let me go. Fuck.

Speaking of Vincent, he was giving me a sarcastic look, something akin to a look as if Karma, herself, had decided to take a giant wet bite out of my ass.

"What the fuck are you staring at, asshole?"

He was grinning his horrible crooked grin, "Nothing, just, yaknow, something funny, I guess."

"You guess?"

"Yeah, I guess. How about we get back to the point of this meeting? I don't have all night, either." For the first time since we'd met up, he did look tired, almost used up.

"So we're back to the money, again, or the lack thereof."

111

Vincent had his gaping mouth open again, nodding. I said, "Vincent close your mouth you look like the fucking Cheshire Cat. It's creeping me the fuck out."

He instantly complied, but then opened it again, a moment later. "Think about it, yes, we are back to the money again."

"OK, so we're back to the money. What does that prove? You also mentioned murder, but so far I've heard about a lot of unlucky coincidences."

Vincent, nodding again, "Yes, but now think about this crooked cop. Where did these supposed receipts go, and for that matter, where did the actual money go? Someone had to end up with the cash."

I was dabbing at my damp crotch with a small stack of napkins so rough I could have filed my nails with them, "If this cat was pilfering money from the drug deals and dealers he was working, there would have been some sort of record, or public outrage about it. I mean, in a town like this, someone is bound to notice. There just isn't enough separation between the layers for corruption of this size to go unnoticed."

That fucking Cheshire grin of his, "And there you have it!" He clapped his palms together and spread his arms wide, as if a magician revealing the trick.

I was puzzled, "And there I have...what...?"

"Did you ever hear of an uproar about crooked cops? No. You are correct, in a town this size, someone would take notice. This isn't Phoenix, Los Angeles, or New York City, hell even Detroit. This is a small town where people know each other and if someone was going to try and filch a chunk of money that size, someone would have a shit fit about it. The entire city fucking council would be up in arms demanding some sort of explanation as to 'how this could happen in there fair city' and all that bullshit."

I shrugged my shoulders, "OK, so no one said anything. So what does that prove, exactly? Maybe this guy was smarter than your average bear."

Vincent pulled some folded papers out of his pocket. "I'll grant you that, but here's where it really gets hinky. Remember me telling you about Cayman National Bank? Remember our friends from the gas station in New York?"

"Yes, I do."

"Well, when I was investigating the matter, I found out that there was indeed a deposit to the bank. I'm still working out the particulars, but it seems that a deposit, in the amount of one hundred and twenty thousand dollars, was placed into an account that was traced to a limited liability company, based here in Bozeman; something called Nuclear Winter Industries, whatever the hell that means. Maybe they build bomb shelters, or apocalypse shelters, something like that?"

I shrugged my shoulders. I wasn't sure if I was supposed to care or not, should answer or not, or just keep listening.

"What I'm thinking is that it's your garden variety shell company where money seems to get parked. I'm still trying to crack what they do, exactly. *If* they do anything, exactly."

My ears perked up at this, and upon seeing this Vincent seemed to grin even more. I swear to God, I was going to punch him in the face by the end of the night, if not worse.

I said, "Well that's a pretty solid coincidence, but aren't a lot of companies in Bozeman shell companies for others? I thought it was a good tax haven thing, or something?"

"True, they are, and it is. But to get back to the hinky part, this same company also made a deposit, just a few years earlier, in the amount of seven hundred and fifty thousand dollars, into our very same Caymanian bank. Who else do we know that is associated with a number of that importance?"

For the first time, tonight, Vincent had my complete and undivided attention. "Holy shit, Vincent, how did you find all this out? And better yet, who else knows about it?"

"Right now, it's just you and I. It's taken me quite a while to put this together, that's why we haven't spoken in a while. Did you think I was kidding you?"

I had to admit, "I thought you were full of shit, there, for awhile. This is great stuff. How much do you want for the intellectual property on this?

"Honestly, man, when we first sat down, I had thought about ripping your ideas, reworking them and making a new novel out of it, but shit, this is too good, as is."

"Are you asking to buy me off? Are you actually trying to buy me off? For God's sake man, stop being so damn petty!"

Interesting choice of words, "Yes, actually, I was going to quote a number. I can run with this. What are your thoughts, I mean, can we do business?"

"I thought we were doing business. Do you have your checkbook with you?"

I was actually reaching into my pocket when Vincent burst out laughing. "Wow, you really are that petty, aren't you? Don't worry, just yet. I think that you and I can come to an agreement before the night is over.

"Before we get to that, though, I have another story to tell you. This, too, is a doozy."

This time, Vincent had my rapt attention.

DIME STORE WHORES

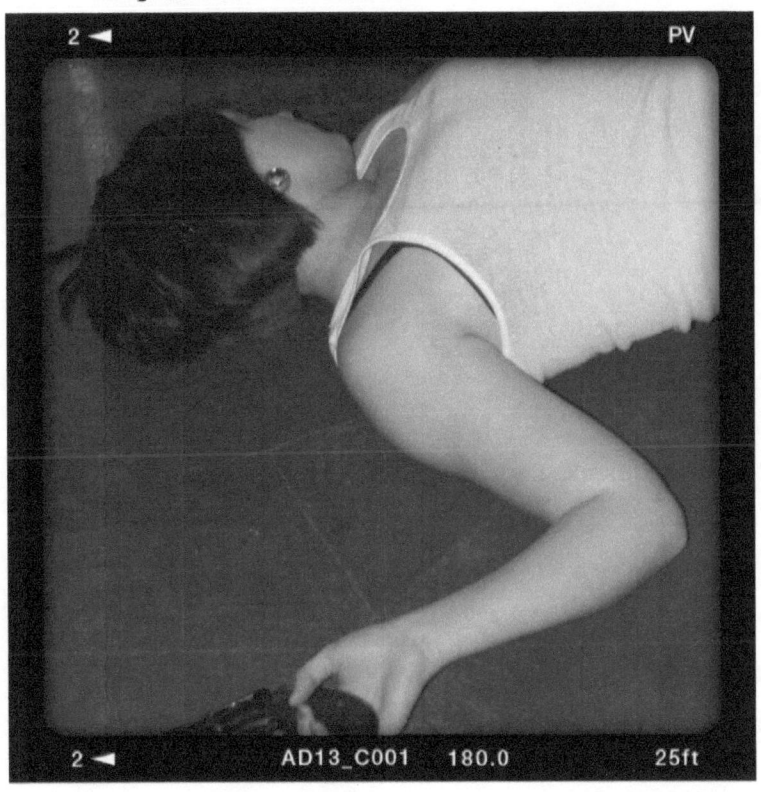

July, 1986

Louis Hennepin sat on a worn wooden barstool at the front counter of the store, adding numbers in old fashioned paper ledgers, just as his family had always done, making notes on bills that needed to be paid. The antique cash register never had more than two hundred dollars in it, but the safe was plenty well stocked. Rarely did Louis ever need to get into the safe. Even the last few holiday seasons barely kept him afloat. Might have been just as well that he kept to the old ways, like his father had done, and his father before him.

"Louis, you got any more coffee?" Sheriff Rasmussen always stopped in for a cup on his morning rounds. It was his way of keeping the peace in this sleepy little town. It also ensured that the green metal Thermos that the Sheriff carried was never fully empty, either.

Without lifting his head, Louis nodded to the office behind his counter. "Pot's on. It's fresh."

Technically Sheriff Rasmussen's term had ended about ten years ago. When no one stepped up to run against him, though, people just left Rasmussen to run things. He still drew a paycheck because no one wanted to be without a legitimate sheriff. When the town's only squad car finally went tits up, old Jim Rasmussen simply took the lights off the cruiser and put them on his shit brown 1979 Ford Bronco. He didn't even bother with a logo because most people who saw the Bronco coming down the road knew it was Sheriff Rasmussen. About the only time the sheriff ever saw trouble was when Dave and Andrea Palmer started a solid night of drinking and took to using each other as a punching bag. Even then, a night in the drunk tank, some stern lecturing and a cold gaze from one of the deputies usually cooled them off for a few weeks.

Sheriff Rasmussen helped himself to the pot and poured a generous amount into his Thermos. "How's the day looking for ya, partner?"

Louis didn't think that the Sheriff really gave a good God damn, but to know his people, a sheriff has to mingle just a bit. Louis said, "Yesterday wasn't too bad, Sheriff. The State Class B boys track team came through, on their way to a meet over in Omaha, picked me clean on sun lotion and lawn chairs. I guess they didn't wanna sit on those metal bleachers, again."

Rasmussen nodded, "They gearing up for the season, already? School's still over a month out.

"That coach of theirs, what's his name, Coach May, he better watch himself, or he's gonna give those boys a heat stroke. We need those front running seniors if we're gonna have a chance this season."

Louis lifted his head, "Some sorta exhibition match and they'll be running against the Class A boys. It's good practice for the season.

"Besides, the coach is a solid guy. He'll bench the boys if they start looking peaked and he knows full well what's at stake this season. I think that he's got a right head though, making 'em run against some tougher people. The boys'll be able to see who they're apt to be up against."

Sheriff Rasmussen grunted his agreement at this and took a long pull of the hot coffee. Louis may not have always done the new and best things, but he certainly didn't skimp out on the coffee.

Hennepin's Department Store was a simple affair nestled on the east edge of town, out on Highway 12, also known as the Outlaw Trail Scenic Byway. Rumor has it that the highway so got its name because it was once a cattle rustler's trail used to smuggle goods and cattle through the wild prairies of Nebraska.

118

The original wood floors of the once great department store that Louis's grandfather, Joseph installed were still waxed once a month, polished to a high mirror shine. The eighteen foot ceilings still had the original white washed tin tile squares and the stained glass above the newer, energy efficient windows on the east and south walls were still held together in their pewter frames. A simple rough-hewn wood counter sat on the west wall, surrounding the office entrance, were Louis kept the store's books and meager necessities to keep the store in the black. It also housed the private toilet that even the Sheriff didn't ask permission to use.

"Well, I'm off, Louis. Got rounds to keep." By that the sheriff meant that there were other free cups of coffee to cash in on, and the occasional free lunch at the Stormcastle Café on South Wood Street. With his coffee mug raised in salute the sheriff departed the store.

"Sheriff, you take care. Sounds like it'll be a half ways decent day out there." Louis's words chased the sheriff out the door. When he looked at his watch and saw that it was already almost noon, Louis's stomach started to grumble. The lunch he'd packed was in the mini fridge, in the office. The sheriff got into his Bronco and pulled an illegal U-turn in front of the store, tooting the torn and waving as he drove by.

Louis had never married, and while he wasn't a queer, just didn't really care that much for the dating scene. So he rarely went home for lunch and today his afternoon guy, John, wouldn't show up until two o'clock. Today, like most days, Louis would eat his lunch at the counter and not mind when small dollops of mustard dripped down from his egg salad sandwich on to the worn planks.

Valentine, Nebraska, was the sad hope of a town that could have been a metropolis but never progressed beyond the small

Midwestern dream. There were barely 2,800 breathing souls within the town limits and that was if the fair happened to be nearby. Locals agreed that the only reason it was still there was because it was the seat of Cherry County and that some damn fool had gotten the idea to send mail through the barely capable hands of Violet Schumacher who was probably the oldest person in the town, as well as the town postmaster, so that every year on the 14th of February, you could have a stamp added to your envelope's back with a sad and sappy greeting that made a Hallmark card look about as noteworthy as a Shakespearean sonnet.

Hennepin's was the other reason that the town was on the map. Joseph Hennepin first opened the doors of his fine department store back in 1931. Folks around the budding town thought he was plum crazy, what with the Great Depression raging. There was no way that a store could raise walls, much less capital, in a time when the depression was literally sucking the life out of similar towns.

But Hennepin had the financial backing of sound investments and he was bound and determined to see people get some work and so he hired all the local labor he could find and used every soul willing to wield a hammer or pour concrete and within four months the first story of Hennepin's Department Store was open for business. The winter of 1931-32 wasn't a particularly cold one, no worse than any other winter, but the laborers all had ranches to attend to, and grain silos to button up, so work ceased. When spring poked her pretty little head out of the frosted summer fallow fields, however, work resumed and by June of 1932 the second story was operational.

Home goods and groceries were available aplenty on the first floor, while the second contained all the latest fashions that Hennepin could bring in. There was quite a stir at Good

Samaritan Bible Church for a few Sundays when it was discovered that ladies could get their hands on some of those French cut silk undergarments that were being mentioned in the new fashion magazines. Sears and Roebuck didn't carry those provocative items and if they did, they certainly weren't in the catalog. Life magazine was most certainly not going to do an article on them, either. It didn't matter that Matt Freiburg, at the Amoco station on Green Street, next to the Cherry County Hospital, had all manner of pinup magazines and calendars behind the counters; even a few tacked to the walls in the service bays, because they were hidden from the boys. Hennepin put those sexy undergarments on display, and while they were tucked in the corner, boys often wandered far from their mothers' disapproving glares to catch a glimpse of the whore's red silk on the plaster white mannequins. It would have shocked more than a few boys to know that their mother owned silk garments very similar to those on display, purchased especially for their husbands on those rare and special occasions when they had a night to themselves.

During the Soviet red scare of the 1950s, Hennepin even brought in an excavator to extend the basement and create a bomb shelter that could easily hold 100 people. It didn't matter that most of the surrounding farms had their own tornado cellars, Joe Hennepin used good marketing skills and a little dose of fear to play to his customers' needs. By letting them know it was there, and that all were welcome, he'd make sure that all were going to come back for their shopping needs. When he brought in some new firearms to, as he advertised, "fend off those Commie bastards," sales shot through the roof, pun quite intended.

A single shot, 20 gage, breakaway shotgun made by Remington firearms of New York was the most popular sale item. For thirty five dollars a customer could get themselves a brand new range gun, and a great home defense weapon. Hell, Hennepin even threw in a box of shells to go with the handshake. These weren't the cheap paper shells that some companies were selling, no sir, these were the original brass cartridges that resembled the enormous howitzer shells used in the bombers over Europe.

Soon, boys all over town were setting up old tin cans and blasting them to bits and hunting jackrabbits and coyotes in the back forty. Even with the sales skyrocketing, Hennepin was smart enough to keep the selection of these firearms small, and as a result there were very few injuries. Common sense and a strong background in outdoorsmanship were common things that today's society seemed to now be lacking.

Things went well for Joseph Hennepin who turned the ownership of the store over to his son, Jacob, in 1962. Kennedy hadn't been shot yet, and things were looking good in the Whitehouse, though that good for nothing president was talking about spending more hard earned tax dollars in this new space research crap and was promising to send a man to the moon.

Things ultimately did not go well, though, for Jacob Hennepin. He had inherited his father's smarts and gone to Harvard Medical School when he made the choice, at the last minute, to switch majors and go into business management. Medical school seemed like a long ways off, and with the grades he was pulling, he could easily go back. Besides, with the money his father was making, Jacob wanted a piece of that pie, too. Graduating in spring of 1961, twenty one year old Jacob Hennepin returned to Valentine, Nebraska, with the full intentions of taking over his father's business, with Joseph's blessings, of course. Old Uncle Sam, though, had other plans.

In a little thought of corner of the world, trouble was brewing in a rarely heard about country called North Vietnam. By 1966, the twenty six year old Jacob wasn't worried about being drafted, he was closer to thirty now, than he was twenty. There was no way in hell they would take an old man like him.

His childhood sweetheart, Erica, had just given birth to their son Louis barely nine months after the wedding vows were exchanged. Things were looking well and prosperous for the Hennepin family. Erica came from a wealthy cattle family and while she knew her place in the home, her wealth brought an equal voice to the table, and the marriage. It brought further stability to the family business, as well.

The United States government felt differently, though. Jacob's medical schooling wasn't lost on the War Department and soon a telegram arrived with Jacob Hennepin's name on it, orders to report for basic training, Fort Sam Houston, Texas.

Specialist Jacob Hennepin breezed through his training and soon found himself in the middle of battle he knew little about, in a corner of the world he had never heard of, and as a newly minted combat medic of the 1st Cavalry Division, healing the wounds of men and women from cultures and religions he'd never dreamt about. His conservative Lutheran upbringing certainly couldn't have prepared him for any of this.

For twelve long months, Jacob operated out of Tay Ninh, north of Ho Chi Minh City, walking soupy rice paddies of Vietnamese deltas, as well as the hot and arid plains of the highlands, his M16 rifle took as many enemy lives as he had saved. Regarded as a gifted combat medic, more soldiers lived under his care, than perished. No thanks to the concerted efforts of the North Vietnamese Army.

When his tour was up, Jacob shouldered his gear that was now battered and trail worn, boarded a transport plane that would take him to Guam and was taxing down the runway when a mechanical failure caused it to veer off the runway and crash, killing all aboard. A simple failure of a circuit or switch or hose or pump did less in five minutes than what the entire NVA could not do while he was one full year in country.

Because of the nature of the body's condition, a closed casket was sent home for the family to bury and that's where Jacob resides, to this day, in plot 317 of the Mount Hope Cemetery, just off of the section of Highway 83 South, known as the Blue Star Memorial Highway, named for his service.

Jacob's infant son, Louis, grew up hearing tales of his father's heroism in Vietnam, looking at pictures of his father while he was in country and being regaled with tales of his father's shenanigans as a spirited youth. Jacob's widow, Erica, took over the family business and with some quiet and sage advice from old man Joseph Hennepin himself, she made the flourishing department store an even grander jewel of a small Midwestern town.

By the time that Louis Hennepin took over from his mother, the gas crisis of the 70s seemed to have passed and the 80s looked ripe for some new opportunities. Economic downturns that were forecasted hadn't seemed to hit the self-sustaining, insulated community of Valentine. Louis didn't have a college degree, but that didn't matter to him. It was pretty widely known that he would inherit the family business and Louis had a pretty keen eye for the public side which kept people coming in. He may not have been as smart as his father, but he damn sure had the smile to charm the old widows and the young maidens, alike. Men could easily talk to him, and kids didn't mind him. Louis quickly became the new fixture at the counter and that's about where he most often stayed.

When Erica Hennepin passed away, her inheritance and fortune kept the store running high in the black even during the dark days, but slowly those columns had started to drift closer to the red than Louis would have liked. It was Louis's keen eye that kept things going, but even after years of floundering business Louis was forced to close the second floor for business, and when the Masons offered to renovate it for their meeting hall, it was an offer he jumped at. The monthly rent wasn't a big influx but it was cash coming in. Columns in the black side of the ledgers started to go back up, again. Jacob even resorted to renting out basement space for private storage and soon had people renting out small offices for themselves in the newly remodeled basement. Once again, it was easy income, and he knew that his father would have approved of his sound business models and practices.

Jacob had all but forgotten about the bomb shelter that his grandfather had built, assuming he even knew it was down there to begin with, but to Francis Moore, who rented the office that had been built around the bunker's entrance, it was an unexpected find that turned into a gold mine. Wooden shelving units had been built in front of the door, but when stacking papers on the shelf, Moore discovered the loose plank that activated the door's catch. When the twelve inch thick concrete door swung open into the bunker, he couldn't believe his eyes.

Moore was an independent financial analyst when it was still something to be proud of. Guys like Bernie Madoff hadn't hit the scene to corrupt people and while Moore worked with some unsavory people he still attempted to make an honest buck, doing what was still considered an honest trade.

Discovery of the bunker changed all that. While most of the original cots that Joseph Hennepin has stocked the bunker with had fallen into disrepair there were still a few ratty metal frame beds with even nastier, mildewed mattresses still sitting on the sagging springs. The crate rations had all spoiled and the water had turned moldy. Most of the military surplus gear was still in sealed footlockers, though and in solid, most importantly, perfectly saleable condition.

Crates of metal canteens, field gear and gas masks were stacked to the ceiling. Mess kits, ammo pouches, helmets and riot gear were packaged in wooden crates. Tents and ponchos, knives and bayonets, flashlights and even some ancient radios were packaged and ready to go at a moment's notice. Old man Hennepin had surely thought this one out. If the Commies had attacked there were certainly a few people that would have been very well off, down here.

If Louis Hennepin had known this stuff was down here he most certainly would have hauled it up to the sales floor; there seemed to be a market for this stuff, as of late. Those skinhead punks would drive from as far away as Omaha to get their fascist looking gear. Teenagers and outdoorsman alike seemed to be adopting a military lazy look as well. It seemed to be the new vogue fashion as many of the teens showing up for class at Valentine High School were wearing the three color camouflage pattern of greens and browns.

Since it seemed that Louis Hennepin had forgotten all about this little portion of history, Francis Moore was more than happy to line his pockets with profits he made from selling off the gear, sometimes in small quantities, sometimes in large quantities to religious nuts, private militias, and the occasional collector. It was a chance, off-hand conversation though, with one of his less than truly legitimate clients that had really gotten things rolling for Moore.

"Yaknow, if a guy had a half a mind, he could run his own little brothel, yaknow, party palace outta that thing." Normally

Moore didn't tell people about the find. Drake, however, was a repeat client who was willing to pay a bulk price and drive some of the goods up to Montana, if needed. Montana was its own separate paradise of buyers who seemed to love the idea of the state splitting off and becoming its own nation, surrounded by the rest of a sovereign nation.

"Not a bad idea, but who'd wanna run shop outta this dungeon?" Moore wasn't too keen on subletting his new find and women of ill repute weren't known for keeping their tongues. Well, not keeping their tongues silent anyway.

Drake smiled, "Who says they would have to be a legitimate whore? Hmm? Plenty of runaways hanging around that travel center, up in Murdo. It's only about an hour's drive up to South Dakota and you could have your pickings of the ladies.

"I reckon it wouldn't take much to entice 'em and hell, they're just like a wild horse. Ya just gotta know how to break 'em, partner."

Fran Moore appeared as if someone had slapped him. "Hey, man, I don't know..."

Drake held up his hands in a defensive posture, "Hey, I'm just thinking out loud, here. No one said anything about anything. Just spit balling, as the phrase goes."

Murdo, South Dakota, seemed to have been a product of necessity, a town built up around the intersection of Interstate 90 and Highway 83 South. There were indeed plenty of various folk, including your typical, as well as atypical runaways that hung around the truck stop. It was, in the simplest definition of terms, basically four ways to get the hell out of this tiny little section of the country. Roads led to all four corners of the country and it was widely known that truckers who ran through there had big mouths and stories of adventure.

West led to the mountains and skiing of Montana, north to the endless wheat fields of North Dakota, and east to Minneapolis and Rochester, Minnesota. So many ways to escape unnoticed, no one would notice a girl or two go missing every now and then, would they? Drake certainly didn't think anyone would miss a person from that area.

As Drake collected his merchandise, packed into a canvas duffle bag he brought with him, he said, "Might be something to think about, yeah?"

Moore had no intention of graduating to kidnapping. Certainly not for what, in today's language, would be known as sex trafficking. He had to admit, though, there was a certain novelty when it came to the thought of easy money. Fran Moore loved the easy money.

By this time, Moore had just about had his mind made up but he certainly wasn't going to tell Drake that. No, that greedy bastard already took more of a cut from Moore than he wanted, and Moore did have a long weekend planned, up in Pierre, next month. Maybe he could pick up one of these young gals and see what would come of it. He said, "Indeed; something to think about." It was already something that had been thought about, and was soon to be acted upon.

August, 1986

Moore had been sitting in the parking lot of Sumptner's Travel Center for the better part of an hour watching the influx of girls as they walked to and fro. He hated to admit it but Drake was right. All manner of girls, both old and young, were walking around the tarmac of the gas station. An odd mixture of leftover 70s bell bottom fashion was mixed with the 80s new wave raver fashion and the whole scene made for a motley

128

blend of individuals. It was as if a deranged Paris runway show had come to South Dakota, all for a show, just for him.

It wasn't that there weren't the right girls to choose from; Moore was trying to figure out how to balls himself up for something like this. It wasn't that he wasn't prepared, he had done all manner of preparation and gotten all the necessary supplies, spacing the purchases out so as not to attract attention. Turns out it wasn't that necessary since Jennings Lumber Company, on Hall Street, didn't really think it all that odd when Moore said he needed some paint stripper, tarps, tape and twine.

"You looking to do some remodeling?" The kid behind the counter at Jennings wasn't a complete idiot, but he was close. He belonged to one of the families on the city council, but Moore couldn't remember who. Moore knew that this punk had been in trouble with the law a few times for drugs but it appeared nothing too serious since he was still working the counter. Nothing was secret in a town like this.

"Yeah, the office needs to be spruced up and it's a little quiet so I figured I'd get a jump on some refreshing." Moore was surprised by how easily the lie slipped past his lips. What the hell was he getting himself into? Moore didn't think it really would be that easy as he loaded his freshly purchased supplies.

Now Moore was sitting in a parking lot, across state lines, about to commit a felony as far as he knew, all because he had an idea pop into his head to make a few more bucks, under the radar, and maybe satisfy a few primal urges in the process.

There... She was the one right there. No one would miss here, would they? No...

Strutting across the parking lot in a pair of severely worn sandals and some horribly cutoff jean shorts was a red headed chain smoking gal; her hemp shoulder bag swinging and bouncing against her ample ass cheeks while stubby nipples pointed through the worn cloth of her aged tube top. There was certainly no bra to restrain the little nubs.

Making eye contact with her, Moore motioned for her to approach his vehicle. The rented cargo van could be, in theory, tracked back to him, but again, in such an out of the way, anonymous place, who would remember a rented cargo van with plates that didn't come from a state near at all to South Dakota? He really couldn't have been more anonymous if he was invisible.

Miss Redhead came with her hips swaying suggestively up to the driver's side of the van, leaning in through the open window. "You looking for a little company, hun?"

"Maybe I am, what are you thinking?"

Her smile was about as fake as her enthusiasm at being in this pitiful stop in the middle of nowhere. "Well, you got this nice ride, so maybe you and I can take a ride down the road a bit. Sun's gonna set here in a few, maybe you buy me some dinner and we go find a place to be alone?"

Nodding, Moore motioned for her to get into the passenger seat. Dinner was a greasy sack of burgers from a roadside stop and while he didn't think he was going to get a disease from the food, Moore didn't think that it couldn't be ruled out completely.

Sure enough, they found a place to park and as soon as the sun set behind the horizon, clothes came off just as fast the darkness enveloped the van. Rocking back and forth, Melody, probably not her real name, was soon screaming in ecstasy. Probably not real ecstasy but Moore certainly didn't care. She was hitting all the high notes at all the right times. And while Moore was no wizard in bed, the way this girl was riding his heated crotch he knew he had picked a winner. Without realizing what was happening, he let loose and gave her every ounce of man juice he had. Instantly her face flushed and her moans turned into a sweet smile of satisfaction.

Melody's sweaty breasts bounced up and down, and her smile grew even wider when she realized what had just happened. "Oh, is that for me?"

Moore, gasping at his own actions panted, "And there's plenty more where that came from."

This was going better than expected. He had planned it and it was working right into the plan. Dismounting him, Melody sat her naked body against the rear doors of the van, knees drawn up, splayed open, revealing everything to her new friend. Reaching into her bag she produced a battered cigarette pack that contained expertly rolled joints. With the practiced flick of a seasoned addict, she tapped one out of the pack.

"You want one of these?" The brief glow of her lighter illuminating the sweat on her naked body made her appear almost beautiful. Her adventures on the road had aged her body quicker than she would have liked, making her actual age almost impossible to tell. The only real vibrant hue was her hair. What had once been perky breasts now slightly sagged, and her small, protruding gut resulting from a steady diet of poor meal after poorer meal. Melody didn't look old, rather *worn out* was a more appropriate term for her. Life on the road had sucked the very soul from her. Scars from drug abuse, piercing, torment; all of the above adorned her body.

But, in that brief moment of post coital ecstasy she almost looked youthful and vibrant again. Almost beautiful again.

"Sure, c'mon over here." Moore, himself still naked, had a cloth, wrapped in a plastic sandwich bag, soaked in the recently purchased paint thinner. Opening the bag he brought it out and as Melody crawled towards him he covered her mouth and nose with the near toxic fumes; she never had a chance. Her eyes went wide with surprise but by the time she could register what was happening, the fumes overtook her and she collapsed, unconscious but still breathing in a shallow, jagged rasps. Her sweaty skin trembled as her body fought to expel the toxic vapors of the foul substance.

Working fast, and still naked, Moore wrapped Melody's body in the plastic, in a tight roll, securing the roll with the packing tape. Even if she awoke she would have no place to go. Placing a strip of tape over her mouth to ensure that she wouldn't be able to scream, but still allowing her to breathe, he would be able to get her back to Valentine and get her into the bunker before the sun came up, if Lady Luck in any way decided to bless this perverse little operation.

Moore redressed himself and gathered up all the food wrappers and other items that didn't belong. Placing them in a bag, along with Melody's personal belongings he intended to stop somewhere along the way and place them in a trash dumpster. If not, he could bring them back and burn them in one of the many burn barrels around town. Hell, even the town landfill would be safe. Moore had even thought to purchase a few plain white T-shirts and a couple pairs of men's white basic cotton boxer shorts for Melody (or some such similar victim) to change into. He thought she wouldn't be able to get far if she didn't have proper clothing or footwear. In the recesses of his mind, Moore was certain he had heard something about if a victim was able to disassociate from their identity, they would be less likely to try and mount an escape. Basically take away all thoughts of a personal identity, all thoughts of hope.

The other purchases Moore had made were for a length of chain and a secure padlock that was now bolted to the concrete bunker wall. If she were able to get free of that, she wouldn't

132

be going far. *If.* Heavy chain links had been secured to the wall with a secure eyebolt and another padlock. Marley's ghost would have had a hell of a time escaping those chains.

Driving back to Valentine he worked out the rest of the details in his head, while the AM radio played some distant honky-tonk station. Just loud enough to keep his mind from wandering back to the rear of the cargo van and just soft enough to not attract any attention should he get himself stopped. Even if he was, he rather thought the rolled bundle in the back would resemble a small roll of carpet, which had been his intention, for the duration of the trip. Moore was pretty sure he could talk himself out of just about anything, if he was stopped, except for the pot smell. He rolled the window down, a bit, to bring a small breeze into the cab. Cool prairie breezes helped to dry the sweat on his skin.

Sure enough Moore rolled into Valentine well before sunup. With the drive of only about 90 miles, and never going more than one mile above the posted 55mph speed limit, it was safe to assume he was going to make it back unmolested. Melody was another story... Unconsciously Moore chuckled to himself when he thought about the adventures he was going to have.

Backing the cargo van up to the rear doors of Hennepin's, that also served as the entrance to the basement offices, Moore first went in and ensured that the basement was clear of other occupants, and also that his office was unlocked, as well as the door to the bunker was open. This was going to be the most dangerous part of the journey, making sure that no one saw him unload his cargo from the back of the van. Again luck was with him and Moore was able to get Melody into the basement, and chained to the far back wall of the bunker, without anyone noticing she was there, or even better, before anyone including Melody herself knowing that she was awake.

133

Her naked body was still covered in the stench of paint thinner and sexual sweat. Moore couldn't help but admire her naked form, the white skin dotted with an occasional freckle. Her pink nipples and shocking read thatch of pubic hair almost called to him, nay screamed to him. Truly the carpet matched the drapes and it was only with the greatest of restraints that he could keep himself off of her. Instead he dressed her in the loose fitting white undershirt and the ill fitting boxers and then laid her on one of the bunks. There was a carton of rations next to the bunk, along with a couple of canteens of water and a battery powered lantern. In the corner, still within length of the chain, was an old five gallon bucket with a makeshift toilet seat attached to it. Primitive was too good of a word for the setup inside the bunker.

The bunker walls were a solid 12 inches of concrete and as far as anyone knew, soundproof to the world around it. To be safe, Moore had strung wire from one end to the other in an X formation, in essence dividing the room into a grid of four squares. On this wire he hung the heavy woolen military surplus blankets that would create extra sound and light barriers between Melody and the entrance to the bunker. No one would know she was here unless Moore wanted them to. And that was only if they were willing to pay the right price. Admittance to this show did not come cheap.

All in all Moore felt he had a pretty solid setup. By this time Melody was starting to stir and with the dosing he had given her, Moore suspected she would have one hell of a nasty hangover when she awoke. He had thought about this, though and brought some aspirin to help ease that pain. He wasn't a total sadist, after all. Opportunist was more like it. Time would tell if this would turn into a lucrative endeavor.

Moore shut the door to the bunker just as Melody was beginning to stir. He wasn't sure if it was really his ears, or if it was his imagination that heard the soft sobbing as he latched the bunker door from the outside.

September, 1986

Sheriff Rasmussen stepped out of his battered Bronco and turned the collar of his worn ranch coat up against the overcast day. His three day stubble growth of coarse grey hair on his neck had consistently rubbed against the very same collar for many years and there was a decidedly worn spot on that old brown corduroy. His Thermos was empty but he knew of one place that always had a fresh pot of the gourmet stuff on.

Louis Hennepin didn't even raise his head when he heard the door creak open. It was only September but the last few days had been bitterly cold. Clouds had been racing across the sky, being chased by a fierce wind out of the west that drove flocks of birds from their migratory watering holes and their peaceful fields. Colors on the trees were rapidly changing and fading as if the very life heat were being sucked out of them. Leaves fell, broken and dead, trampled to a fine powder beneath the pedestrian foot. It was going to be an early winter, by the feel of it, and a long one, to boot.

"Mornin' Louis." Sheriff Rasmussen had long since stopped asking for permission to walk behind the counter and Louis could have raised a fuss about it, but what would have been the point? The sheriff was a good guy, a real solid citizen and he always made a nice show of force when he was out and about. Not that there was much crime in these part to be aware of, regardless.

"Mornin', Sheriff." Louis had the morning copy of the *Valentine Sun Times* folded over as he shamelessly worked the crossword puzzle in ink. He was daring that way. If he were to make a mistake, who would care, right? Hell, who would even notice? John, his afternoon man wouldn't dare make a mention of it, not if he wanted to keep his job. Not that Louis would fire him over something as petty as a crossword puzzle, but he wasn't sure that John knew that, and a little healthy dose of fear kept his employee in line.

Sheriff Rasmussen reached over the counter and grabbed the paper out of Louis's hands. "You see that business up in Murdo? Girls 's been going missing near that truck stop. Local law enforcement thought they 'as a couple of runaways, at first, but now they are seeing more of 'em going missing. They think some people got it in their heads to start nabbing them girls. Who knows where they'd'a ended up by now."

Louis, not a father, nor a husband, nor an uncle that he knew of, was really more annoyed at this point over his apparent inability to finish his crossword. He had seen the article as he skimmed the front page headlines. The *Sun Times* had a mediocre, at best, nationwide section that did their best to cover events that were happening around their area. Most of the information that was printed in the article appeared to be second hand sources, and there was no AP accreditation. While Louis was no journalism expert, he was pretty sure this was nothing more than slicked up gossip and didn't really pay attention to it.

"Yeah, I saw the article. Sounds to me like some girls got into trouble and probably run off with their boyfriends. Hell, maybe a few of 'em got pregnant and are now trying to make sure they don't get themselves in a bit of trouble with their dear old dad."

Sheriff Rasmussen didn't look all that pleased, "Well be on the lookout, nonetheless. I'm sure them girls are miles away from here, but ya never know. We got a lot of interstate traffic starting to come through here, these last few years. Who knows what kinda people that'll bring through these parts?"

Louis just raised an eyebrow. He seriously doubted that if that kind of trouble was bouncing around, that it was likely to end up in his world. Besides, those girls were long gone and Louis doubted that anyone was ever going to see them again. If he had only known how right, and oh so wrong he was.

"Sheriff, if I were to see that kind of trouble in this town, I would more likely shit myself than to play tough guy. I figure I'll just call you because that would be a better way to stay alive then if I decide to play hero."

Sheriff Rasmussen lifted his coffee in his customary salute and walked out the door. Cold breezes buffeted his coat as he climbed into his battered truck. Yeah, it was going to be a long winter all right.

Just to be sure, Louis checked the cubby under the counter. Sure enough, the battered old shotgun, one of the very same that his grandfather used to sell, was resting comfortably in its nook, a small box of shells at the ready. Not the brass cased ones that his grandfather had sold, but the more modern plastic cased loads. Louis had never once had an opportunity to pull that shotgun, let alone use it, but there was a small moment of refreshing security knowing it was there. Louis turned his attention back to his crossword. Five down, a seven letter word for scoundrel, starting with the letter "D"...

October, 1986

Moore came into the office early, like he always did, for the last couple of months. Checking on his merchandise before he opened the office doors had become a daily habit. His legitimate clients thought he was bordering on insane because he was always at the office. One even gave him good natured chiding when she said, "Yaknow with all this new found wealth you have, in working the world's most horrible hours, you should be able to find yourself a nice gal, settle down and relax a bit." Her sly grin belied the good natured ribbing she gave him and suggested that if she weren't married and maybe a few years younger, she could have been that gal.

His illegitimate clients didn't care if he was obsessive, insane, or downright fruity. These clients had a taste for young and illegal flesh and Moore was happy to provide for those desires for the right price. It was amazing how quickly he could turn a blind eye, and a deaf ear, to the muffled grunts and occasional cry that he thought he could hear from the interior of the bunker. When there was business being transacted inside the bunker, he kept himself out of it.

Fran Moore was no stranger to the dating scene. He wasn't bad looking, either. But, like any good addiction, once it got its hooks into you, all other matters seemed to fall away and become less important. Runs to Murdo had become more prevalent and after a few times of renting a van, he was starting to run out of excuses and while he was flirting with danger, it would have been infinitely more dangerous to start a pattern of behavior, especially on a matter like this.

Melody had been a fantastic experience. Once she realized what her new role in life had become, she was eager to do whatever it took to remain alive. *Eager. Whatever.*

These were words that potential customers loved to hear, and even more eager to experience. Moore had learned early on that Melody had a small penchant for prescription medications. Pain killers kept her docile enough to keep from running away but not so doped as that she was unresponsive. Even the sickos that seemed to find their way to his bunker drew the line at unresponsive and comatose patients. Besides, there was no thrill, no danger in it.

But, like so many things, Moore became lazy and lax and one fateful day he left that bottle of pills within reach of Melody. She might have had a chance if she was within reach of the hospital. *Maybe.* However, after ingesting a small handful of the remaining pills, and a few good shots of fine liquor from her newest client, her poor body just couldn't take the stress anymore. While said client was in the middle of his own personal ecstasy, Melody's heart quite literally gave up the ghost and to make matters even worse, said client had no idea he was fucking a corpse until he had finished his business. His screams, when he found out, were about enough to alert the neighbors. Thankfully, Moore had the good sense to not take clients such as these while business hours were in operation. No one was around to hear the muffled wailing coming from what Moore was quickly beginning to dub as "the tomb."

There had been other girls. Moore had been careful not to go for a particular type, lest he attract attention. He was still chiding himself over his carelessness with Melody. He wouldn't make that mistake again. He chose indiscriminately his victims. Whoever seemed interested in taking a ride in a rented van, with a seemingly nice guy. There were a few apprehensive ones, but with a little coaxing, Moore was able to get them into his vehicle.

One look around the truck stop and seeing the alternatives was really the only motivation that a girl needed to get the hell outta Dodge, or Murdo, or wherever the hell they were.

Moore was only scared one time during these trips and that was a particular Wednesday evening when he attempted to get his hands on a Native American girl who had turquoise beads woven into her hair. Moore didn't give a shit, at this point, who he was getting his hands on. Again, his customers weren't all that picky. This girl, well she just screamed "feisty" and Moore liked that about her.

Her name was Danielle and Moore liked her instantly. She, just like every other girl he had picked up, had a story and Moore had become quite adept at listening and sounding like a sympathetic ear. Danielle was no exception with her story and as Moore listened to her drone on about how she had run away from her foster home and was trying to make her way back to Oklahoma, and her people (Moore rolled his eyes when he heard that) she continued on about how she had been forced to become an exotic dancer at the age of seventeen.

"How old are you?" Moore had asked.

"Old enough to know better, but still young enough to try the stupid stuff," she replied with a sly grin.

Something about the math and the story didn't add, and in the back of his mind Moore could already sense trouble, but he put it off to nerves. There has never been trouble before, why should now be any different?

Moore saw a now familiar turn out coming up, that led down some country bumpkin road with the fancy name Grandview Street. To call this jutted dirt path a street was more credit than it was due, and there certainly wasn't a damn thing grand about the view. He began to slow down and pull over. This was a great place to pull off and test his goods.

"Why are we slowing down?" Danielle had stopped talking and Moore was so lost in his own thoughts, he hadn't even noticed, or realized what he was doing.

"Well, there's a nice spot over here, by the looks of it. I thought you and I might take a few minutes to get to know each other, yaknow?" His best and toothiest grin wasn't able to convince Danielle, however. Apparently her street smarts extended beyond the tip of her mascara brush and her ability to hide it was a surprise to Moore.

"Um, you said you'd be giving me a ride to town. I didn't think that this was going to be a situation where I was going to have to pay for my ride, if ya catch me.

"I could have just as easily blown one of those filthy trucker fuckers back at the station. I stepped over to you because I thought you were a decent guy."

Oh, honey, if you only knew the truth, is what Moore was thinking. Out loud he said, "Honey, gas, grass, or ass. But no one, and I mean no one, rides for free."

Just like that, the twinkle in his eye was gone. Danielle saw it go and immediately she was scared. She had been in these situations before and there was no way in hell some dirty white boy was going to get his hands on her. Not after the way that her last pimp had treated her. That fat lazy fuck of a man had felt that her flesh was his flesh and he had marked her, fucked her, and defiled her more times than she could ever had hoped to count. No, this guy in his cheap and shabby van, with work stained clothes wasn't going to take advantage of her.

Danielle hadn't planned on doing anything, drastic or otherwise, until the door was already open, surprising her as much as it did Moore. The van was still rolling at a good clip and Danielle didn't quite grasp the physics of what was going to happen. Her body half fell, half rolled out the open door, and as

141

gravity did its thing, she was promptly run over by the rear tires of the van.

Instantly her pelvis was shattered, as well as her right femur and left wrist. Unable to move, let along get up and run, she was a mortally wounded animal lying in the ditch next to a deserted country highway.

Moore got the van pulled over, and jumped out, tire iron in hand. He knew that he had to finish her off, and quick. He should have listened to that little tingle of a voice at the back of his head.

"Why are you doing this? I just needed a ride." Danielle's breathing was labored and raspy. Had she punctured a lung as well? Road rash marred her tanned and pretty skin, turning the soft textures into a disarrayed patchwork of shredded flesh and muscle. To Moore this appeared more hideous than the scars that showed through her torn top.

"Listen, honey, it's nothing personal. This was a business venture. You and your feisty attitude were going to make me a lot of money. I'm sorry that you chose to end it this way. It could have gone a whole lot differently, yaknow. You could have had a very nice life; comfortable and all the pills and booze you could handle.

"I just want you to remember that you chose this."

Moore had became quite good at rationalizing himself in the face of his nefarious and heinous deeds. If his old self could have seen his new self, it would have been mortified. Addictions have a way of altering that perception, though.

Defiant to the last, Danielle looked up at Moore and sneered through a mouthful of blood and pain. Bright red, frothy blood was foaming at her lips. Moore thought she had indeed punctured a lung, though he had no idea how he knew that.

"I'm nobody's whore." Her sneer had started to falter, just a little bit, but Moore sensed it, and Danielle knew he did. "I'd rather be dead in this ditch than property to some faggotty old man who can't keep his pecker hard unless he's got a bitch tied to the bed. Fuck you, and the van you rode in. Curse your fucking life!" One final wad of spit and blood exited between her torn gums and broken teeth.

"If that's the way you feel about all of this... Well... That's too bad." Raising the tire iron, he brought it down in one hard stroke connecting with her skull. It shattered instantly. Danielle got her wish; dying in a ditch, along a deserted road. There would be no grave, no marker, no one to know that she was there. Fran Moore doubted that there would be much left of the body soon enough to even identify her.

After Danielle, another trip north had produced a brunette with a horrible Brooklyn accent who claimed to be searching for her long lost brother and mother. Moore, being the Good Samaritan that he was, offered to give her a ride to the next town. Sure no problem, but would she mind sharing a bite of dinner with him, first?

Tana was her name. Her look of surprise was almost identical to that of the previous ones. The wide brown doe eyes never saw the cloth coming out of the sandwich bag and before she could even register what was happening she was choking on a mouthful of greasy fries and paint thinner. She didn't even require a tarp roll, but again Moore wasn't going to take chances. He had her bundled in a tarp in less than ten minutes. Again, the drive was uneventful. Again, the unloading and transfer process was uneventful.

When Moore got Tana back to the building, he again did a quick sweep of the premises to ensure that no one would be skulking around. No one but him, that is. Again, the alley and parking pad behind the store were deserted. This little burg never did see much traffic this early in the morning.

Moore brought his new acquaintance into the tomb and proceeded to strip her down, and get her changed into a shirt and pair of boxers. As he removed her shirt, he saw that she had a steel barbell in her navel, with a little jewel hanging off of it. He knew that people were putting bars and rings into their appendages, as it had been made mention of recently when Karen Hensleigh, the new waitress at the Stormcastle Café showed up for work with a small ring in her nose. Her nose for the love of God! How the hell did she even blow her nose without having snot hanging off of that God forsaken bull ring? Moore didn't give a shit one way or the other what people were using for jewelry, or where, for that matter. Those neo-Nazi faggots coming in from out of town, looking for their military surplus to give them that sharp look all had earrings in their ears. Both ears. If that wasn't a sure sign of a queer, Moore didn't know what was.

But here, as if a small and shameful secret had been revealed to only him, was something Moore had never seen before. The glistening stainless steel, the way the light hit the purple topaz looking jewel. The battery powered lantern seemed to ignite the very essence of the piercing and caused the stainless steel to radiate. Moore couldn't help himself. His unconscious victim never had a chance. Her long brown hair, the same shade as her doe eyes, her curvy hips, ample breasts and full backside didn't entice him near as much as this secret and delicate piercing did.

Naked and helpless she had no chance but to submit to him when he, too, stripped down and mounted her. Her shapely breasts bounced up and down while her hips seemed to almost beg to be parted. Moore left no part of the young, helpless

144

victim unexplored. While Moore was pretty sure that she was still unconscious he had no idea that she had begun to slowly vomit out stomach contents. Engaged in his own carnal explorations he didn't see her eyelids flicker and a brief moment of consciousness before she again passed out.

When he flipped her over to explore other parts of her, he had no idea that she had been vomiting and the contents came spilling out. However with her face pushed into the pillow of the cot, there was nowhere for the ominous liquid to go, and she slowly began to inhale it back into her lungs. Like Melody, Tana was dead before Moore knew was going on. When he reached to flip her over, his hand slipped through the vile stomach contents and instantly Moore knew. Panting, naked, sweaty and shivering Moore knew that he could dispose of the body just as easily as Melody's. The town landfill was only a short drive and looking at his watch, Moore knew it wouldn't be sunup for at least another hour. Cleaning himself he redressed and placed the body of his newest victim inside one of the many dilapidated crates he emptied from the tomb.

Once upon a time there would have been a very large part of Moore that would have been horrified at what he was doing, and what he had become. Now, maybe the initial shock, like a drug addict, had worn off and he was never going to reach that "high" again. Now, it was just a matter of business. Business was good, and this was just a nasty side effect of it. Ample stacks of cash locked in other crates, in the tomb, attested to the fact that this was indeed just a nasty side effect.

While it was bulky, the crate wasn't overly heavy, or maybe it was the surge of adrenaline that now coursed through his body. Either way he got the trunk up the stairs of the back entrance and loaded into the back of the very same rental van he had just brought her in not a few hours earlier, alive and still breathing. Now, not so much.

Tough luck, baby, Moore thought to himself.

Driving to the landfill he wasn't too worried about the body being found. It was an old pit dug into an already existing small box canyon and every two weeks or so, someone from the city maintenance crew would show up and pour a few gallons of diesel into the pit and flick a lit kitchen match into the works. In those times in between the burn times, generous amounts of horse manure would be spread over the trash to keep the scavengers at bay, and keep those pesky people, now known as dumpster divers, out of the pit. In the past, it seemed that the adage of one man's trash often overtook the common sense of some, and in attempting to get into the pit to grab a new piece, some unlucky bastard would get caught up in the garbage and either slice his flesh to ribbons, or in the case of Harold Bates, break his ankle and die of exposure because he was trapped in the pit for three days before someone came out to empty their waste and saw his bloated body swelling under the spring sunshine.

No, Moore figured he had a pretty fair shot and it was almost time for the bi monthly burn session. It would appear, though, that luck was not with him. When he pulled up to the edge of the pit, Jason Shanes was there, himself unloading a horse trailer full of scrap material and waste material into the pit.

"Morning Fran!" Jason called out. "Too damn early to be out, yeah?"

Fran nodded, the initial shock of seeing someone at this time of day faded pretty quickly, "Yeah, started doing some cleaning and remodeling in the basement office and lost track of time. I've had this garbage stacked down there for a while now, and been meaning to get rid of it. There's no goddamn windows

146

down there and I didn't realize how late, or early, it was." His forced chuckle came out as a grunt.

Jason's head bobbed up and down. "Shit, don't I know it? Me 'n Candy was cleaning out the barn and I didn't realize how much time had slipped by. Finally got that old harvester stripped down and salvaged all the scrap metal I could think of, but the rest of that shit has been stacked up and taking up too much room in the old hog chute. Hell, we might even be able to get a few hogs this year, now that we got room for 'em.

"But, dammit, the horse show is coming up on the 19th and we need to be ready. Thinking if we can unload a few of these colts that have been hanging around the stable, we might be able to turn a nice profit for the winter, yaknow?"

Moore nodded. He knew that Jason and his wife, Candy, were big into horse breeding and himself a transplant, Jason made no secret in town that he hoped to have a sizable ranch to turn over to his kids one day. Moore also knew that Jason Shanes was a talker and wouldn't shut up for the better part of the day, if you let him go on about it.

Walking over to the doors of the van, Jason said, "You need a hand with that? Say, that's a nice trunk. Where'd you get that?" He reached out to give a hand and Moore recoiled as if he had been stung. The hollow look in his eyes flashed fire, ever so briefly, but Shanes caught it.

"Easy there, partner. Just trying to lend a hand." Jason looked at Moore with squinted eyes; the sun was just peeking over the horizon. Shanes thought Moore looked a little strung out. Either he was working himself to death, or he just got over one hell of a bender. Well, these money making types, Shanes has heard, they were more apt to work themselves to death before they were able to spend their riches.

"Sorry, man, been a long night. Yaknow? This damn trunk has been giving me fits and I'm just overtired."

Jason nodded, "I understand. No worries.

"Hey, yaknow I was in the Corps back in '83. Left Beirut just before that shit went down. Reason I ask about that trunk is, if you had any more of 'em I'd buy one off of you and store some of my gear in it."

Fran Moore had recovered himself by this point. "Well, Jason, if this one wasn't stock full of spoiled rations, I'd let you have it. It came with the office, and yaknow I had it as an end table for the longest time, but lately it has been smelling a bit putrid. Finally cracked the lock and damned if there wasn't some spoiled cheese and I think pork in there. Bought knocked me over when I smelled it."

Jason nodded again, "I was gonna say, brother, you are smelling a bit ripe." His hearty bellow of laughter broke the tension, immediately. "But I know those rations. Not bad when they are still sealed, but shit, you let one of 'em get damp, or spoiled, well hell, you might as well burn it, cause that's all it's good for."

Fran hefted the side of the crate in agreement, even laughed nonchalantly, and said, "Don't I know it? Well, I'll keep my eyes open. If I see anything you might have an interest in, I'll let you know." He had no way of knowing that this dismissive comment would eventually lead to his undoing.

November, 1986

As was his usual perch, Louis Hennepin sat on his high backed bar stool, crunching numbers in his ledgers when Jason Shanes walked in. Setting aside a leftover turkey sandwich on marble

148

rye bread, leftovers from last Thursday's festivities, he wiped the excess mayo on his shop keeper's smock.

"Good morning, Jason. What can I help you find today?" Again, small town, everyone knew everyone.

"Louis, I ran into Fran Moore a while back and he had this old military trunk he said he got from his basement office. Said it came with the office, but it was too beat up to use. He said he'd keep an eye open for another one, and I was wondering if you might have one down there, yet, you'd be willing to part with?"

Louis, like everyone else in town, knew that Shanes was a military vet, and that he had been "over there." What exactly he did, no one really knew, but he had a wall full of medals and citations to prove it, as well as quite a few stories, some amusing, some bordering on the downright bat shit insane. According to local lore, and depending on how many beers Shanes had ingested, the story got more and more fantastic, he had stolen a Libyan chopper, right out from under their noses and flew it back to his barracks in Beirut. Again, depending on the number of beers he had, the story changed as to what kind of chopper it was, and just how severe his punishment was.

Many a bar patron, though, can attest to the fact that he is regarded as firing one of the first shots in the Middle East conflict. Often you'd hear him, tuned up by about three or four pitchers of lager, starting a story with, "So there I was…"

Regardless of the truth, most people knew about his service, and were eager to indulge an old war vet, if someone in their late thirties could be an old war vet. Certainly he had "been there" though, because the lines around his eyes didn't lie. Shanes had the look of a man who had seen some shit.

Louis shook his head, "Sorry Jason, I don't think it came from this building. We've never had any surplus like that. I'll see a few pairs of those camo pants now and then, the green ones all the teen kids like, but nothing in the way of hardware.

"And I decorated those offices, myself, when they were built. Nothing military in 'em. Pretty basic furniture. Desk, chair, sofa, the likes. Nothing like that trunk you're saying.

"But, I know Fran's downstairs right now. Saw his car parked out back, on the pad this morning when I got in. He must be burning a lot of midnight oil because I got here at 6:00 and he was already at work. You can run down the staircase back by the toilet, if you wanna, and see what he's up to."

The Stetson on Jason's head bobbed. "Yaknow, I might just do that. It was a pretty slick trunk. Looked to be about Korean War vintage, if not older. Again, if I could get my hands on one, it'd be a nice piece for my stuff."

Louis jerked a thumb towards the back of the store, "Sure. Head on down."

Jason headed on down, just as Louis had suggested. Fran was indeed in his office, the man was bordering on obsessive with all the time he spent here. He really was going to be able to retire with a nice profit. Long hours of hard work and dedication were manuals for success. Shanes told himself that little pearl of wisdom quite often and the ranch was doing all right for him and Candy. They had indeed sold the colts and the profit was more than enough to see them through the winter, even get them the hogs that he and Moore had chatted about.

Walking through the open door, he barely paused while he rapped his knuckles on the hard wood frame, "Fran you down here, buddy?"

Fran was indeed in his office, his new office as well. He didn't have a chance to close up the entrance to The Tomb before Jason Shanes walked in. Whatever debauchery had been going on in the concrete encased tomb was now open for the world to

150

see, including the contents. The legitimate, the illegitimate, the trafficked and the kidnapped, all on display.

"Whoa, partner, that is one slick storage room you got there!" Jason was instantly impressed. The size of the office belied the nature and scope of The Tomb. So well crafted was the entrance that it was impossible to know it was even there, at all. That had been its intended purpose and even this many years later, it was dutifully serving.

Horrified, Fran rushed out meaning to stop Jason from saying anything else, or seeing anything else. "Jason what are you doing here?! I'm not open for another hour or so. You can't be here right now. I'm very busy."

Fran's breathing was labored. He had just finished cleaning out the room and was preparing to make another trip north to procure another girl. The stench, mixed with the dampness of The Tomb, was near impossible to clean out and it had taken quite some time to disinfect the space, and be rid of the contaminated and soiled materials. Tana had been the last, for a while, but the news reports of the disappearing girls from Murdo had almost seemed to draw more potential victims, rather than deter them. The panning camera shots showing the candlelight vigils and stuffed animals wired to the chain link fence of the truck stop that Moore liked to frequent did nothing but serve as a menu to Fran Moore.

Danielle's body had been found, by some local hillbilly who was out checking his cows and fence lines. Her body was so badly decomposed and torn apart by scavenging coyotes that the local Sheriff surmised it would be next to impossible to figure out what had happened to the body, much less give an identity to the victim.

All they knew for sure was that it probably was a girl, based on the clothing tatters found near the body, and that the poor girl had probably been killed there. Her skull, if it indeed had been a "her", said the Sheriff, had been smashed and that the poor thing had died right in that ditch. He further continued that whoever had committed this crime was a most heinous person, indeed.

"Fran, you all right, buddy? You look like you are about to have a heart attack. You need me to call someone?"

"Jason, I really wished you would have called, or made an appointment. This is really a bad time right now."

"Fran, it's all good. I can come back."

Coming fully into his regular office, now, Fran said, "I'm afraid it's not that simple. No one can know about this room, ever. At all. No one. I'm sorry, my friend, I think that you just really picked the wrong time and the wrong day."

Producing a small pistol, fitted with a matching suppressor on it, from the drawer of his desk, Fran motioned Jason into the office, and to take a seat on the sofa. Jason, terrified and completely perplexed obeyed without a further word of protest. Fran knew it was a clichéd, and risky, move to keep the pistol there, but when a time like this comes along...

Fran's pistol had been a gift from one of his earliest customers, Drake, and when it was given to him, Fran didn't think he'd ever need such a thing. Especially since it wasn't registered and the bulky can on the end of it, Fran was pretty sure, was something that required special permission from the sheriff. Permission that he most certainly did not have.

However, since Fran had taken up kidnapping as a sideline business, he had started to carry this little dandy just in case he ran into trouble. He never figured trouble would come find him, certainly not in his own office. He never figured it would be Jason Shanes, the Sheriff maybe, but not Jason.

"Fran, I'm not sure what's going on here, man, but as far as I'm concerned I didn't see a thing. Honestly, I really didn't see a thing."

"Jason, I know you're a standup guy, I do." Fran wasn't really liking where this was going. "The problem that I have is that you might accidentally let this slip. And then someone else is going to be asking about this. Then all of a sudden I've got people asking questions that don't need to be asked."

"Fran is this about the trunk?! Shit, man I won't say a word about the trunk."

"Dammit, Jason, this isn't about the damn trunk! It's about where the trunk came from. I mean, how do I explain this? How am I supposed to explain why there is a bunch of military surplus buried underneath a fucking department store, in a concrete bunker that isn't supposed to be there? How do I tell people that hookers have been fucked and have died inside this fucking bunker?! Do you know it's a godforsaken, cursed death trap in there?!

"You tell me, how the hell should I explain this to people when they start to ask questions? And you know they will, because in a town like this, someone will ask about it and then it'll be the new fucking gossip at the hardware store and the café and every other fucking joint along the highway."

"Fran, what are you talking about? Hookers? Who said anything about hookers? Did you stumble across something?

"Fran, does this have anything to do with the girls that have gone missing up in South Dakota? Did you have a hand in that?"

Moore was really coming unglued and Jason could sense it. What was happening, Jason couldn't begin to understand but he knew that there was something really freaky going down. He needed to get out of here, and fast. Hell, the sheriff might even need to be notified about this. How he was going to accomplish this little miracle, though, with a madman and a gun raving about hookers a few feet from him, he wasn't quite sure. If he could make it to the door, he might have a chance.

"Jason, haven't you been listening?! Yes, this all has to do with those fucking girls and their weird hypnotic ways and that asshole, Drake, and his fucking loud mouth. If he wouldn't have said a word about this to me, shit, I could have still been making normal money with normal clients, during normal hours. Not fucking dumping bodies at the landfill before sunup!"

Slowly, Shanes began to inch closer to the edge of the sofa he was perched on. The door was still open. He didn't hear anyone else in the basement. Jason was sure that if he could make it upstairs he might have a chance, there was no way Moore would start anything upstairs with Louis behind the counter, would he?

"Fran, who is Drake? Did he put you up to this?" Shanes was more scared now, than anything else.

Jason didn't know that Moore didn't know about the back stairs next to Hennepin's private toilet. He decided that while Moore was raving about some girl lying dead in a ditch he would make his move. He bolted off the couch, his old military instincts kicking in. It was pure survival and escape at this point.

While Moore was facing the entrance to the tomb, Jason rushed him, pushing him into the entrance. He came right out of the office, down the hall and up the stairs. Did he hear Moore behind him? Did he hear him howling, he wasn't sure.

Moore was so surprised by the attack he forgot that the gun was in his hand and when Jason hit him, his body tensed. Jason could have pointed out that by holding the gun the way he was, with his finger on the trigger, there was a very good chance of an accidental discharge happening. That's exactly what happened.

Fran Moore pulled the trigger and a suppressed bullet slammed into his own thigh. His howl of rage was so primal and so raw, even Shanes was caught off guard for a moment. It wouldn't have mattered, though, because Moore was crumpled in the entrance to The Tomb.

Whether luckily, or unluckily, the bullet missed the femoral artery and what could have killed him in minutes, was now a gaping and raw flesh wound that, by another miracle, had also missed his bones. Even with the pain, the adrenaline was coursing through his veins and allowing him to remain upright.

Shanes ran upstairs to the main floor of Hennepin's. "Louis! Call the Sheriff! NOW! Moore's got a gun. He tried to shoot me!"

In all his years in business, Louis Hennepin had never been robbed, strong armed, or even joked about having his cash taken from him, by force. Every local in town knew he kept one of those shotguns his grandfather used to sell, near at hand under the counter. Louis had never once used it but on a rare night he had been known to pull it out, make sure it was still properly oiled, and that a box of shells was near at hand. Just for such an occasion. By the way that Jason Shanes came running up the stairs, screaming at the top of his lungs Louis knew that now was such a time.

Pulling the shotgun from the spot under the counter, he opened the action to ensure a live shell was indeed in place, and brought it up to bear, the long twenty plus inch barrel aimed right for the stairwell. The box of shells was on the counter, also near at hand. In his other hand he held the receiver for the phone and had dialed 9-1-1 without even really having to think about the action. So focused on the back stairwell he should have remembered that not most folks knew about it, and therefore didn't think to use it.

"Dispatch. What's your emergency?" Was that Sandy Nichols on the line? Louis had met that fiery redheaded gal at previous town social functions and the two had seen each other socially, in years past, not that anything had ever come of it. In his heightened state, though, he couldn't be sure.

"Hello? This is dispatch. Do you have an emergency?"

"Yes, this is Louis Hennepin. I need the Sheriff at my store. NOW!"

"Louis, the Sheriff is out at the dump. Seems someone found a body buried in a trunk out there. Can he get back to you? Can I send another officer?"

"No. I need the Sheriff to be radioed right now. I need him at my department store right..." Louis never got a chance to finish his sentence that there was a madman with a gun shooting at one of his customers. He forgot about the front entrance to his store, so focused on the back stairwell was he. He forgot that Moore only ever came and went through the rear entrance of the building and that's how he had gone around, out the back door, through the alley space between buildings and in the front door. Staring at the back of Louis Hennepin's balding head, Moore knew that he had the drop on the man. And was Hennepin holding a shotgun? Moore knew he needed to be dispatched and without a second thought, he fired two successive rounds into the back of Louis Hennepin's head.

Hennepin didn't even have time to think about a last thought because he was dead before the phone dropped from his hand onto the sawhorse plank counter, line still active and the dispatcher, it was indeed Sandy Nicholas, frantically asking if everything was all right. She would be sending an officer over, right this very minute, don't you worry.

156

Moore grabbed the receiver and ripped the phone cord from the wall, and Jason Shanes who was standing just off to the side of the counter, at this time unnoticed by Moore, used the opportunity to pick up the shotgun that the recently deceased Hennepin had discarded. Again, pure military training and instinct took over and he shouldered the shotgun, placing the BB welded to the end of the barrel functioning as a rudimentary sight, right over Fran Moore's right eye, and pulled the trigger. *CLICK!*

"FUCK!" Shanes screamed as he grabbed for the box of shells. How the hell had Hennepin kept a shotgun near at hand and not kept it loaded. Opening the action he saw that there was indeed a shell in the chamber, but it was either a dud, or the gun was old enough that it could no longer function properly. His military discipline was screaming at him to clear the chamber, reload and go again. Shanes did just that, cleared the action, and locked a new shell in place.

His outburst has made him noticed by Moore and just as he was about to pull the trigger Moore fired three ragged shots at him, two harmlessly slamming into the polished wooden floors, and the third connecting with Shanes' hand. Completely in shock that he could make it through Beiruit without being shot, and now, here, in this shitty little Nebraska town he gets tagged by a whacked out kidnapper with a suppressed pistol?

Rage boiled over and he brought the shotgun back to center on Moore's head and fired. The explosion from the barrel was deafening and instantly the right side of Moore's head disappeared in a cloud of pink mist and white and grey fragments of skull fragment and brain matter. Pink vapor and blue gun smoke hung inside the confines of the store. Shanes, deafened by the blast moved forward to make sure that Fran Moore was down, for good.

157

Officer Donald Wilson, who went by Officer Don, thank you very much, showed up on scene, and though he had no real clear indication of what was going on, he was damn sure that this shit wasn't going to happen in his town. Sheriff Rasmussen was on his way back in from the dump when he had gotten the call, immediately clearing Don to take point. Officer Don had his gun drawn, a .38 Special, and his long black flashlight, an aluminum job that carried about four D-cell batteries in it. It also doubled as a rather effective Billy club, when it had to.

If Sheriff Rasmussen had been the first to arrive, things might have gone different, because he knew Jason Shanes. Hell, he liked the man. Shanes had a colt he was going to hold on to for him, break him, and sell him to the Sheriff. Sheriff Rasmussen knew Jason Shanes quite well, but Officer Don Wilson didn't know Jason Shanes, didn't know him or recognize him at all.

All he knew was that Dispatcher Nichols had sent an all cars alert over the police net and that someone was trying to rob Louis Hennepin, and possibly trying to kill him, if they hadn't already done so. When he his cruiser came skidding to a stop in front of the department store he was just about to make entry when the shotgun went off. Officer Don stomped on the brake pedal and the cruiser skidded to a halt, thinking he was being fired on. When he realized there wasn't anyone firing at him, he kicked the door of Hennepin's Department store with his right foot, to announce his presence.

Inside the store Jason Shanes had grabbed the box of shells and was reloading the shotgun, moving forward toward the counter, ensuring that Moore was down for good. Through the glass door Don saw the man with the shotgun move forward and moved quickly, to save himself and anyone else who might have been trapped in the building. Using his flashlight Officer Wilson smashed out the glass of the window, the noise of the

158

commotion causing Shanes, still half deaf, to swing his weapon towards what he perceived as a new threat. That was all the threat that Officer Donald Wilson ever needed.

Jason Shanes never had a chance and when Wilson fired, he emptied all six round of .38 caliber ammunition into Shanes' chest. He too, was dead before he hit the ground. A look of utter confusion masked Shanes' face as his eyes became cloudy and lifeless. More blood and acrid smoke filled the already tainted store, the paltry haze of death hung low over the department store mannequins and clothing racks.

Officer Don didn't waste another second and immediately reloaded his weapon from spare cartridges kept on his belt. Within seconds he had retrieved his flashlight and was clearing the building. When the Sheriff and other deputies showed up, they found Officer Don Wilson clearing the building in the precise and effective manner in which he had been taught.

Within minutes the scene was secure and the Sheriff even managed to keep that asinine photographer from the local newspaper outside the building until a preliminary investigation had been completed. If there was going to be anything going to press about this matter, it was going to go through the Sheriff, and no one else. There would be no rumors, no half assed attempts at guessing as to motives or anything else. Try as he might, the Sheriff couldn't keep everything quiet and eventually rumors did make it out, but no crime scene photos ever did.

January 3, 1987

The coroner, the very same fellow dispatched to examine the remains of a human found in a ditch some months before, concluded that it was indeed bullets from Fran Moore's pistol that had killed poor old Louis. With no living dependents that anyone knew of, the city assumed control of the building. Even the Masons, upstairs, wanted no part of the building anymore and vacated soon after what became known as "The Incident." A dark day for the residents of Valentine, Nebraska, it was rarely ever spoken of. If it happened upon a mentioning, it was always in hushed tones, usually by locals at the Stormcastle Café who were trying to drum up mystery and intrigue to the few random travelers who happened through their little town. Most of these travelers were from places north who were escorting their senior citizen parents to Arizona for the winter, and didn't put much stock in the local lore.

Officer Donald Wilson, cleared by the state investigators never got over the shoot. He quit the law enforcement business the day after the shoot, turning in his badge and weapon, and retreated to the relative safety of his family farm, back in Kansas. Some say he made a go of things with farming, but those same folks also said that eventually the darkness won out and when his neighbors didn't see the combine out during harvest season they came to check on him and found him dead in his favorite easy chair recliner. That was the local lore, but with no one to refute the story, as most fables do, it gained traction and became fact. It was said that bottles of whiskey had been piled up in the trash can near the end table. According to the story, he had been dead for about a week, judging by the smell.

But, nothing could clear his conscious of shooting an innocent man, and threats from Candy Shanes of lawsuit after lawsuit certainly hadn't helped matters. Eventually she dropped all suits, but the damage had been done. She, too, pulled up stakes not longer after The Incident, and moved the family out of state. Where they went was anyone's guess, but some say they had moved south. They were never heard from again.

Government agents from all manner of agency swarmed over the small town of Valentine. The nearest FBI field office, in Denver, dispatched agents to immediately make sense of what was going on. Aided by Sheriff Rasmussen they excavated the town landfill and found a number of human remains, presumably the missing girls from Murdo, South Dakota. However, the extent of decay, as well as the burning of the town trash pit only worked against the agents.

More agents were sent up to the town when it was discovered that there were surplus crates in the basement of a department store containing piles and piles of money, as well as military relics, probably even munitions. It was first assumed it was fake money but when the Secret Service declared it to be legitimate currency, a brief turf war broke out, each government agency claiming the money was necessary for their investigation. In the end it went to the FBI as it tied directly to the kidnapping cases they were working. It was a pretty flimsy argument considering the remains couldn't even be accurately identified as the missing girls. There were no personal artifacts from the missing girls to return to the families. In the end, just when the families of the missing had though they were going to have closure to their own personal nightmares, they were left with just another mystery.

Over time the remains were identified, through dental records, and other medical signatures, but by then The Incident had long faded from the memories of the nation's residents.

To this day, only one mystery remained. An agent, claiming to be from the Denver field office, showed up at Sheriff Rasmussen's office with a written statement indicating he was under orders to transport all the confiscated money, as evidence, back to Denver. Sheriff Rasmussen had had enough of government officials in his town and was happy to comply with this agent's request. Regardless of his cheap suit and handlebar mustache that seemed so tacky and out of place, he had the right badge, the right documentation, and he was helping to clear one more problem from the Sheriff's desk, even if his mirrored aviator sunglasses were a bit off regulation.

By the time the real agents from the Denver field office of the Federal Bureau of Investigation showed up with documents very similar to the ones the previous "agent" had, he was long gone.

The Sheriff was cleared of any complicity in the heist, netting quite a few million dollars. It seemed that the kidnapping and sexual slavery business was far more lucrative than anyone could have ever guessed. When a purveyor of such services has clients from as far away as Idaho and Iowa who are willing to transport themselves, and their sick friends, and pay top dollar for anonymity... Locals still swear they thought Fran Moore was an exceptionally hard worker and if they would have known what he was up to...

Eventually the entire story of The Incident faded from the town's memory and even the building that had once housed Hennepin's Department Store was demolished to make room for further growth and expansion. Only the ghosts of that terrible day still remained.

Saturday. 18 July 15. 0040 hours.

I sat, mouth agape, as Vincent finished his story. I had no immediate response to this particular story. I had heard, and seen, some real horror shows in my time, but this was by far the nastiest and darkest thing I had ever heard about. I only wished that I could have written down the particulars and details, as it would truly be a perfect way to preface a new novel. I might even be able to break into the non-fiction world with a book like this.

"OK, so now I'm starting to see the pattern. The money *IS* the pattern. You were right, it had nothing to do with the victims, nothing at all. It was always about the money, wasn't it?"

Vincent now looked beyond tired, beyond used up. He looked as if his very essence had been drained, now that his stories had been told. "You see it now, don't you?"

I was actually starting to see it all, now. Maybe this evening hadn't been a total wash after all. I was starting to get up again, fully intending to actually refill my soda, this time, when a figure caught my eye. "Vincent, do you know that guy?"

Following my gaze towards the cash register, and the man at the counter, he said, "No. Should I?"

I shrugged my shoulders, "I don't know. I had one of those weird moments when I feel like I should know someone, even though they're a complete stranger, that kinda thing."

The man at the counter paid little attention, if any, to myself and Vincent who were blatantly staring right at him. However, his obviously drunken gait, if it was a drunken gait, or possibly a limp, implied that he probably wasn't even aware he was out in public. I'm sure that with the stupid mirrored aviator sunglasses and obscenely plaid shorts he wasn't really aware of much of anything, not at this point. Maybe he knew that he was talking to an invisible girlfriend, but who knew?

As I got up and made my way to the soda fountain, again I was struck by him. Again, I was freaking myself out over something as simple as a drunken jackass who was navigating a late night restaurant.

With a fresh soda in hand, I returned to the table. Vincent was looking haggard. "Dude, a few hours ago I was thinking you were going to be raving all night long. Now..."

As my voice trailed off, Vincent managed a smile. "I know, I think we've about gotten to the end of the night? I'm feeling pretty worn down, but we have one more matter to settle."

He produced the leather satchel he had walked in with. I had forgotten all about it, until this moment.

Reaching for my checkbook again, I was fully intending to pay top dollar for this story. I had a feeling that this was going to make my career. They say that only dead authors become famous and I was damn sure to beat that superstition.

Waving his hand at me, Vincent said, "No, not yet. We have this one last matter to go over, and this is the cherry on top, I think. And then we can discuss a price, and whatever you pay, I think that it's going to make your career."

Vincent wasn't grinning right now. For a moment I was worried about him and then I remember that godforsaken grin of his misshapen teeth. This was the karma that I had been waiting for all night? Yeah, he looked like shit, but at least I didn't have to see him grin. So much for the better, I thought.

"Listen, I'm gonna take a piss. While I'm doing the business, you can look over my notes. See if there is anything in here, that you can use to piece together these instances.

"I've been following this for so long, I honestly can't see straight over 'em anymore."

As he now stood, his back cracking in the process, I felt compelled to warn him of the two people having torrid sex in the bathroom when I first came into this dive tonight. It felt like a month ago that I had walked through the door, but in reality only three hours had passed, according to my wristwatch.

"I'll make sure to watch out for cum stains on the toilet seat." He nodded and sauntered down the hall, and as I watched him walk away, I noticed he was sweating hard enough to leave a sweat print on the seat, and there was a sweat stain ringing the crack of his ass. I could even see the sweat pouring down the back of his neck. Fuck. Did Vincent have the fucking flu, now? I swear to God if I get sick from this bastard...

Opening his satchel there were stacks of loose white paper that had either been typed up, or scribbled on. There were printed photos of people, with names, dates and locations. He had even taken a basic desk calendar and started marking it with various names and times, associated with the dates.

"Sonuvabitch...," talking to myself, I had no idea that Vincent really had been doing some serious work. I thought he was a half assed amateur, but this work was straight professional. Who the hell was this guy?

Once again the rest of the world disappeared to background noise as I started to piece together the notes that Vincent had in his case.

SUPPOSITIONS

-persuasive
arguments-

⚙ Dispatch Call Sheet

556 North Main Street
Suite # 005

••

Call Sheet To Be Witnessed By Supervisor Prior To Shift Checkout
Failure To Turn In Call Sheet At The End Of Shift Will Result In Disciplinary Action

For Official Use Only

Dispatcher:	Nichols, Sandra
Shift:	0600 - 1600
Extension:	1663
Date/Time:	22 November 86
Support Call:	
Location:	Central Dispatch
Sector:	5

Call #	Start Time	Duration	Description	Desired Result	Badge # Dispatched
1	0813	0:14:37	MRS LAWSON'S CAT IN TREE AGAIN	OFFICER DISPATCHED	14
2	0921	0:16:01	BURGLER ALARM TRIPPED AT PRIVATE RESIDENCE	OFFICER DISPATCHED	10
3	1000	0:05:03	JUVENILES IN POSSESSION OF POSSIBLE ILLEGAL NARCOTICS	OFFICER DISPATCHED	17
4	1005	0:09:01	FURTHER OFFICER DISPATCH NEEDED - MULTIPLE JUVENILES	OFFICER DISPATCHED	13 ; 15
5	1317	0:15:15	MOTOR VEHICLE ACCIDENT EAST OF TOWN WITH POSSIBLE FIRE	OFFICER DISPATCHED	14 ; 10
6	1501	0:01:00	MRS LAWSON MISDIALED EMERGENCY NUMBER	NONE TAKEN	N/A
7	2119	0:06:10	DISTURBANCE	NONE TAKEN	N/A
8					
9					
10					

Why is there no record of the call on the
evidence log for that day?

Why is there no record of Officer Donald Wilson
being on duty that day?

What was the disturbance that was recorded?
Why were there no officers dispatched to the
scene of the disturbance?

Why is there such a lengthy gap between calls
when it seems that calls happen pretty regularly
for that dispatcher shift?

Cayman National Bank

Nigel Avenue
George Town, Grand Cayman, BWI
Phone: 1.555.945.

DEPOSIT #	DATE
560167	Date Unavailable

DEPOSITOR

Rev. Ricky Willard
Church of Nuclear Winter
   Industries
PO Box
Bozeman, MT 59047
1.555.219.
fallofatom@

DESCRIPTION	AMOUNT
Deposit *** Secure Account 25817379958 ***	5,560,000.00
International Tax @ 3.5%	-194,600.00
Direct Transfer Discount @ 0.5% *** Seattle Merchant Marine – Gig Harbor Branch ***	27,800.00
Thank you for your business! **TOTAL**	**$ 5,393,200**

Please contact our office during normal business hours with any questions regarding your transactions.
For faster service, please have your account and routing numbers readily available

Cayman National Bank

███████ Nigel Avenue
George Town, Grand Cayman, BWI
Phone: 1.555.945.████

DEPOSIT

DEPOSIT #	DATE
324365	Date Unavailable

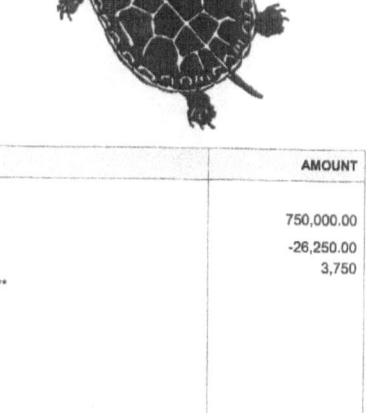

DEPOSITOR

Rev. Ricky Willard
Church of Nuclear Winter
  Industries
PO Box ███████
Bozeman, MT 59047
1.555.219.████
fallofatom@████████████

DESCRIPTION	AMOUNT
Deposit	
*** Secure Account 25817379958 ***	750,000.00
International Tax @ 3.5%	-26,250.00
Direct Transfer Discount @ 0.5%	3,750
*** Seattle Merchant Marine – Gig Harbor Branch ***	

Thank you for your business!	**TOTAL**	**$ 727,500**

Please contact our office during normal business hours with any questions regarding your transactions.
For faster service, please have your account and routing numbers readily available.

Cayman National Bank

████ Nigel Avenue
George Town, Grand Cayman, BWI
Phone: 1.555.945.████

DEPOSIT

DEPOSIT #	DATE
447711	Date Unavailable

DEPOSITOR

Rev. Ricky Willard
Church of Nuclear Winter
   Industries
PO Box ████
Bozeman, MT ████
1.555.219.████
fallofatom ████

DESCRIPTION	AMOUNT
Deposit *** Secure Account 25817379958 ***	128,500.00
International Tax @ 3.5%	-4,497.50
Direct Transfer Discount @ 0.5% *** Seattle Merchant Marine – Gig Harbor Branch ***	642.50

Thank you for your business!

TOTAL $ 124,645

Please contact our office during normal business hours with any questions regarding your transactions.
For faster service, please have your account and routing numbers readily available.

175

Why are these deposits all sent to a branch of a bank on the West Coast? What's the significance of having them funneled to a specific branch?

Who is the Reverend Ricky Wilson? Is he the bag man for this particular assassin fella?

Need to find this fella...

Vincent must have returned while I was reading through the invoices and studying the information. He had even gone so far as to type notes and attach them to the back of each of the copies that I was now reading. I was wrong about him, he was certainly not amateur hour and this was certainly going to win me a Pulitzer Prize for non-fiction. Hot damn!

"I see you've dove into the research, haven't you?" Vincent was sitting across from me, still sweating profusely.

"Vincent, I get it, I see why you've been out of contact for so long. This is some exceptional work, my friend."

Eyeing me, with just a hint of disdain he said, "Oh, so now we are friends? A few hours ago I thought that you couldn't wait to rid yourself of me.

"It's amazing at what just a hint of money and the promise of some notoriety can do for two people, isn't it?"

He was actually enjoying this moment, the pompous little shit. He was actually getting off on the fact that he had something over me. Maybe my initial impression was correct.

"Vincent, I'm sorry, I get it. I fucked up, and you hold the hand on this one. My bad. I get it."

"No, obviously you don't get it. Have you even been paying attention to these narratives? Haven't you made the connections, yet?"

I gave him a quizzical look.

"Think about it, man. Just take a step back and think about it. Who do we know that once went by the name Reverend?"

Slowly, I could imagine a light flickering to life over my head. Clichéd as it was, it was a very accurate representation. Vincent could even "see" it. Still sweating like a whore in church, he nodded with a small smile forming at the corners of his mouth.

"Exactly! Now you see it, don't you?"

I, too, began to nod my head. "Yeah, I see it. But if something like this happened, how did he get from Nebraska to Bozeman? Wouldn't that show up on a background check?"

Vincent looked at me with a blank stare. "You're serious? Think about it, man. It's 1986. There's no internet. There's no search engines. Hell the phonebook barely made it to rural areas like Valentine.

"Donald Wilson was his real name. Schaap is his mother's maiden name. Who the hell would think to look at a maiden name for a guy who had blatantly stated he's never been anywhere but Bozeman. Who knows, maybe he concocted a story to say that he was somewhere else, somewhere that was anywhere but damned Valentine, Nebraska?

"This was a man who was used to concocting stories, backgrounds and alibis for his undercover work. You don't think that it just 'came with the territory' did you? He had to have had a good start on that career."

Once again I was nodding, the light bulb was burning brighter than ever. I said, "You said, though, that they found a body in his family farm. How do you explain away a body? There has to be at least a coroner's inquest or report."

Vincent, sweat dripping off his brow said, "Who said there even was a body? Hell that could have been the local lore, or there certainly could have been a body. It's not like this guy didn't meet up and obviously know some crazy motherfuckers. They could have planted the body, got the story rolling, paid off the right amount of people and *WHOOSH* instant alibi! It's like Donald Wilson never existed."

I said, "OK, so we see that he's got the money. But we don't have dates on the transactions. Where and when did that money come from?"

Vincent said, "They probably sat on the money for a while, washed it through a few other companies, made sure it was completely sterile, not even remotely traceable back to them. After a few months, hell maybe a few years, they start parking that money in an offshore account where the feds can't be snooping around."

I said, "That would explain your notes on the back of the call log. Why there was a gap in the time logs. He switched it, didn't he?"

Vincent said, "Oh, he did more than that. Look at some more of the paperwork and you tell me what you see."

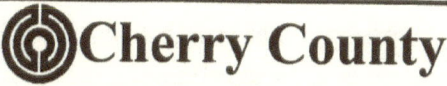

Cherry County

Sheriff's Office
Phone: 402.555.3761
556 N Main St #37, Valentine NE 57555

Top Copy to Sheriff's Office
Bottom Copy to Evidence Locker

Evidence List

Case Location: Hennepin's Department Store

Responding Officer: Donald Wilson

Date: 22 November 86   Case No: 72163427

Evidence Transfer Date: 22 Nov 86   Transferring Officer: Donald Wilson to Rasmussen

Department Name: Police Dept

Evidence Description	Total Quantity:	Evidence Tag Num:	Discovering Officer:	Witnessing Officer:
Shotgun	1	1-01	Wilson	Wilson
Shotgun shells - live	19	1-02	Wilson	Wilson
Shotgun shells - fired	1	1-03	Wilson	Wilson
Shell casing - .38 caliber	6	1-04	Wilson	Wilson

Special Info:

Evidence Appears In Keeping With Robbery Call

Rasmussen
Sheriff's Signature

For Official Use Only

What does this evidence list pertain to? There
is no robbery listed on the call log for the
particular day in question.

Supposedly all evidence has been turned over to
the federal agents. There is no paperwork to
suggest that any federal received anything
pertaining to this matter? Was this an
oversight? Wasn't properly filed in the first
place? Why didn't this raise a red flag?

If there was a robbery committed and this is the
evidence list, where is the pistol that was used?
Why is there no record of the pistol?

"So, Vincent, explain this to me; what is it that Wilson, I mean Schaap, is afraid of? Why would he cover his tracks so thoroughly? He was involved in a righteous shoot and while it's totally unfortunate, he was cleared of any wrong doing.

"I've researched cases like this, in the past. These guys basically get stripped down, head to toe, and take about thirty seven different drug tests, and who knows how many polygraph tests. He was cleared of all of it. It was a clean shoot."

Vincent looked like he was melting. "Was it clean and righteous? We're back to the money, here. What happened to the money?

"The Bureau claimed that it never received any of that money that was supposed to go into evidence and that there might not have been any money to begin with. It's all suspect, remember, because everything happening so damn fast. That sick ass pimp could have cleaned the money out well before anyone ever got there. Or, at least a very large chunk of it. Who knows if there was any real money?"

I looked at Vincent. "You think that Schaap made off with the money? That would explain the whole name change. It would explain why no one ever heard from Wilson again. Did he become a paid bag man for some greater and more nefarious characters?"

Vincent nodded, "I think so. I mean, I think that he saw an opportunity, he took it, and in doing so either got hooked up with some very dastardly folks, or he himself became one of the dastardly folk.

"I think that he got hooked up with the wrong people, though, as we know that he's now dead. There are no doctored reports to suggest otherwise. If I had to guess, I think that the higher ups were starting to cover their tracks and the fact that anyone of any importance had anything to do with him is now dead, makes me believe that."

I was looking at the paper, suddenly it hit me. "Vincent, all these forms are in the same handwriting. Why would a female dispatcher name Sandra have the exact same handwriting as a guy that she worked with, but otherwise had no contact with?"

Vincent tapped the table for emphasis, "Bingo! If he wasn't hiding, why did he switch out all the logs? Look at the misspellings on the Sheriff's name. You think that the Sheriff would actually misspell his own name? You think that he wouldn't notice that if there was a crime scene, that certain crucial evidence was missing from the evidence log?

"There's one or two more papers I want you to look at."

POLICE REPORT

Case No: 72163427

Date: 22 November 63

Reporting Officer: Donald Wilson

Prepared By: Donald Wilson

Incident: _____

Detail of Event: Arrived on scene at Hennepin's Dept Store to find disgruntled customer arguing with owner regarding what customer felt was a bad sale and owner disputing the sale. Customer wants satisfaction. Owner wants customer trespassed from property.

Actions Taken: Customer's money was returned to them. Customer was asked to leave and has agreed never to return. Owner is satisfied with this agreement.

Summary:
No further action needs be taken at this time.

Vincent was tapping this particular paper. "Why would an officer write a bogus police report to put him at the scene of a crime that supposedly never happened? Why would he attempt to explain his whereabouts if he had nothing to hide?

"I think that he did clean up the crime scene, just a bit, before everyone else showed up. They didn't see the crime scene until *after* the shoot occurred and even the Sheriff couldn't attest to who or what was on scene. He was off on the other side of town dealing with the corpses found in the burn pit. When he got the shooting call he had to haul ass across town and by the time he got there, Schaap could have stashed the weapon, and made the scene more appropriate to what he detailed."

Of course, I had forgotten all about the pistol. "There is no record of the pimp, what's his name Moore, having been found with the pistol, was there?"

Vincent clapped his hands together and opened them palms up, as if a dealer clearing the table. "Indeed, we're missing money, we're missing an untraceable weapon, and we're missing a few crucial characters. I think that we found the key, here. A cop, normally who's a good fella, gets a bit dirty on the takedown, for whatever reason he's thinking.

"Somehow he gets pinched by these dastardly characters and now he's their bitch. He's feeding 'em bits of intel on where to score major cash and major drug hits. These people, who knows who they are, they are using him until they decide that Schaap is no longer of value and they decide to take him out of the equation."

Picking up the last piece of paper, I ask, "So what's this all about?"

Cherry County

556 N Main St #37
Phone: 402.555.3761

Employee Monthly Pay Stub

Official Pay Stub
Pay Year Jan 1 – Dec 31, 1986

Name of Employee / Badge #: _Wilson, Donald_

Period of Payment: _1 November 86 – 30 November 86_

Scale of Payment:

Description	Amount	Description	Amount
Standard Working Days in a Month	var	Daily Pay Rate Per Hour	5.00
Standard Working Hours on Daily Basis	10	Overtime Rate Per Hour	7.50
Holiday Rate Per Hour	7.50	Overnight Differential	6.75

Computation of Gross Salary to be Paid for This Month:

Description	Amount	Description	Amount
Regular Hours Logged This Month	160	Pay For Regular Time Hours	800.00
Overtime Hours Logged This Month	13	Pay For Overtime Hours	97.50
Holiday Hours Logged This Month	20	Pay For Holiday Hours	150.00
Overnight Hours Logged This Month	9	Pay For Overnight Hours	60.75
Total Accrued Sick Hours	276	Salary For All Paid Leaves * 1380.00 *	
Sick Hours Used This Month	0	Pay For Used Sick Hours	0.00

Break Up of Deductions for the Month

Gross Monthly Income	1108.25
Social Security Withheld	-68.71
FERS Withheld	-55.41
Additional Tax Withheld	-10.00
Total Deductions	-134.12
Net Monthly Salary	974.13

Prepared By: _Rassmusson_

Received BY: _Wilson_

For Official Use Only

"What about this? It's a pay stub."

I nod to Vincent, "Yeah, everything looks square and in the means. There doesn't appear to be anything out of scene with this. I mean, my math is a bit fuzzy but it doesn't look like he was skimming hours, or having money withheld that shouldn't be, yaknow?"

Vincent said, "Think about it. This guy's in the prime of his life and this is what he's making for salary? I think we have the motive, right here. Good old fashioned greed. He sees his take home and he thinks, 'Fuck it' and when he has a chance to get a bit dirty behind this shoot, maybe he doesn't consciously make that leap, but he sees an opportunity to move beyond the stages he is in. There's money all over the basement."

"You think that the greed just got the better of him?" I ask. "You think that this all started with a bit of jealousy because he wouldn't be able to get that new fishing boat that year?"

Vincent, who was positively soaked with perspiration, nodded, "Yeah, I do. I think he walked into what he felt was a can't miss deal, and sadly it was with the wrong people, and plain and simple greed was what got the better of him."

I replied, "Yaknow, I think that there is more to the story, but I honestly think that right now you and I have a killer byline together in at least one article, possibly a series of articles. We're gonna be famous, buddy."

Vincent held up his hand in deference, "Well, that's why I came to you. If anyone knows how to get this stuff out there, it'll be you.

"Right now, I feel like ten pounds of shit in a nine pound bag and I'm ready to go home and get some rest. I think that I got the fucking flu or something. I need some rest."

I stood and extended my hand. Dripping with sweat and bodily fluids or not, I was going to shake this man's hand because he was going to make me one famous sonuvabitch. I owed him at least a solid handshake for that very favor.

I replied, "Well, make sure you don't wait another two years to get in touch with me. We got headlines to make, yaknow? I'm thinking some serious book negotiating. Maybe, just maybe a movie title."

Vincent nodded, gave a half hearted salute and gathered his case with him. His sallow skin was looking like melted wax under these late night flood lights. He did not look well.

Suddenly this restaurant was too bright, it was too loud, it was all together too much for me. I needed to bail. I gathered up the papers Vincent had left for me, folded them into fours and stuffed them into my back pocket.

I was in so much of a hurry I didn't see Vincent stop near the back entrance of the restaurant, just next to the men's room. I didn't see him take out a package of cigarettes, ready to shake one loose and light it up outside. Not that it would have done much good. Thunder echoed off the urban canyon walls and rattled the old iron door and window frames. Rain pelted the hot concrete, as if Mother Nature herself was disturbed at this story and demanded vengeance for it.

I didn't see the man in the mirrored sunglasses, loud print shorts and polo with the popped collar wrap his arm around Vincent's neck and herd him into the bathroom.

So focused on the mental notes that I was making I headed out into the early morning storm, oblivious to the dangers lurking in the shadows, lurking in the rain.

The Ballad of Agent Diabrava

Thursday. 16 July 15. 2215 hrs.

Agent Diabrava sat alone in her orange peel colored 1979 Dodge Grand Monaco. Her raven black hair that was normally kept shoulder length, at minimum, to better accentuate the look of her 1950s pinup face was now cut short in a spiky pixie cut giving her the appearance of a sinister and deviant sprite. Her full and pouty lips that once sported thick candy apple red lip paint were now painted jet black, to match her hair. Even her favorite frilly dresses had been replaced by slinky black clothing that had more lace and mesh than actual cloth. This was especially troublesome because it was cold as shit out tonight and Agent Diabrava, "AD" to her superiors and just "Addy" to everyone else, was now pretty damn sure that her legs were going to fall off, or she was going to cut the windows out of her car with her rock hard and frozen nipples.

West Coast weather simply was not her style and this nasty cold, dampness wasn't doing her any good. There was some great action out here, but these were supposed to be the summer months, it might have been a bit warmer. This wintery cold shit had to end sometime, didn't it?

Considering her curious mix of Italian and Spanish heritage she was simply not built for this weather. Warm sunset breezes and tropical weather were much more her style. In the spring of 2012 she had visited Puerto Rico and fallen in love with the entire scene; the culture, the people, the very essence that exuded from the very island was something that she wanted to drink in, and embrace. Not this hideous damp weather that made her bones ache and shiver. Addy didn't care what time of year it was, the breeze coming in off the bay was positively bone chilling.

As if to remind her, the old shoulder would of her teen years seemed to cry out in torment, the surgical grade stainless steel staples dug further into the bone, their icy tendrils threatening to suck the marrow, the very heat and life from her core. While extremely flexible, surgical rubber bands that had long since replaced the shredded tendons seemed to rake their way across the tender bone and worm their way under the tormented flesh of her shoulder.

Absentmindedly she rubbed at her shoulder, hoping to will away the phantom pain, and simultaneously snapping her fingers of her left hand in a vacant attempt to return feeling to them. Puerto Rico didn't have this issue. No, she could easily get away with her bikini and sarong wrap to make herself at home on the beach.

Addy desperately wanted to turn on the car, if for nothing else than to get the heat running and at least maybe some circulation back in her dolled up toes. It didn't matter a whit because the monster goth boots she was wearing may have covered her flesh up to her knees but the leather and fishnet stockings didn't go a damn bit of good for keeping her legs warm. Even her ass felt frozen to the seat of the car. Ancient leather and vinyl seemed to crack and groan every time she shifted her weight to restore the circulation.

This was no ordinary assignment and she wasn't really thrilled with it. Her partner Tana Barnes was at least comfortable, sitting in some police station somewhere, being interviewed for a possible position and transfer assignment. Apparently it helps when your sister is already on the police force and willing to give you a good recommend.

But, that was also in some backwards weird little town called Bismarck. Where the hell was Bismarck, anyway? North Dakota? Addy was pretty sure that at one time there had been some big name German official or prince with that particular name, but she wasn't sure about some backwater town in a frozen wasteland that was more often mistaken for a part of Canada, and not the United States.

There was oil money, though, flowing through that state and there was a desperate need for anyone who could sling a gun to come work the streets in any damn town. That was why Addy sat alone on her stakeout waiting for her target to show. Agent Barnes might have been getting the lion's share of the action, but she was going to have to put up with a frozen wasteland to make it happen; which, when you got down to brass tacks, was pretty much what Addy was doing right now. If Addy could have changed one thing about her past, it would be to not have believed all the movie hype when big guys would kick down doors with sexy chick sidekicks, wielding fully automatic weapons. Nope. More often than not, her job was here, sitting in a shitty car, waiting for a mark who may or may not show, and if he did show, to photograph him and send the intel to the higher ups.

The Drug Enforcement Agency was pretty straightforward, as far as government agencies go, but once in a while they employed agents such as Addy to work in places that no male agent could get to. And that was why Addy found herself sitting in this damp and cold car in a parking lot just off of Harborview Drive in the historic district of Gig Harbor, Washington. What had once been an up and coming Mecca of trade, this port town was now more resort town and the line of expensive sailboats tied off to the piers in various private marinas suggested that wealth was something that could easily be tossed around in this town.

There was a cold front coming in off the water and the temp was dropping rapidly, but just across the street, according to intel, her target was going to be arriving at the house of a known provider of female services for gentlemen. Her breath was starting to form small moisture clouds inside the cold and silent car, but Addy's assignment was to be ready to go and be that "lady" when her specified target did arrive. She tried not to be self conscious and had to keep from checking herself out in the mirror every five minutes. While Addy was a very good undercover agent, this was well outside of her established boundaries. She's played and mirrored some shady characters in the past, as her career had played out, but nothing to this extent and this whole goth look, while sexually enticing to a certain cliental, really was starting to make her tits chafe.

Madam Lee an ancient looking Oriental woman, by anyone's standards, who ran the establishment that dealt out the particular services such shady men like to partake in, had cut a deal with the DEA the year previous to ensure that her business was overlooked from future operations when she had agreed to supply agents with information concerning certain suspicious cliental. Most specifically, a certain young gentleman had started frequenting her establishment just recently. While his penchant was for the Oriental ladies that Madam Lee had on hand, he also had a deviant fetish for 90s era goth hookers. That was how Addy found herself in this getup with no backup, not even a cell phone, just her Sig P238 compact pistol tucked into a garter holster inside her right boot. If she got into a gunfight she was going to be royally screwed, but at least the seven rounds of .380 caliber ammunition in the magazine gave her better than a snowball's chance in hell of escaping certain death. Not by much, though. Hollow point ammunition could do a fair amount of damage and Addy didn't care who you were, you weren't walking away from a hole in the head, but for that kind of work you had to be up and close and personal. This

196

pistol's tiny little barrel wasn't good for much more than that, and Addy didn't really like being that close in a gunfight, anyway. Regardless, it was sometimes the nature of the beast.

Addy didn't know the target's name, which was in keeping with her cover. All she knew was that this man had requested a date for the evening, to escort him to a fancy restaurant where he would meet with another gentleman, to exchange some information. She was to get a look at faces, memorize them as best as possible, and listen for names, dates, associates. Under no circumstance was she to intervene in any dealings, as the men of the evening were to believe that they were meeting for soft shell crab and fine champagne. She was to look as dumb and bimbo as possible so as to let the alcohol do its job and loosen some tongues.

Addy saw a limo pull up out front of the chic renovated two-story Cape Cod that faced the waterfront. Many of the homes in this area of town had been renovated to house small, family run businesses, and Madam Lee was no different. While most of the business that served this waterfront neighborhood catered to family and tourists and just about everyone in between, Madam Lee made sure that she was particular about the cliental she catered to and was sure not to attract the wrong crowd. That fact that her doors didn't open until after sundown certainly added to the mystique of the property.

Addy exited her car, not bothering to lock it, as there was nothing in it to steal anyway. Patting her right calf she ensured the pistol was still secure and that it hadn't gone anywhere. Her small clutch contained everything a working girl would need; lipstick, mascara, gum, breath mints, even a few condoms just to ensure the part was looking right. She highly doubted it was going to come to that point, but if it did, she was going to be ready and do what needed to be done.

She had once proudly given head to another woman in the back of a Lincoln just to elicit information about a possible drug dealing pimp and while she was pretty sure the taste of that woman's crotch was going to be on her lips for a month, Addy did indeed get the information, and better yet, got the collar, and another drug dealing pimp was off the street. His rap sheet ensured that there was no chance he was ever going to see the free world again. To this day he was housed in Cell Block B of a federal maximum security prison somewhere in Colorado because of his interactions with suspicious and shady characters as well as his history of using his ladies as punching bags. Addy had no regrets about her behavior that night, not for the information it provided, or the asshole that had been removed from society.

Walking the long way through the parking lot Addy headed north on Harborview Drive, circling to her left and heading back south, along the sidewalk, coming in behind the parked limousine and giving all the appearance she was either heading to work, or returning from another client. Once again she wished she had decided on a better costume as the cold breeze, accentuated by the horn of the Boston Whaler parked in the harbor, seemed to announce the mournful wind that was now blowing down her exposed back and threatening to freeze her ass cheeks clean off. Coastal weather was a real bitch.

Right on cue Madam Lee opened the door and in a thickly accented voice proclaimed, "There you are! Right on time! We have a guest!" Addy hadn't even made it to the front steps of the house when she found herself being turned around and herded towards the open and beckoning car door of the limo. Guests were always treated to the best treatment that Madam Lee could afford.

Addy smiled her best smile and needing no further indication that this was her fella; she linked arms with the mystery target and walked him over to the curb, entering the limo first, as a proper girl should do. Madam Lee was all smiles and waves, a matriarch sending her teenage daughter off on her first prom, for the entire world to see. In reality, she had just bought another four months of silence from those bastard federal agents that loved to raid her place, inexplicably at the precise times she was about to give one of her special massages, looking for all manner of illicit drugs. If they had known where to look for the cocaine and the heroin she would certainly have been in a world of trouble, but even with all the evidence presented in the movies, they never, ever seemed to find the compartment in the baseboards where she kept the stashes that kept her ladies docile and manageable, and kept her clients on an even keel. Another benefit of these guests was that many times they paid for services in products that often times found their way doubling or tripling her benefit, and their value.

As it was Madam Lee had a special guest waiting on her, a woman in her early 40s with the body of a goddess and long, curly red hair. Her name was Serena and she was an absolute treat to massage as she usually tipped well, and once in a while, threw in something extra for Madam Lee, herself, if the service was especially good. Men, women, old or young, Madam Lee didn't mind. She loved the feeling of human flesh in her hands as it melted, transformed and became workable clay in her hands under her expert technique and warm oil. Madam Lee only stayed outside long enough to ensure that her most recent client was safely off.

Now she needed to return to Serena, whom she certainly didn't want to keep waiting.

* * *

Addy actually found herself attracted to the gentleman whose arm she was clinging to. His handsome face and rugged features were only marred by his bizarre mustache that he seemed to be so proud of, a closely trimmed affair screaming a Howard Hughes meets Wild West Gunslinger. Spencer Tracy with a set of wicked mirrored aviator sunglasses that he refused to remove. For the love of God, it was dark outside, it was nighttime. No one cared.

But her job was to dutifully laugh at this man's jokes and she did. She even managed a few genuine bellows when he told a joke that could have been funny under different circumstances. And when she did, her breasts would heave within the confines of the corset she wore and she would catch his eyes through the sides of his sunglasses, as he turned his head to watch them dance. She knew she had him and that was all right with her.

As the limo drove Addy swayed with the motion of the car and occasionally she would bump into her client, allowing her to get an occasional grope on him. This proved to be fruitful because she could discern no obvious weapon or firearm stashed beneath his finely tailored suit jacket. If this cat was rolling light, so much the better because she needed him to be as minimal threat as possible. This was a quick, one night deal, and if he liked, her so much the better. But she couldn't risk him going off half cocked if she did get up in his business, not if he was carrying a firearm.

Pulling up in front of the restaurant, a place also on the waterfront, called *Harbor Monsoon*, Addy was instantly impressed. This wasn't a joint she would ever eat at, not on her meager federal salary. No, this was a place that she felt as if she would need a credit check just to enter the front door. Even from this distance Addy could see designer labels of all kinds gracing the finely lit tables and brands of champagne that she had read about were scattered over the tables like so much cheap soda pop. Instantly she felt under dressed and out of place, as her "date" in the expensive suit led her to the side entrance. Her brief glimpse inside the front windows showed men and women, all in suits and dresses that would cost her a month's salary, eating from fine china on little tables that revolved around like the ones in the bar in Indiana Jones. So much fine food, fine wine, fine people, and here she was, dressed like a cheap hooker, begging to get a peek inside; or maybe an even darker, sexier version of the Orphan Oliver?

However, the front entrance was not their destination. Moving to the left of the building, a hinged metal door, resembling the bulkhead of a battleship, stood atop a metal grate loading dock. Years of neglect had taken their toll on the paint, and even the once regal murals on the side of the building were now faded to sad tattered paint scraps that were in serious need of a makeover. No sign or label marked the door. There was no address to even discern that this was an entirely separate entity from the glamorous restaurant just around the corner. Just twelve feet away, an entirely new and different world awaited her.

With a single knock on the door, a portal slid open and the man in the suit spoke a few hushed words. Without a verbal response the portal was slid closed, and the door opened to reveal a grand staircase leading up to the rooms above the restaurant. This particular staircase had taken its cues directly from Al Capone's personal stylist. Red velvet draperies hung on the walls, while worn and threadbare carpet was tacked to creaky wooden stairs. Velvet ropes looped up the risers and runners giving a truly theatrical aspect.

Addy had assumed that they were apartments for rent, or other business offices. Perhaps even private rooms for rent, for whatever reasons a patron could think of. The reality, however, was far more stunning, even a bit overpowering.

As she and her date mounted the staircase, men and women of all legal ages, and some, Addy presumed to herself, probably not so legal, were seated all across a vast expanse of a converted ballroom that had draped tables with opulent silver, china and incensed candles as centerpieces. All of the furniture was of exceedingly fine quality and the people that occupied that furniture were no less than perfectly dressed. Just as Addy felt out of her depth, especially in her get up, she felt equally out of her depth with the company she was now keeping. Assignment or not, this was a world all unto its own. To a woman sporting a cheap fetish hooker costume she was certainly turning heads, and not in the ways that she would have preferred.

Gig Harbor was a town that was supposed to have a ban on indoor smoking, but that rule certainly didn't apply here. Cigarettes, both domestic and exotic, cigars, hand rolled Puerto Ricans from the streets of old San Juan, even marijuana cigarettes no doubt brought in from some far away cartel were being puffed on, passed around, and creating an intoxicating atmosphere. Addy was instantly euphoric and when what she presumed was a waiter, appeared out of nowhere with a glass of champagne, she accepted and as graciously as etiquette would allow, began to imbibe. She was playing a dangerous game, and she knew it because she was "on duty" and she was carrying a firearm, but she couldn't let her date suspect anything to the contrary. Duties aside, she was also a single woman, under so much cover that not even the police knew who she was or what she was doing here. Her own agency and handler barely knew what she was up to. If anything were to happen, she would have a very hard time explaining how she got here, why she was dressed as she was, and most importantly, why she was carrying a concealed firearm that she had no business owning. That was assuming she wasn't led out of here in handcuffs, or shot dead by a thug or an overeager rookie policeman.

Her date saw that his evening escort was already loosening up and this brought him great pleasure. With luck his meeting tonight would go smoothly and he would be able to close the deal before his date got too bored, and if he was really lucky, maybe, just maybe fuck her brains out as they rode back to Madam Lee's place. But, that was for later. Now...

* * *

"Ah, Steven, you made it!" The man in the expensive suit approaching Addy and her date was clearly enjoying this atmosphere and it appeared that he had already been sampling some of the beverages. Or the cigars. Hell he could have been snorting cocaine out of a Faberge egg that he kept in his suit pocket. Addy didn't know what was up with him, but she was sure that this fella was not on the up and up.

Steven, though that was not his real name, came alive at the sight of this man and Addy made a mental note of both her date's name and the man in the suit. The man had taste, and money, as his European cut, single breasted suit suggested it had been hand made in one of London's finer clothiers. Addy was too busy staring at the man to notice that he was accompanied by two teenage girls who appeared drugged and dosed to the gills.

Their staggered gate, their ragged makeup, and whorish clothes suggested that they were not here of their own volition.

If they were drugged, Addy presumed that they were most likely victims of traffickers, though with all the makeup on, it was hard to tell who they were, and in here hastening state of dazedness, she wasn't sure she would be able to pick them out of a lineup, even if they were the only two females.

Steven, removing his sunglasses, said, "Aldrich, of course I made it. When you sent an invitation for me to join this party, I couldn't resist! I love what you've done with the place!"

With his right hand, Steven placed his glasses in his inner jacket pocket and shook Aldrich's hand in a show that they were not casual acquaintances. His left hand he kept open, to gesture around the grand trappings of the room.

Aldrich Wilson smiled a big, toothy smile, "Steven you adorable little shit, you, there is no need to suck my dick just yet, what's mine is yours and after your last few bits of business you've assisted me with, how could I not invite you?

"This whole spread is because you have helped to remove some barriers and obstacles for me, and now I've got various dignitaries and other regal gentlemen and ladies from all over the world paying me more than ten thousand dollars a plate to come and enjoy the best food, wine, song, and uh, company, if you know what I mean..."

Steven did indeed know what Aldrich was referring to because he had helped lay some of the foundation work for this particular endeavor.

"Aldrich, why don't we get a table for ourselves, and we can chat about what you have in mind for me, next?"

Aldrich clapped his chubby hands to his chubby cheeks in a mock comical expression, as if he had forgot he was standing in the middle of an enormous party. If Benny Hill could have come alive, Addy would have sworn that he was standing right in front of her. Though, to be safe, Addy wasn't sure she could pick Benny Hill out of a lineup, either.

"My god, Steven, where are my manners?!" Aldrich snapped his fingers and pointed to a man in an equally expensive tuxedo standing off to the side. Immediately this man turned and spoke into his right cuff, and as if by magic, a door in the wall was opened, from the inside, and the guests ushered inside. Steven placed his right hand around Addy's waist, his fingers riding just high enough to grace the side of her ample breast. She didn't back away or flinch when he did this and Steven didn't bother to move his hand or adjust the location of it.

Walking into the inner chamber, Addy was taken aback. Gothic ceilings arched to darkness that even the bright torch lights of the walls could not pierce.

If the party going on outside was opulent, then this room was down-right blasphemous. Paintings and draperies hung from the walls, hand carved wooden chairs from ancient trees lined a gigantic banquet table that looked as if Odin himself has assembled it with stones of Asgard and planks from his very own ships.

Rough hewn beams stained with a dark molasses color spaced the walls to support equally rough and dark beams spanning the rooms. Addy half expected to see wild birds roosting in the beams, but instead the faintest of ancient cobwebs was blowing gossamer threads in the electric breeze created by an unseen HVAC unit. This was truly a hall for kings and leaders of men, and as Addy thought to herself, of the damned.

On the table sat piles, heaps, mounds of meats, fruits, vegetables, pastas and other exquisite dishes that looked as if they cost a small fortune. In truth, they did cost a small fortune, paid for in copious amounts of illicit cash and more than a fair share of blood spilled in the name of illegal fortunes and lifestyles. Spilled by men, and some women, with no more moral character than the table upon which this feast was placed and the chairs upon which they sat.

Aldrich motioned his guests to sit and without a word began to help himself to the large piles of food and indulge his hideously gargantuan appetite. Without regard for his expensive attire, or his manicured face and hands, he ate as if an animal himself. Meat juice ran down the jowls of his face and into the creases of his fine collared shirt. Smears of food matted against his hands as he wiped away the excess from his massive lips.

His guests, likewise, sat themselves down and more delicately began to pile their plates with the various meats, cheeses, and pour large goblets of expensive and fine wines with names that Addy couldn't pronounce and was pretty sure she couldn't afford. Dutifully, she sat to the side of Steven, and slightly behind him, so as to appear out of sight, out of mind. Men were discussing business, and she could more easily roam the room with her eyes. Only then did she truly notice the women that Aldrich kept as his company. She wanted to enter into conversation with them, but it was not her place, nor was this the appropriate time for such a discussion. Addy also wanted to feel for the comforting bulge on her leg, but that would have been too easy of a tell, a rookie move indeed, and she could not blow her cover now, not while the tongues were loosened and the conversation was flowing.

Aldrich was speaking, "Steven I can't believe our luck. Your work down in Nebraska, all those years ago, really caught the eyes of my associates and ever since then..." His voice trailed off as he motioned for his guests to look at the two girls, still doped and out of it, as they sat on a velvet covered lounge chaise. Aldrich motioned for one to come over, and she stood, wobbling on her feet. Her slinky black dress left little to the imagination and her brown hair swayed with her body. Without a word of protest she knelt in from of Aldrich as he pushed his chair back from the table and lowered the zipper on his pants.

Addy didn't need to see the girl's head bobbing up and down, the noise was enough to disgust her.

In between labored gasps, Aldrich continued, "Your work in removing that competition was brilliant. As far as I know the feds had no idea what was going on. They still think it was a shit storm robbery gone bad in some back water little town!"

Aldrich threw his head back and laughed, the violent motion causing the poor young gal to gag, to which she received a swift smack on the side of her head. He pushed her off of him, and proceeded to expose himself to the entire group while he used a fine linen napkin from the table to clean himself. There was no shame as he exposed his flaccid genitalia to the group, even a perverse smirk crossed his face as he caught Addy eyeing him.

"Young lady, would you like a turn, as well?" Aldrich was fairly offering her a turn and she did her best to turn a polite smile and demure, while at the best trying not to vomit on her plate.

If any of this was offensive to Steven he didn't say a word, just looked on in bemusement while Addy was doing her best to hold her stomach contents down. The poor, abused servant girl that Aldrich apparently kept on a short leash slunk back to the chaise where she was comforted by her companion while silent tears streamed down her cheeks. Her cries were so subtle and shuttered that Addy could barely hear them. Her hitching chest and slunk down shoulders were impossible to miss, though.

"Just so damned hard to find good help, nowadays," Aldrich had stood and was zipping himself back up, "but that's the price you pay for the finer things in life."

Steven raised his glass in salute and agreement, "Aldrich, we need to talk. You've been very generous with your money and your opportunities. Your partners have been more than generous with their time and money, as well. You have all made me a wealthy man. What I need from you, now, is to talk about this last endeavor of ours. I need some specifics so that I can finish up this assignment and be on my way.

"This is truly a young man's game and I'm getting too old for it. Please don't take this as a sign of disrespect, as you have for almost twenty years given me the chances to travel, to see new places, meet new people..." Steven's voice trailed off.

Aldrich continued, "Given you the opportunity to kill a few people, too, as I recall."

Steven motioned for Aldrich to let it go, but Aldrich continued. "Honey, you don't care, do you? You'll be a good girl, and keep your mouth shut, won't you?"

His eyes, as well as Steven's, were locked on with Addy. Their combined looks could have bored holes through the very walls.

Addy stammered out, "I'm... I'm sorry, what were you saying; I was lost in the art on the walls... This is some truly beautiful work, here. This painting isn't this from the early collection of..."

Aldrich cut her off, "Oh, Steven, you do know how to pick them, don't you? Drop dead gorgeous and dumb as a sack of hammers.

"Oh, darling, what I wouldn't do to you, if you'd give me ten minutes of your time."

Steven held up his hand in mock protest, "Aldrich, be careful my friend, she's a friend and she's paid been paid for. Madam Lee wouldn't look too kindly on her merchandise coming back damaged."

Steven ran his hand down her exposed shoulder and while Addy's skin nearly crawled she kept her composure. Her initial attraction to the man was all but gone after seeing, and grasping, what this man was all about, and more importantly what his partners were all about.

Aldrich waived his hand dismissively, "Steven you have nothing to fear, I have my own specimens to explore, I wouldn't dream of taking this lovely beast away from you."

Steven nodded, "Thank you. Now, if we may get back to the task at hand?"

Aldrich smiled, "Yes, of course. I have one last obstacle that needs to be removed. The man is a crackpot, he's probably a raving lunatic, but he's also starting to put some things together and rumor has it that he's going to be meeting with some people who might listen to his crackpot theories with more than a passing interest. If this should happen, it could be trouble. I seriously doubt that he would be of any concern, but we still need this person dealt with.

"You can take care of this situation, in any manner you see fit and then as far as my partners and I am concerned, you are free to go and do as you please. If the situation were a bit more mainstream I would write you a letter of recommend, but alas our arrangement is far from mainstream and I very much doubt that you'll be advertising your services all that much."

Aldrich slid a digitally printed photo across the table and Steven picked it up, studying it. The man in the photograph looked strung out and tired.

"Aldrich, who is this guy; he looks like a nobody. Why do you want me to spend any time or energy on him?"

"Steven you are correct, my dear boy; he is a nobody. He's a retired cop, burned out on the job, and spent the last few years doing piecemeal private investigation.

"His talents are not all that exceptional, but he's apparently made a few friends, talked to a few people, and can generally bullshit his way in and out of a conversation with enough authority to make himself sound legitimate, but that's about where his credentials end."

Steven nodded, "And you want me to ensure that he doesn't talk to anyone else? Why, just because he might have seen something, stumbled across something, and had no damn clue as to what he saw?"

Aldrich's face immediately grew serious, "Steven our arrangement has always been that you get paid for services rendered. You have never asked questions and you have never once dared to interfere in matters that don't concern you. I ask you, now, as your friend, please do not start."

Steven held up his hand, no longer in mock defense, "Aldrich, I would never presume to interfere with your affairs, and I apologize if I've crossed a line. I only ask because everyone else that we've dealt with has had a pretty clear picture painted as to why they had become an obstacle.

"That psycho bitch in New York that killed her husband, I mean that was a sheer stroke of luck that she would go batshit insane and go on a killing rampage *after* she had killed off one of our moneymen. I mean, we couldn't have planned it any better."

Aldrich was smiling again, bobbing his head, "I know. And when her idiot son torched the place, it was priceless. I still don't know how you managed to blow that train, though..."

Steven just chuckled, "That was the dumb damn luck, again. I had injected his dumb ass with enough neurotoxin that he would have been dead ten minutes into the train ride.

"And when he passed out in the damn train station, it was a matter of switching the money with stacks of catalogs and other books. Poor bastard never knew he had been robbed. I can't believe we walked out with that much cash. I figured we were going to have to kidnap the son, torture the mother, do some seriously heinous shit, and these two fools did it all for us."

Aldrich did appreciate that his banker was able to take control of so much cash without having to lift a lot of fingers. In the grand scheme of their operations, it wasn't all that large a sum of money, but it was still an outstanding balance that was owed to him, and his partners, and Aldrich employed people like Steven, though Steven was undoubtedly his best man and Aldrich was sorry to see him go, to ensure that there were no outstanding debts and obstacles to be negotiated. Men like Aldrich, as well as the men he worked with, appreciated that there would be more black in their ledgers, than red ink.

Just then the man in the expensive tuxedo who had opened this room up by speaking into his cuff appeared at Aldrich's side. He spoke a few hushed words into Aldrich's ear and then retreated to the rear of the room.

"Steven, it seems that some of our guests are leaving, will you please excuse me?

"Please, all of you, continue to dine, if you'll allow my absence. I shall return momentarily." Aldrich swept his arms upon the vast expanse of the table and gestured toward the spread.

Steven bowed in acknowledgement and Aldrich stood and exited the room. Addy used this time disruption as a means to excuse herself to the ladies room. "Excuse me, sir?" She looked at the man in the tuxedo.

His professional face, and faraway gaze gave nothing away, "Ma'am what can I do for you?"

"Would you point me in the direction of the little girls' room, I need to relieve myself."

The man's dour expression suggested he wasn't used to being talked to in such mediocre language. He motioned to another man, who in turn came forward to escort Addy to an alcove tucked in the recesses of the draperies. Here she found a small powder room where she did indeed relieve herself and took a moment and check to make sure her makeup was still striking. It was. She checked to ensure that her gun was still riding perfectly in her boot. It was. Lastly she checked to ensure that she was showing just enough cleavage and that her breasts appeared just perky enough to catch Steven's attention. They were.

Flushing the toilet, and washing her hands, she exited the powder room to find Steven standing at the head of the table, with Aldrich, who was back to his seat, with the man in the expensive tuxedo on Aldrich's right. There was no question, at all. Their attention was focused directly on her. Scope locked on her, once again boring holes into her with their eyes.

Addy put on her best feigned surprise, "What's going on?"

Aldrich motioned for Addy to take back her former seat, which she did, but when Steven didn't join her, she became a bit worried. She tried not to nervously twitch, that would have been a dead giveaway. Instead she pretended to absentmindedly pick at her food, pretending to not notice them still staring at her.

Aldrich tented his fingers, resting his elbows on the table. The two brown haired girls that were Aldrich's escorts had disappeared. He said, "It seems we have a problem. Winston, here, received a very interesting phone call from a woman who identified herself as Madam Lee. Do you know this woman?

"Oh, Aldrich, such a silly question, of course you know this woman, don't you dear?" His mocking tone and genial reference to himself in the third person was far more terrifying than Winston's lurking presence, behind him.

Winston, the man in the expensive tuxedo, smirked just enough that Addy couldn't help but notice it was directed right at her. Addy was scope locked on Aldrich, though, and barely had time to think about Winston. How could so many things change in the span of just a few moments?

"Well, yeah, I know Madam Lee, I work for her, and obviously you know that right?

"If there is a problem with hired girls being in here, I can leave. I'm not one to meddle in someone else's business, I'm just here for a night's work, that's all."

Addy started to rise, and utter a few further words of protest, but was instantly shushed by Aldrich who motioned for her to sit back down. She complied.

Aldrich chuckled, "Oh, you're a working girl, all right, though I don't believe for one minute you work for Madam Lee, which is quite the pity because a beautiful specimen, such as yourself, really should learn to embrace the world's oldest profession. You could be rich beyond your wildest dreams. And, something tells me you are used to fucking men over." Instantly the jovial attitude was gone. It was replaced by ice cold emotion, or a complete lack thereof.

He stood and walked around the table, placing himself right behind Addy, with his hands seductively on her shoulders, "I wouldn't shit a penny, though, if you told me that you worked for a man named Uncle Sam. It wouldn't surprise me in the least that you are indeed a whore for an unnamed man, that you peddle your wares and there are certain people who profit and certain people who lose out because of your talents. How close am I?"

Addy's mind was racing. That bitch Madam Lee had sold out Addy, and with what these men knew, it was clear that she had no intention of Addy returning this night. There was no sense in denying it, as it would only have gotten her shot that very moment.

"You're right, I work for Uncle Sam, well, maybe Uncle Sam's distant cousin. You know how this goes. I've got the tits and the ass, and therefore I'm the one who's on the street. I'm the expendable one and the person who's going to get liquidated first. That's just how it works.

"I work vice. I was tracking a couple of low life dope dealers who ran this way, hoping I could catch their supplier. Maybe score a promotion out of it, yaknow? I have no idea who you are, and what you guys are all about.

"I went undercover with Madam Lee because I was told that the pukes liked to frequent her place and I figured it would be a great way to catch 'em."

Aldrich was smiling, now, though Addy couldn't see it behind her, "And you thought that after all you saw and heard this evening, you were going to waltz out of here, and tell your friends back at the DEA that it was all just a fantastic coincidence that you happened to wander into our midst?

"Do you really think we'd just let you waltz out of here? Do you know who is out in that ballroom? There are heads of states. There are corporate executives. There are men and women who stand to lose more than their paycheck. Their very reputation would be tarnished if the world found out what these men and women like to dabble with.

214

"As we sit here, now, there is a woman who is the Chief Financial Officer for a Fortune 500 company. She's slick, she's savvy, and she also happens to have a ravaging cocaine appetite. She'll snort enough snow tonight that she'll most likely be carted off to the local Emergency Room, where her assistant will concoct a bullshit story about her taking too much cold medicine, and because the assistant will hand the triage nurse and on-call doctor some unmarked bills, they will understand it, they will excuse it, and within a few days our lovely CFO will be back at work, after recovering from the flu."

Aldrich continued to keep his vise grip on her shoulders and spoke again, "I have another gentleman out there. He's a fan of young and pure teenage girls. He prefers to indoctrinate them in his own perverse way and he prefers to train them his way.

"You remember the two beauties that were with me, earlier? Well, they are gifts from that particular man. He's been in this business a long… goddam… time! And I sure as hell will not let you ruin these particular business contacts and the businesses they have worked so hard to build and that I have worked equally hard to conceal!"

His sudden outburst startled Addy, who had kept her cool, and was now on the verge of tears, herself. How had it come to this? "Yes, I mean, no, I figured we could walk away, call it a draw, and you both know that I don't know shit about what's going on here. If my superiors ask me about my night, I tell him that I escorted a gentleman to dinner, a very nice dinner, and that he did indeed treat me like a gentleman, and that he dropped me back at Madam Lee's house, and that the two guys I was looking for never showed their faces this evening."

Through all of this Steven stood motionless, he had replaced his mirrored sunglasses and his face gave away nothing. Were the sunglasses hiding a small moment of emotion? Addy doubted that they were, but she held on to that slim hope.

Aldrich cinched his hands a little tighter on Addy's shoulders. They were now starting to cut off the circulation to her limbs and she could feel pins and needles tingling down her arms, "You really are a great story teller, aren't you? I'm sure that this is how you got this gig, in the first place, isn't it? A great piece of ass, a great set of tits, and a fucking story teller to boot, hot damn!"

Addy tried to raise so that she could face him, but Aldrich pushed her back into her chair, his hands "accidentally" caressing the sides of her breasts, as he did so, "Oh, honey, if you'd like to dance before the night is over, we can do that, but not just yet. I have a very nice little room that has all sorts of playthings that you can dance with, much to my own perverse pleasure." Aldrich wasn't even attempting to hide his hideous and grotesque nature at this point. No matter what fine suit he clothed himself in, the monster underneath always seemed to show through.

"No, right now we have some talking of our own to do, and while I'm sure you can weave some beautiful fiction, I need you to know, as if your very life depended on it, as it most assuredly does; tell me a very detailed and accurate narrative, a very thorough dialogue of how you came to be here, this evening. I would love to hear all about your superior, his name, and most importantly the names of his family.

"I have a feeling they are going to become a few obstacles in our near future." Aldrich shot a glance that Addy couldn't see to Steven but she did pick up the subtle nod from Steven's head.

Addy winced and Winston caught the expression as he just smiled and gently wagged his index finger at her, as if to say, "Naughty, naughty!"

This particular situation was grim to begin with, and wasn't looking to clear itself up any quicker. There was only one chance to get herself out of this...

Addy knew that she had to act fast, and so she did the only thing she could think of, pushing her chair back as hard as she could, tipping it back, while reaching into her boot for her Sig. Such a tiny little gun but at this very moment it was her last chance, and maybe, combined with an element of surprise, she might have a chance.

Steven, Aldrich, Winston, and the two other men near the door and the powder room made for some pretty close numbers when stacked with her limited amount of ammunition, but it was her only chance.

If Addy was surprised by her own sudden burst of action, Aldrich was completely taken aback, intend the pun, when he suddenly found himself on his well cushioned ass, with a heavy wooden chair on top of him, and Addy wrestling with her boot.

Years of training and practice now paid off as she lined her sights straight at Winston's head and fired once. The bullet grazed the side of his scalp, tearing away a large chunk of flesh, but leaving a survivable flesh wound. Addy's second round, however, found its mark and entered Winston's skull right above his right nostril. He fell, dead, before anyone had a chance to react.

It was unlikely that anyone in the outside ballroom had heard the shots, as the muffled pops were enough to antagonize Addy's eardrums, but not much more. Guests outside their dining chamber, however, were likely to hear the gunfire that was about to erupt from the H&K compact weapons, as well as the sawed off, pump action shotgun that were produced by the guards at the back.

Addy didn't waste time, though. She jumped up, grabbed the picture off the table, stuffing it into her corset, and ran for the door. When the guards in the back started firing, it would have been difficult under the best of circumstances to hit Addy while she was standing still, much less when she was running away from them. There was a distinct reason these weapons were referred to as personal defense weapons. These were not meant for offense, and close quarter combat was a stretch, at best. Their short barrels and high rate of fire made them a pure "pray and spray" weapon.

Gunfire erupted and shattered glass all around Addy, a gossamer thin flying sliver of it cutting her cheek in the process, just as she reached the door, slamming it closed behind her. Guests stared at her as the disheveled agent gasped for breath, running towards the stairs leading to the exit. What they perceived as a sex slave was breathing heavy, bleeding, and holding a gun. This was not the party these guests had signed up for. Immediately the room erupted into chaos as these well heeled people were now faced with a fight or flight response and since none of them had ever been in much more of a shouting match with a lawyer, they chose flight. What had once been a quiet elegant evening was now chaos as the men and women trampled each other as so much livestock as they buffeted each other in hopes of being the first to escape.

Addy could hear Aldrich behind her, shouting. She didn't even have time to think about where Steven may have gotten off to, but he was the least of her concerns, right now. She just needed to make it to the door. From there she had a chance. Raising her gun in a classic movie pose, she fired one round into the air. This really motivated the patrons and the mass panic created every bit of the human barrier she needed to make her break.

While she wasn't in running shoes, Addy was no stranger to running in all manner of footwear and she had chosen these boots because they were light. She could haul ass long enough to get away and deal with the blisters later on.

Ahead of her was the same stairway she entered from, leading back down to ground level, and as she approached it, two men armed with short barreled AR-15s came running up, spraying bullets at Addy, in her general direction, at the poor patrons, and anyone else who happened to be in the general vicinity. Again, the weapons in the hands of these men showed Addy that they were not trained, but rather hired thugs and had no real inclination to do much more than hose the room in hot lead.

Diners dressed in tuxedos and evening gowns alike fell under the onslaught as Addy dodged through the people. Already the well polished floor was slick with their blood and spilled drinks.

Aldrich screamed, "No you fools! Not our guests, just the girl!" His gesturing only motivated the thugs to really ramp up their firing and soon both men had swapped out their spent magazines and were again firing blatantly and blindly into the crowd.

At the sound of Aldrich's voice, one of the guards spun to look at him, and in the fog of this gunfight he managed to keep firing and one of the bullets clipped Aldrich in the leg, effectively shattering his right knee cap and sending the man to the floor in an ungraceful, cursing heap of blood, expensive tattered clothing and saggy flesh.

Addy raised and aimed her Sig at the misguided guard, fired, and watched as the bullet exited out the back of the man's neck. The dead man's partner, upon seeing him fall, turned to flee back down the stairs when Addy shot him in the back. He, too, dropped without a further movement. When he fell, she picked up his weapon and turned to face Aldrich. With the iron sights pasted right on top of his skull, it was going to be an easy kill, and just as she was about to pull the trigger, two more guards came running from the back of the ballroom. Their sudden appearance forced Addy to adjust her field of fire and what should have been a clean kill forced her to duck back down and the bullets to miss.

Screaming guests blocked Addy's view of the guards, but in a moment of brazen defiance she leapt to the top of one of the tables, kicking the smoldering candle centerpiece aside and fired two controlled bursts at the approaching guards. They, too, fell dead.

Meanwhile Aldrich was screaming, Steven was long since gone, and guests were starting to create a mob mentality and were changing course, directing themselves at Addy. She was their new threat and they wanted her gone. She was the reason their quiet evening of drinks and debauchery and come to a swift and violent end. She needed to get away, quick.

Dropping the rifle with the now spent magazine, she jumped to the floor, and veritably flew down the stairs her feet barely touching the threadbare carpet of the worn steps, managing to exit the building without any more bullets coming her way.

With only three rounds remaining in her pistol, Addy knew that she had been lucky as fuck so far and that she needed to get away, fast. She also knew just how to spend those last few rounds. Luck such as this was tenuous, at best, and rarely held past the first few minutes. Addy wished she was wearing a watch. It felt as if hours had passed, even though her trained instincts told her it couldn't have been more than ten minutes, at best. Adrenaline that had previously been coursing through her veins was now wearing off and she was fast approaching a battle fatigue she hadn't felt since her first days of training at the Federal Law Enforcement Training Center, though at this moment she was glad that she endured the training with little ill effect or throwback. Those long days crawling through the mud and obstacle courses had conditioned her already toned body to something that was akin to a professional athlete.

Without evening knowing where she was heading, she made for the waterline, instinctively knowing that it would get her back to Harborview Drive, and eventually back to her car. Breezes blowing in off the water made it far colder against her sweat stained skin, forcing Addy to control her involuntary muscle spasms with her entire bit of consciousness. When she did make it back to her Grand Monaco, she saw that it had been burglarized.

Burglarized was far too pretty a word for it. The car had been stripped to its very frame, with the pieces scattered throughout the lot, no doubt the work of Madam Lee, or her varied associates. It could have even been one of Steven or Aldrich's men, too. She hadn't made a secret as to the type of car she had driven in, probably the first major tactical and operational mistake that she had made in quite a long time. Apparently there had been a few throwback mistakes from her early training days.

By now, Addy was shaking with pure adrenaline, the walk should have helped her to burn it off, not continue to build it, but now Addy was in a rage; rage that fed off the last bits of energy remaining in her tired muscles. There was nothing in the car that could have tied her to the DEA, or any information that could have linked her to this investigation. There was, however, a significant lack of transportation and she was now forced with a walk back to her place. Addy didn't dare take any form of public transportation lest someone remember a bleeding hooker frequenting the late night drunk run and wouldn't it be her luck that this drunk as a motherfucker asshole would start to run their mouth, and someone who knows someone who heard something about something else would start to put the pieces together and that would be bad for Addy, really bad indeed. She already had a run of bad luck going and it didn't need to get any worse that it already was.

Addy took stock, and what she did have was the picture, and a target to match the picture, possibly, maybe, even a name? Could she hope for that much? Addy was pretty sure that she had a location for this target. She could call her superiors, and have them bring her back in from the cold, both literally and figuratively. It might be the needed remedy in order to get herself out of town. First, though, she had to deal with Madam Lee.

When Madam Lee opened the door, the look of surprise on her face was indeed genuine. She didn't even have time to recover, or to utter a single phrase, as Addy emptied the last three of her rounds into Madam Lee. Her shaking body had held her hand steady enough, just one last time tonight, to level the gun at Madam Lee's face and as Addy pulled the trigger, she felt nothing. No fear, no pleasure, no grim satisfaction.

Addy has just broken the law, well she had broken a lot of laws tonight, but previously it had been justifiable. Everything up until this point had been a defensive reaction, but this, this was so much worse. This was a cut and dried offensive reaction motivated by pure rage and anger, a sense of revenge.

This, yes... This was revenge, pure and simple. Addy had been sold out, and more and more she was starting to think that the desk job in Bismarck was starting to sound good. She wouldn't ever admit it, not to anyone's face, much less in a court of law, but dammit it really did feel good. She wouldn't understand that until later, but it really felt good, if for nothing but a temporary bit of closure.

It was going to be an even longer walk back to her flat.

* * *

Addy made it back to her apartment just as the sun was about to break over the horizon. She hadn't taken a direct route, but a winding and circuitous route, ensuring that she would be able to track and detect anyone who might be following her. She wasn't being followed. A basic surveillance and detection route designed to showcase anyone who might have been following her had given her piece of mind that if anyone did see her, they would be just as quick to dismiss her as a wandering and drunken hooker. It wouldn't have mattered, though. From the moment that Madam Lee had spilled her secret to Aldrich's man, Winston, all of her secrets were up for grabs. She had to get out of here, and fast. Every moment she spent waiting was another moment closer to being caught. Addy didn't know the names of the men that worked with Steven and Aldrich but she knew that they were dangerous men and that they were pissed off, angry men. These could lead to vengeful and desperate men. This was not a scenario that Addy was willing to explore.

She didn't know any of this, outright, but she felt the pressure of the situation and knew she needed to be moving, and it had damn well be soon.

Upon entering her flat she made a quick sweep to ensure that it was empty. She didn't need to be jumped now, or worse have some half ass punk pick now as the time for an even more half assed home invasion or robbery. The place was empty and she felt safe enough so she mentally prioritized and got her ass in gear.

Grabbing her cell phone, a 20 dollar burn phone purchased at random from a gas station about ten minutes after landing her gig in this dive, and this town, from the rickety card table that she used as a desk she immediately dialed a completely random and seemingly innocuous set of numbers and pushed SEND. This activated a modem in her laptop computer that was a high tech version of 90s era dial up modems. The idea behind it was to have something low tech that no one would think to look for. When the modem activated, it sent out a distress signal via encrypted email that announced her need to bail out, and if things worked the way they should, she should be getting a phone call with confirmation in three... two... one...

After the second ring she answered, "This is Helen." Helen was her code word for duress.

"Helen, this is Troy, from Majestic Travel. I see that you have placed a reservation with us, and I also see that you are leaving later this morning. I wanted to confirm your travel arrangements.

"Do you have a pen and paper handy so that I can give you a confirmation number?"

If anyone was listening in, and they probably were, it would seem odd that she was receiving a travel confirmation at 6:30 in the morning, but it was better than nothing. Hopefully she wouldn't be on the line long enough for anyone to even really make sense of any of this, anyway. Hell, she didn't make a whole lot of sense of it, herself, right now.

Addy answered, "Yes, go ahead with that confirmation number, please."

She wrote down the numbers, actually GPS coordinates that would designate her pickup point.

Troy said, "Helen, I have you scheduled for departure at 10:30 this morning, is that correct?" Addy knew it was the best they could do on short notice. She'd have to roll with it.

Addy also knew that was a long way off, but it was better than nothing. She said, "Yes, that is correct. Would you please inform the driver that I am traveling light but will need arrangements to assist with my luggage?" Code for traveling with weapons.

Troy responded, "Sure. Is there anything else I can do for you, at this time?"

Addy said, "No, thank you. I'll see you at 10:30."

She ended the call, and tossed her phone on the floor. With one giant stomp from her boot she smashed the cheap plastic phone into so many plastic shards. Once again, a skilled tech could probably piece the hardware back together but the phone wasn't high tech, and there was no real hardware to assemble. She grabbed her travel bag and blow out kit from where both bags were stashed under the bed of the shabby apartment, and of all the things in the place, they were not in shabby condition. These bags remained stocked, prepped and ready to go at a moment's notice.

Her travel bags were really high tech bug out bags and go bags, prepped to go at a moment's notice, each stocked with enough clothing, gear, and a few weapons, to help her get out of any scrape. Addy was sure that this counted as one hell of a scrape.

Opening the two bags, she laid the contents of the first bag on her meager bed. Broken down components of a highly modified M4 rifle that she could assemble with her eyes closed if she had to, and she had had that opportunity once or twice. Assembling a rifle in total darkness can save a girl's pretty ass. Normally chambered for a NATO 5.56x45mm cartridge, Addy had ordered this particular beauty from a certain builder out of Oklahoma City who ran a crew of veteran special ops soldiers and former Marines. When hearing her request Clint, the owner, eager to cater to the needs of a fellow defender of the Constitution, had promptly turned out a precision rifle with a 10.5 inch barrel that had a fully integrated suppressor, giving the barrel a total length of only 15 inches. Instead of the standard NATO cartridge this particular nail driver was chamber in the ever increasingly popular 300 Blackout cartridge. It looked like someone had stuffed a bullet from an AK-47 into the shell casing of a 5.56mm.

However after only one session of test firing at a private DEA range Addy was quite sure she was in love. Custom furniture on the rifle allowed her to grip and hold it in a stance and style that was all her own. Anyone else holding Addy's rifle would feel off balance and out of sync with the rifle. To Addy, it felt as if she was born with it in her hands. Clint had certainly lived up to his reputation as a master craftsman with this little devil of a rifle. She had even taken to having "Priestess" engraved on the lower receiver as it was most likely going to be dealing out some last rights.

Coupled with the top shelf optics installed on it, Addy was putting half inch groupings at 100 yards on the first try. This was more than accurate for what she needed it for, and right now she needed a friend. Fully assembled with a fresh magazine seated and round chambered she now had half of a fighting chance.

Reloading her Sig she slapped a fresh mag in, chambered a new round and placed it on safe. Now she felt ready to move, should she need to, and that need was fast approaching, she thought.

In the corner sat her beloved and battered guitar case, an equally battered secondhand, but entirely serviceable Fender nestled inside. Addy wasn't much a guitar player, but enough people had passed her on the front stoop, enough people had seen her trying to master the chords of some obscure Nine Inch Nails or Guns 'n Roses that she could safely travel the streets with it and not be questioned, or even noticed. She hoped that the latter was going to be the norm. That her custom rifle, a scant 33 inches, when fully collapsed, fit perfectly in the guitar case was no coincidence. Maybe it was a bit desperado mariachi but it was camouflage and that was another thing she sorely needed right now.

Her second bag contained clothes that were far more adaptable to this getup that she was currently encased in.

Not bothering to unlace the corset, she grabbed a knife from her weapons bag and slit the side of the garment effectively peeling herself out of the outfit. Sweat soaked and covered in others' blood, the garment fell to the floor, leaving her breasts to actually feel normal and allowing her to take more than a shallow breath for the first time in a few hours. Her boots came next and even though the fishnet stockings were hideous, she was going to miss the pinup look they gave her legs. Her gothic skirt was tossed to the corner and the g-string underwear she wore followed.

Naked she grabbed a pair of drawstring olive green hemp cargo pants, and her favorite Echo 8 band T-shirt. A local band, they had opened for another equally local and mostly unknown punk band called Sofa Glue a few years ago, and while she was on a stakeout, watching the kids pass ecstasy pills back and forth, she had managed to enjoy a bit of the show. When the band played an acoustic cover of Sibery's "It Won't Rain All the Time" she knew that she had to have their album. Hell it was the perfect cover and she got to charge some items to the DEA expense accounts. Not a bad night's work. She had even managed to secure an arrest through the local police department narcotics team.

Addy was not a typical DEA agent and she wasn't a typical girly girl either. Instead of traditional ladies' undergarments, she preferred a pair of men's boxer briefs and a tight white strappy tank top. The combination was not near as restrictive and she felt she could easily blend in better.

With the hot water running loud in the bathroom and the steam already creating a fog in the small apartment space, she didn't hear the men walking down the hall, or see the door to her flat creep open as they expertly picked the cheap lock.

As Addy looked at her face in the mirror, placing two small precision stitches in her cheek, she reflected that she hadn't detected anything amiss on her route back because the henchmen that had been dispatched already knew where she lived and had spent the evening waiting outside her place. Madam Lee had made sure that she knew everything about her little double agent and she had promptly fed that information to both sides and so not only did her small task of backup agents know where she was, but so did the bad guys. It was a simple matter of waiting to see who showed up first, and when the bad guys saw men in federal windbreakers approach the building, they simply exited the minivan they had liberated from an unsuspecting soccer mom earlier that day, and without a hesitation, placed their silenced pistols to the heads of the agents. *BOOM.* Two men dispatching four federal agents before they ever had a chance to go for their guns, or their radios.

Now those men crept through the apartment, bathed in early morning sunlight, waiting for their prey to step into the shower.

If they could catch her in the shower, it would make it so much easier, the hot water would even clean up their mess for them.

Addy was letting the hot water and suds from her body wash go to work into her tired and taut muscles. As she leaned her head against the cheap tile of the shower, a movement caught the corner of her eye.

Without making movement to notify her guests that they had been noticed she turned her side profile to the men, making as if to reach for a towel. Addy had no illusions that this view would for a second slow her intruders, but underneath the towel, on the cabinet was her Sig. If she could reach it...

"My dear, that's enough reaching. I'm going to ask you to put your hands up, and step out of the shower." Nope. No such luck.

"Who sent you? Was it Steven? Madam Lee?" Addy knew that the answer was immaterial, but if the conversation kept them occupied long enough, she could possibly reach the counter...

The slug hitting the counter sent a puff of dust up where it hung in the humid air. The smoke wafting from the barrel of the man on her right indicated that he, too, knew she had more than a towel on the counter.

With her hands up, naked to the world and dripping water she stopped moving. The man on her right was clearly in charge, and the man on her left was either a lackey or completely new to this game. Either way with his eyes fixated on her breasts, she knew he wouldn't be much of an issue. Was that... Sonuvabitch, the twisted asshole even managed to have the start of a woody going in his ill fitting suit pants. Yeah, he was new to this.

Addy focused her attention to the man on her right. He was going to be the trouble maker, all right. Without a second to hesitate, she ran forward, closing the distance between herself and the man. With the added length of the silencer on his pistol he wasn't able to bring it up properly and the weight of Addy hitting him forced the barrel down, and when he pulled the trigger, he hit nothing but floor. It had been close, though, as Addy could feel the wind of the slug pass her thigh. The man to her left just continued to stare. Either he didn't know what to do, had forgotten that he had a pistol himself, or was too busy in his own dreams to realize that his life was about to end.

Whatever his final thoughts were, Addy threw an elbow into Right's face, grabbed his pistol and point blank shot Left in the chest. He was dead before the second and third slug hit him. He was certainly dead before he hit the floor.

Focusing her full attention back to Right she couldn't get a clean level shot, not being this close, not with the silencer on the end. Instead she reversed her grip on the pistol and proceeded to smash Right in his face until she heard the crunch of bone breaking, most likely his nose or eye sockets, if she was lucky, all of the above. She continued to smash his face until it was a bloody and broken mess, indistinguishable from that of a human face. Right wasn't moving anymore, but she didn't want to take a chance.

Addy once again grasped the pistol proper, and standing, fired one shot into his head. If we was not dead before, he was now.

Gathering the weapons she placed them on the counter and went through the pockets of the two dead men. She had no hopes of finding and identification but if they had anything, something to give her a clue as to who they were, it might help in her escape.

No dice. In left's pocket she did find a gangster wad of rolled up hundred dollar bills. These she took, and with the cell phone from Right's pocket, she laid them on the counter with the pistols.

Back into the shower she went to clean the new blood off of herself. This time she was able to clean, and for just a small minute, forget the spreading pool of blood on her bathroom's wooden floor. She would have to act fact lest it start to leave a noticeable stain.

Satisfied that she could indeed pass muster, she toweled off, careful to step over the blood and the bodies. Dressed and ready she hefted the bodies and placed them in the tub of the shower, and turned the water on again. There were a few smudges of blood on her pants, but nothing that would attract attention. Washing her hands, and drying the blood with the few towels she gathered the money and the cell phone and placed them in her clothes bag.

Intruders who would be assassins were so fixated on their prey that they failed to notice her rifle in the corner. Removing the guitar, she really did hate to leave it, Addy placed the rifle inside, along with her newly acquired and stripped pistols.

Money, cell phone now with the battery removed, and various other clothing articles went into her other bag. It was time to leave this place. She would have to call in a cleaning team, but there was time for that later. Harvey, the man who handled that group, was a little off, but he was good. They would make it look like no one had ever lived here, or at least not within the last few years.

After one last look around, Addy was satisfied that nothing would immediately be taken for as amiss, at least until someone looked into the shower. She planned on being long gone by then.

Like most Washington cities, Gig Harbor had a coffee shop that was open well before any normal human needed to be ingesting it and Addy had no trouble finding a place where she could check her surroundings and relax, maybe not fully relax, but take a small load off, even if for just a few minutes. She didn't need to look up her coordinates, and risk exposing herself to anyone who might have been searching her online. This particular coffee shop had WiFi and computers for public use, but Addy just booted up the liberated cell phone long enough to pull the most recently dialed numbers and most recent texts. When she had the info, she again pulled the battery and dumped it into the wastebasket with the wrapper from her onion bagel and cream cheese. If anyone had *ping'd* the phone, she would be once again gone before these people showed up.

Addy knew the coordinates given to her were for the train station. Just a scant two mile walk from the coffee shop she now sat in, she could easily make it, get lost in the crowd, and be picked up before anyone else were to notice. Paying for her breakfast, with a small tip, she left the coffee shop. As planned, the walk to the train station was indeed uneventful and when her extract picked her up at 10:30, on the dot, she was grateful to just be getting the hell out of Dodge in one piece. This last night had been a night near misses and she had no desire to go into any more scrapes, gunfights or brawls with anyone. She needed to be out of this state and back with her people so that she could pass along the information. She had a feeling that there was a stopwatch ticking and that it was going to run out of time really damned quick.

Within the hour she was airborne on a private jet that was leased through a dummy corporation that in turn was a shell company of another company that was a subsidiary of another shell company that was owned by a group that was really just a holding firm for yet another company that didn't even exist, except on paper. In truth, and reality, it was owned by the DEA and no matter how many layers separated her, and her parent agency, Addy was glad to be back on her home turf, for however short of amount of time it was to be. Addy had a feeling, and she was soon to be proven right, that she would once again be wheels up and back into the fray on the tail of her new target, and that Bozeman would be a stop in her near future.

That was all the future. Right now, she needed sleep, and that was exactly what she got. Ten minutes after the plane left Gig Harbor, Addy was asleep in the back passenger compartment with a small protective detail watching over her from up front.

Four agents' bodies had been found on the front steps of Addy's place and the loss had been especially tragic to this team as they were a tight unit and when one of their own goes down, they made the perpetrator pay in spades. That they had lost four agents was inconceivable. Yes, blood would be spilled for this tragedy.

Saturday. 18 July 15. 0135 hours.

"Martin, wake your ass up!" I was shouting into my cell phone, and my editor was not all that happy to be talking to me at this hour. Fuck it, that's why he gets paid the money he does, to deal with guys like me at the hours we deem necessary.

"Yeah, what do you need? It's three thirty in the morning, do you know that? Are you even in Boston? It sounds like a hurricane is going on. Did you go straight to Florida?"

I shouted, "No, I'm still in Bozeman. I need you to cancel the Florida trip, or at least reschedule it for me. We've got a whole new project that we are working on, as of right now! You feel me, on this?"

Martin, now more fully awake, probably shaking the sleep and the wine from his head, while he sprawled out in his king sized bed, complete with satin sheets and matching pajamas, replied, "Yeah, I feel you. What's so important that you need to wake me up, though, at this hour, that couldn't wait until tomorrow morning?"

I said, "I need you to dig up all the information you can on this guy, Vincent. I think it's an alias, but see what you can find. I need backgrounds, I need known associates, everything."

I could hear Martin nodding his agreement on the other end of the line. He was scratching notes on to a pad, I could hear the pen moving furiously over the paper, while he took down the information I gave him, as well as making notes for his own personal checklist.

Martin knew a lot of people. He could put a lot of people in touch with a lot of people.

I was just about to end the phone call when I asked, "Martin, one last thing, why in the name of all holy God did you give that crackpot, Vincent, my cell number?

"You know that stuff scares the shit outta me. Why would you give him this number, of all numbers?"

Martin's pause was both genuine and palpable. "I never gave him your number. I didn't know who you were meeting until about ten minutes ago, remember? You didn't tell me a thing. I didn't give that number out. Hell, I don't know if I even have this number."

I stood in the pedestrian walkway of the alley, "Well, if you didn't give him the number, who the hell did?"

That's when all hell broke loose.

Thursday, 2310 hrs

"Aldrich, this is most unusual. Why are we talking on the phone like this? We have usual channels and methods of contacts. This... This is too risky."

Steven sat in a rented apartment that had a long term lease and was in the name of one of his many aliases. It was one of many cutouts that he kept, and used for this very purpose. Sparsely furnished and very low brow it was designed to avoid any attention yet still be serviceable if, or when he should need it. Tonight was one of those nights when he truly needed it.

When his cell phone had chirped it had sent a wave of near paralyzing fear through him. People didn't call him, he called them. That's the way he had worked from day one. Steven was never caught off guard, he was always in control. Well, until tonight that is. This pretend prostitute had gotten to him and had gained access to the uppermost levels of the organization that he had swore himself to protect. Not for a sense of pride, or honor, but because the money was fantastic and now it all teetered on a very fine tipping point because of one fucking miscalculation.

"Steven I don't give a good God damn about your protocols right now. You seemed to have left your ass and your brains in the same bucket, back at the party tonight.

"Do you know that I have a crew of over two hundred men cleaning up the mess you caused? Yes, a mess that YOU caused! All because, you had to get your dick wet and impress a few people? Do you know that there are thirty seven corpses that are being hauled out of a building that isn't supposed to be able to host a gathering such as the size of the one we had tonight?

"Steven it's not even supposed to be able to hold gatherings. It is supposed to be a God damned warehouse that holds party

239

decorations, because that is precisely what it says on the rental agreement, and now all of a sudden there are even more people who are going to be asking questions that they have no business asking!"

For the first time in a long time, Steven was at a loss for words. He did his best to stammer out, "Aldrich, I don't know what happened. I really don't. Madam Lee never mentioned anything like this to me. If I had known…"

Aldrich cut him off, "If you had known that she was an agent for the fucking DEA you wouldn't have brought that sweet honey pot into my party?! *How very fucking considerate of you Steven!*"

Steven continued to stammer, "Aldrich, I swear, I'll fix this. You have my word on it. This will be made right."

Aldrich replied, "Oh, I know it will be made right, because if it isn't made right with the blood of this little wench, this dirty little whore, being spilled out all over the ground, it will be made right with your blood being spilled out. Do you have any questions whatsoever, or do I make myself so clear that it appears to be crystal?"

Steven, who had regained his composure just the slightest bit said, "Yes sir, perfectly clear."

Aldrich had himself regained his composure and said, "I have a small team of men staking out her apartment. Apparently there was some very valuable information imparted to my people by Madam Lee before her untimely demise."

My people? That Aldrich had always said "Our people" when referring to the organization, but now it was "my people," that signified to Steven that he truly was on the outs with this particular crew. It certainly didn't bode well for a man in his position. He would certainly have to bust his ass to ensure that there were no more foul ups, lest he become a foul up, himself.

"Madam Lee is dead?" Steven couldn't believe it. Just less than four short hours ago he had seen her alive and well.

Aldrich replied, "Yes, apparently she met an unfortunate end, and if I had to wager, it would be through the business end of your fleshy girl's holdout piece. I'm guessing it would be the same one that did my poor Winston a nasty turn, as well."

"Fear not, Aldrich, I'll make this right." Steven hoped that the bit of bravado in his voice served to cover the sheer terror that was gripping his mind. Never, in all the years that he had worked directly with Aldrich, had Steven been so in fear of losing control of any particular situation. This was the very reason that he had been "hired on" and had risen to the position that he now found himself at. He was most certainly not "amateur hour" and he certainly wasn't going to be played like a new hire who was. He had to act fast, quickly and rationally. There would be time for reflection, after the air had settled.

Before he clicked the END button on his phone, Aldrich said, "I'm not the one who is afraid, Steven. You are the one who needs to be afraid. Make this right."

Friday, 0720 hrs

Steven had received the information from Aldrich, as promised, as to the location of Addy's flat, though Steven had no idea what her real name was. He immediately gathered a fair amount of kit and prepared himself to end this, hopefully while she was still stone cold asleep and passed out from the previous night's activity. He could slip in, and if the gods were with him, he could certainly think of a number of ways to end her life. None gave him more pleasure though, than the thought of waking her, just so that she was fully awake, and alert, just so that at the very end, she fully comprehended who had, and more importantly why someone had, done this to her. She would be awake just long enough for that look of recognition in her eyes to turn to terror and then that would be it, lights out. Goodnight Gracie. That'll be all she wrote.

As he passed the entrance to the flat, his heart sank. Marked police squad cars, unmarked sedans that could only have belonged to the various fleets of numerous federal agencies, and various other vehicles were lining the street in front of the entrance. Thinking fast he pulled his vehicle off to the side, dug through his kit bag and came out with a very official looking, if very false, set of credentials and a legal pad clipped to a metal clipboard. His pistol was already holstered on his right hip. Slipping the chain over his neck, he donned his favorite mirrored aviator sunglasses and stepped out of the vehicle.

"Excuse me sir, you can't be here. This is a crime scene." As uniformed officers go, there is bored, and then there is bored to tears. This poor officer was apparently stuck in the middle of those two poles. He'd worked crime scenes before, and there was nothing new about this crime scene. What caught him off guard was the amount of federal agents that had come swooping in, without so much as a word of explanation and taken over the scene.

He'd known better than to stand between these agents and their scene as that was the surest way to find yourself working the weapons cage for the local SWAT team, if you were lucky, and if you were totally unlucky, find yourself on the curb with a cardboard box full of your personal desk belongings and a pink slip stuffed inside. That was no way for a career to end, especially when you were looking at a healthy pension, in the near future.

Steven held up his fake badge, "It's OK, son, I'm FBI. What's going on here?"

Officer Koessel stared at the badge, and said, "Sir you aren't aware? It appears that there's been a rather large homicide here. I don't know the specifics but I do know that there are two men upstairs, who are dead, and that there are at least four federal agents, out here on the front steps, who are also dead. Beyond that, sir, I don't know a whole lot else.

"I've heard a bit of conversation, going back and forth, and it sounds like it's a robbery gone bad, that kind of thing. I think that there might have been some drugs involved, but I'm not sure. There are enough alphabet soup jackets around here for you to check in with any one of them and they would probably be able to give you better information than I could."

Steven smiled at the man, "It's OK, son, thank you for your time." He turned to leave the scene, fully prepared to call it in to Aldrich when Officer Koessel called out to him.

"Sir, don't you need to be here? Do you want me to let the other officers know you are here?" He had his duty radio, already in hand. "You need to get upstairs? I could call it up, real quick like." Officer Koessel also knew enough about federal agents to know that a little ass kissing went a long way. He was prepared to get on all fours, if necessary, in order to get away from this god awful duty and if it made it happen, he would gladly do it.

Never removing his sunglasses, Steven came back to the officer. "Son, don't worry about it. I appreciate your help. I was looking for a crime scene and I don't think that this is the one I'm needing, right now. I appreciate your help though, and please know that I'll be sending a note to your supervisors, informing them of just how helpful and courteous you were."

Steven knew how the game was played, as well. He made a show of writing down Officer Koessel's name and badge

243

number. When he had done this, he made a further show of reviewing his meager notes and tipped his head to the officer.

"Thank you, sir! You let me know if you need anything else!" Officer Koessel was truly elated. He couldn't wait to get home and tell his wife his good fortune. He had no idea that he, and his lovely young wife, would be dead in five hours.

Friday, 0900 hrs

"Aldrich, it's Steven. Our girl's in the wind. We need to do some serious recon, find out where she went. I couldn't even gain access to her flat. Apparently someone beat me there and now there are bodies stacked up all over the place."

Aldrich let out a long sigh. "Steven I know about the bodies. I sent the two men to take care of our, excuse me, *your* girl. It sounds as if they weren't my best men."

Steven couldn't see Aldrich rubbing his temples on the other end of the line, but he could feel the tension. He was starting to feel the fear creeping back into his mind. "Aldrich why didn't you tell me you had sent two guys over? I would have not even bothered to show up had I known there was already a bloodbath going on!"

Once again Aldrich let his two sided behavior slip loose, "Fuckin' don't I know it?! If you had gone there...when I asked you to...last fucking night... I wouldn't have had to send men over to watch the place! I wouldn't have had to lose two of my men to a woman who is starting to get under my skin, like some irksome sexually transmitted disease!

"Did anyone see you while you were at the apartment?"

Steven said, "I spoke with one officer, an Officer Koessel, and he assured me that it's pretty much a cut and dried robbery homicide logic that the police are working off of. I don't see him being an issue, whatsoever. Hell, I barely made it five steps

244

from the car, and I know that the feds didn't see me, or even know I was there."

"Uh, huh. This, uh, Officer Koessel... What's his badge number? Do you know what precinct he's with? I'll have a gentleman come over and have a chat with him to make sure he knows his place in the world."

"Aldrich, I told you that I would make this right, and I will. There is no reason to involve this officer. He doesn't know anything, not about me, especially about you. You have my word on that."

"Steven, your word means nothing to me. You have abused my good nature far too many times, and you have used up whatever credit you and I had with each other.

"I'll make sure that there are no problems with this particular officer and that it goes no further."

Steven had a sinking feeling about that.

Aldrich continued, "If you want any chance of redeeming yourself, I would suggest that you get your ass to Bozeman, Montana where this Vincent is about to blow the lid off of everything we have done for the last thirty years, and I'm no detective, but I am guessing your fair haired fake prostitute is on her way to do what she can to save this man from a fate worse than death.

"A fate need I remind you, that will certainly be visited upon you, should you fail me, one more time."

Without waiting for a chance to respond, Aldrich ended the call. Steven, back in his apartment, put down his phone and sat back in the sofa now knowing that he was in really deep. There wasn't going to be any talking his way out of this one. He needed to get to Bozeman right now and see what he could find out. He needed to eliminate this threat before it became his undoing. Things being as they were, were already going to be his undoing and he didn't need anything else fouling that up. He needed to get away clean.

Steven pulled his very expensive luggage out of the closet. He needed to get gone, right now. While he debated over his clothing and wardrobe choices, he dialed a number that he knew by heart, into the keypad of the speaker phone on his desk.

"Emerald Travel, this is Richard, how can I help you?"

"Richard, this is Jeffery Boehm (the very same alias under which this particular flat was rented) and I just had an unexpected meeting pop up, in Bozeman, Montana. I am wondering if you could arrange a flight for me, to get me there by this afternoon, so that I have a chance to prep for the evening meeting. I'll also need a car waiting at the airport.

"There won't be any passengers, other than myself, however I do have a fair amount of luggage, and need to be ready to go when the plane hits the tarmac. Can you make this happen, my friend?"

Richard Sanford, no stranger to the business of Jeffery Boehm, delighted at the sound of his customer's voice. Such requests like this weren't all that uncommon and Richard knew that his client would pay dearly for it, regardless of the price. He even tipped a very generous amount that he insisted stay off the books, so that no one could claim a part of what was rightfully Richard's.

"Mr. Boehm. So lovely to hear from you again! I can indeed accommodate your request. How soon would you like to leave? I have a G5 that is due to return within the hour and I could have it prepped with a fresh crew on a return flight to Bozeman about thirty minutes after that.

"Would that be sufficient to your needs, sir?"

Steven / Boehm checked his wristwatch. "Yes, Richard, that will be perfect! I think you just saved my bacon, and I know that I have one client who will be particularly happy that you were able to accommodate me so quickly."

Richard positively beamed, the joy streaming in his voice, "Sir, it's always a pleasure doing business with you! If you'll be at the usual gate within the hour, I will have the plane ready to go as soon as possible and get you to your meeting on time."

Friday, 1100 hrs

"Good morning, Mr. Boehm. Glad to have you with us again. Will there be anything you need before we land in Bozeman?" The stewardess provided by Emerald Travel was a stunning and buxom young brunette thing that Steven had no doubt would get on all fours and spread 'em for him, if that's what he asked of her. Certainly her low cut uniform blouse and skimpy mini skirt hinted that she could fulfill multiple needs at once, and the tone of her voice suggested that she had indeed done so on many occasions.

While that very thought was temping, he said, "No, thank you. Is my car and my room ready to go?"

Ms. Buxom answered with a demure smile. "Sir, there is a two door Avenger parked in the hanger, as per your request. I understand that the keys will be in the ignition for you.

"I further understand that the card key to your hotel room will be tucked in the visor of the car. Directions to your hotel and the room number should be on the envelope. I know that it's not the usual accommodations that you request but Richard did all that he could to ensure that there were no hiccups in your flight plan."

Steven / Mr. Boehm smiled at her, his best movie star smile. "Well, now, that's a beautiful turn of events. How long until we land?"

Ms. Buxom checked her beautifully sculpted wrist that contained an expensive wristwatch. "We should be on the ground in about thirty five minutes.

"Can I offer you a drink, or anything else...?"

Steven knew exactly what that tone meant and since he was the only passenger on the plane, he didn't hesitate to unzip Ms. Buxom's miniskirt and let it fall to the cabin floor.

Emerald Travel knew that passengers like this did indeed exist, and as such they staffed their airplanes with pilots who were trained to turn a blind eye, and a deaf ear, to the sights and sounds that emanated from the cabin behind the cockpit. Today's pilot made a mental note to get the carpet's shampooed before his next hop as he locked the cockpit door.

Friday, 1300 hrs

Steven stopped at the hotel just long enough to drop his bags, and make sure he looked respectable. He was flight worn and he was tired, but a cup of coffee and a drive through town with the windows down would make it all better.

Steven loved this town. It wasn't his first time here, and he remembered the cool air, the feel of the fresh mountain breeze, not tainted by smog and chemicals, flowing in the open windows. Yon stewardess had even managed to procure an Avenger with a sun roof in it. The summer sun felt good streaming in.

One look to the west, however, told Steven that it wouldn't last. There was a storm brewing and it was going to be a big one. The purple thunder heads looked angry and ready to burst. If you stood still long enough, you could almost feel the electricity building in the air. It was either the storm or the anticipation of the night's events, but there was certainly a charge to the day.

With any luck the storm would hold until the night's business was concluded. Then he could be back in his room, and up with the sun, and out of this fucking town for good. Out of this fucking country, forever.

Today's disguise was that of a photo journalist. It was a play that he had learned from a previous encounter here. While it had worked, up to a point, for the previous owner of that identity, it was magnificent as cover for Steven. All he had to do was jump out of the car, snap a few frames, ask people some random questions, and he was off. No one would be the wiser and no would ever know that he had snapped a frame of his subject in question. No one knew that they had most likely just had a brush encounter with death. Whomever was Steven's mark would know it soon enough, but that was always at his own discretion.

Today, he was a photojournalist and he was studying the graffiti for an expose in a major metropolitan newspaper Sunday section. Is graffiti art? At what point does art become graffiti and vice versa. Who decides?

This way he had the credibility of cruising through back alleys snapping frames, without anyone questioning it. He even had a few great quotes from some excellent folks downtown, which was more the pity because not one of those quotes would ever see the light of day. Not in a Sunday newspaper, anyway.

Or maybe Steven could find a nice place in Goa, India, and publish his book, and let the royalties pile in and even with the substantial money he'd already made, this would make easy street all that much closer. Something to think about...

Now, his main priority was to locate his place of meeting, for tonight. Intel provided by Aldrich suggested it was a restaurant, downtown, and with a few other specific details, it didn't leave a lot of room for imagination as to what particular restaurant was in question. If it was a late night meeting, and Steven thought that it would be, there was only one restaurant that fit that bill. He would stake that one out, first, and then if necessary check out the others.

Friday, 1400 hrs

Agent Diabrava entered the conference room of Bozeman's DEA Field Office. Sleep deprived and tired from her flight, she was now three states, two hours and one cargo flight east of where she had been just last night, hell even this morning. Her go bags were slung on her shoulders and her guitar case still carried her fully assembled Black Label AR-15. He pistol was holstered on her hip, and for the first time in a long time, she wore her badge openly on a chain around her neck. It was about the only thing identifying her as a federal agent because her clothing and luggage suggested a travel worn hippie on spring break.

"Addy, pull up a seat. Ya look like shit, kid." Her supervisor was never one to mince words and right now he was all business. It would have been no stretch of imagination to say that he was pissed at the results of the stakeout, the night previous.

"Sir, I apologize for my attire, I had to beat feet and get out of Dodge. I'll be dress more appropriately for my formal debriefing, tomorrow, I promise."

Lead Agent Arnold Thomas stood up to his full six foot frame, and with his piercing brown eyes and olive skin, he was indeed a formidable person and commanding presence. His regulation brown mustache flirted with the lines of propriety and often looked more akin to a gunslinger's handlebar mustache than on a law abiding federal agent. "Addy, I don't care about your clothing. I care about you. I care about the op. We got some great intel from you last night, but dammit you were playing with fire kid.

"I'm looking at your face, it's all scratched up. You've got a nasty cut and frankly, kid, your hair's all out of place. You gonna be able to make it through another few rounds?"

Addy didn't realize he had slipped that last line in as a joke until she saw the corners of his mouth curve upward into a mischievous smile. "Sir, I'm fully good."

He walked over to where she was seated, and seated himself on the chair next to her, "I know you are. And I know you need some downtime, but the intel you pulled is matching up with some chatter that the boys in our listening posts are also picking up. We need to go back under, tonight, and see if we can flush this cat out. You down for another op?"

Addy had to suppress her smile, "Sir, you know I'm ready for it. Will my partner be joining us?"

Thomas looked wistful, "Addy, I think she's gone to the dark side. Nothing official, yet but it sounds like she might be signing a contract with the PD in Bismarck; sounds like there is a lot of work for her, there, in their undercover and narcotics units. I think they may have made her the offer she couldn't refuse."

Addie exhaled slowly, "Well Sir, I can do this, but it'd be nice to have a crew that I know. I don't have the time to train up an entirely new bunch of kids." A running joke between her and Agent Thomas, as Addy was barely more than twenty five years old, herself. "Are you absolutely sure we can't get Tana back, at least for tonight? We can't get a chopper out there, and have her back me up?"

Lead Agent Thomas looked into Addy's eyes and what he saw wasn't pleading, but a sense of remorse of having to work without the one woman who Addy knew had her back. Pulling a stack of personnel jackets from his briefcase he slid them over to where Addy was sitting.

He said, "I'll see what I can do. In the meantime, you have about four or five guys to pick from. There aren't any ladies available, right now, so you are going to have to use the fellas we have, here." He tapped the table and pointed to the folders, for emphasis.

"These are some promising young guys. One of them, I think his name is Bodhi, he came directly to us from Air Force Special Operations; PJ's I think. His evals are top draw and his performance critiques put him at the top of his class. He was medically retired when he blew out a knee during an insertion jump. He's weapons qualified and when push comes to shove, he knows what his role in this operation. I won't tell you what you need to do, or who you need to pick, but I would highly recommend him. If you choose him, he'll act as your second in command.

"But, everything points to him being a solid team player, and a great tactician. There are a few other fellas here, like I said, and I don't know much about 'em. This is your op, though, and these agents are your chess pieces."

Addy looked respectfully at the folders. Of course these men were all solid and proven leaders. They'd have to be to work undercover, and if they were getting Lead Agent Arnold Thomas's stamp of approval, they certainly weren't going to be wet behind the ears noobs, either.

Addy nodded then spoke. "Sir, you're right, it was selfish of me to start making demands. These guys probably are as best as we are going to get on short notice, but I just would love to bring some of the old crew back, yaknow?"

Thomas nodded, "I know how you feel. Promotions, transfers, retirements, and hell, even death have their own unique ways of changing the chemistry in a group such as ours. I know you'd love to run with the original crew, but like you said, it's short notice. Can you still make it work? If you need me to help you game this out, I'm all over it, but I'd prefer to let you run the op, while I be the God voice in your ear, giving you support assistance, and just generally being a voice of reason."

Addy stood, shook her superior's hand and said, "Sir, we're gonna end this tonight. These fellas and I are going to make sure that we have no worries."

Picking up the stacks of personnel folders she thumbed through them quickly, gleaning the highlights of each person. No, this wasn't bad. Certainly it could have been a lot worse.

"I know you're still gleaning the intel, but anything you can tell me up front, so I can brief the boys?"

Thomas nodded, walked to his briefcase and pulled a single page of typed paper. "The guy who's pic you nabbed, well his name is Vincent. We have a few nods to think that this might be an alias, though we aren't sure. We think he might have been in, or more likely around law enforcement personnel at some point in the past, though we aren't a hundred percent on that. The chatter indicates he's meeting someone downtown, tonight, and as to whom this particular fella is we have no idea. As soon as we get that intel, you'll have all the fresh and raw cuts. Will that suffice?"

Addy stuffed the folders into her bags, shouldered them, grabber her guitar case and snapped off a crisp salute. "Sir, that'll have to do."

Friday, 1615 hrs

"Gentlemen, this is our op. This is our target. We need to end this quickly, and preferably as quietly as possible tonight.

"It's going to be crowded downtown, and I know you're no strangers to working crowds, but I cannot stress this enough that if we lose this guy, there's a good chance he's gone for good. If we nab him, we gain access, a literal doorway into an entirely new syndicate that's just coming to light."

Addy passed the photo of photo of Vincent around the table. Her operatives, her chess pieces as Lead Agent Thomas had said, each took their turn looking the photo over, memorizing all pertinent facial details and any other identifying marks. There weren't many, and these men rarely needed more than a second look.

Addy was in another room of the local office, this one was far more secure than the conference room, though it would have been no easy task to gain access to either room.

Soundproof insulation had been built into the walls to ensure that whatever was said in this room, stayed in this room. Electronic countermeasures were employed so that if someone were lucky enough to get a listening device near this room, or into this room, they would only be picking up white noise static. Cell phones and even the tactical radios employed by the agents were useless in this room. It was truly as secure a room as anyone could make it.

Two secure computer terminals were connected to the database but had no access to the outside world. If intel was needed, they could easily access it but wouldn't have to worry about contacting anyone, or breaking their silence regarding this operation. There was no web browser history that would remember searches to show what agents had been pulling from the database. If there was a downside to this particular method

254

is that the agents were limited to the information already on hand that had been entered into the database, but that was updated on a daily basis. It would have to do.

Addy was in front of the kidney shaped conference table while her three picks were seated and spaced on the other side, facing her. These three men really were quite fantastic picks and to have them so close at hand was without a doubt one of the best blessings of this whole operation, thus far.

* * *

Bodhi had indeed come from Air Force special operations and while he wouldn't speak a word of it, rumor had it he had seen a bit of action in and around Afghanistan. His jacket stated that he had been awarded numerous medals and commendations though most of those had been redacted due to the areas in which he was operating.

He had indeed been medically discharged but thanks to some titanium hardware and some serious rehabilitation he was fully able to perform at a level that still far exceeded even the talented the agents in this field office.

His code name was a reference to the one and only Patrick Swayze and his beautiful surfing movie in which he shared the same name. Bodhi was truly a Zen master when it came to coolness and level headedness under fire. He was one with the chaos that is battle and never shied away from the sound of gunfire and combat.

Reading through his jacket, Addy saw that one of the few things that hadn't been redacted was an operation in Iraq where he was dispatched to aid some Special Forces soldiers who were trapped, out of ammo, and taking heavy casualties. Tasked with a chopper pilot who was equally as solid as Bodhi, they had flown into the heat of battle, bullets coming from all directions, with enough tracers to make it look like the Fourth of July.

Landing in the midst of the chaos the pilot discovered there were more men than they had been aware of and these new calculations would have put them over their max load. While they already were going to be flirting with those numbers, it would have been physically impossible with these new passengers for the chopper to even take off.

Bodhi treated all the men he could with the gear he had on board, as well as in his person kit. These Special Forces boys were no slouches either, and had made great preparations for the inbound PJs, and the chopper flight out.

In the split second that they had to make the decision, Bodhi and the Special Forces ground commander immediately leapt off the bird, allowing the pilot to throttle the overtaxed chopper into the night sky, ensuring the salvation of the men on board.

When the pilot reached the base hospital he immediately relayed the information, directly and in person, to the base commander, who in turn dispatched a rescue chopper to the area where Bodhi and the SF commander were last seen. Fighting was so intense that they only had one chance for a flyover and in that short span of time they were not able to locate the two missing men.

Three days later, severely dehydrated and out of food and ammo, both Bodhi and the SF commander staggered into the base. Both had been severely wounded and were supporting each other in an effort to just stand.

These men would not be defeated and in a sheer display of determination and fortitude they had fought through the enemy lines, according to after action reports, killing as many as nineteen enemy combatants and using old fashioned grit and will power to get themselves back to friendly territory.

The Silver Star that accompanied this citation stated that due in no small part to the actions of these men all of the trapped Special Forces soldiers lived and returned to their families.

Ranger was a lanky red headed agent who directly after high school, went on a mission for his church, spending two years in California and almost getting himself sent home when he disobeyed a direct order to not get himself involved in the matters of a family he was overseeing.

When he and his companion had knocked on the door of a particular household, whether by pure luck or something higher, he and his companion happened to walk into the middle of a domestic assault and though he was strictly forbidden to intervene, his sense of decency would not let him turn a blind eye. From the small amount of details in the file, it sounded as if he had asked his companion to step aside while he walked into the house, and escorted the male counterpart of the battered couple outside the back door for a less than friendly chat about what was, and was not, proper behavior when it came to treating the women in his life.

While not officially condoned by his church as a course of action most appropriate for a missionary, after a stern lecture on personal safety nothing more was said of the matter.

Where things really got hairy was when Ranger had discovered surfing and spent the last month of his mission on the beaches of southern California's coast, working with and meeting the locals of the area. If he happened to have his swim trunks with him, and if they happened to have a nearby surfboard with them, who was he to refuse?

Sadly, the mission leader didn't agree and this time the lecture was a little more stern, and if Ranger hadn't been on the downhill slope, headed home, he would most certainly been more severely reprimanded.

257

After returning home, he immediately enlisted in the Army and soon breezed through basic training, his advanced individual training, and earning a slot in Ranger School and jump school, he earned the tab that earned him his code name.

His experience downrange in the poppy fields of Afghanistan had made his name pop up on the radar of the DEA and when his enlistment was up, the agency scooped him up without a moment's hesitation.

Ranger was young, and still very headstrong, but he was a fine example of a team player, able to take orders, and think on the fly. This behavior model had earned him the high marks from his superiors.

Zach was the last man of the team, but in no way the least member of the team. He had no high school degree and no college degree, but what he lacked in paper, he made up for in his mechanical and intel abilities, as well as his mental fortitude.

One of the strongest agents in computers and technological abilities, he was a coveted team member in the field for being able to relay information on the fly, as well as maintain a team player status. He was capable of juggling mental tasks and calculations that would have college educated doctoral candidates crying from the overload. Often he was the voice in the ears of many agents, utilizing the latest in thermal, night vision and areal technology to make sure that his teammates had the best view and information on any given space or battlefield.

In high school, Zach was often the student in the back of class, cutting up and causing trouble. Teachers and educators alike had threatened to have him put on a strict regimen of prescription narcotics to control his mood. What these educators didn't realize until much later was that he was just bored, with an IQ of 127 he was smarter than most of the educators in the area school system.

On a suggestion from his uncle, a law enforcement official in his home town, Zach had applied with the DEA, and when they realized the potential of this would-be agent they immediately accepted him and went to work molding him into precision agent and putting him to good use and to serious work.

It was impossible to calculate but it was though that in his first year alone, Zach had saved over fifty different agents' lives. His distinct ability to read a situation, and to propose a technological solution, paired beautifully with the groundwork that many agents were used to and soon the overall effectiveness of local operations began to spike.

So confident in his abilities was he that Zach refused to use a call sign or code name. While Bodhi and Ranger refused to give out their Christian names, Zach was the only one to insist that Addy call him by his first name when they had done the initial meet and greet.

* * *

Bodhi was the first to speak. "Ma'am, how are we gonna pick one face out of a crowd of, what, hundreds? Thousands? Do we even know what the venue is, tonight?"

Addy slid another piece of paper across their planning table. "We've got a basic satellite image pulled from our imagery library, and a few agents have already done a quick drive by and drive through of the area. There's nothing that's changed, in terms of structural, since the imagery was obtained. I've outlined a few places that we should be looking at.

"It's going to be pretty tight quarters, like I said, and I don't know what kind of people we are going to be dealing with. The good news is that we've got solid fields of fire, and if we are tight, we can keep them overlapping and we shouldn't have any blind spots."

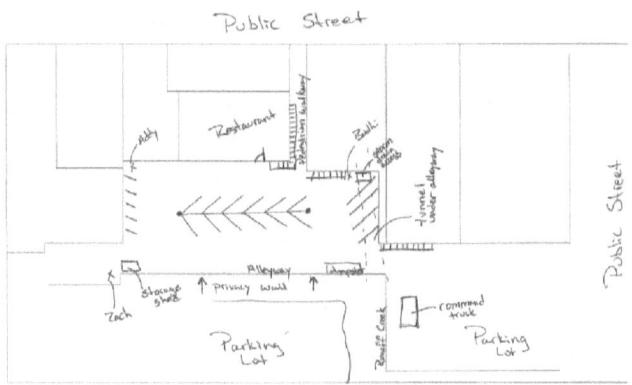

Addy continued, "Gentleman, this target of ours, as you can see from the photograph, he's a pretty outstanding guy. Our intel points to this being a pretty recent photograph. So unless he's had some elective surgery in the last week or so, we should be able to spot him, even if he decides to go the usual routes of hair cutting, and colored contacts.

Ranger looked up, "Ma'am, do we have a position for me? Where am I in all of this?"

Addy, who had anticipated this said, "Ranger, I need you ghosting the scene. I don't want you tied down to a specific spot, because I'd rather have you being able to support any specific spot as needed.

"I've got Bodhi attached to the spot in the corner because I need him to be invisible. Until we get better intel, he's a strictly observe and report support role."

Looking at Bodhi she said, "I need you looking as strung out and as hobo as possible. Take a sidearm, but nothing else. I can't have you sticking out like a sore thumb."

Bodhi nodded his agreement and said, "I like the field of vision between these three positions. We should have cover over almost the entire space in terms of visual confirmation."

Addy continued, "Zach, you're our comms guy. I've been told that you have access to the toys that can help us see all over the place, is that correct?"

Zach nodded his agreement. "Yes, ma'am. Images that you pulled from this area were actually from our very first drone trials and I'm already coordinating with support personnel to have one overhead. It's being fueled as we speak so we should have no less than seven hours on scene before we lose our eye in the sky."

Addy gave him a thumbs up. "Perfect. I don't want to be on station for that long, but a solid insurance policy is what we are going to need, at this point.

"Zach I want you tac'd out as much as possible. Bring whatever gear you have to and use that particular storage shed as a gear dump, if needs be. Gain entry, the world is yours, you know this."

Zach was nodding his agreement and Addy wasn't going to insult him by telling him what to do when he was already gaming the space in his head.

She continued, "Ranger, I need you loaded down as well, and ready to roll at a moment's notice. I'd have you take up a position behind this particular wall, wherever looks to be the most efficient use of your space.

"Plan on being the ammo bitch, if we need it, and have an extra med kit that you can dump with Bodhi, and that way we should be covered."

Once again all three men were nodding their agreement. They didn't need to be giving out the usual praises that new and sometimes ineffective leaders needed as encouragement. Obviously this was a gal who knew what she was doing and that made them a lot more comfortable. For as young as she was, this Addy character had done her homework when it came to leading a team.

Pointing at the corner of the map Addy said, "I'm going to take up position in this corner, here, so as to have the best field of view, because if this cat walks in, I want to be able to see him right off the bat. I'll be in plainclothes for most of it, but I'm going to have my gear stashed in one of the metal barrels that are along the wall, here. I should be able to slip into it and be in position at a moment's notice."

Ranger raised his hand and motioned to the map. "Ma'am, that's a long way around the back of these buildings, especially without being seen. Are you sure you can make it to your post when we need you to be there?"

His question wasn't asked in a demeaning manner, nor did Addy take it as such. She said, "It'll be a stretch, but it's a risk we have to take at this point. If we switch up the order, we may lose the element of surprise that we need. Also, I need to be able to scout the interior of the restaurant. I want to see who's already in play."

Opening up her shoulder bag she produced a few college textbooks and a binder. "If I play this right, I can be the 'lost and lonely school girl waiting on a study buddy' character that if we're lucky, won't get a second look.

"Bodhi, the only electronics I want on you is a comms piece and a burner phone. If you see anything that looks like our guy, send me a quick text and dump the phone. That'll be my cue to get into place and we can be in place for as long as necessary and wait to scoop our guy up. Otherwise you are in listen and receive mode, only." They both knew it would be far easier to dump a communication earpiece and a burner cell phone, than an entire tactical radio rig, if he were to be spotted.

More nods of agreement. This really was a professional crew and Addy was lucky as hell to have them. This felt right. It wasn't perfect because she didn't have the right people with her, but these were the people she had and they were great at what they did. Under these extraordinary circumstances, she couldn't have asked for better than that.

Zach spoke up, "Ma'am, I'm thinking that we need to have at least one or two support people, on sight, just in case things get hairy. I've got an RV that's beat to shit, but has been renovated with the latest gear. We can stuff the people inside and have them on comms with us."

Addy agreed, "Already with you. Lead Agent Arnold Thomas will be our God voice and he'll take up that position in the parking lot just to the east of our location.

"We are going to have tactical control and operations of the space, but he is going to be our ace card to play if shit gets too weird. We won't have to wait on usual channels. He'll be there and if we need him to be, the voice that supersedes all other channels and can call down the thunder if we need it.

Once again, silent nods. "All right gentlemen. Let's take a few hours of personal prep before we kick this thing off. Gather what gear you need, whatever comms and weapons you need. We'll launch from the loading dock as soon as it gets dark.

"Lead Agent Thomas is going to be already on scene to give us the heads up. Bodhi, you are going to get dropped a few blocks away near the alley behind the bowling alley. This should give you sufficient cover to stagger your way over to your perch. Zach you're next to set up surveillance and Ranger you are last to insert. I need you to stash our vehicle, but keep it close for a quick getaway, if we need it."

Ranger nodded, "Ma'am, where are you inserting at?"

Addy pointed to a coffee shop that was a diagonal block from the restaurant, but in direct visual distance. "I'm going to set up there, hang back and see what I can see. I'll make my way over to the restaurant and take position inside.

"Zach I need you to be the one to stash the gear. You good with that?"

Zach said, "Yes, ma'am. That I can do easily."

Addy looked around at her crew, and nodded one last approval. Without a further word they dismissed for prep and departure.

Friday, 1645 hrs

Steven easily found the restaurant where Aldrich had said his mark was to be meeting. His only concern was how Aldrich had come upon this information in the first place.

Situated near the corner intersection of two larger streets in downtown Bozeman, it had two entrances. The Main Street entrance was by far the most used and the most heavily trafficked, but with the back entrance facing a well used parking lot and thru alley it was going to be a crapshoot as to where to look for his target. Thankfully he had a way he could deal with this particular issue, but that wouldn't be until later on.

For the time being he would have to content himself by hanging around the area and watching the comings and goings, and managing to stay under the radar of the locals and the police, who conveniently had a precinct cross corner from the restaurant. That could be a problem, if he wasn't careful about it, though if he did this right, no one would even know he was ever there, in the first place.

A quick walkthrough of the restaurant had informed him that shift change was about to happen as the staff were happily counting out their tips for their shift. This particular restaurant was designed to be quiet and cozy in the daytime, with the close quarters, and a funnel chute to get the drunks fed and back out into the late night hours.

Walking to the bathroom, the men's room was equipped with the basic two stalls and a urinal, no real place to hide, but in the middle of the nightlife, it could prove useful. There could be a nice play to dispose of a body, if necessary. The lighting was poor to begin with and maybe if he needed to, he could disable one of the far lights, giving him the advantage of shadow.

In the lot out back there were various staircases and other building amenities that could offer him concealment and a place to watch the goings on. The public access walkway was a straight shot from the back parking lot to the street, but other than that, unless some fool was going to be scaling a decorative brick wall on the south side of the alley, there was only two ways into this back alley. An east west road allowed one car at a time through, unless an opposing car could wind through the myriad of parked cars. It was a veritable traffic nightmare but would be great for traffic control.

There was a creek that was running north south, with a pretty fair sized tunnel that ran under the street, and where it let out was anyone's guess, but it was something to tuck away in the back of his tactical mind.

Steven's phone buzzed in his pocket.

"This is Steven."

"Steven, this is Aldrich. Have you found the meeting place?"

"Sir, yes I have. I'm working on a plan for entering and exit of the situation, as we speak.

"What can I do for you, sir?"

Aldrich's voice was foul in his ears. "You can turn around and get in the damned truck that has been following you around town for the last two hours, you stupid fuck."

Steven was positively petrified, now. How did anyone know where he was, right now? Turning around he saw an older model SUV coming down the alleyway towards him.

Tinted windows obscured the figures inside but it was easy to see that there were three individuals inside, two in the front, and one in the back seat, sitting in the middle. The two occupants of the front seat looked both serious and dangerous. They had the look of hired muscle and that could mean only one thing.

The backseat door swung open and there sat Aldrich. His leg was casted, and he looked pissed off and uncomfortable. "Steven won't you join me, please?" His face clearly stated that there was no room for argument, or dissent.

Steven climbed into the back and Aldrich straddled a fine wooden cane with a silver head on it. "Aldrich, I wasn't expecting you. If I had known you were coming to town, I would have prepared a better room, or at least gotten some more preparations done."

"Steven, I am beginning to think that your heart is no longer in this. I know we've talked about you leaving our family, but while you remain with this organization, I must insist that you perform your job to the highest expectation. Do you in any way not understand me?"

266

Steven shook his head emphatically, side to side. "No, sir. I completely understand where you are coming from. I have this well in hand, leaving plenty of room for adaptation and maneuvering."

Aldrich placed both of his hands on top of the cane and bowed his head. "Good. That means you will have a place to incorporate the men I brought with. They are not as good as you are, as you *were*, but they are outfitted and ready to end this little problem so that we can move on."

Steven gaped at Aldrich. What in the hell was Aldrich thinking bringing all of this muscle into a situation that would be better served by one person, alone. Maybe adding one more person, for the double coverage, but that was not how Steven worked and Aldrich knew it. All these extra men were just going to get people in trouble, probably get them killed.

"Aldrich I have this under control. If we start altering this plan, it could be disastrous."

"Steven you were doing better when you called me 'sir,' and I do believe that you said it was flexible. So are the men I brought along. Make them work, yes?"

Steven knew that he couldn't argue this point any further. "Yes, sir. I'll ensure that they are properly employed."

Without a further word, Aldrich nodded and waived him back out of the vehicle. Steven exited without any further prompting and the SUV sped away, down the alley.

When it turned the corner, away from the restaurant, Steven found himself still standing in the parking lot, attempting to process what had just transpired. While he was processing a man he had never seen before, clad in black cargo pants, with a slate blue T-shirt and wraparound sunglasses approached him. His salt and pepper hair cut and style, as well as his swagger, and the fact that he openly carried a pistol on his hip implied that he was most likely one of the mercenaries that Aldrich had mentioned. He was certainly an older gentleman but he didn't appear any less competent. In fact, his age seemed to make him that much more dangerous. His rock solid physique fairly pushed the T-shirt to the limits of its seams and the sinewy muscles of his forearms told Steven that this was a man who was used to working with his hands. Probably getting them dirty, too.

"You Steven?" No name, no introduction, nothing to signify a friendly meeting between two business associates.

"Yes, I am," Steven stuck his hand out, expecting at least a formal hand shake, "and you are?"

Sunglasses stared at him, "I'm the man who has been asked to ensure that you finish the job for which you've already been paid, and that which you have been tasked to do."

Steven said, "I haven't received confirmation about payment, not through the usual channels, anyway."

The man with the sunglasses and the gun produced an overstuffed envelope with cash in it. "Yes, you've been paid."

Steven made no motion to count it. This was truly the end of the partnership, he could feel it. "When do you want me to meet your men? How are we going to coordinate this?"

Finally the man with the sunglasses removed them. His piercing hazel eyes bored right through Steven. There was a small scar that ran underneath his left eye that added a milky, cloudy look to the eye. It looked as if a surgeon had gone through great care to work on the eye and damage it as little as possible.

"Let's get one thing straight, fucktard. I'm here to see that you get your job done. You won't be meeting anyone. You've already met me. If you feel the need to write a note in your dear diary about this, you can make a mention that you met a gentleman named Drake, all right?

"My men will be around and they will be watching, but if anything even seems remotely hinky, I will unleash them and they will bring all the evils of hell and damnation upon you, and whoever this assclown Vincent is, do you understand?"

Steven nodded that he did indeed understand. "Will there be anything else?"

Drake grunted. "Yeah, your guy Vincent, he's meeting a writer here, tonight. They are going to be doing some discussing about some things. What those things are, I don't know. I'm not paid to know. Frankly I don't care one way or the other."

Steven asked, "Then how do you know he's meeting a writer?"

If it was possible, Drake looked even more pissed at Steven. "You stupid little shit. We have electronic measures, same as the feds that we use to listen in on phone calls. We have motorized fucking model helicopters that we have attached little itty bitty cameras to that allow me to fly over peoples' houses so that I can see what they are doing, and who they are doing, in the pool.

"I have guys that have been following this asshole, Vincent since he decided to start his own little investigation and then wag his tongue about it. I've been following this piece of shit for two years now."

Steven could see why this was getting personal. "So do we know who the writer is?"

Drake put his sunglasses back on. "Some fiction writer. He scored a hit on the bestseller list and now he thinks that he's all hot shit. He's going to be doing a lecture tomorrow.

"You are to ensure that this Vincent motherfucker doesn't speak a word to him. If he does, you're going to go right to number one on my shit list."

Steven felt that this was a place he didn't want to be, not in any sense of the word. He nodded his agreement. Even though he didn't smoke, Steven was really craving a cigarette right now.

Drake pulled a battered pack of cigarettes from his cargo pocket with the lighter inside the package. Placing a cigarette between his lips he lit it up and took a long drag. Seeing the reaction on Steven's face he tossed the pack to him and muttered, "Fuckin' junkie."

Shamed, Steven caught the pack and walked back to his Avenger. Turning around he said, "Hey, what's the name of this author?"

Drake was already rounding the corner of the building, following the path that Aldrich had taken, "How the fuck should I know? I don't read that pulp novel fiction shit."

Friday, 1830 hrs

Addy hadn't really had a moment to sit still since the night previous, so sudden was the action and the ferocity of the pace now that she had a moment to stand still, she found herself swaying on her feet. She wouldn't do a bit of good to anyone if she couldn't keep her focus, let alone keep her eyes open. Addy needed to rest, she needed food, and she needed a burst of focus. Her fellow agents had shown her to a series of small rooms at the back of the field office, that could easily have been containment cells, but were explained as mini apartments for agents who were on call, or were needed to be in office for any length of time.

Each room was outfitted with a small bed that was barely a cot. There was a small bathroom that housed a tiny shower, and a toilet and sink combo that were the same stainless steel variety used in just about every prison in America.

The room's tiny size didn't leave much room for the Spartan furnishings, much less anything else. Besides the bed, there was a small table at the door, and a small chair that looked like it had been stolen from a church's youth group program. Metal frame with torn padding, it was only slightly more comfortable than sitting on the concrete floor of the room.

This was dangerous territory for agents such as herself. Many an undercover agent had begun to slide down the slippery slope of narcotics usage, themselves. Often times, in a situations such as this, agents would need a pick-me-up and when the over the counter aides, and the cups of coffee, and the energy drinks no longer worked, agents often found themselves staring at an easy answer, albeit an illegal answer.

Addy had no such intentions whatsoever, she was going to man up, to borrow the sexist phrase, and do what needed to be done for the operation so that she and her agents could get these criminals off the street, and she could start to take a well earned and deserved vacation. Hell, she might even take a look at the opportunities her partner had explored in neighboring Bismarck, North Dakota. It might be nice to slow things down a bit...

"Addy, you all right?" Bodhi had walked into the room that Addy was temporarily calling her quarters. It didn't occur to him to knock because he and his mates never did. He forgot that he was working with an entirely new person, and a female to boot. He wasn't old school, or anything that would suggest a hint of misogyny, but he was used to working with a bunch of guys who lived, breathed, ate and stank just like he did. Here was an entirely new leader, with a completely different set of parts and he wanted no part of a sexual harassment lawsuit.

Addy looked around the room. Sitting on her cot she realized just how tired she really was. "Yeah, I'm good Bodhi, c'mon in. What can I do for you?"

Bodhi hunkered down next to the cot. "Listen, Addy, you need to take a few minutes. Hell, take an hour. We aren't going anywhere in the next hour, anyway. If something happens we'll come get ya. In the meantime, take a few, rack out back here and then we'll prep the team gear.

"Addy, no one doubts you, or your abilities. I just talked with Lead Agent Thomas and he filled me in on what you've been up to the last 24 hours. Addy, you need to crash out for a while, or this op is going to burn, one way or the other. We need you fresh and focused."

Addy reached out and took Bodhi's hand. In any other circumstance it could have come across as a sign of intimate friendship, but in reality both Addy and Bodhi knew that it was a silent affirmation that she was giving in to his advice. "Thank you, Bodhi. I'll get some rest."

Bodhi stood up, any doubts about his new leader's abilities or intentions instantly erased, grabbing a small tray he had set next to the door, on the room's meager table. "While you are resting, get some food in you. How long has it been since you ate any real food?"

Addy's blank look was all the answer that Bodhi needed. She said, "Thank you, I'll eat up and rest up."

As Bodhi walked towards the door, he replied, "Don't thank me just yet, you haven't tasted the food."

Addy barely heard him. She was tearing into the plate of meatloaf and French fries, covered in gravy with buttered peas rolling over the industrial ceramic of the plate.

Bodhi didn't say another word. He just closed the door and headed down the hall to the team room.

Friday, 2015 hrs

Bodhi walked into the room to find Addy still asleep and snoring gently against her pillow. He didn't dare shake her, there was a pretty good chance she slept with a gun, and he didn't want to get his head blown off tonight.

That Addy did sleep with a gun was something that wouldn't have surprised Bodhi. She kept it tucked under the pillow, concealed with easy access should she need it. Never before had there been a need, but one never knew.

In that moment she could have been his little sister. In these brief few hours that he had known here, she had shown her courage and she had shown fortitude by rising to the challenge and making herself a truly adaptable warrior. This was most definitely not a woman to be trifled with. Addy was certainly a leader that people could rally behind, and Bodhi was a good enough warrior to let her have this moment.

It didn't matter what he thought, though, it was time. "Addy. 'S time to get up. We need a pre-mission briefing and then it's time to roll out. We pulled together some gear for you, as it looked like you were traveling light. Hopefully we can make it work, yeah?"

Addy rolled up to a sitting position. Her bare feet touched the cold concrete floor, and in that moment she forgot that she had shucked her pants in an attempt to get at least a few hours of comfortable sleep. Her form fitting boxer shorts didn't leave much to the imagination but Bodhi made a good show to turn his back while she redressed.

"Sorry about that. I've been on my own for so long, I forgot what it's like to work with a partner. My old partner works for a local police force, now, and it's been forever and a day since I worked with a fella." Bodhi turned back around and she was running her fingers through her hair, trying to get the stunted strands to look pixie again, though the bed head certainly added to the college girl mystique that she was aiming for.

Stepping into the small bathroom she turned the cold water on and splashed it into her face, and her eyes. Her mascara, what was left of it, had run to raccoon eyes and it needed to be cleaned up. Even her cherry red lip stain had faded to a nice rose pink. That could stay.

"Hey, Bodhi, hand me my go bag, yeah?" He reached in through the door with it in hand. Her eye liner pencil easily touched up the missing parts of the makeup and in under two minutes she was looking like a spunky 21 year old again. Only the hollow stare of the undercover agent would even begin to belie her status as a college student. Though, Addy surmised that if anyone was looking that close, they weren't interested in her mascara.

"All right, pre mission prep. Let's do it. We've got us some bad ass motherfuckers to take down tonight."

Bodhi put his arm around her shoulders, stalling her just a moment, "Listen up little sister. Your courage, your spirit, hell your piss and vinegar are completely admirable, but you need to sit back and listen to the newsflash.

"You've got three good people out there. Ranger, Zach, Lead Agent Arnold Thomas, and you've got me. Don't strategize the entire mission down to the minute. It's going to happen and when it does, the more fluid we are as a team the better off we are going to be and we sand a better chance of getting our asses home tonight."

Bodhi waited for a protest or a word of defiance, and when there was none, he continued with his speech to Addy.

"Prep the guys on what they need to know. Let them be their specific support role and let them do their jobs. Their job is to cover you, so that you can do your job. Your job is to identify our guy. Identify our threats. We can handle the rest."

Addy initially bristled at the thought of having someone tell her what to do but that quickly dissipated when she realized that what Bodhi was telling her was the very key to a successful op on their part. He was speaking from experience.

* * *

Bodhi and Addy walked into the prep room, just off the loading dock, and on the tables were an impressive array of gear and weaponry. Even Addy's custom rifle had been stripped down, cleaned, re-oiled and had a few of the worn pins replaced. It was just as good as when it was delivered from an Oklahoma gun manufacturer.

Addy walked to the group and said, "Gentleman, tonight it's on. We've got our target, and we know that he's the subject of a very intense search from people who are very hell bent on ensuring he doesn't do a whole lot of speaking to anyone else."

Pulling the folded printed picture out of her pocket, she opened it up and laid it on one of the gear tables. "This is our guy. His name is Vincent, same guy we were looking at earlier, though we aren't sure if that is an alias or not.

"But, he's the guy we need to keep alive, and get out of harm's way. Everyone else is secondary, got it? That includes this writer fella that Vincent might be meeting with. I'd like to keep him around for some questions, but he's pretty much the least of the worries. It's the information that Vincent has that we want."

Heads nodded and Lead Agent Thomas stepped up, "Fresh intel from our listening guys. Chatter has been going back and forth for the last twenty four hours like it was a damned party line. Anyone who we think might have something to do with this has had someone check out their email, their phone calls, anything and everything we can think of."

Zach said, "It's not that I'm against this, but how did we pull this off? I figure that in order to get warrants like this, it would be no less than two business days. How did we get a judge to sign off on it so quickly?

"Or... Are we to assume that we are operating in the black on this one?"

Lead Agent Thomas said, "We are totally legit and this is a white op, however the discretionary means to which we are conducting this op are being classified. I asked for, and was given, permission to utilize any and all necessary means to get these cocksuckers before they go back under.

"Our superiors, going all the way back to the top brass in Washington agree with us and while they have asked to be kept in the loop, they are also taking a decidedly 'hands off' approach to this particular matter. They want these people found and therefore they are classifying this as a Tier One op, and we have the utmost flexibility."

Zach nodded, "That's fine with me, sir. All's it does is open a few more doors for tools that we can use."

Lead Agent Thomas agreed. "It does. Your drone should be up and running within the hour, ready to give us some pregame footage of the area."

Bodhi chimed in, "Sir, any fresh intel on our guy? Are we still operating under the assumption it's an alias?"

Thomas continued, "No, this is the meat of the matter, right here, and I wanted to make sure we had everything else off the table, first.

"Our target, his name really is Vincent. Vincent Boyle, from Phoenix, Arizona... Former beat cop... Resigned do to shady practices..."

Thomas was flipping through a stack of printed pages. "Other than the fact that he might have gotten a little too aggressive on a few takedowns, I can't see anything that would suggest he's a bad dude, just maybe a little too aggressive, a little too happy to lay the hurt on, yaknow?"

Ranger said, "Well, if he's a former law enforcement officer, it would explain how he got a lot of the information he's supposedly got. You don't turn that kind of contact and information supply off like a spigot.

"Hell, he could have been off the force for a year before anyone realized he wasn't a LEO anymore."

Lead Agent Thomas had stopped perusing the papers and was focusing on the last page. "Well, he didn't really leave the life behind, yaknow. It says here that he went to work for a private investigation firm, doing tracking and surveillance for them. Basically searching for rich old ladies' sugar daddies who were currently shacked up with a twenty year old secretary."

Again, nods around the bay. This kind of work wasn't unheard of. Law enforcement officers and retired agents often got into this kind of work because it allowed them to keep up the life they knew and it allowed them a bit more flexibility than working for governmental agencies did.

Lead Agent Thomas spoke again, "There's one last bit of intel, though it's pretty raw so we aren't sure about how authentic it is. But the guys are picking up a name, Coleridge...? Maybe Allard? It could be a cover name or maybe things are getting scrambled in the decoding process, but this guy definitely sounds like a big player in the game.

"Whoever is doing the talking about this particular person obviously is not a first time out of the gate rookie. If the info is to be believed, than someone big is on their way out, too."

Addy stopped dead in her tracks, "Aldrich. His name is Aldrich. He's the guy running this show and if he's here, that means that there's another guy named Steven running around, as well.

"Now, this Steven fella he could be an alias, and I think that he is. But Aldrich, I think that's his real name. He's been so far removed from the scenes of these things that I don't think he's had to cover his tracks in quite a while. I'm betting if we do some digging, we've probably already got some dirt on this guy, even if it is however many years old."

Addy gave some very specific details about Aldrich such as his physical description, as well as his MO, and penchant for drugged underage girls. When she mentioned the last part, Ranger spat a fair sized wad of spit onto the loading dock; his disgust and loathing fairly evident on his face.

Lead Agent Thomas Arnold closed his notebook and went back to his office. He had some research to do. Over his shoulder he hollered, "Carry on!"

Addy and her crew didn't need any further encouragement. She went to a folding table that had been stood up and laid out with a variety of gear.

A black tactical MOLLE vest with soft armor plates had been outfitted with an open top magazine pouch that held three fully stocked magazines. Addy's pistol was also accommodated for with another open top pistol magazine pouch that held two spare magazines for her G19, to the left of the rifle magazines. To the right of the rifle magazines, a first aid kit, outfitted for gunshot traumas, had been attached to the vest. Addy did not find that a very comforting thought. To the top of the rifle magazines were two flash bang grenades, meant to stun and disorient an enemy, or to gain entry into an enclosed area.

With a blast and flash upwards of 120 decibels it could have a suspect's eardrums ruptured within two seconds.

Someone had also left a tactical helmet, fitted with night vision goggles, on the table next to the vest.

Ranger came over, "Addy, I don't know what you have for kit with you, but we took the liberty of outfitting you with a vest and helmet. You've got some next gen goggles attached to the helmet, too, as you can see.

"Your vest is pretty standard because I wasn't sure what you'd want, but I figured if we need more than this, we are already in a world of trouble."

Addy looked over the gear. "Zach, keep the helmet with your stash, if I need it, I'll be coming by your position anyway. Let's get the vest and rifle stashed where we talked about and pray it doesn't need to go farther than that, OK?"

Zach didn't like the idea. Splitting gear between positions was a bad idea, and it put Addy in a line of fire if she needed to retrieve it. But, he also didn't think it was going to come to needing half of this, anyway.

Friday, 2130 hrs

Addy found a seat in Roger's Pit Stop, the very restaurant that the intelligence indicated would be the meeting point; the very restaurant that Lead Agent Thomas had told her about. Her flight from Washington to Montana had been a straight shot dead head and she was beat, and the little bit of rest she had received at the field office was already dwindling. Even the coffee that she had consumed, with the hot dinner that Bodhi had provided her, was no longer able to keep her fully alert.

Intelligence had told her that the meeting with her contact was going down tonight, in this very dive. All she had to do was make sure her guy showed up, and when he did, she was supposed to take him into custody, nothing more. Considering her luck, however, as of late when it came to observation missions, she figured that she had really lay low on this one.

Crowds of people swarmed to and fro, and it was going to be difficult to spot her target, so she needed to be on her game. It didn't help that there was a man was sitting across the way, making eyes at her. Addy wasn't even sure how she could be considered attractive at this time, especially since her last shower had been something like fourteen hours, three states and one plane ride ago. Now she looked like every other haggard, red eyed college student in here. Her pixie cut hair was a mess, and her lipstick had been faded to a sad rose pink, not the feisty red she knew they had once been. Her stitched cut had been covered with enough makeup to ensure no one would notice on first glance.

In another situation this fella might have been cute. He was obviously dressed to impress with his clean hair style, his neatly trimmed shadow beard and freshly pressed button down purple dress shirt. He was waiting for someone for sure. Picking at his food he was apparently waiting for quite some time, and not too thrilled about it, either.

Before leaving the loading dock and prep room of the field office Addy had ensured that her phone was loaded up with a bit of music to make sure to keep her awake. Choosing one of her very favorite albums, *The Iron Horse*, by The Sound Defects, she was able to ensure that she had the tunes to keep her feet tapping and her head bobbing.

Also with her built in microphone / headphones she could remain in contact with her team positioned outside. They had fallen into place exactly like they had predicted. She had even gotten a text from Zach, who had taken the liberty to program her phone with certain headings, again to deter the casual observer. He thought it fucking hilarious that he was listed as 'Honey Bear' in her contacts.

But when Addy received a text from Honey Bear stating that the laundry was done and put away, she knew that he was up, in position, and that her gear was in place for her.

Lead Agent Arnold Thomas had indeed parked the renovated RV in the public lot, out back, so that it looked only less slightly out of place than the school bus parked next to it, that was being used as a tour bus by some low budget local band playing a show nearby. His text stating, "Daddy's home." let Addy know that he was in position.

In keeping with his persona, and not risking any hints or tells, Bodhi sent no text, but Ranger did indeed text Addy stating that the "twins were down for the night."

Addy felt very comfortable with the situation and now she waited. All she had to do was play the role of the college student and if anyone noticed anything out of place, or out of scene, they didn't say a word. There were plenty of other college students hanging around, though Addy was the only one who appeared to be doing any studying at this ungodly hour. She was studying all right, just not the O-Chem book in front of her. No, she was studying peoples' faces, looking for a certain one or two in particular. She knew that they'd turn up soon enough, and when they did, all of this would be the perfect prize for a few days hard labor.

CONCLUSIONS

Bodhi

Bodhi sat in the crotch of two intersecting buildings, deep in the shadows, where even the illuminating rays of the arc sodium lights across the alley way could not penetrate. If anyone did notice him, he would be just another vagrant or bum sleeping it off behind the bar scene. He had taken great care in picking out his outfit for the night and it was a little scary to himself just how easily he blended in to the background scene of the downtown nightlife.

A pair of ragged and faded three color woodland camo cargo pants, a ripped grey long sleeve long john shirt underneath a purple T-shirt that had been left in the break room of the field office sporting a badly silkscreened leprechaun flipping the world off and grabbing his crotch was the perfect combination of dime store chic underneath his battered bush jacket. Black sneakers and fingerless wool glove inserts completed the image.

He carried a small backpack that any bum on the street would have, containing a bus map, a metal water bottle with water in it, a few granola bars, and various other items that any homeless person would carry on their person. His pack was another product of something being left in the lost and found of the field office and its perfectly worn image was right in line for what Bodhi needed it to be.

Already, though, he wished he would have added a sleeping bag or bed roll to his prop kit. This concrete pad that he found himself on was already starting to make his ass numb, and while he was sure that he could handle that, as he'd handled worse, he was worried about the possibility of tripping over his own feet should they go numb and he need to haul ass in a hurry. Damp concrete was already starting to seep water into his pants and if the sitting didn't cause his ass cheeks to lose feeling the cold brackish water pooling in the corner certainly would.

He did remember to grab a burner phone from the tech heads and it was concealed deep in the pockets of the dun colored oversized bush jacket that he wore. It was right next to the subcompact 9mm pistol that Lead Agent Arnold Thomas had insisted he take, as well. Bodhi would have been much happier with his standard fair .45 caliber spec ops pistol and his .308 FN assault rifle, but those were options for another op on another day. Tonight he needed to remain invisible so he had reluctantly given in and agreed to the miniature holdout piece that Lead Agent Thomas had passed him. Besides, this was going to be a quick and easy takedown, he didn't need a lot of firepower to lug around, only to have to break it all down, clean it and reload it when the operation was over.

He could see that Zach was in place, and only because he knew where to look for him. This kid was as good as his reputation, and Bodhi not having worked with him before, was instantly impressed with his attention to detail as well as his talent with his electronic devices. This kid certainly had potential and he was certainly going places.

Bodhi knew that high overhead, invisible to the naked eye, and unheard over the din of downtown life, a gray painted drone was watching over them, blending in with the night sky. Zach had insisted that it had both thermal spectrums and infrared spectrums to more easily identify targets and sort out who was who on the field.

"You sure that this going to work?" Bodhi knew that Zach was sure of it, but he still felt the need to express his doubt, however slight it may be. "I don't want you mixing me up with some dumbass bad guys and lasing an IR beam all over my forehead, with a Hellfire to follow."

Zach had chuckled, "Well, first, it's an unarmed drone; strictly recon with this one. Second, it'll be clear enough that I'll be able to tell when you are picking your nose." Bodhi wasn't sure if that last part was a joke, or not, but he was sure that Zach wasn't joking. Either way, he felt comfortable around this guy and judging by the way he quickly and efficiently went about setting up and deploying his gear, as well as manning his post, Bodhi knew he was in good hands.

Zach had even taken a moment to ensure that Addy's gear was stashed and ready to go, unseen by the casual passerby, but easily accessible to Addy. He really was a solid player.

Ranger's head could be seen bobbing up and down behind the wall. This was not a tactical mistake on the part of Ranger, but rather he was probing the lines of vision, seeing where points of vulnerability were coming from and making mental notes and preparations as to where he needed to be to see a certain area.

Yeah, this kid was another solid pick. Bodhi had worked one op with him before, where they were disguised as local law enforcement officers, Bodhi as the senior, Ranger the junior officer. Instantly they had hit it off and Bodhi could see that he hadn't lost any skill, whatsoever, in that timeframe and in fact was still making great strides. This kid also had a great career ahead of him.

Lead Agent Thomas was in the RV, nearby. His job was to relay information to the field office and headquarters, acting as the go-between for the team and the limited reaction team he could put together on short notice. This would leave everyone in contact, but with only one voice being in the ears of the undercover agents, instead of the many.

Bodhi still wished he had brought a sleeping pad, or at least a length of packing foam that he had seen laying on the loading dock of the field office. His ass, already numb, was now starting to get cold and damp. This was going to be a long op.

Zach

After being dropped at the insertion point near the bank, Ranger had sped off quickly, with Addy in the passenger seat, his intent to deliver her to her destination and insertion point. Zach moved the short distance to the storage shed quickly, and quietly. He needed to be there, as soon as possible, because he was the eyes of this operation, and without a start time, or a start time that was known to them, he was going to need to be ready first, without any sort of delay. And he needed to do this while also coordinating the movement of his team.

He found the storage shed was secured with only a simple metal accessory carabiner and opening it, he saw why. Inside were three overflowing barrels of moldy scrap food that was either going to be composted, or simply discarded. Likely they were remnants from the surrounding restaurants. With the stench permeating his nostrils, he wasn't sure he wanted to go in, but this simple affair of pallet boards and a tin roof was to be his staging area. He been in worse, and he could make it work for a few hours; and, truth to be told, who the hell would think to look for a guy in this little rat infested dump. Zach sure hoped that there weren't rats in this place as he really didn't need a dose of rabies shots on top of this.

Before he settled in, he immediately went across the small alley way to the barrels where Addy needed to be, and with a little creative work stashed her gear. Her rifle was cocked, locked and ready to rock. The vest partially covered it, with helmet tucked underneath. She had specifically said to leave the helmet with him, but Zach just couldn't get it out of his head that it would be a tactical mistake. If Addy wanted to raise hell over this, she could do so after the op was over, and then they could hash it out in the hot wash and after action report.

An old chunk of scrap cloth that served as a tarp inside the door to the food shed was placed over the top of the barrel to conceal any evidence that there was something different about this barrel. After a minute of fidgeting, he decided that it was camouflaged enough and went back to his hide.

Using his best fixed blade Gerber knife, he pried one slat off the side of the shed giving him a very open view of the parking lot and alleyway. This would allow him to remain as concealed as possible, but also have line of sight to his people. He would have preferred to construct a better hide sight, but in the time pinch this would have to do nicely.

He placed the drone, fully fueled and battery charged, on top of the tin roof, ready to launch it into the night sky at a moment's notice. All the sensors and indicator lights on the drone were reading green and that was a very promising thing. With green batteries this thing could remain in the air for up to seven hours. It would be just what they needed.

Taking his place inside the shed, Zach closed the door, and looped a small length of wire on the inside to keep it closed and with luck dissuade any passerby from taking a closer look at the shed. Zach powered up his laptop with the screen shaded, and waited for the action to begin. His M4 rifle also was loaded with a fresh magazine and he carried a chest rack loaded with four fully loaded magazines, as well. There was a multi tool tucked into his pants pocket and he had looped a few extra flash bang grenades into the corded loops of his chest rack, just in case he should need them. He would be ready as he could be, for whatever would be needed whenever it would be needed.

He didn't fail to notice a dirty looking guy come limping into the alley, wearing a well used bush jacket to shield himself against the rain that was already misting through downtown, and take up residence in the corner of the buildings across the way. His team was already falling into place. This was a sure sign of success for this crew.

Ranger

Dropping Bodhi in the alleyway behind the bowling alley, he watched him immediately adopt the drunken saunter that was to be his identity tonight. He moved with the professionalism of a dedicated individual and possibly someone who had spent a bit of time under the bottle, as well. His backpack hung limp on his shoulders and he might have even believed the look himself, had he not known any differently.

He then proceeded to drop Zach at his insertion point, and as he drove down the one way street that ran parallel to their alley of question, he slowed to a crawl and with one smooth motion Zach stepped from the car and continued walking as if this was his chosen path the entire time. He moved with the purpose of a college student, carefree and easygoing, and unless anyone was watching they would never have noticed that underneath his loose fitting soft shell jacket he was wearing a fully loaded tactical vest himself. Even with the hot weather it added a layer of concealment necessary for the Zach to work unmolested. Besides if, or when, the time came for his gear to be necessary, he would already be ready for it to rock and roll. All he would have to do is unzip, drop the jacket and he'd be good to go.

Ranger made his last drop for Addy, at the coffee shop and brought the car around to a lot not too far from where he originally dropped Bodhi. He was sure to lock the vehicle up, but also sure to have the keys handy should he need to make a fast getaway. Addy's drop didn't need to by anything super secret as a guy dropping a gal in front of a coffee shop was far less likely to attract attention than anything else.

Even when Addy moved to give Ranger a quick peck on the cheek, with all the intimacy of a friend saying goodbye, Ranger had rolled perfectly with the impromptu maneuver and again, if anyone was watching, they would have seen two friends departing for the night.

Ranger had all the gear necessary for this op stashed in a store bought hiking day pack. A few extra first aid kits as well as some extra ammo he had placed into the pack for ease of access. He also carried all the necessary restraints and cuffs to ensure that they could safely restrain as many as ten people, should that become necessary, though he sincerely hoped that it wouldn't be.

Ranger didn't wear a tactical vest but he did carry an MP5 sub machine gun in the bag that he could deploy at a moment's notice. Only Zach had chosen to wear a helmet this evening because the rest of them depended on a level of normalcy for their cover legends.

When his time came, Ranger hoped that he wouldn't need to get too involved, as he wasn't as heavily armed as both Zach and Addy, but he was for more armed than poor Bodhi. His ass was certainly hanging in the breeze, if it came down to it. That was not a position that Ranger wanted to be in, himself, but certainly would have appreciated a full on stack up outside the door of an Afghani opium dealer, as he'd at least have some more arms and armament with him. A few more mates, too.

For an operation that had been thrown together at the last minute, this was certainly moving as well as could be, and there had tactically been worse operations that he had run, especially when he was with the battalion. Those had been some hairy and crazy times, and those had been in some pretty insane parts of the world. Based on tonight, Ranger assessed that this was going to be a cakewalk.

For now, he would wander back and forth, bobbing his head up over the wall, checking sightlines, making mental notes of the spots he needed to be working if he needed a line of fire for cover of his teammates.

He caught sight of Zach's night vision goggles as the green light flared from the shed, and that gave him hope, because that meant that they already had eyes in the sky and that he would have the cover they needed.

Steven

Steven walked the length of the alleyway before the sun had gone down and he made a mental note of the places that he could hang out, waiting for his prey to show themselves.

Using the photo and intelligence provided to him by Aldrich, he had committed to memory all the details that his quarry would show. He knew that he would be able to identify his target, this fella Vincent in just about any weather, in any light, in any type of clothing. There would be no way in hell that this guy would be able to escape him tonight. He would ensure that he would redeem himself and retire in glory. Then, just maybe, he could walk away clean.

Donned in his best grungy clothing he carried a shoulder bag that he had filled with fake band posters and other handbills that he could plaster in the nearby billboards and corkboards of the various restaurants so as to better cover his identity.

Making a pass through the restaurant, he didn't notice anyone who might stand out, he didn't see his quarry and he certainly didn't see the girl in the Echo 8 band T-shirt sitting in the corner near the window at the front, else this little party would have certainly kicked off a lot sooner. He did manage to catch a glimpse of a guy in a fine button down shirt and vest giving him an eye. To this guy he gave a small wink. It didn't hurt that the gorgeous Nordic blonde, at the soda fountain, thought that the wink was for her. He then walked out the front door to make another quick change of clothes and make another pass through the restaurant. As he passed the doorframe, he pressed a small nail mounted camera into the soft plaster walls of the restaurant, and with its wide angle lens, it gave him ample visual coverage of the front of the restaurant, and also the door. If Vincent came in the front door, he would be able to see it with the live feed that was being slaved to his smart phone screen.

When his guy showed, he would be ready with a suppressed pistol that a certain fella named Fran Moore would have certainly recognized. It was the very pistol that had disappeared from a Nebraska massacre, so many years before, and this pistol had for the last twenty odd years served him faithfully and never once had a crime, a murder, or even the hint of shenanigans been tied to him. If Steven had been privy to the conversation that Vincent was about to have with a certain writer, he would have also made a very strong mental note of the name Drake, the mercenary fella he had just earlier met. Sometimes though, fate intercedes, if even briefly, for those involved, although, in this case, it only prolonged the inevitable.

He even had a few other toys with him, just in case. Various assortments of cords, knives, and duct tapes would allow Steven to adapt to whatever environment and do whatever he needed to be doing in just about any situation. This would prove useful, he felt, as it would allow him to better tactically adjust to any situation he might come up against this evening.

Vincent

Vincent was terrified of the meeting this evening. He certainly wasn't sure what was going to happen and if he was sure of his theory, there were most certainly going to be people watching. He would have to be on his game and he damn sure wasn't going to let his guard down, not tonight.

Walking in his worst rumpled sport coat, purposely chosen because the jacket, and mismatched clothes were sloppy; they certainly wouldn't attract any attention, he maneuvered himself down the back alley, unaware of the persons already in play, watching his every move. He had no idea that he was about to become the central lynch pin to a story that would shatter quite a few cover stories and bring light to quite a few folks that certainly didn't want light being shined upon them, nor their legends shattered. At this time, it was completely out of anyone's control.

His leather satchel was clutched tightly to his chest, even though he had a shoulder strap securing it to his body. Contained within were the very documents that he was hoping would bring down a certain killer, though he had no idea it was Steven, and he had no idea that Steven was already watching him, all too aware of whom he was, and that he was ready to pounce the minute he had an opportunity.

That's why when Vincent walked past the man in the obnoxious outfit with the mirrored sunglasses, he didn't give the man a second thought, though later he would certainly give said man more than just a few moments of thought, even a few well chosen words, before it all came apart. Of course, had he known how it was all going to come apart, he sure wouldn't have opened his mouth in the first place.

Bodhi

Bodhi didn't even have to do a second look, or a second guess. As soon as Vincent came sauntering into the back entrance Bodhi knew that he was the target he was searching for. He had already programmed a message into the phone, addressed to Addy.

The minute Vincent came into view he selected the message to Addy and hit SEND. In less than two seconds since the message stating TARGET IN POCKET – REAR ENTRANCE popped up on Addy's phone, Bodhi had dumped the burner phone into the storm drain next to him. There would be no back tracing a signal, no triangulation of anything, and if Addy, or anyone else had tried to reply it would have been lost to a black hole of cyberspace.

Did he hear Ranger speaking hushed words into his tactical radio? Was it his imagination? If Ranger was speaking into the radio it was on the alternate frequency that he was using to communicate with Zach and Lead Agent Thomas. Either way, Bodhi knew that his crew was already in motion. He couldn't be more proud of his team than at this very moment.

Ranger

Ranger, as well as Bodhi, saw their target move into pocket and immediately he saw that Bodhi made a few quick motions, and then dump his cell phone into the storm drain. He thought that he could hear it clank down the metal pipe, even the faint splash as the phone hit the creek.

He spoke a few hushed words into his tactical radio and received a double dash back from Zach. Zach wouldn't break silence unless he had to. He knew what to do, what his specific role was, and just how important it was. Lead Agent Thomas, who was in Zach's state of the art RV to the east of Ranger's position also responded with a double dash. This kept the unnecessary chatter off the radio and out of the ears of the people running the play. He was a good enough agent to let his crew run the operation. If they needed him, he would be there, but not unless. Until then he coordinated on yet another channel with the folks back at the field office, and those that were listening in, from Washington, D.C.

So intent was he on the monitors that he didn't notice the man walking around the RV. If he had noticed, he might have stopped to wonder why the man who had already made two previous passes around his vehicle was now on his way for a third pass around when he stopped to press a small metallic object, attached to a magnet, under the main body of the RV. He most certainly wouldn't have heard it click home, or felt the added few pounds of high powered plastic explosive, set on a digital timer that was slowly counting down to ZERO.

When it reached ZERO, it was going to cause a very big bang.

Addy

Addy looked at her phone, retrieved the message and just as quickly hit DELETE. It was almost as if it was never there. She looked up just as a man in rumpled suit carrying a leather satchel walked in the back door. That was her cue. Vincent walked in and sat down next to the man in the fine button down purple shirt. *Holy shit, was that their guy?* She could have had bagged the guy right from the start and this could have been over just as easy.

She gathered up her belongings, and if anyone noticed her they would have seen a girl dumped by either a would-be date or a would-be study buddy, who was finally packing it in for the night.

Addy exited the front door, and turned left, heading down the street to the next block. At the intersection she turned left again, this time breaking into a small jog. Intense moments like this had a way of getting her worked up and she knew that a quick jog, of even fifty yards, would help to bleed that excess energy off. She needed to get to her post, and quickly. If Vincent was here, then Steven couldn't be far behind and she needed to take them both. Steven, alive if possible, dead would be just as good. Either way she needed to have both men in pocket as soon as was humanly possible.

When she reached the halfway point of the block she cut through the drive thru of the bank that occupied the real estate on this side of the street. At the end of the drive thru she again turned left, effectively making a small circle, around to the rear of the restaurant. Metal trash barrels, nothing more than converted fifty gallon drums, have been stacked neatly against the back wall of the bank, and according to plan, she found her gear tucked into the last one, closest to the corner where the bank met the restaurant.

She quickly donned her tactical vest, cinching it tight. Her crew had indeed picked a solid rig for her as it was sitting perfectly against her body, nothing pinching, nothing hanging over. It was as tight as she could make it. From her shoulder bag she drew out her pistol and clipped the Headlock Custom Holster to her pants, the Glock riding a bit low, so that it wouldn't get caught in the vest, should she need to draw.

Zach who had mounted a radio pouch to the rear of the vest and had it tuned to the proper frequencies the team would be using had also disregarded her instructions and placed the helmet in the barrel, as well. Upon turning the radio on, and plugging the earpiece into her ear, she immediately hit the remote transmit kit three times, the triple dash was her designator that she was the final piece to move into position.

She chose not to put the helmet on right now, waiting until she needed it most. It would have been a hindrance, right now, due to the fact that the alley and parking lot were still lit fairly well and it would have been very out of scene for a bug eyed girl standing in the shadows. Not that she would be able to explain the vest and gun any easier. She was going to have a chat with Zach for not following her orders to the letter, but that would come later.

Half crouched and hunched into the dark corner, she wished for a good cigarette to ease these nerves, but that would have given her position away just as easily as if she had been holding a neon sign. For now, she waited. Addy had a feeling it wouldn't take much longer for things to kick off and she was going to be ready, nerves and all.

Movement across the parking lot didn't escape her vision as she watched a very scruffy looking bum in a beat up bush jacket roll over and cough out his phlegm onto the pavement. He shuffled to the pedestrian walkway between their restaurant and the bar, next door. If anyone had noticed they would have seen a drunk looking to score his next shot, not a highly trained agent moving into the next spot of his operation.

Steven

Steven moved into position in the back door the minute he saw Vincent enter the restaurant. He was bound and determined to end this man's life tonight, come whatever may. There was no way that this prick was going to escape his reach. He had just the means to end said target's life with him, in his own shoulder bag. A small syringe containing a neurotoxin that a certain husband of a certain murderous gas station wife would have recognized contained enough of the neurotoxin to take down a small horse, which was more than enough for what he needed it for. It wouldn't be an instant death, but his target sure wouldn't make it past the next few hours.

If Vincent was sitting, Steven's plan was to walk by, jab him in the back of the neck, and he'd be walking down the hall, back out the door, before anyone else was the wiser. A small distraction might even help with this foray. He could play it by ear, as was the old saying. He was flexible like that.

As Steven walked into the back entrance of the restaurant, he noticed the place was now full of rowdy young twenty something's and older teens, all who were quite full of piss and hormones. There were quite a few more people in here than were on the previous passes through; Steven though that this was going to be all the cover that he needed. He wasn't even sure that he was going to be able to walk through the joint without getting jostled.

Steven checked to ensure that his shoulder bag was secured against his body as the contents were far too valuable to lose on a night like tonight. There was too much at stake and Steven knew that he wasn't going to get a chance as easy as this, not for a long time, probably ever again.

Approaching his target Vincent, it didn't fail Steven how creepy he looked. How unhealthy and sickly he appeared and as Steven approached the cashier's counter, paid for a soda and went to fill it at the self serve machine, he noticed that the man smelled vaguely of booze. It was probably a cheap variety normally found wrapped in a paper sack, cast empty and discarded into the nearest alleyway.

As he made his way back to the rear entrance Steven made a motion of stopping suddenly, causing the man Vincent was speaking with to spill his drink on himself, and to curse loudly.

Without breaking stride, and with Vincent consumed in the mess of the man's slacks, Steven expertly and proficiently stabbed the very tiny needle into Vincent's neck. Vincent never even felt the poke, so wrapped up in his story and so distracted with the spill.

Already aware that he was under surveillance, he was anxious to be done with this job. He wasn't sure by whom, but he had a pretty good idea. That little minx from the night previous was most likely behind the RV that was no so expertly disguised in the parking lot. A quick attachment of plastic explosive would certainly take care of that problem, and if it wasn't the people he thought it was... Well, a little collateral damage was part of the profession he practiced. It was a sad ugly truth, but if it helped to cover his tracks, that was just part of the game. Those fireworks should be going off in just a few minutes. Even if they were discovered, there would be no way for anyone to get themselves clear of anything that might not be potentially hazardous, and therefore cause a significant amount of damage to the immediate area.

Steven exited the restaurant and immediately tossed the soda. The needle that had been full of the neurotoxin he recapped and placed in his shoulder bag. With his task done he pulled a package of cigarettes from the bag, and lit one up. That cigarette was very likely his undoing, and he didn't even like to smoke.

Addy

Addy was scanning the back alley when she saw a man exit the restaurant to light a cigarette. Normally she wouldn't have given him a second thought but she saw that the light from the pack of matches reflected in his mirrored sunglasses.

Mirrored aviator sunglasses? At night? Who did Addy know that favored mirrored sunglasses at night? She watched for just a moment to make sure that she was seeing what she thought she was seeing. There was no need to raise an alarm until she was absolutely sure.

Stepping out in the arc sodium light, proper, she saw a man's face, handsome under other conditions, mirrored sunglasses and while his clothes were obnoxious, they were finely tailored. Sure as shit, it had to be Steven. That was her assassin from the night previous. There was no way she would forget his face already. Addy supposed that if a thousand years passed she would still remember every single detail about this man.

"All agents, this is lead. We have a positive ID on one our suspects." She went on to detail his clothing, his stature, physical description, right down to those mirrored aviator sunglasses that he seemed to have a penchant for.

"This is Thomas; I have a visual on the suspect. All agents hold position until we get a visual on our target. If he has the target detained we need him alive so we can get the information on our target." Normally Lead Agent Thomas wouldn't take over like this, but he needed his team to be aware of the risks. He knew that they knew, but this was not the run of the mill takedown operation.

Bodhi

Bodhi heard the warning over his comm piece in his ear, and made his way back to the alley from which he had just come. Surveillance from the front had revealed nothing and he had made a near complete loop of the area without seeing anything of sorts. If he had looked a bit closer he might have noticed something out of sorts...

Now he headed back, and as he did so managed to take note of a small stairway, hidden under a metal and plexi-glass awning that led to the basement, under their target restaurant. He decided to hide here, for just a moment, and see if he could catch any stragglers coming down the way.

There didn't appear to be anything, or anyone, unusual in this area and his job was to make sure that no one would be able to squirt out the back and escape their net that had fallen so beautifully into place.

Steven

Steven noticed movement to his right. It wasn't Addy that he noticed, but rather it was a movement that was out of character, in a place where there shouldn't be movement. Also, there seemed to be a hint of greenish glow coming from a shed across the way. There were a lot of bums that hung out in this part of town and he was pretty sure that it was a transient with a new MP3 player that he'd probably acquired through one of the local pawn shops. It could even be a lady of the night and her john looking for a quick fix, who knew?

When he looked again, there was no glow, that he could see, and whatever had "moved" was now either not moving, or was gone, or had never been there to begin with. Steven knew that there was enough junk and garbage back here that it could have been any manner of things, including a stray animal looking for a quick meal.

There was just one or two more things left to do and then he could tidy up and be out of here, for good. That's when the rain started. Thunder and lightning had been threatening moisture all evening, even earlier in the afternoon when Steven had been cruising around the city. Now, however, Mother Nature made good on her threat.

Steven stood to the side of the restaurant's rear entrance, and did his best to shield his cigarette from the rain that had started to come down steadily and with more intensity. If he had been fully paying attention he would have seen the writer that was meeting with Vincent exit out the back door, take up refuge under one of the many metal stairways in the back parking lot area and place a very hurried call. He should have heard the tone of the man's voice, at least, and the very frenzied nature of it, but the rain was whistling down and causing what sounded like a miniature hurricane in the alley.

Instead he finished what he could from his cigarette and pitched the soaking butt into the alley, returning to the restaurant and seeking out his guy. A quick check to his smart phone showed Steven that Vincent was still sitting at the same table, though he was now alone.

Vincent had just stood and was just walking down the hallway when he saw Steven moving towards him. Vincent didn't know who Steven was, not by name, but he knew what Steven was all about and in his poisoned state he couldn't even think to utter a scream to alert anyone to the danger he now faced. It was as if his mind was racing, trying to fire off all manner of warning signals, but the lines of communication between his brain and his body had been cut.

When Vincent reached out to fend off Steven, he realized that his strength was gone and that Steven was far too powerful. So when Steven grabbed him by his coat and drug him into the men's room, to the back stall that was normally reserved for handicapped access, he didn't have the energy to fight him off. Vincent knew what was coming but he was powerless to stop the man, even when he saw him remove a folding knife that would have been at home in any old timer's denim pocket for farm work, or at the fishing hole, or even

303

around town.   The folding lock blade gleamed under the bathroom light and its menacing razor edge was honed to a point near too sharp to even make out.

It was too bad for Vincent, but he was still very much alive when Steven began to slice at his neck, slowly and deliberately decapitating his head in very long and jagged strokes. Sounds of gurgling water that Steven had heard before, when another person he had dispatched had choked on his own blood, emanated from Vincent's defiled throat and neck.

When he was just about done, Steven sat the corpse on the toilet seat, propping the body in the corner, and with a smooth and swift motion he made a slit at Vincent's scalp, just nearly scalping him clean. With his knife he drove the blade through the scalp, into the wall, pinning the head to the wall. If anyone would notice a defiled corpse in here, it wouldn't be for a while. Even physics were in Steven's favor as the drain for the floor was placed in the far corner, the floor gently sloping away from the door, so that no blood pooled out of the stall.

It wouldn't have mattered anyway. Soon, Vincent's corpse was about to be the last thing on everyone's mind.

One Final Showdown

Even if Lead Agent Arnold Thomas had seen the plastic explosive attached to the RV, there was no way he would have been able to get clear in time. Either way he had about one half second to wonder what that rumble was before the explosion completely consumed the RV and he was incinerated by the blast.

Addy was watching, and waiting for Steven to come back out of the restaurant when the explosion launched the metal body of the RV some fifteen feet into the air, flame and smoke billowing from the column of fire that erupted where their base of communications had been. Their only link to the outside world, outside of their operation, was now gone. They were truly on their own.

Her screams of distress, protest, agony and hatred peeled through the alleyway. She immediately broke position from her spot, and creating her first major tactical mistake of the night, moved towards the explosion, hoping against hope that she could save Lead Agent Thomas. She knew that there was no chance, but she moved, anyway. Addy had barely cleared the barrels when a movement in front of her, instantly reminding her of swarming bees, caught her direct attention.

In one of the nearby dance halls that was currently being renovated in an attempt to modernize and revitalize the downtown night scene, a group of highly trained, highly armed men sat in wait. They had been waiting for a signal from Drake, their commander. While there had been no audible communication, this was the signal they were sure they had been waiting for. Drake could have explained that this wasn't the signal and he had far too much effort involved in this for something so totally horrendous as a gigantic fireball to alert every law enforcement officer in a three county radius.

Without a further thought or mental debate they broke out into the raining night and the scenes of carnage greeted them. These men, men who would not bow under the yoke of an unrelenting government and regime that sought to only further the interests of the inner circle, who had trained for weeks and months for a moment such as this; burst from the door and began to engage their targets.

* * *

Bodhi was waiting in the stairwell when he heard the explosion peel through the downtown. His instincts propelled him towards the sound of the carnage and even if he had wanted to, he could not hang back and wait for the scene to play itself out. He needed to be there where the metal was sure to meet the flesh. So many years of training automatically propelled him towards the danger, and the carnage that was sure to be waiting.

The screams of Addy could be heard throughout the back alley. Even the patrons of the restaurant were paralyzed with fear at the sound of the explosion, the violent shake of the buildings as the shockwave rolled through the downtown urban canyons. Memories of the explosion from the 2009 incident echoed in their brains and few wanted to wander around in the decimated aftermath that they had witness just a few years ago.

Bodhi rocketed himself towards the men who were most certainly not on their team, who were engaging "targets" as they saw fit, generally causing as much chaos and carnage as they could muster. Innocent men and women, whose only crime was being out this late, were being mowed down in the gunfire of hired thugs. These wannabe patriots turned thugs were ending human life without regards to cause or color of the victims they drew down on.

As if on instinct Bodhi began to engage these targets and drop as many as he could with his small pistol. With the way they were moving and the limited ammo capacity of his holdout piece he was only able to drop three of the targets before the magazine was empty. These men weren't even fully dead, either. Not that it mattered to Bodhi, he was only concerned about ensuring that his people had a fair chance. What had been a flexible and finely tuned operation was now a chaotic mess and it would be a true test to see whether his crew would be able to hold together. Bodhi had faith that they would, and sometimes that was all you needed.

Casting aside his spent pistol he grabbed a dropped rifle from the nearest fallen target. This man, a fat slovenly wannabe commando never would have stood a chance. His overweight stature and his ridiculous amount of kit ensured only that he would have been the last to cross the finish line. The black jeans and blue sweatshirt cut into short sleeves fairly strained against their own seams as the behemoth attempted to move with any amount of dexterity, or grace. He was an easy shot and when he raised his AK-47, Bodhi saw that it was not even a real AK but rather a cheap Chinese knockoff, Bodhi was able to drop him with one shot to the head. The obese man's comical ponytail that was made up of graying and matted streaks of hair, greasy and unkempt, flopped to the side as his head made contact with the pavement.

Bodhi hefted the weapon and began to systematically pick his targets. He had to be careful about his shots because in the initial chaos there were so many people running about he was afraid he'd hit an innocent civilian and this was something he couldn't live with.

There were hoards of these armed men and Bodhi had no idea where they had all come from. Where they were still coming from. He only knew that he needed to be dropping everyone of them that presented as an immediate threat before they became overrun. Hell, they were already overrun and the odds were starting to look like a little operation in Mogadishu two decades previous. Bodhi kept engaging and dropping targets until his magazine ran dry, then he grabbed another rifle and went back to work.

* * *

Zach was in place when he heard the explosion, and felt the heat from the intense fireball, that used to be his RV, containing

307

their supervisor. He didn't have time to look at his computer monitor again, there was already a shitload of bad guys swarming the alley way and his team was in danger of being exterminated. Bodhi had thought overrun, but Zach had no such thoughts. He smelled death.

Whoever these dudes were, they were shooting blindly, at anything that was moving. They were dropping people for the sake of killing them and they had zero remorse about it.

How had his drone missed this? All the signals had been green and there was no sign of malfunction. He hadn't even seen anyone scouting around the RV and that was most disturbing of all. He should have seen, and noticed the difference of, someone skulking around their mobile base of operations. It was bad form on his part and he was sure that he was going to catch hell for it, later on.

Not even bothering to gather his computer or his tech gear Zach grabbed for his rifle, unzipped and doffed his jacket, and ensured that the chest rack was still seated properly. It was. Of course it was. It was a specially made SOE Gear chest rack and it was made in the motherfuckin' U.S.A. It was not cheap shit and now when Zach needed his gear to be top notch, it was.

Still with his goggles in place he kicked the door of the shed open and with the moonlight shining through the rain he had almost perfect vision paired with his night vision goggles. Lining up targets was easy. He knew what his team looked like. He knew what civilians looked like. These men who had all sorts of weapons and kit that were indiscriminately shooting people, they were most certainly not on his team, nor were they any of the good guys.

Zach lined up the targets in his red dot sight mounted on top of his rifle and squeezed the trigger. His suppressed rifle let out barely a sound, covered by the din of the crowd and the chaos.

Patrons from Roger's Pit Stop, as well as surrounding bars and dance clubs came spilling out in all directions, creating a veritable feeding ground for the tangos he now engaged. This was going to be a crazy mess to sort through and it showed no signs of letting up.

Zach had just enough time to wonder why the police had not yet shown up, but realizing the nature of this area, they probably couldn't even get to where the action was. Until they could, it was up to his team to keep this band of armed misfit psychotics at bay.

Zach had switched his tactical radio to VOX mode and while he knew that Bodhi couldn't respond, he lived up to his duty and began to inform his team of the battle spaces and what they could do about it. Without shouting he called out the threats most dire of the immediate area. His calm voice relayed the information to his teammates and they in turn used that as the most potent weapon of all to contain the threat, and keep the wolves at bay. If they could keep up this momentum, and if the ammunition lasted, they would make it out of this mess.

Bodies were piling up amid piles of spent shell casings and already used magazines. Zach had already reloaded twice, and with the third magazine in place, it left him with only two more magazines for his rifle. He had his pistol, but if it was going to come to that, it was already a shitty day in paradise.

"All right kids, it's getting a little sporty back here. We need to wrap this up, and quick. I have no visual on our subject, nor a visual on our target. I say again, lost visuals on both men.

"However we have a serious and most immediate threat coming from the unknown number of heavily armed assholes pouring out of that dance hall. We need to cut off the flow of these people, and then regain our visuals." Zach's continuous feedback was amplifying his team.

Ranger's voice cut through the noise, "Zach the RV is gone. I don't know if anyone was inside, but if they were, they don't have a prayer.

"That inferno is helping us though, because the heat is so intense no one is getting though that particular cordon. We need to focus on containing these guys before they get loose into the general public. We also have to figure out a way to keep the rest of the public out of here."

Addy came over comms then, "Push one of the cars against the pedestrian walk way. That should keep people from entering into the kill zone and if any of these assholes tries to jump one of the vehicles, we'll at least see 'em going for it. That leaves one avenue of escape, Zach, and that's right past you. You've gotta lock that corner down and keep the information coming. Clear?"

Zach watched as Ranger, in an incredible burst of strength, with a rage of pure adrenaline, smash out the driver's side window of a VW bug, jam the transmission into neutral, and mash the vehicle into the entrance of the pedestrian walkway. If anyone was going to come there, they were going to have to vehicle hop in order to do it.

"Addy I copy you. I have a visual on Ranger and Bodhi, they have Bodhi's corner locked down and they are engaging targets.

"I've got a heavy volume of fire coming down my way, and I'm about spent on ammo. We need to end this quick."

Addy responded, "I copy. Hold that corner at all costs."

"Roger that, girl."

* * *

"Bodhi we need to close this up. How are you holding for ammo?" Ranger and Bodhi were back to back in corner where Bodhi had started the evening. As he would empty a weapon,

Bodhi would grab another from the pile of corpses that were stacking up around them.

"Ranger we're already in a world of trouble. My holdout piece is gone and I'm down to scavenging. We need to get a resupply real quick if this goes on much longer. And if Zach is about spent, we're going to need to cover his ass pretty quickly." He picked his shots carefully and continued to double tap the enemy targets as they presented themselves.

Ranger nodded. "I'll cover you. Gather all the weapons you can. When you have a stash, I'll take the pack full of ammo and get Zach topped up. I don't know how many more guys we're facing but this is starting to look like a bad movie, here."

Bodhi agreed. "Give me two minutes." He moved out from under the metal stairway they were using as cover and began to grab various rifles and bits of kit that were laying on the ground.

He was just about to head back to his position when a bullet ricocheted off the concrete in front of him, catching him in the shin, causing him to stutter. It was going to be a close call, as it was, but now he was trapped in the line of fire. It took one enterprising thug with a long burst and three shots hit Bodhi directly in the abdomen.

Ranger saw it happen but was powerless to do anything about it. He was already pinned down by a heavy volume of incoming weapons fire. Keying his radio he said, "Bodhi's down. He took rounds to the abdomen and he's not moving. I'm pinned down.

"Zach I need you to create a diversion so I can get you topped up. Gimme a three count and then lob two of those flash bangs and I'll shoot my way over to Addy, and then link up with you."

Zach's reply was to indeed lob two bangers and when the immediate shock of the noise and light hit the hired thugs, Ranger took off running towards Addy, sliding on stomach, in a classic baseball pose, like a runner stealing home. It was the only way he could break the speed of the run.

* * *

Steven didn't know who the "heavily armed assholes," as Zach had referred to them, that were swarming out of the building were, but they were doing a magnificent job of causing more chaos than he could ever have hoped to. He was pretty sure they belonged to this Drake fella, but that was another question for another time. They were allowing for him to move through the battle space, and if he could keep his head down, he could finish up and get the hell out of here.

Right now, though, he needed to find that fucking writer. Steven couldn't be sure what Vincent had told him and he needed to ensure that the information went no further.

Steven found the writer slumped, half underneath a rolling dumpster, unconscious from the force of the explosion, his cell phone still in hand. Had he gotten any information out? Again, it was another question for another time, and certainly not one that he needed to worry about answering, himself.

This time, Steven didn't bother with any theatrics. He removed the cell phone from the writer's hand and dropping it into his shoulder bag and then with that same hand pulled a certain suppressed pistol. Two simple, clean shots to the head ended the fine career of a certain writer, and stopping the flow of information to a certain editor, though Aldrich didn't know that and would certainly see to that loose end at a later date.

Crouched behind the dumpster so content was he to let the battle play out that he didn't hear Drake come up behind him. "Say there, fella, that's a rather nice *pistola* you got there. Any chance you happened to know a guy down Nebraska way a few years ago?"

Steven couldn't even hide his shock at this comment. How had this guy known about that bit of history? How had he known about that particular *gun*?

"Once upon a time, I might have been down that way. Yaknow, there is a distinct possibility that was a thing that could have happened years ago.

"Why do you ask?"

Drake stood up, "Oh, that just happens to look like a gift I gave to a friend of mine, once upon a time," nodding towards the suppressed pistol.

Steven tucked the pistol back into his shoulder bag. "Damndest thing, these guns all start to look alike after a while, don't they?"

Drake moved from the dumpster, back into the fray, "Yeah, damnedest thing."

* * *

Zach saw Ranger slide into the wall and with the thud being audible over the sound of the gunfight he was sure that Ranger was either dead, or severely injured. He was more than a little surprised when Ranger got up, dumped a few loaded magazines with Addy, and then bolted for his position.

"Shit, buddy, I thought you were a goner. How's the head feeling?" Zach didn't bother to check Ranger over, he needed to focus his attention on the remaining thugs that were still pouring large amounts of hot lead at his position.

Almost all of the civilians had either fled the alley, or were lying dead and dying in the midst of the battle. It was truly a carnage the likes that had never been seen in this town, before.

Once again Zach had a moment to wonder where the police were, where the fire crews and first responders were, but he had no idea that these very groups were tied up in a battle of their own with a second wave of Drake's men. These men had almost broken formation when they saw a limping bum in a well used bush jacket come wandering past their position.

They had completely engulfed the force and the dedicated and experienced officers, while taking heavy casualties, were valiantly whittling away at the numbers of thugs that stood in their path.

One officer in particular, Mark Silver, who was just weeks away from retirement, would have loved nothing more than to skip the "reading of the rights" portion so he could go right to judgment. It's not that he was a crazed vigilante cop, it's just that he was still reeling over the news of his brother-in-law's death, in Gig Harbor just this afternoon. His wife's only brother was a career officer, a great man, and being found dead with his wife had left the family in a state of shock. *Now this?*

Each urban terrorist he dropped was a bit of retribution, in his mind, and he felt zero remorse over any of it. They were the ones who had chosen to break the peace of his town. They were the ones who had chosen to create carnage when had so dutifully served the citizens, over a long and dedicated career, to ensure that it remained peaceful.

"Bodhi's down. I think he's gone. Addy's been topped up with ammo, and if she can stay behind those barrels for a while, she should be able to keep pouring fire into that crew." Ranger wasn't telling Zach anything he didn't know, but that he could still communicate under the pressure was a testament of his training, as well as his fortitude in battle.

Zach, still taking down targets said, "Roger that. I need you and Addy to cover that north side, then. Keep pouring fire into that crew. We need you moving again, you good with that?"

Ranger stood up again, re-shouldered his pack and made one last visual of his path. "Yeah I'm good. I'm still good on ammo, and if you can lob a few more bangers that should give us a chance to keep them back on the ropes."

"Roger that, buddy. Hang tight." Zach pulled the pins on two more flash bangs and tossed one up the alley, one over the cars to where body was slumped. The one second delay between the two explosions allowed for just enough of a confusion that Ranger could move back to Addy's position. When she was again topped up on ammo, he moved back down the rear wall to where Bodhi was still slumped over.

* * *

Drake moved down the back side of the wall that Ranger himself had occupied just recently. While he had been chatting with Steven he noticed a man who was hiding in the shadows towards one end of the alley. This man was apparently the central key to their communication strategy and Drake's trained senses knew that if he could remove this one component that he could finally have his men take the alley and sweep up the remaining stragglers.

Normally Zach would be one hundred percent aware of every aspect in a battle space, but this was not a normal scenario and he had completely disregarded his electronics package in favor of keeping these armed thugs at bay. This was the advantage that Drake needed to circle around behind him, and take a key position for attack.

Drake was correct. As he rounded the corner he heard, "Addy two tangos your one o'clock. Cross X with Ranger, put 'em in a fatal funnel.

"Ranger, keep pounding that sector right there, and let Addy walk the tangos your way. That should decapitate that group."

Another flash bang going off next to Addy let Zach know that she was indeed pushing the tangos down a certain path and that this particular path was spelling certain destruction and doom for them. While he talked his teammates on to various targets he kept pouring fire down the lane, towards the open door of the dance hall cum hideout. There were no more tangos coming out of that door, but his third lane of fire was ensuring that bad guys had little room to maneuver.

Drake could hear the entire conversation and he waited until there was a lull in the conversation, if that was even possible. He could hear the chatter of weapons fire echoing off the alley floor, the building walls and mixed with the roar of the inferno that was the molten pile of torched RV.

For all of the gadgets that Zach had at his disposal, electronic or otherwise, he failed to use the most important one, his brain. He became scope locked on the targets in front of him, and failing to remember that the battlefield is a three hundred sixty degree space. Had he remembered this he would have seen the creeping figure of Drake moving into position, behind the position he occupied. That was probably the only tactical mistake he made this evening, but unfortunately, it was a fatal one.

Drake had no sense of theatrics. He had no sense of flair, or panache. His only concern was getting to and putting that target that was in front of him, down in the dirt for good.

Drawing his pistol, Drake stepped behind Zach, placed his pistol to the soft part of the head behind Zach's right ear and pulled the trigger. There was no need for overkill, that single bullet blew Zach's left eyeball right out of his skull, including a copious amount of brain matter.

Zach never knew what hit him, as the saying goes and he was dead before his body could register just what in the hell had happened. His rifle slid from his hands and Zach slumped to a kneeling position on the wet pavement.

Thunder echoed all through the city as if God himself had disapproved of this killing. For a brief moment Drake was outlined in forks of angry purple lightning that charged the sky with electricity so intense that Ranger could feel the hairs on his head standing up beneath his ball cap.

He and Addy both turned their profiles just in time to see Drake, standing over Zach's corpse as he delivered one final shot, just to ensure that Zach was indeed dead. Addy saw the flame spit from the barrel of Drake's gun, she saw Zach's head snap backwards, up off the pavement, as the concussive blast of the round ricocheted off the pavement. Blood mixed with rainwater and the acidic coppery smell permeated the night.

Ranger wasn't sure but he swore that he saw just a hint of a smile in the executioner's face. Though he had no way to know that it was Drake, he knew without a doubt that this man was going to be his next target.

Without regard to his own safety he pulled the pin on his last flash bang, and hurled it right to Drake. Ranger's timing was impeccable as the grenade exploded just as it reached his face, blinding Drake, deafening him, scarring his face and ripping flesh from bone. The sheer force of the blast liquefied his eyeballs and he fell to the ground screaming, himself in a kneeing position, blood and liquid eye remnants dripping through his fingers.

Addy heard screaming and she couldn't be sure if it was Drake, Ranger, herself or a combination of all three of them. There were still armed men milling about, though they had pretty much taken up a piece of real estate that was safe and most refused to show themselves; as the fight was almost gone out of them. Most of these men refused to believe that near fifty of their best warriors could be bested by three minimally armed people, and one motherfucking bum. And one of these people was even a woman. Fucking women and their desire to be in combat.

* * *

Colby Boone was not a native to the state of Montana. He was a transplant from Ohio and while he would always remain loyal to his beloved Buckeyes, he couldn't help but fall in love with the rugged natured and distinct manliness that Montana had to offer. A chance to go to college here, and finish out a Master's Degree, was something that was too good an opportunity to pass up.

When he had first met Drake, who was selling original WWII merchandise at a flea market, he thought the guy was a bit of a lunatic. However as the two men continued to run into each other, Colby decided to take him up on his offer for a beer, and he figured that worst case, he'd give the man two hours tops, and if he didn't like what he heard, well *ADIOS...thanks for the beer... have a good 'un.*

It only took thirty minutes and Colby was hooked on Drake's speech. In all fairness, Drake was no slouch, and this certainly wasn't his first recruiting mission, either. No, he had seen promise in this young man's character, a real chance to have a good lieutenant in his group, a fella that could listen, follow orders, but be able to carry on without being babysat. Drake needed a guy who could certainly get his hands dirty, and in Colby he saw that man.

Colby claimed to be a descendent of the actual Daniel Boone but he had no proof, only a vague lineage and a great bunch of stories. His charisma was enough to propel him upwards in the ranks and turn him into a natural leader. Drake was right, too, Colby certainly didn't mind getting his hands dirty and he sure didn't mind doing any of the heavy lifting.

When Drake had asked for a band of volunteers to lead a mission of mass destruction against the establishment that was the local city government, Colby was the first one to volunteer. He didn't have to step forward, because he was already in front of the rest of the men, itching to lead these dedicated individuals and patriots.

Colby Boone had lived with, trained with, sweated and bled with these men and he would happily be the one to lead the charge. Drake, if he had dared show any emotion, would have hugged him and told him that he was truly the favored son amongst the men. That would have been out of character, however, and he certainly wasn't going to risk losing face in front of the men he respected. They wouldn't have it to be led by a man who got teary eyed at the drop of a hat, and so he nodded his head, and a firm grip of the shoulder was all the thanks and motivation that Colby needed.

Immediately he gathered his best twenty five mates, including himself, and then gathered a handful of other men whose hearts were in the right spot, but certainly were no better than cannon fodder. Such losses were always necessary in a battle such as this as it would vilify their enemies and the sight of their brothers lying mortally wounded on the ground would steel these men further, pointing them onward to victory and to glory.

So that was how Colby Boone, who once had a promising career in law ahead of him, complete with a matching diploma from a prestigious ivy league college, and further education from the local university, found himself kneeling in the wee hours of the morning, behind a car that he was pretty sure had started life as a newer SUV, but now resembled the battered hulks seen in the backgrounds of any post apocalyptic movie. He was kneeling in puddles of piss warm rainwater, probably mixing with blood that was spilled by the government pigs and their hired bitch who up to this point, had refused to come out from the shadows of her hiding place, back in the corner.

He saw the angry forks of purple lighting and he saw Drake, their fearless leader, stride into the midst of battle, and execute one of those government pigs and he smiled while he witnessed the young man's head explode out the front. The crack and report of the final execution was music to Colby's ears and he immediately reloaded his rifle, a vintage M1 Garand that was probably older than he was, but was accurate as hell and had dropped quite a few Vietcong swine, based on the notches carved into the antique wooden stock.

Colby had listened to the tutelage of Drake and had learned how to shoot this rifle with iron sights. He knew every little shake and rattle the rifle had, and moreover, he knew just where to put those iron sights to drop a man at over one hundred yards. When Drake had given him a new set of optics for the rifle, and paid to have them mounted and zeroed Colby felt as if it was Christmas morning, all over again.

Now he was easily reaching out and touching individuals at over six hundred yards. Not that any distance in this back alley was near that long, but the deadly accuracy that he had with the rifle bolstered the sniper spirit in his blood and he continued to drain targets of their very life essence, without regard. There were no innocents, not in this back alley. His brothers in arms were avenging angels sent to do the work of the common man, who needed to be shown what it took to rise up and shuck the yoke of the government regime that now held sway in Washington, D.C.

These stupid young kids had no idea of what it took to maintain their lifestyle of ease and excess, and they lacked the discipline to make the choices necessary for sacrifice. They

320

were no better than the men and women Colby had sworn to eliminate from the earth. You were either with him and his brothers, and their father figure that was Drake, or you were against everything that these men stood for.

It came as a shock to him when he heard the feral battle cry that was coming from the alleyway entrance by Drake. He looked up just in time to see Drake catch the full force of the flash bang grenade in the face, and as the concussive blast hit him, Drake's face seemed to melt away from the very bone that gave it form and shape.

Colby, himself, was enraged to the point of sheer bloodlust. His very mentor, and more of a father than his own capitalist swine father had ever been, was now kneeling in a puddle of his own blood while his face continued to melt, and bits of charred flesh were raked away by the pounding rainwater.

Colby saw motion to his right and he saw that a man in college street clothing was hefting a very powerful sub machinegun towards his leader, and then, there she was... The very bitch that had caused so much trouble these last few hours, she stepped from the shadows.

Both of them, the man to Colby's right (Ranger), and the woman in the shadows no more (Addy), took aim at Drake and opened fire. What was left of Drake seemed to be peeled away in puffs of red mist and the unmistakable sound of hot lead hitting human flesh and bone put Colby Boone at the very breaking point.

He stood up, took aim, and fired.

* * *

Addy was herself enraged at the very battle that had unfolded before them. This was supposed to be a simple extraction and, if possible, capture mission of a man who could lead them to a whole host of nefarious characters that would certainly, with their absence, make a dent in the world's terrorism industry. Now, it was all going wrong. Men and women were dying by the scores out here.

Summer rain was pelting her skin so hard it was stinging needles and causing actual pain in her exposed biceps. Addy didn't know it, at that time, but she had actually taken a piece of random shrapnel from one of the thousands of rounds that had been fired. It had hit the metal trash barrel to her right, causing extra metal to fly up and cut her arm. Blood was flowing freely, but all Addy felt was rage, and anger, pure homicidal rage that Madam Lee might have recognized but certainly not to the extent that she now unleashed in the alley.

When she saw Ranger move into position to fire, she shifted her fire, as well, and in an instant Drake was turned into so much ground meat, his murderous life and light snuffed out by an undercover agent and a militarily trained man who were truly in the fight of their lives.

Addy ejected her spent magazine and grabbed a fresh one from the pile that Ranger had stacked near to her hand. Her plan had been to hold back in the shadows, wait for their target Vincent to show himself, and when he did move up the backside of the buildings and take down Steven, who was sure to be following him. Addy briefly wondered where Steven was, then returned her thoughts to the task at hand. There couldn't have been more than five bad guys out there. So skillful was her crew that they had systematically eliminated a force over ten times their own size.

That's when the unthinkable happened.

Ranger had unloaded the last of his ammo for his MP5 on Drake and with no fresh magazines left, he let the sub machinegun drop to the pavement with a metallic clatter. He drew his sidearm, knowing full well that he was now past knee deep, and was well on his way to hip dip in the shit because there were still some pretty nasty thugs out there, they had armor and they apparently had more guns than he did at this point. Odds like this were never favorable but that didn't mean for one second that Ranger was going to back down from this fight, not for any amount of safety.

Ranger wasn't scared. He certainly wasn't above fear, but he had learned early on that, if you are in the mountains of a foreign nation, outnumbered and low on ammo, the only thing that will save you is your training and your wits. So far this philosophy had served him well. He was going to ensure that they walked out of this gunfight, come hell or high water. With the amount of rain coming down, though, Ranger wasn't sure what would happen first.

As he was scanning for targets Ranger heard a rustle of movement and spun, dropping to his right knee. This action probably saved his life because there was Steven, who had been waiting for just such a moment, and when he heard the metal of the MP5 hitting the ground, he moved in to act.

He would have had a clean execution on Ranger, as well, but his pants caught on the metal stairway and tore them at the knee. This sound alerted Ranger who spun and ducked, just as Steven fired and a bullet tore through Ranger's right shoulder, his gun arm. He willed his arm to bring his pistol up, but the torn ligaments and muscles of the limb wouldn't fulfill his commands.

Ranger instantly switched his pistol to his left hand and fired one round, right at Steven's chest. A look of surprise and agony instantly plastered itself on Steven's face. He had no idea how someone could have gotten the drop on him, and now here he was, bleeding out from a chest would. He tried to inhale, but the pressure of the sucking chest wound was collapsing his lung and he was literally suffocating on the air around him.

As Ranger was preparing to deliver one more shot to put him down, a gunshot to his right rang out, and instantly Steven was blown against the sides of the metal stairs. Ranger looked over to see Bodhi cradling a sawed off double barreled shotgun that was smoking from both barrels.

Blood was running down Bodhi's mouth, painting a macabre grimace on his face, and his eyes were full of blood, making him appear as a demon incarnate. Hell, apparently, had followed with him, tonight. His clothes were hanging in ragged tatters as the damage done to him had literally torn the fabric from his body and his bush coat was now gone.

Shrapnel holes and wounds peppered his pants and he looked as if he had just survived a full assault from Xerxes' army by himself, without two hundred and ninety nine brothers standing next to him. He certainly looked as if he was at the mouth of the Hot Gates, ready to make his last stand.

As Bodhi stood making a valiant attempt to reload the shotgun with shells procured from the body lying next to him a close range blast hit him in the chest, knocking him backwards. He dropped the shotgun, the spare shells, and looked utterly perplexed as to how this could have happened. Falling through the flimsy wooden covers of the storm drain cover, without a further sound he fell down the storm drain pipe and splashed into the cold water below.

Colby Boone, enraged at the loss of his mentor, had succumbed to the very thing that had cost Zach his life. He had lost sight of the big picture of the battlefield and he had assumed that all behind him was clear.

While he was sure that the bum in the bush jacket was most certainly dead, he made no move to check it out, and it had nearly cost him his life. When the bum had suddenly come back to life, and wasted that fool Steven, it had made poor Colby piss down his leg. His initial reaction was to turn and open fire, but that would have been an even bigger tactical mistake. Instead he slunk back down between two cars and slowly turned himself around. There was the bum, quite alive, though probably not so well. He was holding a smoking sawed off double barrel shotgun.

Steven was lying in crumpled heap near the bottom of the metal stairs leading up to the apartment that, unknown to him, was currently being rented out by the master of this terrible three ring circus, Aldrich. Aldrich had foreseen many of the issues plaguing this entire night and he had chosen to not put his faith in Steven, as Steven had so pitifully mewled.

No, Aldrich knew that the only way he was going to finish this up was to step right to the edge of the battlefield, and from one of the large bay windows that overlooked the alley, he spoke commands into his cell phone, and a two way radio, directing certain key players. These particular people were now the few surviving members of Drake's assault team. They were huddled in place because Aldrich had a commanding view of the battle space and the small nuances and spaces that afforded any measure of protection.

If he had had more time to prepare this particular group, he could have eliminated the entire group of DEA agents in just underneath ten minutes and this battle would have been a moot point. What Aldrich didn't know was where the players would be exiting and he certainly didn't want to be left out of the loop, so he had staged a crew similar to the one in the abandoned dance hall, across the street, in a renovated building that wasn't quite open for business.

When the explosion had turned the RV into so much a hellacious campfire, these men had abandoned their posts and come rushing to the aid of their comrades in arms. They were disciplined, but only to a point, and these men certainly weren't going to be left holding the bag if there was going to be gunplay.

Initially Aldrich had cursed at this, but as these men continued to blindly follow the man in front of them, pouring out the one entrance, the sheer numbers causing chaos and confusion, he let it go. They were doing exactly what they needed to be doing and that was causing death, destruction and mayhem. Most of these men didn't even know why they were here, only that they had a chance to shoot their guns outside of a training venue and that they were going to be paid for it.

The six men that still remained in the parking lot, below, these men were the handpicked of the bunch, and Aldrich had ensured that each man was further compensated for holding their trigger fingers to the point that they would plug only a selected bunch of targets. Each man, an enemy of capitalist imperial policies jumped at the thought of having a bit more coin in their pockets and possibly, escaping to a different part of the world, starting their revolution in a new spot, or simply starting over. While it was not lost on each other that they were blatant hypocrites, none of the men chose to speak up regarding the matter. When it came to bounties for kills, there were certain things that even a hefty bunch of banded bills could procure. In this case it was a blinded eye to the actions of the man next to them. Cold hard cash was funny like that.

* * *

Ranger saw the blood spray from Bodhi's chest as he was propelled backwards, into the blackness of the storm drain. He didn't even have time to utter a single word of protest. Instincts kicked in, and he turned, again dropping to his knees, and seeing his target, lined up the center mass of the fellow holding the battle scarred M1 rifle and with his left hand, his off hand and weak hand, he pulled the trigger.

Discipline had gone right out the window and what should have been a smooth, clean squeeze on the trigger was a ragged jerk that sent the bullet, even at this close range, wildly off course of center and at this height, causing the bullet to impact into his target's hip.

Colby screamed in pain as he collapsed. "I can't believe you shot me!" His voice was a high pitched shriek as he attempted to maneuver the rifle as a crutch, to better lever himself up. This was the last tactical mistake that he ever made.

With the wet pavement, and his shattered pelvis, Colby could do no more than wobble against the unsteady rifle and when he slipped, his hand instinctively reached out for purchase, grabbing at anything that would stabilize him. His flailing fingers were slapping at the wet stock of the rifle, the metal trigger guard and the hair trigger.

One final *BOOM* echoed through the alley as the slug exiting the rifle tore through the thin tissue covering Colby's cheek, traveling up through his brain, and exploding out the top of his head like a sadistic fireworks display. Two well placed shots from Ranger were useless when they hit Colby's chest, and just served to further mutilate the corpse. Colby fell dead, so much mangled gore, on to the pavement of the alleyway.

* * *

Addy watched the scene unfold in slow motion. She was powerless to help Bodhi, whom she thought was already dead. Now she witnessed him shot, again, and fall out of sight. He was gone. She saw Colby Boone's head explode as his tactical errors and stupidity culminated in his own demise. She saw Ranger, limping but still alive, begin to work his way back to her.

"Ranger, come to me. My location is safe, for the moment, but there's a few more of them out there. I can hear 'em breathing!" Addy doubted that she could hear them breathing, but she knew her voice was going to carry and if Ranger heard her, then so would they.

She didn't think of it as using Ranger as bait, so much as drawing the enemy out where they could be dealt with. Ranger knew full well what the stakes were, but he came back to her, limping as he went, sweeping the area with his pistol. His wrecked right shoulder was hanging limp at his side, blood flowing freely from the wound.

When Addy saw him she came fully out of the shadows and in doing so committed her final tactical mistake. These men that had been lying in wait, they had been doing so because they were promised the share of a one hundred and fifty thousand dollar bounty if they were part of the crew that brought Addy down. They didn't know her name, but they knew her face, and when she stepped fully from the shadows they had all the opportunity they needed.

They knew that she was hiding back there, but not one of them had dared to fire for fear of giving away their position. No, they would wait until she made the play, and they would react on it. It now appeared that their tenacity and patience and perseverance had all paid off. Now, they found themselves all lining up the same target in the red dots and cross hairs of their automatic weapons.

Ranger was the first to hear the safety selector switch click off. Instinctively he dove in front of Addy and as such he took the full force of the first barrage. No less than ten bullets hit him in various points around his body.

His femur was shattered and he was pretty sure that his femoral artery was severed. There was blood flowing freely down his pant leg that pulsed with each beat of his weakening heart. If he had any chance of saving himself, he needed to be in an operating theatre, right now. Since there wasn't one nearby, he chose instead to make the best of his last few minutes of life and draw out the snakes from the grass.

He opened up on the two targets that he could see, and while the first one ducked down behind a vehicle again, the second wasn't so lucky. The bullet from Ranger's pistol went right through the glass of the front windows, causing the safety glass to shatter and slamming home into the temple of the assassin. One down, four to go.

When Addy saw this, she opened fire, her long burst of rounds catching two of her targets completely unaware that she possessed such firepower. These two targets fell immediately and that made three down, two to go.

These last two men chose a different approach, instead, and the man to Ranger's left pulled the pin on a smoke grenade he had been saving for this very moment, lobbing the canister between Ranger and Addy. Thick white smoke bloomed between the two and in the air that was still heavy with mist from the dying rain, it hung in a thick, cloying cloud that stung the eyes and singed the nostrils of both Addy and Ranger.

"Addy; down!" She didn't need to be told twice. They both fell to their bottoms and sat back to back doing their best to cover their sectors and fields of fire. Ranger was in a terrible position as his right arm was mangle and it was the one facing out. He now had to use his left arm, sweep across his body, and severely limit his range of motion, using a pistol that was already low on ammo.

Addy's rifle was far too bulky to be of any use in a sitting position and while she had a good field of fire, she was still forced to wield the rifle from a sitting position and her smaller frame had to compensate for the weapon.

"Ranger, I think we're down to just two tangos left. We just need to hold out a bit longer and then the cavalry should be on the way. Stay with me, brother. We got this."

Addy wasn't sure if she was talking, at this point, to bolster herself, or to keep the spirits up of the last remaining member of her team. Staring through the smoke she could just make out Zach's corpse where it had fallen. His desecrated body lying face down next to Drake's equally abused body. So much carnage for one man. From one man.

A sudden burst of gunfire snapped her mind back to the present. A gurgle of blood and air mixing in a person's lungs sounded in the still night. "Ranger! Ranger, don't you fucking die on me, man! Jesus don't you die on me, not now!

"We've got help on the way!" Addy was screaming and as she did so, she realized she was all alone. Turning around and kneeling, she saw that Ranger, already peppered with bullets had just taken new rounds, and without any protection from body armor he was bleeding like stuck pig. There was no chance and they both knew it. The puddle of blood beneath his left leg confirmed to Addy what Ranger already had known, his femoral artery had been severed and he hadn't had a chance.

Ranger's last act of bravery had been to use his own body to shield Addy. Addy looked up and was staring into the eyes of the man who had just executed her teammate. She dropped her rifle, and in one swift motion brought her G19 to bear and shot the man six times in the chest, each slug propelling him backwards, bloody spray flying from his lips as he did so. Though Addy had no way of knowing she had pierced his heart with the fourth round, and the following two just hurried what was already an inevitable end for this sonuvabitch...

Addy had little time to savor any amount of victory when three loads of triple aught buckshot hit her in the right side of the stomach and abdomen. It was one of the few places that her body armor didn't cover and protect near as well, and at this close range, the soft armor plates stood no chance against the onslaught of lead pouring from the end of the tactical shotgun.

Force from the blast slammed her against the metal barrels that had shielded her all night long. Addy's breath came in shallow and ragged gasps. She had no idea what mortally wounded was, but she knew that she was in serious trouble. No matter how hard she tried, Addy wasn't able to get an entire lungful of air.

Reaching for her med kit, she knew that she had occlusive dressings in there that she could place over the majority of the wounds to stop the sucking chest wound that was collapsing her lungs. Steven, had he been alive to talk about it, could have mentioned that it wouldn't have done any good. Damage inflicted by the lethal blast had torn her liver, her spleen, her small intestines and a small chunk of her stomach to shreds.

Dropping the contents of her med kit on the ground, she tried to focus her eyes on the gun lying on the ground, in front of her. She tried to reach for her pistol but she couldn't get her fingers to cooperate and each time she bent to attempt to retrieve it from the holster waves of electric flame swept through her body.

Now on all fours, she pawed at her rifle, just inside her reach. If she could grasp it, bring it up, she just might have chance. Addy tugged at the sling, bringing it up to bear, lined up the glowing red dot on the head of the man who had just shot her. Holding what was left of her breath, in a vain attempt to stabilize her body that was near convulsing and well into shock she depressed the trigger.

* * *

Aldrich was pretty sure that the scene was now safe enough for him to make his way to where he was sure Addy was waiting for him. On the table next to the door was a black metallic briefcase that was locked with a combination lock, and contained only one thing.

Thumbing the tiny wheels of the combination lock, Aldrich opened the case to reveal a very ancient British Webley pistol. It had been reworked and retooled over the years and though the original frame was well over one hundred years old, it still fired the custom made cartridges with the force and tenacity of a charging African rhino. Even the illegal pearl and ivory grips that had been made for this weapon shined under the soft light of the overhead lamps in the rented condo.

Before coming up here, Aldrich had insisted that his driver park their rented SUV nearby, such that he could make a clean getaway. With his casted leg, he wasn't going to be running any time soon, and he needed to be sure that he had a clean line of exit. He also ensured that everything that couldn't be disposed of was packed and ready to go.

As Aldrich put his overcoat on, over his expensive silk suit, and his fedora hat complete with a tail feather from an actual sage grouse, he grabbed the silver headed cane, and braced himself against the door. With the Webley in hand, he broke the action to ensure that all six rounds were live, and in good working order. He knew that they were. Closing the action he placed the pistol in the pocket of his overcoat and hobbled down the metal stairs.

Reaching the last step he gave a cursory glance to Steven's body that was lying in a heap, at the bottom of the stairs. Aldrich stepped over this bit of nasty business and was just about to round the corner of the building, into the alley proper, when he heard a gunshot. Had Addy chosen the noble suicide and taken her own life? Aldrich doubted that very much, and he believed with all his heart that she had dispatched the one remaining man who was set to inherit a rather large bounty. As it was, Aldrich didn't have to pay out anything to anyone, now, and that was just fine with him.

As he approached Addy, he saw that his initial assumption was indeed correct, and the last man of the bounty team, who had remained so still that he had appeared another casualty of this battle, now lay dead with a fairly even groove cut down the middle of his head, carved by a high powered bullet from yonder vixen's rifle, a spent tactical shotgun still smoking just inches from his fingertips.

Addy lay against the metal trash barrels gasping, blood running freely down her side and out of her mouth. When she saw Aldrich she made an effort to raise the rifle. She couldn't. Too much blood had been lost and the weight of the rifle, as well as the weight of the body armor proved too much to bear.

Smiling, he said, "Special Agent Micha Diabrava, of the DEA, I presume?" His mock question was a horrifying second only to the fact that he knew her name. Her real, Christian name.

Addy looked up, stunned. "How? How did you know? How did you find out?" Her life force was slipping out of her, and she wasn't in pain, not right now. Addy's body was in too much shock to feel pain, and the loss of blood was making her want to close her eyes and just go to sleep.

"Oh, my dear girl, didn't you learn anything about me last night? I employ people who know things, and who have things to sell; pieces of information to trade for various things." Aldrich was really enjoying this. Temporarily the pain was gone from his leg. Even the dull throb that the prescription narcotics couldn't touch was temporarily abated as he relished this moment.

Addy raised her right hand, blood tattooing her finger and she extended her middle finger. It was one last final gesture of defiance to the man who had caused all this pain and death and destruction and grief. "I found out all I need to know about you Aldrich. I know that you are truly a 'Class A' scumbag. You are one depraved pedophile. You like to poison young girls with drugs and then have your way with them. I know that you have more politicians and CEO's in your pocket than you do dollar bills."

Aldrich spread his hands wide, as if to say, 'Ya got me.' Instead, "Well there you have it. I do have quite a few dollar bills in my pocket, my pretty thing. I use them to grease the palms of people whom I need to work with and it seems to work rather well, in these instances.

"Again I thought you had learned more than that about me. Come on, pretty girl, can't you tell me that you've learned anything that would rock me? What did your informant tell your writer about me?

"Speaking of which, where is our writer friend? Oh, that's right. He appears to be lying dead next to an abandoned dance hall, underneath a dumpster with two bullets in his head. Your informant, I believe Vincent was his name? Well he met a far worse ending, according to Steven. Either way, those two have no further stories to tell."

Addy watched as he produced the Webley from his pocket. She sneered, "You stupid fuck. I learned everything I need to know about you. I learned where you came from, what your true business is.

"All I learned I downloaded into the mainframe computer at the DEA and they are sifting through it right now. You ignorant shit, the best agents the DEA has are currently picking apart your life, your history, and are farming that data out to every government agency and headhunter they can think of."

Was that a slight tremble in Aldrich's hand? He didn't think so, he would lie to himself and say that it was rage. Addy saw something else, though, for just a brief moment. It was something she hadn't seen before. It was fear. She had hit a nerve, certainly.

If Lead Agent Arnold Thomas had done everything he needed to do, all the info that they had data mined from the servers was being disseminated to every law enforcement agency in the country and within weeks they'd pick apart his very organization. Hell, maybe even quicker.

Vincent would have smiled at the irony. He was right, the clues were all there right from the get-go. They had just been so obvious that no one had picked up on them, and it took one night for Agent Micha Diabrava to completely pick it apart.

She sneered, "You really are amateur hour, aren't you? I mean, shit fire and save a match, you stupid fuck, how did you think you were going to escape when the feds know who you are? Fuck me man, they know you're last name..."

Aldrich emptied all six rounds of his Webley into Agent Micha "Addy" Diabrava's chest. At this close range the soft armor, already damaged from battle, had no chance of holding up against the slugs from his high powered pistol. Her dying breath escaped her lips and her head collapsed to her chest. Her rifle lay across her legs, useless now that the trained owner could no longer move, or breathe, herself.

"Oh, Addy, if only you had taken the time to dig deeper. You would have realized that it was our friend Drake who set this whole thing up. But, you didn't even bother to notice that, did you?" Aldrich could have continued but what was the point. Addy was dead. Drake was dead. So much carnage adorned this back alley, it was everywhere.

Aldrich wasn't lying, though. It was Drake who had used his contacts and his surveillance measures to set up the meeting with Vincent and his writer friend, famed Liam Edwards. That was how Vincent had gotten the phone number in the first place. That would have come as quite a shock to the now dead writer, who had done his best to shield that information from the best of the prying eyes and ears of the world. He had almost succeeded.

In the end Addy died cold and alone, in the back alley of a town that was so popular because of its ski resorts and mountain trails. She didn't know if the agency really did have all the information, but her last thought was a bit of grim satisfaction, knowing that Aldrich would be forever looking over his shoulder, jumping at shadows that may or may not have been there, thinking of the monsters that may or may not have been lurking in them.

* * * * *

Aldrich pocketed the Webley, the warm barrel was a comforting warmth against his leg. He pulled his cell phone and dialed a number, speaking in hushed tones.

Within a few minutes there was a rented SUV waiting less than one block away for him, packed with his travel luggage and all the electronic information he needed to start a new life. Just like that, he would cast off the name Aldrich and assume a new identity. He'd done it before, and it was easier than most people thought, even in today's electronic age.

The man riding in the passenger seat jumped out to open the door for Aldrich, who was soon to be no longer Aldrich. Once the man who was no longer Aldrich had situated himself the driver asked, "Where to sir?"

Once upon a time, a man who had grown up in a very different life had assumed a name that was the furthest thing from who he really was. Looking straight ahead he said, "I think it's time to go home. Make preparations, if you please, for a long term stay in our neighboring state of North Dakota.

"I have a man to see about an oil field and a missile silo."

-afterward-

This is usually the part where the author will do their very best to try and explain the work that they have just poured out onto the paper. Maybe have a little fireside chat with you, the fellow adventurer, as we discuss certain particulars of the book. Well, I'm not going to be that author. I think it's a cheap and shitty way to end a book; fluff and filler to expand upon the number of pages.

I will give a small consolation and that is this: I never wrote this for anyone but myself. A long time ago I discovered that writing became a great therapy for myself, and when you witness the things you are apt to witness in a life such as the one I have lived up to this point, it became easier to put those events on to paper and then dress them up a bit, and hell, before you know it, you have a whole damn dialogue going.

Pretty snazzy when you think about it.

What I realized is that your average person is going to have various interactions with various people through the various courses of their lives. Suffice it to say that some of these interactions are not going to be overly nice, or even all that pleasant. So the question begs, how do you cope with these instances?

When I was younger and a lot more immature, I turned to substances to help me cope. Sounds cheap and petty, but the truth I think is not all that grandiose. Pretty soon those substances began to change me. At the age of twenty one alcoholic beverages were already in the past. Marijuana was already in the past. I had moved onto things like heroin. Yup, been down that road before. I tried things like cocaine, ecstasy, mushrooms, and just about every other substance you can think of. Hell, I once took the seeds from a Hawaiian Woodrose plant and ground them up to make a tea that I think was partially toxic, so that I could drink the tea, get violently ill, and throw up and in the process of the dehydration and chemical imbalance learn to really appreciate the stars under a prairie sky.

But, that's enough history about my debauchery. When you do these things there are certain actions that will go along with these things. You will meet certain kinds of people. Take it as you will. Again, I was still young, had no idea what in the blue hell I was doing half the time, I was not even aware that I was about to witness a friend of mine get murdered, that I would witness a friend of mine overdose and die from drinking chemicals, and yet another friend take his own life. Now you throw all of this stuff in a blender and people would say, "Shit, man that's all part of growing up." I would agree. Shit happens.

However, I was ill equipped to deal with these mental traumas and certainly had no clue as to what to do with them. So they became characters. These characters lived in a world where they didn't die, or if they did, they died in such a way as to allow me time to grasp what was happening to them.

As I got older, and I hesitate to say "grow up" because there are those that would argue we are still waiting for that day, and I took various jobs, it became apparent to me that a lot of these traumas hadn't left me, and as I branched out into the world, I would be sure to meet more and more of them.

Working as a delivery driver during college I would often make late night runs to places that we would describe in the most technical terms as "shady as fuck." Roll up to a house, at two in the morning, with a wad of cash, a bag full of food and a Glock in a shoulder holster praying to God that some crack head wouldn't blow me out of my skate shoes. Parties would be going and the shit that went on in those places makes these people we just met in poor Vincent's stories look like halfway normal and upstanding citizens.

After college I worked, and in many ways still do, at a hospital where I met even more characters, with even more stories. It was like supermarket shopping for personalities at a big box store from hell. I had the greatest coworkers and the greatest job but some of the stuff you see come through the doors makes you wonder just how the hell humanity can even survive.

I've held fathers in my arms as they watch their now dead child pass from the room and out of view. I've seen the victims of spousal abuse, on both sides, as they came into my doors. I've seen 80 year old patients beat cancer, and I've 20 year olds succumb to it. And I still have to process it.

So, in many ways the characters that we just met, and discussed, they are the culmination of many people who I have come into contact with, crossed paths with, and had quick little dances with in the this game of life.

Characters that we have yet to meet, in future works, God willing, are yet more processes of these experiences. They are the metaphorical bodies of the experiences I still mull over when my eyes close but my brain won't shut down.

They aren't perfect, none of them are. I wished better fates for Vincent and Addy, but sometimes, even in fiction, we have to play the cards we are dealt and sometimes you come up spades, sometimes you come up snake eyes. Maybe we'll even run into some other friends and characters again. I have a feeling that we haven't seen the last of Aldrich.

The only other comment I will make is that I have been so heavily influenced by some great authors that I hope, in a weird way to make them proud. Stephen King, Tom Clancy, Dan Brown, Neil Gaiman... The list goes on... I'd almost say we were on a first name basis. And then there are men like Dr. Mark Schlenz. "Don't wait for the project, make the project happen," he once told me. Well, Dr. Mark, I did just that.

So here it all ends, at least for a while. There are other threads to be picked up, soon I feel. Others are best left lying. When the day is done, though, I feel as if I was able to weave a small story for you.

Ultimately though, I have to remember that it was, selfishly, just for me...

Patrik
January 2014 – July 2015, Bozeman

-the story of patrik-

Patrik Hill is the author of *Downtown Noir*, as well as the essay and poetry collection entitled *The Five Aces of Israel: reshuffled*. A self-described adventure geek, he has traveled all over North America, Puerto Rico and the Cayman Islands, exploring mountain trails, back country lakes, jungle canopies, and ocean reefs. A certified SCUBA diver Patrik is as at home on land as he is beneath the water. Patrik often uses these experiences and people he meets to mold and shape the characters of his books.

Patrik has a Bachelor's Degree in Sociology from Montana State University emphasizing on Criminal Justice. He has worked as a draftsman, a restaurant manager, and a healthcare professional. Patrik currently lives in Bozeman, Montana, with his family, and is working on his next novels, *Detective Stories after Dark* and *Thru the Glass Darkly: Retribution*.

...one final thought...

In 2014 it was estimated that in the United States, alone, there were as many as 100,000 human slaves being trafficked for the expressed purpose of sexual slavery, and captivity. These are men, women, and children who are being bought and sold, every... single... day... If that weren't shocking enough, according to some statistics, the number of convictions for perpetrators of these heinous crimes is only estimated to be around 18,000. The staggering magnitude of the task makes it near impossible to determine the actual numbers.

Supply and demand have increased through the years partially due to the internet and the ease with which traffickers and customers can discreetly complete a transaction. Traffickers utilize social media, dating sites and online advertisements to market minors and trafficked victims. Ads seemingly posted by a person willingly engaged in the sex trade are often created or monitored by traffickers. Traffickers lie about the victim's age and may even disguise themselves as the person in the ad when communicating with johns via the internet or phone. Some websites try to screen ads for trafficking; however, the sheer volume of ads makes this process a daunting task. For instance, when the U.S. Craigslist Adult Services Section was available, there were 10,000-16,000 adult services postings per day in the U.S. alone. Additionally, it's difficult to determine if the person advertising is independently working in the sex industry or is under a trafficker.[1]

This is an epidemic that is growing, and it didn't end with the abolition of slavery, as we were taught in History 101. Make the call, be the voice, be the change and help put an end to this despicable behavior, once and for all.

If you are the victim of human trafficking, or know of someone who is, call your local authorities. Call 9-1-1. Call the FBI.[2] *Save a life.*

---

[1] http://www.endslaverynow.org/learn/slavery-today/sex-trafficking
[2] https://www.fbi.gov/about-us/investigate/civilrights/human_trafficking